CLOUD CUCKOO LAND

Also by Peta Tayler

Gingerbread and Guilt

CLOUD CUCKOO LAND

Peta Tayler

HEADLINE

First published in Great Britain in 1995
by HEADLINE BOOK PUBLISHING

10 9 8 7 6 5 4 3 2 1

British Library Cataloguing in Publication Data

Tayler, Peta
Cloud Cuckoo Land
I. Title
823.914 [F]

ISBN 0-7472-1435-2

Typeset by
CBS, Felixstowe, Suffolk

Printed and bound in Great Britain by
Mackays of Chatham PLC, Chatham, Kent

HEADLINE BOOK PUBLISHING
A division of Hodder Headline PLC
338 Euston Road
London NW1 3BH

For Alan,
Christopher and Luke
and for all the friends, past and present,
from whom I have learned so much

Chapter 1

'Honestly, Laura, she's impossible! I mean, *really* impossible!'
Laura looked up from the dough she was kneading and surveyed
Daisy. She was dressed in what, to Laura's eyes, looked like a collection
of black rags, and her small feet in their heavy Doc Martens were hoisted
up on to the top rung of her stool. Above the frayed neck of her grandad
shirt, which sagged out of the confinement of a rubbed velvet waistcoat
patchily encrusted with beads and sequins, the blonde head – balanced
with such poise on the slender column of her neck – rose like a miraculous
flower growing in a dung-heap. Laura, who had been brought up on *The
Book of the Flower Fairies*, tried to think what flower this elfin creature
could represent. The black-binliner fairy? She smiled at the fancy, her
hands continuing the rhythmic push and fold, push and fold and the warm
smell of flour and yeast rising up to surround her.

'She is, isn't she?' Daisy, crouched on the stool like a beautiful
hobgoblin, was not going to let her off the hook. 'Impossible, I mean?
You know her better than anyone, I should think. All those years. I bet she
was impossible when she was at school with you. And before. An
impossible baby.'

'Well . . .' Laura considered Anna, her best and oldest friend, her mind
going back to all the different Annas she had known. Anna the widow,
dry-eyed at her husband's funeral, stiff within her son's supporting arm,
while Daisy beside her wept with the easy abandon of childhood. Anna,
nursing Michael through the hideous progression of his cancer with a
bright smile and fierce, desperate eyes. Anna the young mother, glowing
with adoration at the swathed bundle that was Daisy in her arms, while
seven-year-old Guy stood solemnly and proudly beside her. Anna the
bride, her golden hair shimmering through the white mist of her veil,
floating up the aisle while Laura, plump in her pink bridesmaid's dress,
tried to float after her but feared she was too substantial, and thought
sadly that the best man would despise her. The best man, who like Michael
had finished his long training as an architect, and who had joined the

1

same large London firm of which Michael would one day become a partner. The best man, Edward, to whom she had now been married for nearly twenty years.

As girls and young women, Anna had been the pretty one. Laura had envied without rancour the golden hair, the blue eyes and slim figure, the porcelain skin. She felt herself to be ordinary looking, average, but thought that some faint glow of reflected glory from Anna might light up her mid-brown hair, her grey eyes, her plump shape and her skin that, though mercifully clear, still lacked Anna's pink and white perfection. Now, however, at forty-two, her figure was trim, her hair was well cut and still the same soft brown it had always been, her skin was lightly tanned from working in the garden but almost free of lines. It was Anna who was overweight, whose skin and hair were faded by anxiety and sorrow. None of that mattered, though. They were still as close as they had ever been, their friendship unchanged.

Anna in the sixth form, beautiful even in the unbecoming uniform of shapeless flannel skirt and ill-cut blouse of virulent mauve. She had been adored by all the younger girls so that, between them, as head girl and school captain, they had led the school without effort, bathed in the radiance of the golden nimbus that is only to be seen round the great ones of a small, enclosed world. Anna starting at the school, homesick and woebegone, turning to her friend Laura for comfort. An even earlier Anna going to their weekly dancing class, giggling with Laura as they changed into their pink silk tunics. Anna, yesterday, turning to Laura in despair and saying, 'She's impossible! I just can't cope with her, Laura. I don't know what to do with her. For her. It's just . . . impossible!'

Oh dear, thought Laura. What do I say? The answer is, of course, that neither of them is impossible, really, but that both of them are as well. Sometimes.

'Not really,' she at last replied feebly to Daisy. 'No more impossible than anyone else.'

'Oh, *you*,' said Daisy in affectionate exasperation. 'You're just so tactful! Go on, tell me it's me who's impossible, not Mummy.'

'I wouldn't dream of it! But is that what you think?' Laura thought this was rather cunning, but Daisy shook her head.

'No, no, I'm wise to that one. You won't get me to make an admission like that. You forget that I've been trained in the hard school of counselling sessions. After Daddy died. You'll have to be much more subtle than that to catch me out.'

'I don't want to catch you out,' retorted Laura mildly. 'I just don't

2

know what to say to you. What do you want me to say?'

'Oh, just tell me I'm perfect, and wonderful, and the best god-daughter in the world.'

'Well, you are. To me, you are.'

Daisy sighed. 'Wrong again. Poor Laura. I'm a selfish cow, I have no consideration for my poor mother after all she's been through; all I do is shout and scream and slam doors. But I don't *mean* to. I don't want to be like that. When I'm not with her, like this, I can't believe the things I do, the way I behave. And I always mean to stop, to change, to be better; but as soon as I'm at home with her – wham! There's the Wicked Witch of the West sitting inside my head. It's awful.'

She gave a sniff. She was enjoying her self-abasement, Laura saw, as much as she had enjoyed criticising her mother. Revelling in it.

'It's called adolescence,' Laura said mildly.

'Oh, *don't* tell me it's all a stage and I'll grow out of it! I thought I could trust you not to say things like that, God-mother!'

'Well, but it is, of course it is!' Laura let her hands lie idle on the dough. 'That's what life is like. Lots of stages. You move from one to the next, and hope to cope with the new one by using what you've learned in the earlier ones. Sometimes you can, sometimes you can't. I mean, you could just as well say that *I'm* going through a stage, too. If it makes you feel better.'

'No, are you?' Daisy leaned forward, her face vivid with interest. Her skin was so fine it was almost translucent, and the one red spot on her cheek seemed less a blemish than something to accentuate the perfection of the rest, like an eighteenth-century calico-patch. 'Not the Change, already? You're far too young! Does that mean Mummy is too? Is that why she's so impossible? Hot flushes? HRT? How fascinating!'

'As a matter of fact, no.' Laura was amused. 'And even if I were, it doesn't have to follow that your mother is. We're not linked like Siamese twins, you know. As I remember it, I started my periods months before she did. She was terribly jealous, though I can't think why, now. But no hot flushes, or HRT. We haven't reached that stage yet.'

Daisy sat back again. 'No. Sorry. You don't mind, do you? That I said it, I mean? I did say I thought you were too young,' she added disingenuously.

'Thank you, I noticed. And no, of course I don't mind. But what I *do* mind – bother it – is that my dough has stuck to the worktop now I've stopped kneading it. Pass me that knife, please, I'm all floury.'

Daisy twisted round, contorting her body rather than getting off the stool.

3

'There you are. How long do you have to do that for?'

'The kneading? Ten minutes, usually. Longer, if I'm feeling stressed. It's a good way of getting rid of aggression.'

'Aggression? You? You're kidding.'

'Ah, but that's just what I mean. If I didn't make bread once a week, I'd be the Mad Axewoman of Ashingly.'

'Yeah, I can imagine.'

Laura put the ball of dough back in the bowl to rise, turning it to coat it with the spoonful of oil she had added. She stretched clingfilm over the top, and put the bowl on the side of the Aga. Daisy leaned forward and scraped a little lump of dough from the worktop with her thumbnail, then sat, like a large and sinister toddler, with her thumb in her mouth. Her nails were painted matt black.

'You'll get worms. That's what my granny used to say.'

'Yuk.' Daisy reached out for some more. 'It's quite nice, raw. You can taste the yeast.'

'Perhaps it will ferment inside you, and turn into beer or something.'

'And I'll go home drunk – don't I wish! It's the most boring Easter holidays ever. I still can't believe Mummy wouldn't let me spend those three days in London with the others. I mean, everyone else was going. Why have I got to stay in prison?'

Laura considered the large and beautiful house, with its tennis court and indoor swimming pool, bought by Michael at the height of his career as a successful architect, where Anna still lived.

'Yes, it *is* hellish, your home, isn't it? How you must be suffering. Only one swimming pool, no helicopter pad, not even a private disco . . .'

Daisy grinned ruefully. 'Oh, you know what I mean. But seriously, don't you think I should have gone to the concert with the others? And the party? It was all organised, and we were staying at Emma's house with her parents and everything. It wasn't an orgy.'

Laura thought that Anna was, understandably, a bit over-protective of her daughter, but she had no intention of saying so.

'I thought you had GCSEs to revise for? Haven't you been working on them?'

Daisy shrugged, looking sullen. 'Stupid. They're a complete waste of time. Why do we have to learn all this useless stuff?'

Laura remembered herself and Anna saying much the same thing about their own O-levels, but didn't think Anna would thank her for saying so.

'Because our whole aim in life, my dear god-daughter, is to make your existence a burden and a misery to you. You must have noticed?'

4

Daisy laughed, unselfconscious as the child she still nearly was. 'Oh, Laura, I do love you! You're really great. Why is it I can talk to you and I can't talk to Mummy? My friends come round and talk to her all the time, they keep saying how wonderful she is and how lucky I am; it drives me mad. They go on and on about how easy she is to tell things to, and how understanding, and how brave she is about Daddy and everything, but it isn't like that for me. Oh, I know she is brave, was brave, all of that, but she never would talk about it. She never told me what she was thinking or feeling, or anything about Daddy. And I wanted to know!'

It was, quite suddenly, a cry from the heart. Help, thought Laura. I think I'm out of my depth here. How could I have thought it was over, finished with? Michael's been dead for three years, Daisy was thirteen then, eleven when his illness was diagnosed. We thought she had to be protected.

'She wanted to protect you,' she said carefully. 'You were only a child.'

'You can't *protect* people from their father having cancer,' said Daisy with passionate bitterness. 'You can't protect them from him dying. Not even if it's a child, which I wasn't, not really. Not inside.'

'No,' said Laura. 'I'm sorry,' she said, inadequately. 'She – we – meant it for the best. There aren't any blueprints, you know. No one comes along and gives you an instruction manual. You just do what seems right at the time, what you can, what comes to you. There isn't anything else.'

Daisy drew in a shaky breath, running careful fingertips beneath black-rimmed and heavily mascaraed eyes.

'I know,' she said, 'I'm sorry. For the outburst. I do know, really. I know, but I can't . . . understand. Oh, Laura.' At last she climbed down from her stool and came to lean against Laura, who put her arms round her, amazed as ever to feel the slender fineness of the girl within the bulky, tattered clothes. At sixteen she was still not much bigger than she had been at twelve, and Laura had wondered from time to time whether it was possible for unhappiness, at a certain age, to inhibit growth.

Daisy rubbed her cheek against Laura's shoulder. 'You smell nice,' she said inconsequentially. Laura, knowing what she was trying to say, tightened her hug a fraction.

'It's such a pity you never had any children. You'd have made a marvellous mother.'

Laura felt Daisy's body stiffen into rigidity within her arms before the import of the words had even registered. Then she felt the usual mixture of embarrassment for the other person, and slightly bored resignation for herself. Daisy tried to pull away from her, and she patted her on the shoulder before releasing her. Little white puffs of flour floated up and hung in the air, white handprints marked the black cloth.

'It's all right,' Laura said soothingly, before the other could speak.

'Oh, Laura!' Daisy's face, raised piteously to hers, was aghast. 'Oh, Laura, I'm so sorry! I shouldn't have said it! How awful, how stupid of me to be so thoughtless! I didn't mean it!'

'You didn't mean I'd be a marvellous mother?' Laura tried, without much hope, to lower the emotional level, but Daisy was well into teenage over-reaction, and shook off the attempt like a bird in a puddle shedding water.

'No, of *course* I didn't mean that! Of course you would be! That's what makes it so awful, it's such a waste, I mean, it's so sad for you!' Tears flooded her blue eyes without staining the clear white of them and without, Laura was interested to see, smudging the black eyeliner and mascara that rimmed them. Here we go again, she thought.

'It was a pity, yes. And I did feel sad about it, very sad, for quite a while. But it's over now. I don't mind any more.'

Daisy looked unconvinced. She was near enough childhood herself to feel that a child is the centre, the pivot and keystone of a family. She thought how lonely her own mother would have been without her. And, of course, without Guy, though that seemed easier to imagine.

'But . . . you're so alone!' she wailed.

'Alone? Of course I'm not alone! I've got Edward, for a start – and don't let him hear you saying I'm alone, he'd be mortified! – and my old dears, and my sister, and my friends. Anna, of course, and Jane and Cassandra. And you, and my other god-children. And the cats. And the house. I can assure you, darling Daisy, that my life is very full and happy, and I think I am a very lucky woman.'

Laura believed what she said. In all the forty-two years of her life, nothing had ever happened to her to shake her belief that life was fundamentally a pleasant and rewarding business. A happy, unremarkable childhood had been followed by an adolescence marred by no more *angst* than was caused by puppy-fat, spots, or the delicious misery of falling violently in love with a succession of film and pop stars. Marriage to Edward had given her the added security of a close and loving relationship, and the real sorrow of their childlessness had drawn them still closer together. And even that anguish, and the present anxiety about Edward's finances, had not shaken Laura's intrinsic belief that the balance of life was weighted on the good side. Rather, it reassured her with the feeling that she was getting her share of the bad things and that she was, rather commendably, coping with them. She saw herself as someone who could not only deal with disasters, but who could help her friends with theirs as well. Her strength came from the conviction that every down was balanced by an up, that beyond the darkness was light, and that ultimately there must always be some kind of happy ending.

'A very lucky woman,' Laura repeated. 'In fact, I sometimes think, too lucky.'

Daisy was not altogether convinced. Even though, at times when they had been fighting more bitterly than usual, her mother had been known to utter vehement words of regret that she had ever had children, Daisy's life nevertheless rested firmly on the bedrock of being loved and wanted. She was adult enough to see, however, that the best thing she could do was to appear, at least, to accept Laura's assurances.

'Yes, I suppose so.' Her tone was dubious. She tried again. 'Edward is *really* nice. The nicest man I know, in fact, now Daddy's died.'

'Yes, he is, isn't he? I suppose, statistically, that puts me well ahead. It's much harder to find a really nice husband than to have babies, after all.'

'I hope I do. Find a nice man, I mean. I'm not so sure about the babies.'

'Oh, you'll be all right. You know they say girls usually marry men like their fathers. And you couldn't do better than that, could you?'

'No. But I'll have him thoroughly checked over first. Like when you buy a horse. I'm not going through that again.'

Laura laughed. 'There you are, now. Making jokes about your father dying.'

Daisy's smooth brow wrinkled. 'You're not shocked, are you? It's only a way of talking . . .'

'I know it is, and of course I'm not shocked. But if you were to say something like that to someone you don't know very well, perhaps someone at school, how do you think they'd react?'

Daisy put her head on one side, thinking, and brushing absently at patches of flour on her shoulders and on her black skirt.

'They'd be a bit shocked, I should think. And embarrassed. Very embarrassed. People are, I find, when I mention Daddy. They don't know what to say, and I have to sort of reassure them.'

'Precisely. And that's more or less what happens with me, and not having any children. Isn't that what happened just now?'

Daisy was surprised. 'Yes. Yes, I suppose it is. But . . . does that mean you like to talk about it? Like I like talking about Daddy, only hardly anyone will?'

Laura was rubbing her hands together over the sink, scattering a little shower of floury dough-crumbs. She turned on the tap.

'Not really. At least, it's not that I don't want to talk about it in the sense that it's something I don't like discussing. But I don't *need* to talk about it any more. It's finished with. Like a dress I used to wear all the time; I've folded it up and put it away. Sometimes I might take it out and look at it, but I don't wear it any more. Does that make sense?'

'Mm. Will I feel like that about Daddy, one day?'

'I don't know. Perhaps. Probably not. After all, he was a real person, someone you knew and loved and who was and always will be a part of your life. You don't want to put him out of your mind. But my children that I didn't have weren't real like that. Of course there were many years when I minded, quite desperately. I thought and talked about it all the time. Your poor mother, and Jane – they were wonderful. I could never have got through it without them.'

'It's the other way round, now,' said Daisy wisely. 'They depend on you. I know Mummy's always saying she doesn't know how she'd cope without you. And Jane. You ring her a lot, don't you? Since Bill the Pill went off?'

'Yes,' agreed Laura, disregarding the soubriquet to which she had, regrettably, become accustomed, and with which she was basically in agreement. 'It's something I learned from her and your mother. They used to take it in turns, you know, to ring me every day, at the time when my periods were due. Every month, without fail. Not to say, "Has anything happened", but just to chat, and to see that I was all right, and to let me know they were thinking of me. It was such a comfort. Then, of course, we did it for your mother. And now, unfortunately, for Jane.'

'She's coping well, isn't she?' Unasked, Daisy picked up the kettle and took it to the tap. Jane's daughter, Candida, had been her best friend since they had started nursery school together, and neither their total dissimilarity of character nor the fact that they were at different schools had done anything to draw them apart. Daisy, with the memory of the loss of her own father still painfully recent, had wept almost more tears than her friend when Bill, Jane's husband, had announced a year and a half earlier that he was leaving them for another woman. Or, as they all tended to think of it, Another Woman.

'Amazingly well. I really admire her. She always seemed to be so, well, so quiet, really. Meek, even. I always thought she deferred to Bill all the time, let him run everything, and to be honest I would have expected her to go completely to pieces, wouldn't you?'

Daisy was profoundly flattered by being included in this adult viewpoint, but too honest to pretend she shared it.

'I suppose I never really thought about it – Jane, that is. Up until Bill went, she was just Candy's mother. Not as strict as Mummy, but of course I thought that was wonderful! I never really thought of her as a person. How awful.'

'Not at all. It's perfectly normal. Coffee, tea, or chocolate?'

'Oh . . . chocolate, please.' This, Laura knew, was a compliment. With people she didn't know very well, Daisy invariably asked for coffee, black and sugarless, because she thought it was more sophisticated. Chocolate, which she loved but felt was rather babyish, was a private treat to be enjoyed with those she felt close to. 'Candy still minds about her father. She cries about him a lot, but not in front of her mother. We talk about it, you know.'

'I know.' Laura measured out chocolate into a mug, put milk to heat and spooned freshly ground coffee into a pot. Real coffee was her greatest luxury, and she sniffed the heart-warming fragrance as she stood the pot on the side of the Aga. 'You can probably help her more than anyone. Just like Jane and your mother and I help each other.'

'Yes. It's good, isn't it? Friends, I mean. Mummy says it's something women are best at.'

'Yes, I think it is. Men don't talk to each other the way we do, or not often. Although I have to say, Edward is still my best friend, if that doesn't sound childish.'

'No, it sounds lovely. Oh, Laura, you are lucky.'

'I know,' she said soberly. 'I am lucky. Very lucky.'

She passed the mug of chocolate to Daisy, then poured her own coffee and added a splash of the heated milk. They sat opposite one another at the kitchen table, and sipped companionably. It was cold for late April, the sky grey and forbidding as it had been for what seemed like weeks, and the warmth of the Aga was welcome in the large kitchen. Outside, the garden was very green, but the few flowers that had showed themselves were tinged with brown by the incessant damp and rain, and in the evenings Edward swore he could hear the champing teeth of the snails and slugs as they wreaked havoc among the borders.

Beyond the garden was a band of woodland, then fields rising up to the Ashdown Forest. Laura, born and brought up in London, never ceased to be amazed and enchanted by the view, and blessed the day that had brought her and Edward to Ashingly. They had been visiting Anna, who had just moved into the large house on the edge of the village with Michael, Guy, and two-year-old Daisy. They had fallen in love with the place, with its village green bordered by church, pub and village shop, and when some months later a house that fronted the green came on the market they had been overjoyed. Edward, kindly and generous and deeply concerned at Laura's unhappiness at failing to conceive, had seen the presence nearby of Anna and her family as a blessing to be encouraged. He had not, thought Laura fondly, a possessive bone in his body.

'How's school?' asked Laura, who really wanted to know.

'Oh, ghastly as ever,' was Daisy's automatic reply. 'I really hate it. It's so repressive, worse than prison.'

'You were the one who begged to go there,' Laura pointed out. 'You could have stayed on at Princess Mary's.'

'Well, that was just as bad,' said Daisy gloomily. 'Worse, in a way.'

'No boys?'

Daisy had the grace to smile. 'Quite. And there's much more going on at Abbotsford. If only they'd let us do it, that is.'

'And you don't mind boarding?'

'No, not really. It's a relief, actually, to get away. Is that horrible of me?'

'No. I expect your mother finds it a relief too.'

'Yes, she does.' Daisy swirled her chocolate moodily round her mug. 'But I still feel *guilty* about her,' she burst out.

'Don't. There's no need. She's fine.'

'I know, but—'

The warble of the telephone interrupted them, rather to Laura's disappointment. She would have liked to hear more about Abbotsford, a minor public school that had recently opened its doors to admit girls, and which Daisy had begged, with tears, pleading, and promises of impeccable behaviour, to be allowed to attend after two years at Princess Mary's.

'Hello?'

'Laura!' The voice was instantly recognisable.

'Cassandra, how are you? I was going to ring you later, I haven't heard from you for ages. Well, days.'

'No.' The sound of a sniff. 'I'm . . . oh, Laura, could you come round? This afternoon? Please?'

'Yes, of course. You're not at the shop?' Cassandra, some years younger than Laura and Anna, ran a small and exclusive children's clothes shop in the nearby town that still managed, in spite of the recession, to do very well.

'No. Jenny's coping, I didn't feel up to it. You will come, won't you?'

'Yes, of course. This afternoon? Or now? I could if you like.' She raised an eyebrow at Daisy, who drained the rest of her chocolate.

'No, not now. This afternoon's fine. About three? Oh, thank you, Laura, I feel better already.'

'Good,' said Laura comfortably. 'I'll see you at three. Bye . . .' She waited a moment, because Cassandra sometimes liked to continue the leave-taking ceremony, dragging it out as though she couldn't bear to put the receiver down. She was, Laura knew, lonely. This time, though, she gave one last sniffle and was gone.

'Do you want me to go?' Daisy, obedient as always in other people's houses, was rinsing her mug at the sink.

'No, it's all right. I'm going round this afternoon. She seems to be having a bit of a crisis.' She paused. What do I say? she wondered. Does she know? It's not really the sort of thing you discuss with a sixteen-year-old. And she wouldn't know about the time she had the . . . No. I don't think Cassandra discussed that with the others.

Daisy blinked at her. Should I tell her I know? she thought. She might be shocked. Mummy would have been. Better not, perhaps. She had been shocked herself, though she would never have admitted it, when her mother's friend Cassandra had told her about her long-standing affair with a married man. Cassandra, though younger than her mother (and indeed, with her slim figure, lovely clothes and beautifully styled hair, looking far less than her thirty-seven years), was still old in Daisy's eyes.

They sat in thoughtful silence. Then Laura, rousing herself, finished her coffee. 'Do you want to stay for lunch? I can make some of that dough into a pizza, if you'd like.'

'Oh yum. I think about your pizza at school, when they give us spaghetti and sick.'

'Daisy!'

'Sorry. That's what we call it. Because it looks like . . . yes, well. It's the bits of carrot, you see. Have you ever noticed . . .'

'Daisy!'

'Yes, yes, sorry sorry sorry. I've stopped. And yes, I'd love some pizza, if it isn't a nuisance.'

'Of course not. Should you tell Anna?'

A mutinous look. 'I'm not a baby!'

'Of course not. And that means you're old enough to know that if someone is likely to be getting lunch for you, it's a good idea to let them know you're not going to be there.'

'You sound just like Guy.'

'Thank you. I'll take that as a compliment, though I don't suppose it's meant as one.'

Daisy kicked at the table leg. 'He's so hideously good, it's quite revolting. Never late, never in trouble, never rude. What have I done to deserve a brother like that? He's not normal.'

'He's setting you a good example.'

'Well, he shouldn't. It doesn't work, and it only makes me worse. You can't imagine what it's like at school. Even now, when it's – what – five years since he left, they all go on and on about "Guy did this" and "Guy never did that" until I could puke. Oh, sorry. I'm not supposed to talk about sick any more. But that's what he makes me.'

Laura couldn't help thinking that Guy, who was polite, thoughtful and sober, was also the most boring young man she had ever encountered. 'Completely without a spark', as Jane had once said. 'Asexual. Or just not interested in other people. Selfish.' Jane, since Bill had left, had become rather cynical and acerbic about men.

'It's not easy, having an older brother who's clever *and* well behaved,' said Laura with some sympathy. She fetched a bag of pizza-topping from the freezer and put it in the microwave. 'Still, if it's any comfort I'm sure he finds you just as aggravating as you find him.'

'When I think,' grumbled Daisy, 'of all that potential going to waste! Wouldn't you think that a brother of twenty-three would be bringing home all sorts of interesting and attractive friends for his little sister to meet? My friends at school were dead jealous at first, couldn't believe I wasn't holding out on them. That was before they met Guy.'

'It seems to me,' said Laura with mock severity, 'that there are quite enough boys in your life already, without getting entangled with Older Men.'

Daisy giggled. 'It's quite impossible to have too many boys in your life. Safety in numbers, that's what I tell Mummy. And hasn't anybody told you that girls are *far* more mature than boys at my age?'

'Some girls.'

'Oh, very biting. Can we have bits of salami on the pizza? And anchovies? And pineapple?'

'Yes, yes, and no. I don't have any pineapple. Unless you want to go to the shop and get some?'

'Can't be bothered. It's too cold out there. Was that a car in the drive?'

'Possibly. I'm not expecting anyone. Probably a double-glazing salesman. Or a posse of Jehovah's Witnesses. I'll rely on you to frighten them off.'

'No, they always come on foot. Witnesses, that is. I don't know about double-glazing salesmen. Shall I go to the door?'

Laura was greasing a pizza dish with olive oil, and nodded.

'Brush the flour off you first. I seem to have left white handprints on your waistcoat, and it rather detracts from the *tout ensemble*.'

'It *is* good, isn't it?' said Daisy happily, brushing ineffectually at her shoulders and back and sending a sprinkling of sequins and glass beads to the floor, like a small sparkling snowstorm. 'No one's rung the doorbell. I'll go and look. Perhaps it's burglars. Oh! Edward! It's you!'

Laura turned round. Edward home before lunch on a Tuesday was unheard of. She felt a small leap of pleasure which turned into gut-twisting anxiety as she saw his face. She laid down the pizza dish very carefully.

'Hello, darling. It's lovely to see you, but is anything wrong? You're not ill, are you?'

Edward's face was the colour of lard beneath the faint tan that he never altogether lost. He was tall, with a thick head of springing brown curls that the damp had made even wilder than usual. Laura loved his hair, and was secretly proud that his hairline showed no sign of receding. Only a dusting of silver at the temples betrayed his age, for his tall body was still muscular and lithe, his step springing and his hazel eyes bright and keen.

Not, however, at the moment. He seemed unable to meet her look but, even averted, his eyes looked blank and shocked. He blinked at Daisy, as if he had no idea who she was.

'Ill?' he said vaguely. 'No, I'm not ill. I just came home . . .' He came to a halt, standing in the middle of the kitchen with the helpless look of something that has been washed up on the beach. 'Hello, er, Daisy. Not at school, then?' He had seen Daisy a few days earlier, and had listened with his usual interest to her plans for the rest of the holidays.

'No. Term starts next week. Um . . .' Daisy flickered an anxious glance at Laura, who gave her a little smile but shook her head very slightly. 'Um, I ought to be getting back. Mummy will be . . . Thanks for the drink, Laura . . . um, goodbye, Edward.'

He smiled at her, the kind of smile that chilled Laura's blood.

'Daisy . . . ring Cassandra for me, would you?' Laura kept her tone casual, but Daisy gave her a stricken glance and nodded before slipping out, closing the door with exaggerated care.

Laura leaned with both her hands on the floury worktop, as if grounding herself in reality. As always, she looked for the worst and most likely thing, and tried to accustom herself to the idea of it. Bankruptcy, she thought. I knew things were bad, but I knew he probably wasn't telling me how bad. I always knew the risks when Edward decided to leave London and start up on his own down here. Things were going well, too, until the recession. We may have to sell the house. Well, if we must, we must. I can bear that. I can get a job. Yes, it'll be all right. She straightened herself, lifted her head to look at him.

'What is it, Edward?'

He ran a hand over his face, as if it were clogged with cobwebs. He still didn't look at her.

'Something to tell you. Something I have to tell you, Laura.'

'I think we'd better sit down, don't you?' Laura drew in a trembling breath, and tried not to remember Michael finding that he had cancer. 'Come on, darling. Whatever it is, it'll be all right.'

Make it true, she said fiercely to God. Make it be true.

Chapter 2

Edward seemed unable to move from the middle of the kitchen floor. Laura walked round him to get the kettle, round him again to take it to the tap, and again back to the Aga where she lifted the lid and put it on the hot ring. It was an automatic action; something to do, to occupy the vacuum they seemed to be in. From the look on Edward's face, whisky or brandy might have been more appropriate, but neither of them liked drinking at lunchtime. Later, when he had said what he had to say, that might be the time for alcohol. Coffee, at least, would be warming.

The familiar ritual of grinding the beans, measuring the coffee into the rinsed jug, setting out mugs, was reassuring. This was not the time, Laura told herself, to wonder whether they would in future be able to afford real coffee. Most people lived quite happily with instant, after all. When it was poured, milk added, she put the mugs on the table.

'Come and sit down,' she said gently. Meekly, as obedient as a child, he did. It was strange to see him sitting there in his business suit in the middle of a weekday. Scruffy by inclination, he was in the habit of changing into jeans and a sweatshirt the minute he set foot in the house, and a site visit was the signal for an instant change of clothes.

It seemed odd to be sitting opposite him in the old denim skirt she kept for days at home, the cotton jumper she had worn over her cream blouse discarded in the warmth of the kitchen. She put her hand up to her hair, knowing that the short style she preferred was unlikely to be untidy. She found herself wishing she had renewed her lipstick after the earlier cup of coffee. How ridiculous, she thought, to be worrying about lipstick at a time like this. She gave her head a little shake.

Edward's hands were gripped tightly together; she had the feeling that he was restraining himself from burying his head in them. She drew in a deep breath, and reached for the coffee. It tasted sour in her mouth, and she put the mug down abruptly.

'Please tell me,' she said. 'Please tell me what it is, now, because seeing you sit there like that is frightening me to death. You're not ill? Promise you're not ill?'

'Ill?' Again he sounded as if this was a word he had never encountered before. 'Ill? No, of course not. You know I'm not.'

'That's what Anna thought. About Michael,' she elucidated at his blank look. 'She thought he was perfectly well. Until he found that he wasn't, that his cough was more than just a leftover chest infection.'

He shook his head, not so much as a negative as to clear it, she thought. At last his eyes met hers. She saw worry in them, and fear, and something else.

'No, no, it's nothing like that. I'm not ill, I haven't got anything sinister wrong with me. You mustn't worry about that. It's . . . oh God, I don't know how to say it. How to tell you. I can't bear to hurt you, I don't want you to hate me . . .'

She had seen the anxiety in his eyes. Now she recognised the guilt as well. She sat up straighter, lifted her chin. 'It's not money, then? You know I wouldn't mind about that.'

He shook his head. An idea came to her, so commonplace that most women, she thought, would have thought of it at once. But Edward? Her Edward? It was so improbable that it seemed preposterous. Yet it had been guilt she had seen. 'Someone else?' Her voice was hard, accusing, but it was too late to change it.

'No! Yes, but not . . . I'm not in love with anyone else. You must know that! You're the only woman in the world that I love, I couldn't bear to be parted from you, ever . . . Unless you don't want me any more,' he finished with a humility that was more frightening, to Laura, than aggression would have been.

'So, you're not going off with a dolly-bird?' She tried to make a joke of it, but her voice shook.

'No,' he groaned. 'No, that's the last thing I want.'

He sat looking at her, as if he had forgotten what she looked like or as if to imprint her image on his retina. He seemed unable to continue.

'So, what was it? A one-night stand?' she asked, to help him. Dumbly he nodded his head.

It was bound to happen some time, she thought. He's an attractive man. He meets people all the time. Women like him, and he likes women. I've always known that. I've seen them at parties, we've laughed about it afterwards, together. So he got carried away, had too much to drink. It happens. It happens all the time. I can live with that. I don't like it, but I can live with it. Come to terms with it, put it out of my mind, try not to imagine . . . no, don't think that. I mustn't damage things, make them worse than they already are.

'It's all right.' She tried to sound convincing. 'I know these things happen. I do understand. But . . . oh, Edward, I wish you hadn't told me. I'd much rather not have known!'

It was true. She, who had always thought that honesty and openness were the foundations of a good relationship, suddenly found herself wishing with all her heart that he had done anything – lied, cheated, whatever – rather than tell her. Her mind spiralled into overdrive.

'She's not blackmailing you, is she? Is that why you've come rushing home to tell me? I mean, I assume it didn't happen this morning, over a cup of coffee and a digestive?' Steady, she thought. You're sounding a bit shrill.

Edward's brow furrowed, perplexed.

'Blackmail?' He almost smiled. 'State secrets, thousands of pounds in a numbered Swiss bank account? No, nothing like that. Of course not.' He sighed, his momentary flash of humour dissipating beneath the burden he still carried. 'You don't understand. I haven't told it yet.'

'You mean, there's more? Worse?'

'Yes. Much worse, for you. For us.' He sucked in air, a drowning man. 'It's not a recent thing. It was years ago. Before we moved here, before I stopped working in London. A Christmas party, fifteen years ago. You didn't go, you weren't well, you were actually down here, staying with Anna.'

Fifteen years ago. Fifteen years ago she had been unwell, regularly, every month. Every third week the building hope, the anxious self-examination. Are my breasts tender? Do I feel sick this morning? Then the fourth week, putting off going to the lavatory because she knew, deep down, that there would be a spotting of blood to tell her that another period, regular as clockwork and as soulless, had arrived. Then she would withdraw into her shell, surround herself with a cocoon of warm drinks and hot-water bottles and soothing books and telephone calls from friends, until the sharpness of the pain skinned over with the fragile scar tissue that was, so soon, to be torn open again.

'Go on.' Her mouth was dry. She drank more coffee, felt sick.

'Well, as you say, it happens. I had too much to drink, knowing I could stay the night in town and thinking it wouldn't matter. She was a temp., nineteen. Pretty, I suppose, though I can scarcely remember what she looked like. Aggressive, certainly. Out to prove that she was as good as any man and better than most. Bright. Argumentative. That's what

17

attracted me, really. We argued all evening, it was . . . stimulating. Exhausting, but . . . And in the end we went back to her flat.'

He scrubbed at his face with his hands again. 'That's where I went wrong, of course. I should never have gone back with her. I swear to you, Laura, that I didn't go intending to . . . in fact, if I'd thought it was likely, I'd have run a mile. She told me she was sharing a flat, you see, with three others, two girls and a young man, and she thought they'd be there. They were like her, she said, they had endless discussions and arguments, just like we'd been doing. And I suppose, in my stupid fuddled way, I thought they'd be there, we'd talk and laugh and have a take-away . . . but they were out. She didn't expect that, either. But when I said I'd go, she fired up, got all heated, said I was being sexist and did I think she was incapable of having a rational discussion with a man without falling into bed? So I stayed. And . . . and it just happened. Afterwards, in the morning, we were both furious, both blamed each other, had a blazing row and that was the end of it. I was so ashamed, so bitterly angry with myself, but I swore I wouldn't tell you. I thought I could cancel it out.'

But. The word hovered in the air between them, like a hologram, like a laser light display. But. There could be only one but, and Laura felt her insides shrink and harden. Her skin contracted as if she had been exposed to a blast of sub-zero air; if she moved, she thought it would crack and split. A mummy, she thought, preserved through thousands of years in its sarcophagus, imploding into dust as, unwrapped, it met the air. A mummy! The word could scarcely have been less appropriate.

Edward knew, they both knew – although it was never spoken of between them – that their childlessness was on her account, not his. They had both had tests. Both of them, at the time, had been pronounced healthy and normal. No one, none of the specialists they had visited, had ever been able to come up with an explanation of why she did not conceive. Nevertheless, the presumption remained that the flaw, if flaw there was, lay in her. Come on, she thought. What was it you were saying to Daisy, how this was all in the past, didn't bother you any more? Let's get it over with.

'But she got pregnant?' She listened to her own voice saying the words, and was amazed at how normal it sounded.

'Yes.' He looked at her. His brown eyes were full of anguish. 'I'm sorry.'

'Not your fault.' It sounded ridiculous, but he knew what she meant. Not your fault that she could do, so casually and easily, what I spent all those years trying to achieve. They were both quiet for a moment, the silence a requiem for lost hopes and babies that never were. 'Go on,' she said. 'You'd better tell me the rest.'

He nodded. It wasn't over yet. The worst, perhaps, but not all of it.

'She telephoned me three months later. Said she was pregnant, that the baby was mine. I was . . . well, you can imagine. Horrified. Appalled. Disbelieving. I said it couldn't be mine. She assured me it was, but I couldn't believe her. Actually, I've never been a hundred per cent sure . . . but how could I argue? I could have asked for blood tests, I suppose, but I was so terrified you'd hear about it, all I could think of was hushing it up, keeping her quiet.

'I told her I'd pay, if she wanted to, you know . . . Pay for the best, private treatment, nursing home, whatever she wanted.' Laura winced. For Edward to have suggested an abortion, when at that time she herself was desperate to conceive – it was grotesque. Edward looked at her. 'I know. It's appalling, but . . . I couldn't believe in this baby as *mine*. All I could think about was how it would affect you. I suppose I just wanted to negate it, to make it not have happened. Anyway, it didn't make any difference. She said it was her baby, she wasn't going to get rid of it to suit me. She . . . screamed it. Over the telephone.'

He drew in a shaking breath, looked at his hands as though wondering where his cigarette was: he who hadn't smoked for twenty years. Laura felt she should reach out to him, take his hands, reassure him, but she was frozen. She thought that if she moved she might crumble into little pieces, and as for touching him . . . She looked at his hands, that had been intimate, however long ago, with this girl, and shivered.

'Go on.'

'So I said . . . if she had the baby, that I, that we . . . we would have it. Adopt it.'

The word fell between them like a stone into mud.

Adopt. They had discussed it, of course. Discussed it endlessly, together and with their friends. Knowing with every day that went by that their chances diminished. Knowing that, however quickly they acted, the likelihood that they would be offered a baby, a healthy, unhandicapped baby of any colour, let alone their own, was minuscule. Discussed the possibility of adopting a child of mixed race, an older child, or a child with a handicap. Laura had spent days and weeks imagining herself with a child that was blind, or deaf, or Down's Syndrome. There were times when she thought she could manage anything, bear any future difficulties if only she could have a child in her empty arms, now. Her hands and arms would ache, physically, with the longing to feel that small body against hers. She had held Daisy, and wept over her while Anna wept in sympathy with her.

In the end, however, she had not done it. Partly because she could never be sure that she could manage it, but mostly, she knew, because so many people had told her that if she adopted she was almost sure to become pregnant soon afterwards. Conditions such as hers, where the cause of barrenness was unknown, frequently resolved themselves like that, she knew. That possibility, oddly, had frightened her, because deep down she felt that if she were to find herself carrying her own child in her womb, she would never be able to give an adopted child, particularly one with special problems, the undivided care and attention it would certainly need.

So she had slowly come to terms with it, fought the mental and physical longings and forced them into submission. Sublimated them not by working with children, which she felt would be inviting more emotional problems, but by doing voluntary work at a local old people's home. Now, all the memories she had thought were tamed and subdued shook themselves and rose up alert and untamed, as she imagined, for the first time in many years, holding a baby – not hers, but at least Edward's – in her arms.

'Oh, Edward.'

'If I could have given him to you . . . I thought it would have been anguish, in a way, but perhaps . . . perhaps it might have made up for it. A bit. A kind of give and take, you know?'

Laura swallowed. Tried to imagine how it could have been. Saw, ridiculously, Edward coming home from the office with a baby in his briefcase. 'Hello, darling, I've brought you something from work. A little present. Here you are, I knew you wanted one, I hope it's the right kind.' Like a book, or a kitchen gadget. Would she have taken him? It was, she gathered, a boy. Could she have done it? Even now, she could not be sure. She was not, now, the same person she had been then. Now older, more secure, less emotional perhaps, she thought it would have been all right. But then? The blow to her pride alone might have been insupportable. Quite suddenly she was relieved that it had not happened, that the moment had been postponed until now.

She swallowed, a gulp that made her fear, for a moment, that she might vomit. Breathed in through her nose, slowly, held the air as though she could not bear to let it go, exhaled through her mouth at last. 'She wouldn't agree. Obviously.'

'No. More shouting. I was trying to buy her child, like a commodity. Buying and selling, she said, was all I knew. And she was not for sale. It was . . . unpleasant.'

'Yes.' She did not say, though she could not help thinking it, 'So it should be. You deserved to suffer for what you did.' There was no need, anyway. She could not, she saw, blame him more bitterly than he did himself. 'So what happened? You must have arranged something. Or would she not let you?'

'She *allowed* me,' he said bitterly, '*allowed* me to support the child. The boy. Permitted me to pay her an allowance for his keep. Not a great deal. Not as much as I would have liked. But enough so that they could live comfortably, and so that she did not need to work, for the first few years at least. Not blackmail,' he said wryly. 'Far from it: she didn't want to take anything from me. But she was practical enough to see, at least, that she needed my help if he – and she – were going to have any kind of decent life. As he has grown, I have increased the amount, and every time there has been a battle with her.' I bet, thought Laura with uncharacteristic sourness. Why did she ring you in the first place then? Why let you know about the baby at all, if she didn't want anything from you?

'All these years,' she said reflectively, 'and I had no idea. How strange. All these years, when I thought I knew you, I thought we were as close as any couple could be.'

'But you do! We are!' His eyes were desolate, full of tears. It was one of the things she had always loved about him, that he was not ashamed to cry in front of her. Now she hardened her heart to pity and shook her head.

'What should I have done?' he burst out. 'What could I have done for the best? How could I tell you, as things were then? How could I bear to hurt you like that? I couldn't bear to lose you. I still can't bear it. If it comes to a choice, he is nothing to me. Nothing, compared to you.'

'Your own child . . .'

'A moment of pleasure, a memory of a girl I can't even visualise any more, that's all. Of course I wanted children. Not as desperately as you did, perhaps, because I don't believe any man can understand what bearing a child means to a woman – but badly enough. But the children I wanted were your children, yours and mine. Part of us, of our marriage. An expression of our love, an extension of it. That's why I never pushed for an adoption. It's not just any child I want. How can I feel this boy is mine? I'm not even sure he is. I feel more for Daisy and Guy and Candy and Ben than I can for him. You love the young ones you've seen as babies and toddlers and children. I can't love an abstract, an idea, just because he was – perhaps – created from my sperm.'

Laura looked at him, astonished. 'Do you mean you've never seen

21

him? Your son, and you've never even set eyes on him?'

Her tone was accusing. She felt as if the ground were giving way beneath her, or she were trying to breathe air that suddenly contained no oxygen.

'She wouldn't let me,' he said simply. 'I've never even seen her from that first time to now. And I've never seen the boy. Not even a photograph of him. In fact, I suppose I've never even checked to see that he actually exists.' He smiled mirthlessly. 'Only I'm afraid he does.'

Laura ran her hands through her hair, tugged at it as if the pain would clear her head.

'All these years you've paid for him, and never tried to see him? But you knew her address?' I would have done it, she thought. I'd have waited outside the house, hung around near the local schools. The girl had only seen Edward that once, too, Laura realised. She probably wouldn't remember him any better than he does her.

'I gave her my word.' His gentle voice was implacable. She knew him well enough to know that, having done that, made that one quixotic promise, he would never go back on it, however much it cost. And she found that she did know him, after all. He was still the man she thought he was. Oh, Edward. Oh, my poor love.

Her face must have been revealing, because for the first time he reached out to comfort her. Their hands met across the table, and clung. His fingers were icy cold, and she tried to project warmth and reassurance through her touch.

'What's his name?' That, at least, he must know.

'Mark. Mark Alcantara. Her name, of course. She wouldn't give him anything of mine, not even my name.'

'Mark. It's a good name. I've always liked Mark.'

'Yes.' He half smiled. 'Have you ever noticed how many people there are called Mark? It's sometimes seemed to me that every book I read, every play or programme I watch, has a Mark in it. It was unnerving. Like being haunted.'

'Mm.' There was more, she knew, but she was content to wait for a moment in this oasis of calm.

He gave her hands a little squeeze, and let them go. Laura braced herself.

'She telephoned me this morning,' said Edward without preamble. 'The first time, since the beginning. Every other time it's been a note in the post, to the office, asking me to call her at a particular time, giving the number. Different numbers. So I knew it was . . . important. A problem. She said she has to go to the States. For several months, she's not sure how long. Three or four, at least, maybe more. I don't know why, she didn't say, and I didn't ask. She had intended, she said, to take him with her. Mark. But she had decided not to. She said he'd been difficult recently. Argumentative. Aggressive. In trouble at school.'

'Not unusual at his age.' Laura tried to be positive, but already her heart was sinking.

'No. Anyway, he doesn't want to go, and she thinks it better not to take him. He wants to stay with friends, but she's worried he'd be too unsupervised, get into trouble. She saw the headmaster of his school, and he suggested Mark might respond better to a man. Might need, he said, a father-figure. She was furious, I could hear it in her voice. Furious with Mark, and with the headmaster, and with me, too.'

'So would I have been,' said Laura fairly. 'She's managed all this time, presumably, as a single parent. It's a bit of an insult to be told that some man can do a better job than you.'

'I know, I know, but . . . well, anyway, she said he had better come to me. To us. She sounded a bit desperate about it . . .'

Laura had known it must be coming, but the reality of hearing the words was still a shock. 'When?'

His look expressed gratitude, and pride, and fear. 'Soon. This weekend.'

'But – what about school? The term's about to start.'

'Yes. She thought he could go to the local comprehensive, if we could fix it. He's not started his GCSE coursework yet, thank goodness, so it's not as crucial as it might be. And it's a good school, isn't it? Jane is quite happy about it for Candida and Ben, isn't she?'

'Under the circumstances, yes.' Bill, a few months after leaving, had also announced that since he would be running two homes he would be unable to continue paying the expensive school fees for his children. Ben, who was clever and possibly even brilliant, had been on a scholarship but had refused to stay on at public school if his sister could not do so. 'So . . . what did you say to her?'

'I said I'd have to talk to you. That you must make the decision. She was angry about that, too, and yet she'd be the first one to say that a man should always consult his wife – sorry, his *partner* – about important decisions. Particularly as you'd be the one most affected by it. After all, I'll be at the office all day. It would be you who'd have all the work, all the looking after to do.'

'I don't mind that.' Laura waved a dismissive hand, knowing that the practical issues were the least of the problems. 'But fourteen, going on fifteen, in trouble at school, aggressive . . . supposing he's into drugs?'

'She said there was nothing like that.'

'She would, wouldn't she?' Laura thought some more. 'I don't know. I don't see how we can say no. He's your son, after all. Or she says he is, which comes to the same thing. We can't turn him away. And it's only for a while.'

He took a mouthful of coffee, cold by now. His hand, she saw, was shaking. He had known, of course, that she would be unable to say no. She had never been able to, whether it was to a beggar or to friends needing help with some boring or unpleasant chore. Telling her about Mark must have been, she knew, perhaps the worst thing he had ever had to do. Her skin prickled. She needed time to think about this, to digest it and plan for it. For now she felt the necessity of moving, of doing something, of being busy. The anodyne properties of physical activity were only too well known to her: in the past she had cleaned and polished, stripped down walls and woodwork and redecorated them, dug furiously in the garden.

Briskly she stood up, picked up their mugs and took them to the sink. 'Pizza for lunch, OK?'

'Of course. Anything. I could take some time off work if you like. The first few weeks, say.'

She fetched the dough from the Aga, floured the worktop and flopped the risen mass out of the bowl. It hissed gently as she squashed it down, breathing out a beery gas. She sucked it into her lungs like a smoker inhaling the first cigarette of the day. She spoke briskly.

'Let's see how it goes, shall we? After all, he'll be at school most of the day. Are you home for the rest of today? If you ring the school, perhaps we could go over and see them this afternoon, sort things out, fill in forms and things.'

He was grateful for her practical attitude, understanding that she would as always want time to absorb and contemplate this change in their lives, and that until she had done so she would say little about it, to him or her friends.

'I wonder what he thinks about all this. Poor kid, it must be a strange feeling. He probably knows as little about you as you do about him.'

'I wrote to him.' Edward's voice was quiet and sad. 'I used to send him presents, at Christmas and birthdays, but she always sent them back. So I wrote, three or four times a year. Just chatty stuff, as if he were a distant relative in Australia. Told him about my work, and the house and garden, and the cats. About our holidays. It was difficult not to sound as though I was being patronising, or trying to tempt him away, but I tried to tell

24

him a bit about me. I had to. If he's my son. I couldn't let him grow up in a vacuum.'

Laura nodded, her hands busy shaping the dough into loaves and patting a portion into the pizza pan. Edward, born in the last year of the war, had never known his own father, who had been killed a few months after his birth. His father, for Edward, had been a fading photograph of a man in uniform, and the sanctified memories of his mother and his paternal grandparents. He had always felt, she knew, an incompleteness in him, as if he had been born with some vital organ missing. Some of the things she loved about him – his sensitivity, his kindness – stemmed from that feeling.

'He must have liked that.'

'I don't know. He never replied, but then children don't write letters, do they? And when I started, he was only about three. Too young even to read them.'

Laura spread tomato and herb topping over the pizza, added grated cheese. 'Do you suppose – I mean, would she have read them to him? If she wouldn't let you send him presents?'

He sighed. It was not a new thought. 'I don't know. I used to address the envelopes to him, right from the start. I thought . . . it sounds silly when I say it, but she was a very . . . *upright* sort of girl. You know, women's rights, gay rights, racial equality, ban the bomb, save the whale. Very serious, very worthy. It was what I liked about her in the first place. She really minded, minded passionately about things. She was so full of enthusiasm, so sure she could change the world. It was . . . touching. Inspiring, even. And somehow I just can't see her doing away with someone else's letters. But I wish . . . Even a postcard would have been . . . Anyway, if he's had them, at least he has a bit of an idea what he's coming to.'

He was looking happier now. His face had lost its pallor, even his hair seemed to spring with new vigour into the wiry curls damp weather always gave him. His hand came up to tug at his tie, pull it off.

'I think I'll go and change,' he said vaguely. 'Or should I stay in a suit to visit the school?'

'I don't suppose it'll matter too much, as long as it's the new jeans and a clean top.'

Laura put the bread to rise, the mixing bowl to soak, and laid the table. Her hands worked automatically, tidying, grating cheese, washing lettuce for a salad. She was still numb, but the awareness of pain to come was like the first warning twinge of toothache. You ignored it, hoped it would go away, while knowing with horrid certainty that it would soon erupt into furious throbbing. What's the point, she told herself sensibly, of

25

minding so much about it? The wrong was done so long ago, it shouldn't hurt me now. Edward is still Edward, I am still me, we are still us. Many women, most women, put up with worse things than this from their husbands. Look at Jane. Look, come to think of it, at Cassandra.

It will be all right, she thought. Edward and I will be all right. There will be tension for a while, resentment and anger and guilt. I won't want him to make love to me for a few days. but though at the moment I feel I could never bear him to touch me like that again, it won't last. What we have is too precious to throw away.

And the boy. How will I cope? At least I'm used to teenagers. I know what they can be like. My friends will help. It's only for a few months, anyone can stand that. Then he'll probably go back, and be out of our lives again. We'll send him Christmas and birthday presents, he'll visit from time to time. Everything will return to normal. It isn't as bad as what Anna had to go through, or Jane. Not nearly as bad. I can deal with it. Yes, everything will be all right. And maybe, who knows, he might be all right? It might even be fun, having a boy to stay for a while. Not just a boy. Mark. Edward's son, Mark. My – good heavens – my stepson, I suppose. Hello, Mark.

Chapter 3

In the lobby outside the kitchen, Daisy stood for a moment before facing the outside world. It all looked the same as always. The freezer hummed; wellington boots and outdoor shoes stood in their serried ranks below raincoats and a selection of Barbour jackets in various stages of dishevelment (used, depending on their state, for going to the shops, going for walks, gardening, or mucking out the chicken shed); the cats' dishes stood in a clean row on their plastic mat, empty except for the water bowl. Its ordinariness and familiarity should have been reassuring, but Daisy could still feel the unpleasant sickish feeling that had come over her at the sight of Edward's face.

When she had been younger, fourteen or so, Daisy had for a brief spell fallen in love with Edward. She had haunted the house at weekends, volunteering to help empty the lawnmower when he cut the grass, or to pick up hedge clippings and hold the ladder – oh, the thrill when he steadied himself with a hand on her shoulder – when he climbed up it to trim the top of the hedge. That was in the past, of course, and she had long since got over what she now felt to be a childish and embarrassing crush. Edward was still, however, the nearest to a father-figure that she now felt she had. She admired him, liked him, loved him, even though not, she told herself, in a silly way. If he had noticed her earlier infatuation he had treated it with the cheerful calmness with which he had treated the temper tantrums or the practical jokes of earlier childhood.

Even-tempered, kindly, funny Edward was the man in her world that she knew best, trusted most, relied on. There was Guy, of course, but although he was twenty-three she scarcely thought of him as a man: he was her brother, and she remembered him as the spotty adolescent he had been in her childhood.

Never in all her life had she seen such a look on Edward's face before. She hardly knew how to name what she had seen there – anxiety? bewilderment? guilt? Any or all of them, and he had seemed somehow diminished in stature. It was frightening, and because she was only sixteen the fear made her angry and resentful. How dare Edward come back in the middle of the day looking like that? And poor Laura, she thought belatedly, who must be frightened too. Though Laura would cope, of course. She always did.

Through the closed door she heard the hiss and rumble of water running into a kettle, the clink of a lid, the creak as the Aga top was lifted. Suddenly she realised that she should not still be there, that she was eavesdropping. With stealthy haste, and blushing as though she had been caught peering through the keyhole, she let herself out of the back door.

The air was wet and cold, not raining but spongy with suspended droplets that collected and hung dismally from every twig and new leaf. She shivered, hugging the stiffly decorated velvet of her waistcoat round her. She almost wished she was still young enough to wear her old school duffel coat, but of course that was impossibly un-stylish, even here in the village. One had one's pride, after all.

She walked down the path at the side of the house, careless of the shrubs and trees until she brushed against a branch and received a shower of icy water that ran down the back of her neck. At the front gate she paused, one hand on the latch and the other rubbing absently at the clammy patch where the water had soaked her sweatshirt. In front of her was the village green, its triangular space deserted but for a foraging dog. She could turn right and go down the lane that led to home. She could cross the green to the Old Rectory by the church, where the Babbages lived, only it occurred to her that term had already started at the comprehensive, and Candida would not be at home. Jane, she knew, would welcome her, but Daisy wanted to talk about Laura and Edward, and she wasn't very sure that she felt able to have that kind of conversation with Candy's mother.

Cassandra, then. Her spirits lifted as she remembered that she had an excuse, anyway, to go there. Laura, after all, had wanted her to tell Cassandra that she, Laura, would not be able to go and see her this afternoon. True, she had asked Daisy to telephone rather than turn up, but since she was here, where was the harm? Briskly she snapped the gate shut behind her, and strode along the road to the left, her boots making a satisfying crunch on the loose chippings.

Daisy admired Cassandra, though she found her rather alarming. She was six years younger than her mother, a gap in age which was more significant to Cassandra herself than to Daisy, to whom anyone over twenty-five was middle-aged. Still, she often seemed to regard herself as more of Daisy's generation than that of Anna, Laura or Jane, and Daisy found this flattering if, at times, embarrassing.

Cassandra's little cottage, at the apex of the triangle of the green, was tiny and so picturesque that strangers driving past were inclined to slow or even stop their cars to admire it. The timber framing had been cleaned of its sticky black paint and contrasted gently with the cream-coloured walls beneath the dome of thatch, silvery with age and smocked with intricate straw decorations. The front garden, behind a low wall set with flints, had raised beds with edging tiles that looked like neat rows of hard-boiled brown eggs between narrow paths of rose-coloured bricks.

Cassandra had filled the beds with an indiscriminate mixture of traditional flowers: lavender, roses and hollyhocks rioted, in summer, among pinks, columbines, lilies, marigolds and clumps of herbs. Now, in April, miniature tulips flaunted their satin colours among the green rosettes of lily of the valley, and a small pear tree scattered drifts of petals like snow. In this jewelled setting the cottage looked as though you could lift the roof like a lid and find it filled with pieces of home-made fudge, or clotted-cream toffees, which was Cassandra's idea of a joke.

Daisy knocked at the door. There was a long pause, and she began to fidget, wondering if she would be unwelcome. At length she heard the sound of unlocking and the door opened a crack, a safety chain rattling through its hasp and restraining it after a few inches. Daisy thought miserably that everyone seemed to be behaving oddly today. Cassandra, though she lived alone, was far more inclined – though constantly warned not to by her friends – to fling the door wide to any caller, known or unknown.

'It's me. Daisy,' she said unnecessarily. 'I've got a message from Laura.'

There was another pause, then the door closed in her face. Before she had time to feel hurt, she realised that the chain was being undone and then Cassandra was opening the door to her. Not, however, with her usual exuberant welcome, but hanging back in the shadows of the hall, keeping out of sight of the empty road.

Rather wishing she hadn't come, Daisy stepped over the wooden threshold. The little hall was floored with wide oak boards, polished to a deep brown shine, so that it was like walking over still, peaty water. To Daisy's dismay she saw that Cassandra was in a dressing-gown. Even more unheard of, her face was pale, without make-up, her hair straggly and somehow dusty-looking. Cassandra, who never went even across the green to the shop for a newspaper until she was dressed, her face carefully made up, her dark hair artfully arranged in its immaculately careless style so that each curl lay in its allotted place. Daisy came to a halt.

'Oh Cassandra, I'm so sorry! I didn't mean to get you out of bed!'

'It's all right.' Cassandra was already leading the way to the sitting room, from which Daisy now felt a blast of warm air scented with woodsmoke. The little house was always warm, for Cassandra had installed a new heating system, but today the fire was lit in the big inglenook as well. 'I wasn't in bed.' She flopped down on the sofa, ultra-modern like all her furniture and upholstered in linen as white as the pear blossom, that still bore the imprint of her body in its massed cushions, and waved a hand at the armchair. Daisy stood irresolute.

'But if you're not well . . .'

'I'm not *ill*,' said Cassandra irritably. 'For heaven's sake sit down and stop *looming* over me. It makes me nervous.'

Daisy, at a slender five foot one, had never thought of herself as looming before, but she sat down obediently, perching on the edge of the chair ready, if necessary, to retreat.

'I'm sorry,' she said again. 'I'm afraid Laura won't be able to come and see you today, after all.'

Cassandra frowned. Without the delicately tinted foundation and carefully applied powder and blusher her skin looked pale and shiny, yet somehow dry as well.

'I was there when you phoned,' Daisy continued hastily. 'At Laura's. We were going to have lunch together, but then Edward came home.' She paused to allow this dramatic news to sink in.

Cassandra hitched her dressing-gown up where it was slipping off her shoulder. She looked puzzled. 'He doesn't usually come home for lunch, does he? Or was it a special occasion?'

'No, it was . . . well, I don't know what it was. There was something wrong, I think. He looked – oh, awful. Pale, and wobbly. And his eyes didn't seem to see me, if you know what I mean. So I thought I'd better go, and Laura said to tell you. Well, she just asked me to ring you, actually, but I knew what she meant, so I thought I'd come round. But I didn't mean to disturb you. Shall I go? Or can I get you anything? A hot drink? Anything from the shop?'

Cassandra smiled. The skin round her eyes creased in a way that Daisy had never noticed before. There were dark smudges of tiredness there, too.

'Poor old love, you're not having much of a morning, are you? And Laura . . . I wonder what's wrong?' She looked slightly more animated.

'I don't know.' Daisy heard the wobble in her voice and was annoyed with herself.

30

'Oh, I'm sure it's not anything too serious,' said Cassandra soothingly. 'I mean, Edward and Laura! The happiest couple I know, in spite of everything. In fact, practically the only happy couple I know,' she added rather plaintively.

'Yes, and that's why it would be so awful if . . .'

'If nothing. They'll be all right, you'll see. And so will I, I suppose. Tell you what, if you've got time, why don't we have some lunch together? I do believe I'm hungry, after all. There's some soup in the fridge, and French bread, and a nice bit of Cheshire, if that'll do you?'

'Oh, lovely! That is,' Daisy said carefully, 'if you're quite sure. That you're well enough, I mean. And you must let me do it all.'

'Oh, I'm not ill. At least . . . no, I'm not ill. But I am a bit lonely. I was going to tell Laura all about it, but that will have to wait till another day. And I'd love the company.'

'I'll go and heat the soup, then,' said Daisy happily, who never lifted a finger in her own home, expecting her mother to wait on her there.

The kitchen, like all the rest of the inside of the cottage, was aggressively modern, which was another of Cassandra's jokes. Daisy thought it was wonderful, and enjoyed heating the soup in the little built-in microwave. She laid the small table, a slab of black glass, setting out the severe white plates and bowls, the bread, cheese and butter on stainless-steel platters, sticks of celery in a glass jug. When Cassandra joined her, Daisy was relieved to see that, although she was still in a dressing-gown, she had brushed her hair into its usual glossy disarray, powdered her face, and put on mascara and the vivid shade of lipstick that contrasted so wonderfully with her pale skin and thick dark hair.

'That smells good! Shall we have a glass of wine?' Without waiting for Daisy's answer she went to the fridge and took out an opened bottle. Daisy disliked white wine, and particularly the very dry Chablis that Cassandra invariably drank (fewer calories, she maintained), but she would have died rather than admit it. She took two wine glasses from the cupboard, and sat down.

The soup was delicious, and Daisy said so.

'Marks and Spencer,' said Cassandra, who seldom cooked. She kept as little food in the house as possible, on the principle that if it wasn't there she wouldn't eat it. Daisy sipped at her wine, shuddering a little at its cold acidity and washing it down with a hasty mouthful of soup. Cassandra poured herself half a glass.

'I suppose I shouldn't really . . .' she said, looking at the bottle as if she thought she might find instructions on it about how much she was allowed.

'I expect it will do you good,' said Daisy helpfully. Cassandra looked at her rather oddly, but said nothing.

The Cheshire was rich and strong. Daisy, who loved it, made good inroads into it, and into the bread, while Cassandra watched her in some amusement, sipping at her wine and picking at a piece of dry bread. The cheese, she had found, tasted horrible in her mouth. They finished off with some grapes, then Daisy cleared the table.

'Shall I make some coffee?' she asked helpfully. Cassandra shuddered.

'Coffee? Ugh, no, don't even mention it. Just the thought of the smell makes me feel queasy.'

Daisy, who had been stacking the plates into the little dishwasher that was hidden in a cupboard by the sink, turned round and stared at her.

'But you always drink coffee! I thought you were feeling better?'

'I am, but . . . not fancying coffee, just at the moment.' Daisy frowned. She remembered, quite suddenly, being seven years old and staying the weekend with Candy. Candy's mother being sick in the morning and rushing out of the room when Bill made himself a pot of coffee. And Candy telling her, as they lay whispering in bed that night, that Mummy said they were going to have a little brother or sister . . .

'Are you going to have a baby?' She tried to sound mature, sophisticated, but found that her voice had risen upwards, so that she sounded like a little girl. Cassandra grimaced wryly.

'Actually, yes. But don't tell anyone, will you?'

'Oh, no, of course not! I won't breathe a word, I promise! Um, congratulations.'

Cassandra gave a hollow laugh. She had only eaten half of her soup, and very little bread. The two glasses of wine, on a stomach empty from earlier vomiting, had brightened her eyes and dulled her senses slightly. The shock of discovering, the evening before, that she was pregnant had given her a sleepless night and exacerbated the sickness that, stupidly, she had thought came from a slight case of food poisoning from a meal the weekend before. And she had been, she thought, so careful! After last time . . . Her mind returned to its rat-run, scurrying frantically along the familiar dark grey maze of paths that led, always, to the necessity for decision, for choice. A choice she had made once already, and which she did not think she could bear to make again. She gave a choking sob, and buried her face in her carefully manicured hands, careless for once of her eye make-up.

'Cassandra! Oh dear, Cassandra, don't cry! Please don't cry!' Daisy hesitated only a moment before coming to put her arms round Cassandra's shaking shoulders. She felt ineffectual, and her first touch was tentative, but somehow the narrowness of the older woman's body, from which every surplus millimetre of fat had been honed by diet and exercise, combined with the helpless heave of her breathing, brought a gush of warmth and sympathy so that her arms tightened comfortingly.

'There,' she crooned, 'there, it's all right. It'll be all right. There, don't cry.' She smelled of soap and some light, flowery scent.

Cassandra, who always wore Joy, buried her face in the scratchy surface of the velvet waistcoat, and sobbed aloud, luxuriously. 'Oh!' she wailed. 'Oh, it's all so awful! I didn't mean . . . not after last time . . . but I do want . . . only I feel so ill, and I don't know what to do!'

'Poor Cassandra!' Daisy felt mature, even motherly. The sight of an older person weeping had always been something she'd found intensely embarrassing before. Her mother's rare tears were the worst: they made her feel guilty, and worried, and ashamed of herself for feeling like that. To see Cassandra, in general so elegant and poised, behaving as if she were no more than Daisy's own age, was somehow rather gratifying, now that she had got over the shock of it. Wisely, she continued to murmur platitudes and hold Cassandra until her sobs died away to occasional shuddering breaths. Then she gave one last squeeze, pulled a double piece of kitchen paper from the roll, and handed it to the older woman.

'I'm going to put the kettle on,' she said in slightly bossy tones.

'I feel sick,' said Cassandra limply.

'That's the crying. But I'm sure it will have done you good. Why don't you go and put some cold water on your face, and I'll make some tea. A cup of tea and some dry biscuits will settle your stomach. I know that's what Jane lived on when she was expecting Toby.'

'All right.' Cassandra went meekly to the bathroom. Daisy made the tea, put it on a tray with some Rich Tea biscuits on a plate, and carried it through to the sitting room. There she replenished the fire, plumped up the sofa cushions invitingly, and when Cassandra returned made her recline again.

'Put your feet up,' she said.

'For heaven's sake, Daisy, I'm only two months pregnant,' snapped Cassandra. 'I'm not lumbering around with varicose veins and swollen ankles yet. Any minute now you'll be putting kettles on for boiling water and telling me how to breathe.'

'It's the first twelve weeks that are the most risky,' Daisy said seriously. 'You don't want to have a miscarriage, do you?'

'I don't know. That might solve everything,' said Cassandra sadly.

33

Daisy, who had been caught up in her role as ministering angel well primed with information from a sensible course called 'Personal Development' at school, returned with a bump to the real world and looked at her in dismay.

'Oh, don't! Don't say that!'

'Well, I am saying it.' Cassandra, exhausted and miserable, was beyond self-control. 'It has to be better than having an abortion, anyway. At least I wouldn't have to feel so guilty about it.'

Daisy poured the tea to give herself time to recover.

'You would, if you didn't do anything to prevent it,' she pointed out. Daisy was young, but she was nobody's fool.

Cassandra looked at her with some surprise. She accepted the cup of tea without demur, and took a biscuit. 'Yes, you're right,' she sighed.

Daisy sat on the floor, hugging her knees and leaning back against the armchair. 'Have you told Stephen yet?' she asked, rather shyly.

Daisy had never met the married man who was Cassandra's lover. When she thought of him, her mind alternated between the image of a tragic romantic figure – a Mr Rochester tied irrevocably to a dreadful wife, whose only snatched moments of happiness were the ones he spent with Cassandra – and a sordid, deceitful figure, balding and paunchy, who lived a double life and made both women unhappy.

'No,' said Cassandra. 'I haven't told anyone yet. You're the only person who knows, and I probably shouldn't have told you.'

'I won't tell anyone, I promise,' repeated Daisy. 'Do you want me to go away?' She wasn't sure whether she wanted to or not.

'Not unless you want to.' Cassandra knew she should probably not be discussing this with a sixteen-year-old, but she desperately needed someone to talk to. Daisy's life had been more sheltered than the lives of most girls of her age; too sheltered, perhaps. And there was the advantage that she already knew about Stephen. Some of this must have showed in her face, for Daisy showed no signs of leaving.

'What do you think he'll say?'

'I know exactly what he'll say,' replied Cassandra bitterly. 'He'll say, how could you be so careless? Not we. You. Me, that is. He doesn't like having to take precautions, you see. Not so spontaneous. Not so romantic. So he leaves it up to me, and then if something goes wrong it's my fault.'

Daisy said nothing. She looked down into her teacup, as if consulting a crystal ball. Cassandra saw her face.

'He has three children already,' she said, more gently. 'He loves them. More than he loves me. He's never made any secret of that. He won't do anything to hurt them, and that includes leaving his wife. Of course. And if he were the sort of man who would, I wouldn't love him. So . . .'

'So you're stuck.' Daisy thought about it. Thought about Laura, who had Edward, but no children. 'So you'll never have him, will you? Even if you don't have the baby? But if you do, at least you'll have her. Or him,' she added as an afterthought.

'One or the other. That's the choice. Or neither, of course. If I had any sense I'd be looking for a nice, unmarried man to settle down with. That's what my mother keeps saying, what everyone keeps thinking.'

'Oh, no!' Daisy was young enough to believe that there was value in going against the ideas of an earlier generation.

'I might do it, if I thought I had any chance of success,' said Cassandra gloomily, 'but nice unmarried men who want to settle down are pretty thin on the ground, particularly when you get to my age.'

Daisy was inclined to dismiss this as an irrelevance. Nice unmarried men to settle down with sounded pretty boring, she thought.

'So that's not really a choice, then, is it? It's Stephen, or the baby. Um . . . something you said . . . have you thought about this before? In the past, I mean?'

Daisy kept her eyes fixed on the toes of her Doc Martens, now satisfactorily scuffed so that they had lost their original hard black shine. If I've got it wrong, she'll be furious with me, she thought. And even if I'm right, she might still be furious. 'I don't mean to be nosy,' she said humbly.

Cassandra sighed. 'I was hoping you hadn't caught that one. Your mother would never forgive me if she could hear us now. Yes, it's happened before. Three years ago, actually. I thought – really, I must have been mad – I thought I could force his hand. He kept saying, when the children are older, when things are more settled, when Sarah's had time to get used to the idea, when I've got my partnership . . . and I believed him. I actually believed all that shit, and even then I knew that if I heard anyone else saying it I'd laugh myself sick at anyone gullible enough to be taken in by it. But I wanted to believe it, you see. So I kidded myself, and waited.'

Her fingers twisted together. She thought of the empty evenings, when she dressed up just in case he managed to get away, come and see her. The hours spent, breathless, by the telephone that so seldom rang. The stolen weekends, so few that they were rarer than a white Christmas, which she anticipated for months beforehand and relived for months afterwards. A life of expectation and memory, when the actual events seemed almost unreal, even unenjoyable while they were happening, because she was trying to slow every second, savour and keep every minute, make the most of every hour. Her longing had been not for the kind of bliss she had when they were together, because she was realistic enough to know that it could not survive on an everyday basis, but for something settled. Something wholesome and real: toast and Marmite as well as oysters and champagne. And so she had tried to manipulate, to take charge of their life.

'Then, I couldn't wait any longer,' she continued, almost forgetting she was speaking to Daisy. 'I knew he loved children. Loved his own children. And I thought . . . I thought if I were to tell him I was going to have his baby, it might give him the lever he needed to push him into making the choice between me and Sarah.

'But there wasn't any choice, not for him, or if there was he had made it long ago. He was furious. Nothing else. Angrier than I'd ever seen him before. I was terrified. I thought I'd lost him, that he would never forgive me. And I found that my choice was made, too. I chose – I had to choose – him.'

'You had an abortion.' How can I be shocked? thought Daisy. If I were to find, tomorrow, that I was pregnant, would I want to go through with having the baby? Throw away school, and A-levels, and university, and all the things I'd planned to do? And would that be any worse? If it were me, or one of my friends, I would be sad but not shocked. Why should it be different for Cassandra, just because she's older?

'Yes. They call it a termination, it doesn't sound so bad. But it's . . . not much fun. I thought I wouldn't mind, but I did. I kept telling myself, it's not a baby, not yet. Just a blobby thing, a kind of growth. But afterwards I felt . . . oh, bereft. Guilty. I can't find the words for it. And Stephen was very loving, very kind, bought me presents, took me out for expensive meals, took me to Paris for a weekend, even. But he never mentioned it, would never let me talk about it. It had to be on his terms, you see. I had chosen him, and I couldn't grieve because that would mean that I regretted my choice. And, perhaps, I did.'

'Poor Cassandra. He sounds a pig. Oh, sorry. I shouldn't say that.'

'Well, he does, I suppose. But he was a pig I'd made. Created. Like that witch in the Odyssey, can't remember her name, who transformed men into pigs.'

'Circe.'

'Yes. The benefits of a good education. Having a name like Cassandra made me permanently allergic to anything to do with the Greeks.'

Daisy was not going to be diverted.

36

'But this time you haven't done it on purpose, have you? It's an accident, isn't it? Not your fault?'

'I suppose. But he'll never believe it, not really. And he may be right. Perhaps somewhere, deep down, I wanted this to happen, and that's why it did.'

'So . . . have you made your choice already, then? In a way?'

'Maybe. But if I have, it's not a conscious one. The only thing I am sure of, at the moment, is that I don't want to have to choose.'

Cassandra yawned, suddenly, like a cat. 'Goodness, I feel a bit better. The tea and biscuits seem to have done the trick and settled my insides after all. Thank you, Nurse Lambert.'

Daisy glowed. 'Oh, good. Do you want to go back to bed? Shall I get you a hot-water bottle or anything?'

'No,' Cassandra yawned again, 'I think I'll just stay here and drift off. You couldn't fetch me the blanket off the spare-room bed, could you? I seem to be feeling the cold even more than usual these days. Aah!' She yawned a third time. Daisy fetched the blanket, and spread it carefully over Cassandra.

She stood for a moment, watching the dozing woman. In repose her face was young, as vulnerable in appearance as Daisy felt herself to be. She felt exhausted, not physically, but emotionally, even spiritually. All her childhood she had thought that when she was grown up everything would be easy, clear, understandable. Now, on the verge of the adult world, she was beginning to see that this might not be true, that the actuality might even be the reverse. It was all rather alarming, and she felt that she needed to do something very silly and childish and reassuring, like watching a cartoon on television, or reading a comic, or curling up with a book and a bar of chocolate and her teddy bear.

With a lift of her spirits she realised that it was four o'clock, and that Candida would be home from school by now. The company of her friend, plump, cheerful, and as wholesome as brown bread, seemed suddenly the most desirable and comforting thing in the world. She crept from the house, and made her way round the green to the rectory.

Chapter 4

As Daisy had known they would be, the Babbage family was gathered in the kitchen consuming, variously, a full-scale meal (Toby), a snack with a few extras (Candida), and nothing pretending to be something (Ben). Jane, her brown hair tousled but still attractive, was stirring cheese sauce for lasagna on the Rayburn and picking, from time to time, at Candida's discarded crusts and the broken biscuits out of the tin. She had a fondly cherished theory that if she only ate the fragments they would be less fattening, and since she was careful not to add the fractions together and discover how many whole biscuits she had polished off, she was able to enjoy them with a clear conscience. She had lost two stone after Bill had left, when for some months even the thought of food made her gag, and had been so pleased with this unexpected bonus that, on the strength of it, and to give her self-image a boost, she had let the hairdresser put some blonde highlights into her hair, disguising the strands of grey and making her look, he enthusiastically told her, at least ten years younger.

They made room for Daisy at the table as a matter of course. Jane passed her a clean plate as she went by to fetch the pasta from the larder, Ben lifted a languid hand in greeting while keeping his eyes on his book. Candida cut her a slice of bread, and Toby offered her his private jar of crunchy peanut butter. At ten, Toby still thought that girls were more or less a waste of space, but he found Daisy's slender blonde prettiness, so different from his sister's rosy roundness, pleasing to the eye and interesting, in a disquieting kind of way.

Daisy, who found peanut butter about as easy to eat as putty with bits in, took a little out of politeness, and smothered it with chocolate spread. Candida watched her enviously.

'It does seem unfair,' she said without rancour, 'that you can eat all that kind of thing and stay so skinny. And it's not as if you do games, or take any exercise at all, either.'

'Daisy's not skinny. She's slim,' said Toby, surprising himself more than anyone and turning so pink he had to drop his knife and dive under

39

the table to retrieve it. Jane turned from the Rayburn and, meeting Candida's eyes, smiled fondly.

'Metabolism,' pronounced Ben, still reading. 'Hereditary.'

'But Mummy's fat!' protested Daisy. 'Plump, anyway,' she amended, meeting Jane's reproachful eye.

'When I first met her, your mother was as slim as you are, almost. When you and Candy started at nursery school. Don't you remember? I was the fat one, then.'

'She's still got tiny wrists, and ankles,' said Candida, stretching out her hands and regarding them hopelessly. They were well shaped, the nails smoothly rounded and buffed to a soft shine, but they were large hands. 'Capable', she thought gloomily. And who, at sixteen, wants to be thought capable? Not me, anyway.

'Cup of tea, Daisy?' Jane remembered, yet again, that she didn't want conversations about being fat, or being thin, taking place in Ben's presence. She glanced quickly and anxiously at his plate. It had some crumbs on it, and the edge of a piece of bread, but Jane was fairly sure that it was the same piece he had started with, not even a whole slice, but one he had cut diagonally so that it tapered away around the middle of the loaf.

'How about some cake?' she said generally to a place in the air somewhere above the middle of the round table. 'Banana cake,' she enlarged. Ben had loved banana cake, once.

Before anyone had time to answer, Jane went back to the larder. Large and cold, with shelves tiled in antiseptic lavatorial white, it was as large as a small room, and belonged to the days when the rector was expected to have not only a numerous family, but also three times as many servants to care for them. She brought the cake, still just warm, and set it on the old wooden table near enough to Ben so that he would smell the fresh-baked fragrance of it.

'Banana cake! Great!' Toby spoke thickly round a mouthful of peanut-butter sandwich. 'Cut me a bit, Ben.'

Jane knew she should not be watching, but even as she assembled the lasagna in its dish (another of Ben's old favourites), she was aware, out of the corner of her eye, of the movement of his hand reaching out to the cake-knife. Such a thin hand, the lumpy knuckles echoing the protruding bones of the wrist. He cut a generous slice and passed it over, scarcely raising his eyes from the pages. The hand with the knife hovered tantalisingly over the cake, then he laid the knife down as gently as if it were made of fine crystal, and brought his hand back to turn the page. Jane blinked away the tears that blurred the sheets of pasta she was arranging into the dish – why couldn't they make circles instead of squares that were so difficult to fit into an oval dish? – and reached for the pan of meat. The lean beef had been eked out with soya mince, soaked mung beans, mushrooms and tinned sweetcorn. Bill's maintenance payment was late again.

Candida saw her mother's face. 'Cut me a bit of cake too, Ben,' she said. 'And I expect Daisy will have some. Don't you want any?'

Her tone was casual, but Ben raised his face for the first time, tossing back the long lock of hair that hung between his eyes. Dark brown, like hers and Toby's, it framed a face from which all surplus flesh had melted, leaving the fine bones of the skull delineated like an anatomical drawing. His eyes, the same brown as hers, gazed blandly across the table, and a little smile curved but did not part his lips. Since he had had a brace attached to straighten his teeth, Ben had ceased to smile properly. Jane, at least, found this evidence of vanity obscurely encouraging.

'Cake?' he said, in the tones of an elderly professor encountering some strange and uncouth object for the first time. 'Cake? No, I don't think so. Don't want to spoil my appetite for supper. Lasagna, my favourite. Yum. Yum.'

He smiled again. It was not a pleasant smile, and Candida's eyes fell.

'What are you reading?' Daisy's tone was a nicely calculated blend of interest and being kind to someone younger than she.

'*Ulysses*. By James Joyce.' His tone mirrored hers exactly. Daisy reflected that she should have known better than to try that kind of trick with Ben, who could run rings round her, intellectually as well as physically. By the time he was ten it had become apparent that Ben was not just bright, but possibly even gifted in some directions. Utterly uninterested in the sciences, bored by maths and geography, his work in English was, from time to time, brilliant. Where his attention and interest were captured, he was capable of extraordinary feats of retention and analysis. At his preparatory school the masters had been ready to tear out their hair because he refused to apply more than a fraction of his intelligence to his work. At public school, before he had left a year earlier, he had been the despair and the delight of the staff room, their attitude depending on what they were teaching him. At the comprehensive, fortunately, they were prepared to allow him considerable leeway, recognising that he could be led but never driven.

'I've never read any Joyce.' Daisy knew that she could only reach any kind of understanding with Ben by being completely honest. 'Is he good?'

'Brilliant. If you like that kind of thing.'

'I tried *Ulysses* once. I couldn't understand a word of it, I thought it

41

was completely pointless,' said Candida serenely. She was fiercely proud of her brother, but felt that it was important not to allow him to get too carried away into the realms of intellect.

'Never mind, sweet sis. We love you anyway. Even if you are intellectually challenged.'

'No more than you, dear bro. Really, Ma, you made a big mistake calling him Benedict. He keeps coming over all Shakespearean. Sweet sis!' Candida snorted.

'I don't know why you have to keep complaining about your names. I put a lot of thought into choosing them.'

'It's like noses,' said Daisy thoughtfully. 'I mean, have you ever met anyone who really *likes* their own nose? No wonder God invented plastic surgeons.'

'Yours is nice.' Candida put her fingers up to caress the straight line of Daisy's nose. 'Not like my horrid little piglike snout.'

'It isn't! Piglike, I mean. Or a snout. A dear little retroussé number, darling, and very fetching.' Daisy spoke in fruity tones, like a busty contralto. 'And at least your name's unusual. I mean, Daisy! Just a weed you have all over your lawn. In a manner of speaking.'

Toby, who was heavily into smutty innuendo, sniggered.

'Aahh, flobalob,' murmured Ben. ''Allo, ickle weeeed.'

'Weeeed!' repeated Daisy in a rising squeak. It was a routine they had perfected in their childhood, before Bill left home.

'I'd rather be called after a nice little flower than a disease,' said Candida gloomily. 'Thrush,' she elucidated. Daisy's eyes, which had narrowed in thought, widened in sympathy as she tried not to laugh.

'Oh no! Poor Candy! I didn't know!'

'Nor did I, until someone at school had it and I saw it on the tablets she had to use. And I mean use. Not take. Internally. She told us all about it, in all its sordid detail.'

'What's thrush?' Toby was always in desperate pursuit of adult information.

'A bird,' said Candida shortly.

'A yeast-like infection,' said Jane at the same moment. Jane was a great believer in giving honest answers to children, preferably in an incomprehensible form. Toby's eyes turned appealingly to Ben.

'Itchy fanny,' said Ben succinctly. Daisy's giggle was drowned in a chorus of 'Oh, *Ben*!' and '*Really*, Ben!' from Candida and Jane. Toby, his eyes veering sideways towards Daisy, blushed crimson and dropped his knife again.

'Well, I am *sorry*, darling,' said Jane apologetically. 'I'm afraid I honestly didn't think at the time. I just thought it was a pretty name. *Candide*, and all that,' she finished plaintively, appealing to Ben.

'Haven't read any Voltaire. Is it good?' His interest captured, he raised his eyes from his book.

'Very, at least I remember thinking so when I read it. There's a copy around somewhere, in the Penguin set I think.'

'No thanks.' Ben was dismissive. 'I'll wait a year or two until my French is up to scratch, and read it in the original.' He paused for a moment, his eyes fixed dreamily on his sister. She looked wary. Candida knew that particular look.

You could always use another form of your name,' he suggested kindly.

'Candy, you mean? No, thanks. I may be sweet, but I don't want to be named after a Hershey bar.'

'No, I was thinking of Mavis.'

'Mavis? Why? It's a horrible name. Why should I call myself Mavis?'

'It's another name for the thrush. Avianly speaking,' he informed her gently.

Candida looked at him. She had half a mind to throw the remains of her banana cake at him (which she had only taken to encourage him, sacrificing her figure on the altar of sibling affection, she thought crossly), but her sense of humour got the better of her, and she fell into laughter. Daisy, who had been struggling, joined her, and they leaned against one another, giggling helplessly. Toby laughed because they did, and Jane, who had been tensed for an outburst, relaxed against the rail of the Rayburn and smiled. Her pride was divided equally between Ben's quick wit and Candida's sweet temper.

Ben smiled quietly down at his book. Jane's eyes suddenly flooded with tears again at the hollow curve of his cheek, the bony spinal knobs at the back of his neck that once, such a short time ago it seemed, had been so sweetly and softly chubby. Her lips could still feel the downy smoothness she had kissed; she remembered the smell of him as he had wriggled, ticklish, on her knee, the smell of soap and baby shampoo and clean, childish flesh.

Now he was already needing to shave twice a week and his father, who should have been there to advise and encourage at this initiation, this important rite of passage into manhood, had abandoned them for another woman. Candida and Toby had wept, and pleaded, and talked it over endlessly with their mother, their friends, even with their mother's friends, Laura and Cassandra. Ben, who had admired and respected his father as well as loving him, had for nearly a year refused to believe that it had happened. Bill, wanting perhaps to keep his options open, or simply unable to understand anyone's needs or feelings but his own, had hinted from time to time that he just needed to 'sort himself out' and that when he had done that, everything would be all right. Bill, presumably, had in a typical fashion meant all right for him, but his son had believed, because he desperately wanted to, that it meant his father would come home again and that everything would be as it had been.

For some reason Ben had settled it in his own mind that his father would be home by Christmas. All through November and early December he had waited, with rising expectation. Jane, not unnaturally, had made special efforts for that Christmas, determined to exorcise the memory of the previous year when, with Bill gone barely two months before, every carol, every familiar tree decoration, every smell from mince pies to turkey to the cool fragrance of the tree itself, had brought a flock of memories that mobbed the mind and the emotions, like Hitchcock birds, to rend and tear at the fragile equilibrium she sought to achieve.

Ben's birthday was only four days before Christmas, and traditionally had always marked the beginning of their festivities. This year he would be fourteen, leaving childhood far behind him as he embarked on the GCSE courses that would culminate, they all hoped and believed, in a place at Oxford or Cambridge. Jane, desperate to make him happier, had chosen him an expensive radio and double tape-deck, with a CD player incorporated, resigning herself to the thought of the impending decibels competing with Candida's music by reminding herself of the large rooms and thick walls of the Old Rectory.

Ben had planned the whole thing in his head. His father would, he knew, come to see him on his birthday, perhaps take him out for the day as he had done for Toby's in October. Ben, in his privileged position as Birthday Person, would be able to talk to him, would persuade him that now was the time to return. Surely, by now, whatever sorting out had been necessary must have been done. And, even more surely, his father couldn't really want to leave him, and Candida and Toby, and his mother who was looking so attractive these days, and the big comfortable house he had always loved, for some other woman he'd only just met? Ben had been so certain of success, he had bought several small presents for his father's stocking, a habit the children had started some years earlier and which last year had been allowed to lapse.

Then, the day before his birthday, Bill had rung. He was very sorry, he had said casually, but something had come up. In America – Los Angeles, actually. He was flying out there later today. And since the company were paying, he thought he might as well stay on over Christmas. Sorry, old man, to miss your birthday, but what shall I buy you out there? A guitar? Some Levis? Baseball kit? Roller boots?

'Nothing, thank you,' Ben had said stiffly. The fact that none of the offered gifts was anything he could have been the slightest bit interested in hurt almost more than anything else, at the time. 'No, of course it's all right. Yes, of course I understand. Have a good time.' Putting the telephone down, very carefully, on the table where it quacked to itself for several minutes before Toby picked it up, he had walked from the room. His stiff back and frozen face were so eloquent that not even Jane dared to say a word, or try to follow him to his room.

Since then he had mentioned his father as seldom as possible, and while he had never actually refused to see him, had found excuses to be elsewhere when he visited, unavailable when he telephoned, and inextricably committed when he invited them out. He had appeared to retreat into his reading, and Jane had left him to do so, unsure of her ability to help him, and afraid of doing more harm than good by trying. She was well aware that, intellectually at least, he was in a different league to her. Sometimes, without meaning to, he made her feel rather silly.

It was not for some while that she noticed that Ben wasn't eating. He had been a chubby little boy, with a round football tummy and a matching round bottom. When, at twelve, he had started to grow rapidly, he had developed an appetite to match, and though he had lost some of the childish plumpness, his intake of food, along with his habit of skipping games to find a quiet corner to read in, ensured that he was never thin. Then, the previous month, Jane had taken a fresh look at him and seen that the trousers and jeans, which before had fitted so snugly, were slipping down his hips, while beneath the baggy pullovers and sweatshirts his stomach was concave, his ribs making striped shadows above it.

She realised, suddenly, that he had quietly been refusing food. Rushing off in the morning he would say he had no time for breakfast, he'd miss the bus, and Jane had formed the habit of making him sandwiches to eat on the way. Now she wondered who was eating them: she was fairly sure it wasn't Ben. Nor, she thought, was he eating the school lunches she gave him money for. Candida, when Jane questioned her, looked blank and said that she never saw Ben at lunchtime, but that since they were in different years and the school held nearly a thousand pupils, this wasn't very surprising. Ben would come home, make a pretence of eating tea, and at supper would announce, loudly, how hungry he was and how much he was looking forward to his meal. This smokescreen had worked for a while, but Jane now noticed that the portions of food on his plate were tiny, and invariably unfinished. When she produced puddings he would lean back in his chair and say, with apparent regret, that he was far too full.

During the Easter holidays she had been vigilant. She was fairly sure that Ben had noticed her watching what he ate, but he'd said nothing, casting only the occasional quizzical look as she tried, without success, to trick him into eating more. She had been reluctant to involve Candida, feeling that it was difficult enough for teenagers to have good relationships with their brothers and sisters, without one of them being used as a kind of double agent. At the same time, she knew she was going to have to do something. There were, of course, several reasons for sudden weight loss. Drugs, diabetes, cancer . . . the possibilities had haunted her mind until, panicking, she had gone to see her doctor. He had asked a lot of detailed questions and then reassured her that it was unlikely Ben was stricken with a mystery disease, or that he was taking drugs. Nevertheless, he said seriously, anorexia among teenage boys was on the increase, and under the circumstances . . .

Jane had gone home and telephoned Bill. He, who had not seen Ben for at least two months, had been unwilling to believe that the boy could be as thin as she said.

'All boys get thinner as they grow,' he said impatiently. 'I remember I did, at his age. Hormones, all that kind of thing. Shooting up. Outgrowing his strength. Get him a tonic, or something.'

'The doctor said something about anorexia . . .'

Bill's voice was sharp. 'Anorexia! Nonsense! Load of rubbish, chap doesn't know what he's talking about. He's just jumping on the bandwagon, going for the fashionable disease. You'd better watch out: next thing he'll be saying the boy's being abused, and sending platoons of social workers round to drag him away in the middle of the night. They're all the same, these medical types. Full of theories. He'll grow out of it. Anyway, anorexia's for girls.'

Jane had tried to explain that boys, too, were increasingly at risk, but Bill was unwilling, or perhaps unable, to accept it. The idea that his son might be in danger from something so effeminate, in his eyes so weak and pathetic, as a slimmer's disease, was unacceptable to him, particularly if any of the responsibility of it could be laid at his door. Jane, fearing what he might say to Ben, had given up trying to discuss it with him.

In the end she had turned, as she found herself doing more and more, to her women friends. To Anna, who had gone through the teenage problems already, and who had faced the ultimate loss of her husband also, and through her to Laura, Anna's old friend, who had faced neither but who was intelligent, and sensitive, and who above all always had time to listen. If neither of them had been able to make any positive suggestions, they had at least not dismissed her worries lightly.

'What about his school friends?' Laura had asked sensibly. 'They must have noticed a change in him. When I was that age I never listened to anything my parents said, but I'd always take advice from my friends.'

'He's such a solitary boy,' Jane sighed. 'He's so clever, you see, that they tend to find him rather disconcerting. Interesting, but odd. He doesn't like most of the things other boys of his age are keen on, like sport, or pop music, or getting drunk. Or even girls, though I don't think . . . I mean, he just hasn't really had time to notice them, yet.'

'I think you should talk to Candida, then. And to Daisy – or I will, if you like,' said Anna. 'To be honest, they're more likely to be able to help him than we can. And I'm sorry to say this, but perhaps you should go back to the doctor . . . just to work out some kind of contingency plan, in case he gets any worse. There are special counsellors, I know, for that kind of problem.'

'It would need to be a very special kind of special counsellor,' said Jane with gloomy pride. 'He doesn't miss a trick, and he'd never take any notice of someone he didn't think was at least as clever as him, Arrogant little beast.' The pride in her voice was not altogether hidden.

'What about the school? They must have encountered this kind of thing before.'

'Yes.' Jane nodded gratefully at Laura. 'I'll go and have a word with his tutor when the term starts again after Easter.'

That had been three weeks ago. Jane, reviewing in her mind what Ben had eaten during the holidays, thought that he had probably not lost any more weight, but that he certainly hadn't put anything back on. Her tentative remarks, prepared so carefully that they tended to come out sounding like well-rehearsed set speeches, had not provoked any kind of backlash, and the book on nutrition she had left casually lying about had certainly been looked at.

The telephone rang, startling Jane out of her reverie so that she noticed she had grated all the cheese over one end of the dish of lasagna, and left the other end bare. She made no attempt to pick up the phone, merely leaning back to avoid the general rush of bodies as her children raced to be first to it, each one convinced it was bound to be for him, or her.

'Hello?' Toby, as usual, had wriggled through the crush and reached the phone first. He adored the telephone, and was convinced that anyone who called was equally eager to chat with him. 'Hello? Oh, hello, Anna. How are you? Yes, fine, but I had a *pig* of a time in maths today. I mean, talk about unreasonable! But I've got into the athletics team . . . yes, great, isn't it? . . . Hundred metres, and triple jump, and relay. Will you come and watch some time? And bring one of those . . . yes, with the chocolate fudge icing . . . great. There's a meeting in two weeks . . . oh, Daisy? Yes, she's here. Did you want to speak to her, or was it Mummy . . . OK, here she is.'

He held the receiver towards Daisy, who had retreated somehow into her chair, as if she had taken root in it. 'It's for you. Your mum. Here she comes,' he said cheerfully into the receiver, waving it at Daisy who hadn't moved. Reluctantly, Daisy stood up and went over.

'Hello.' Her voice was wary, distant. It could have been a different person from the cheerful girl who had been giggling with Candida only a few minutes before. 'Yes, well, I meant to ring you, to say I was going to have lunch with Laura, but . . . yes, I *know*, but can't you just *listen* for a moment! I would have rung you, but just at that moment Edward came home, and . . . yes, Edward. E, D, W, A, R, D. I'm not, you just . . . Well, anyway, I could see there was something wrong, so of course I just cleared out.' She fell silent, listening.

Jane noticed sadly how sullen her face was, and wondered yet again why Daisy, who as far as Jane could see had a mother every bit as loving and caring as she felt herself to be, seemed unable to speak with Anna without bickering. She felt her usual upsurge of relief as she looked at her own daughter, whose brown eyes met hers briefly in a moment of shared understanding. How Candida – who at the vulnerable age of fourteen and a half had faced the trauma of her father's rejection – had managed to avoid all the usual horrors of teenage difficulties, was a mystery to her. She was simply profoundly grateful, and tried hard never, ever, to feel smug.

'All *right*! I *know*!' Daisy's voice was rising. 'But I haven't *finished* telling you! Laura asked me to give a message to Cassandra, so I thought I'd better go straight away, before coming home, only when I got there Cassandra wasn't very well, so I got her some lunch and waited until she felt better, and dozed off. I mean, I couldn't just *leave* her, could I? You're the one who's always saying I ought to be more thoughtful for other people.'

She wound a strand of her blonde hair round her finger, and tugged it hard as if she were trying to pull it out by the roots. 'Yes, Cassandra does have a telephone, actually. And no, I didn't think to use it, because I was worried about her, and . . . for heaven's sake, I'm not a child! I didn't need to call for help! I'm perfectly capable of looking after someone who's not very well, and anyway . . . Well, then it was late and I knew Candy would be back from school, so I came in to see her. After all, I'll be going back to that hell-hole prison in two days, and then I won't see her for ages. Well, I'm sorry, but I never asked you to make me lunch. Don't bother, another time.'

Judging that nothing was to be gained from allowing this conversation to continue, Jane silently held out her hand for the telephone. Daisy, without a word, handed over the receiver and slouched back to her chair where she slumped, picking at the crumbs on her plate and scowling.

'Anna? Yes, it's me. No, don't worry, it's fine. She'll be . . . Yes, I know. Look, why doesn't she stay for supper, and you come and join us too? Only lasagna, and there's plenty. I'd like a bit of rational adult conversation.' She saw Daisy looking mutinous, and shook her head at her with mock exasperation. 'Good. Seven-thirty, then. And what's all this about Laura? No, I haven't heard from her either. I hope there's nothing wrong . . . Yes, perhaps we both should. Tomorrow, I think, don't you? Mmm. Right. Bye.'

Jane replaced the receiver.

'Really, Daisy,' she said mildly, 'you are nasty to your poor mother.' She wondered, as she spoke, whether this would provoke an outburst, but Daisy gave her an apologetic grin.

'I know, I'm sorry, but she's just so . . . so *fussy*, and I'm not a baby. Besides, I really *did* feel worried about Laura, and about Cassandra too, and I just forgot. I mean, everyone forgets things occasionally, don't they?'

'She'd better forget to make your lunch, then.'

'I wish she would.' Daisy's voice held an undercurrent of despair, and Jane thought she'd better change the subject.

'So Edward came home in the middle of the day? And looking awful? What sort of awful? Not ill?'

'Not really. I don't think so. Just worried, and . . . scared, perhaps. Not like he usually is.' She gave a little shiver, and felt the hairs rise as the skin on her arms puckered. 'I hope they're all right.'

'I expect they will be. It will probably turn out to be something quite trivial. Or perhaps he was just coming down with flu. I'll give Laura a ring in the morning, and so will Anna.'

'The Ashingly Women's Support Group leaps into action,' murmured Ben.

'And why not?' said Jane stoutly. 'That's what friends are for.'

'And thank you too, Patience Strong.'

Ben could never resist trying to have the last word. Jane opened her mouth, then looked at his fine-drawn face, and shut it again.

Chapter 5

The weather, which had remained cold, wet and windy throughout the school holidays, with temper tantrums in the shape of hailstorms over the Easter bank holiday, changed its character with the suddenness of a fractious child on Friday and smiled benignly. Laura looked at the garden, at the borders where new weeds were growing apace and the spring-flowering shrubs needed cutting back, and decided to ignore it and go for a walk.

Pulling on a pair of boots (for the footpaths would not have dried out yet) she wondered whether to telephone Anna or Jane and see if they wanted to go with her. But that would mean struggling out of her boots again, and she might also feel obliged to change out of the old gardening jeans she had put on earlier, an earnest of good intentions. It was all too much bother and besides, she rather thought she preferred not to have to talk, or listen, or even think.

I should make the most of this weather, she thought. Enjoy it while I can. The sense of impending doom was like a distant thunderstorm. It hovered over her head, pressing down her mind and spirits until even her movements seemed sluggish. The arrival of the boy, Mark, on Sunday seemed to be rushing towards her like a tidal wave, ready to engulf her and carry her into a maelstrom of conflict and emotion that she felt ill equipped to face.

Her friends had been supportive, helpful, encouraging. Naturally. She had expected nothing else. She had also been surprised and dismayed to find how difficult it had been, telling them. She had shrunk, in advance, from their pity and their sympathy. Even their interest – and who could fail to find such an extraordinary event fascinating, when happening to someone one knew? – had been intrusive. In the end, rather than discuss it with them, she had taken refuge in brisk practicality. She had consulted with Jane about school, checking out the basic necessities in the way of uniform, making sure she knew about bus times, cost of lunches, names of key members of staff.

Anna had been busy, to Jane's secret relief, with the inevitable beginning-of-term whirlwind of last-minute shopping trips ('But you *knew* I needed a new pair of shoes for this term!'), panic over bits of summer uniform that had mysteriously vanished since last year and were eventually found, dirty and crumpled, in an unlikely corner, and a tearful session when Daisy suddenly announced that she was miserable at Abbotsford, that she had no friends, that all the staff hated her and that she was sure she was going to fail all her GCSEs because they hadn't taught her properly and she had not been given enough encouragement to revise during the holidays. By the time she had driven Daisy back to Abbotsford on Thursday evening (to greet and be greeted with enthusiasm by everyone she met), Anna had developed a grinding headache, and was unable to think of anything but spending several hours in bed, if not a week.

Cassandra, predictably, had been too much bound up in her own anxiety to react very much to anyone else's, which Laura found unexpectedly restful. She was, of course, shocked, horrified, astounded – but she felt so sick that nothing pierced through the barrier of her physical discomfort for more than a few minutes.

'This is horrible,' she wailed. 'I can't keep taking days off like this, the shop will go bankrupt, but every time I stand up I get this buzzing in my head, and my stomach feels as though it's about to come shooting up through the top of my skull. I didn't feel like this last time. There must be something wrong with it. Or me. I'm too old for this. And Stephen will be furious. I'll have to go back to the clinic and have another – you know. Termination.'

Laura, who was feeling decidedly negative about the whole concept of illegitimate children, agreed rather more enthusiastically than she would ever have dreamed of doing before, since she knew how risky it was to give advice to people who might be in danger of following it.

'Yes, you probably should,' she said. 'I'll come and hold your hand, if you like.' Last time she would never have been able to make such an offer. The thought of seeing someone throw away, so lightly, so wantonly, what she had longed for in vain for so many years, would have been impossible. Cassandra, startled, looked at her blankly and with faint resentment. This was not the kind of answer she expected or even wanted.

'Seriously?' She was at all times very conscious of being six years younger than Laura, and had an instinct to defer to her that was entirely absent in her relations with her mother. Laura sighed, shook her head, and smiled slightly.

'No, not seriously. Don't take any notice of me, Caz. I'm a bit warped just at the moment. You must do what's best for you.'

'Well, I would, if only I knew what that was. Have you swum this week?'

'No, I couldn't face it. The trouble with swimming is that it gives you too much time to think.'

'Mmm.' Cassandra's agreement was heartfelt. Although they lived quite near one another, they had originally met not in the village shop or at the Christmas church bazaar, but at the early-morning sessions at the sports centre in their nearby town. Laura, during the years when she was trying to get pregnant, had set herself to keep her body at peak efficiency, watching her diet and taking regular exercise. Cassandra, for her part, worked with quiet desperation to keep her figure as perfect as it had been when Stephen had first seen her.

These early swims, up and down the long pool in the company of a band of regulars and fanatics, engendered the camaraderie of those who were united in suffering. Laura and Cassandra had progressed from the comparative merits of different shampoos and goggles, to the quirky idiosyncrasies of other people's swimming styles, and had found themselves friends without ever really noticing the growth of friendship.

Cassandra, only child of elderly parents, whose mother disapproved violently of Stephen and never hesitated to voice her opinions, was lonely. Many of her evenings were spent sitting, dressed and made up and discreetly perfumed, listening for the telephone to ring. Friends of her own generation had married, produced children, and tended to regard her either with superiority or with a kind of awed pity at her single state. Laura, married but childless, filled a gap in her life, and she was aware, without anything being said, that her own frequent emotional crises provided a necessary outlet for Laura's need to have someone to care for.

Cassandra, whose relationship with her mother and father had deteriorated to a complete lack of sympathy and comprehension on both sides, envied Laura her parentless existence, while Laura, though she admitted she found Mr and Mrs Happold uncongenial, missed her own parents badly. Her father, older than her mother, had died of a stroke soon after Laura's marriage to Edward, and her mother, six years later, had been stricken with rheumatoid arthritis. The disease had progressed with alarming rapidity until it became clear that she could no longer live at home, even with Laura's help and support. Laura and Edward, with equal sincerity, had begged her to move in with them, but she had refused.

'My dears, it would be disastrous. Too much of a strain on all of us, and with the best will in the world you would start to resent me. As it is I can scarcely move without help, I can't dress myself, or go to the loo, or feed myself properly. I know you'd do all those things willingly, and with love, but even so I'd feel a burden, and it would depress me. Far better to pay for professional help, and thank goodness your father left me with enough to go to somewhere good.'

Laura had been greatly distressed, and had even gone so far as to summon her sister Anne back from Mexico, where she now spent most of her time. A dedicated archaeologist, she lived happily and in extreme discomfort on a series of digs with her lover, also an archaeologist. The idea of marriage had always seemed irrelevant to them: neither wanted children, and both were so deeply involved in the distant past that the mundane world of the present day meant nothing to them.

Anne had stood in Laura's pretty sitting room, shivering slightly in the trousers and pullover she had pulled from the collection of warm clothes she kept stored in a trunk in Laura's attic.

'Bloody cold place, England, even in June,' she pronounced without rancour. 'I don't know how you stand it. No wonder the poor old darling's got rheumatism.'

'Rheumatoid arthritis. It's not at all the same thing,' Laura had almost snapped.

'No, I know, sorry. But she's right, you know. She's better off with professional care.'

'I don't mind! I can do it! After all, what else have I got to do?'

'That's just it.' Anne's eyes, on the rare occasion when they focused on the present, were shrewd. 'You can't make her into your child substitute,' she said bluntly. 'It isn't fair on you, or on her. Don't you see that she would simply hate to be dependent on you? She'd keep quiet rather than ask for help, because she wouldn't want to disturb or bother you, and she'd end up ten times more uncomfortable and unhappy. Find her somewhere nearby, visit her as much as you like, but leave her her dignity.'

Laura had continued to protest, but in her heart she knew Anne was right. Their mother had settled into a nearby nursing home and Laura had visited her almost daily until her death five years earlier. By then, going to the home had become so much of a habit, and so many of the inhabitants had become friends, that it had seemed natural to continue to go there as a kind of unpaid assistant. Now, Laura found herself wishing that she still had her mother to confide in, that she could discuss this extraordinary change in her life with her.

Laura walked along the verge of the lane, one ear automatically tuned to approaching vehicles so that she was ready, if necessary, to squeeze into the hedge and avoid being mown down by a passing Range Rover. A gentle breeze floated small white powder-puffs of cloud across a sky of limpid blue, and flirted with the pheasant-eye narcissus that lifted their heads among clumps of wallflowers in cottage gardens. Drifts of anemones starred the vivid green of new grass by the roadsides, and a faint haze of blue showed where the first bluebells were coming out. It was so beautiful that Laura, who had hoped to be cheered and uplifted, found herself demoralised.

She found to her horror that the glittering green new leaves in the hedge were blurred and rainbowed by tears, and felt a sob of pure self-pity rising like a bubble through her chest. There was a car coming, too. It's bound, she thought, to be someone I know. Probably someone I know and don't much like, who will see me snivelling in the hedgerow and go back and tell everybody in the village. 'That poor Mrs Melville,' she'll say. 'Something must be terribly wrong; she was in floods of tears out in the lane this morning . . .' She speeded her walk until she was almost running, then dived with relief into a gap where a small, seldom-used footpath meandered through some boggy land to a small wood.

She squelched through the mud, breathing deeply in through her nose and holding the air for a moment before expelling it sharply through her mouth. As was her habit when beset by emotional turmoil, she tried to unravel her mind, pick the various feelings apart and examine them objectively.

First, she was so angry. Not a clean, blazing anger, but the sullen internal glow of old coals, grey on the outside but dull red within. Angry with Edward, with the boy's mother, with the boy himself, and most of all with herself, Laura, for being angry at all. She hated this anger that burned so steadily inside her. It challenged her own view of herself. She was not an angry person.

She was, she told herself, very tired. Physically tired, from housework. She had been overtaken by a kind of frenzy of spring cleaning. For the last two days she had turned out cupboards, polished furniture and floors and silver and brass, washed down paintwork, and washed and ironed every cover and curtain that was washable. Now the house gleamed, garnished with bowls and jugs of spring flowers that she had picked earlier that morning. The cats, their incipient paranoia exacerbated by all this activity, took to cowering resentfully under dripping shrubs in the garden. Edward, anxious and awkward, had come home to meals of leftovers from the freezer and eaten them meekly, wondering whether this frantic activity was meant as a welcome or as a territorial statement. Laura, had he asked, could not have told him. A bit of both, probably, fuelled by the need for physical work to still her thoughts.

In the little wood, the remains of hazel coppicing had left clumps of fantastically contorted roots and trunks that were straight from a Rackham illustration. The catkins were over, dry and beige-coloured, but the new leaves were bursting out and the air smelled of growth, and leaf mould, and wafts of heavy balsamic sweetness from a nearby row of poplars. A solid, moist smell that you could have cut into slices, like a fruit cake. A tangle of twisted roots formed a natural seat between two trees, and Laura sat down, breathing rather heavily, for it had been heavy going through the mud and she had taken it at a rapid pace.

Today was Friday. Today, at his office, the telephone would ring and she, the girl, the woman who was Mark's mother, would speak to him to make arrangements for Mark to arrive during the weekend. I don't know her name, thought Laura. How ridiculous. Alcantara, I know that, at least, from registering him at the school. Mark Alcantara. Spanish, I suppose, or Italian. Portuguese? Somewhere in South America? She pushed aside the picture of flashing dark eyes and a mane of dark hair with a red carnation pushed into it, banishing the black satin dress frilled with red flounces, the comb and mantilla, the clicking castanets and the high-heeled shoes back to the childhood storybook where they belonged.

What am I going to say to him? How do I greet him? If he were little, perhaps I could kiss him, but at fourteen . . . and anyway, do I want to kiss him? If only we were French, and could shake hands as a matter of course. Do adults shake hands with young people, ever? She tried to remember if she had ever seen anyone shake Daisy's hand, or Ben's. Guy's, perhaps, but he was that kind of person. I suppose I could ask Ben, she thought wildly. Another vision – of herself performing a version of the hand-slapping routine she had seen on American programmes – had also to be banished. Calm down, now, you're getting silly.

If only I knew what he looked like, she thought, knowing that was silly too. She wanted, badly, to know whether he looked like Edward. How it would affect her if he did, she had no idea. It might perhaps lend some superficial feeling of familiarity and make her feel more at ease with him. Or, of course, it might make her feel bitterly resentful. All she wanted, for the moment, was to be able to make some kind of imaginary construct, a lay figure round which she could invent a script for that first meeting.

She already knew that he would be arriving by train. That, Edward had said, had been made clear to him from the start. There was no question of him going to Primrose Hill to fetch Mark. He would not see where he lived, or meet . . . her. Primrose Hill. It sounded so pretty. Laura couldn't remember ever going there; she had looked it up in the *A-Z*, and found it was on the edge of Regent's Park, by the zoo. Lucky Mark, then. She racked her brains, remembering visits with a little Daisy. The elephant house, sad and dreary concrete; Guy the gorilla, in whose eyes she had, anthropomorphically, read reproach and despair. The reptile house, warm on a bleak winter day but shivery with snakes. Something they could talk about? Hardly.

A gibbering crowd of worries flew round in the Pandora's box of her head. Smoking. Drinking. Drugs – oh no, please. Not that. Aggression. Silence. Homesickness. Truancy. Shoplifting. Vandalism. They seemed to breed as they flew, multiplying like flies in a speeded-up film. Laura batted them away as if they were in reality flying round her, then buried her face in her hands. She felt the roughness of her fingers – she hated wearing rubber gloves – and could smell on them a comforting residue from the wax polish she had used that morning, overlaid with the scented geranium she had picked from the greenhouse to eke out the flowers. He is a child, she told herself firmly. A child. He needs food, and a bed, and a school. He needs a welcome. He needs . . . love. And if I can't manage that – as I don't know that I can – then at least kindness.

She pulled her hands from her face, detaching each adhering finger as if sticky glue were forming strings between the two surfaces. She sat up straighter, breathed in deeply, opened her eyes. I'll pick some of these leaves before I go, she thought. Put them in the copper jug I polished yesterday. And then I'll make a cake. Some biscuits. Pasta sauce ought to be safe. Boys of fourteen are generally hungry. If nothing else, I can feed him.

Walking home, her body felt tired and limp so that it was an effort just to keep moving, but her mind was more at peace. Dr Green, she told herself wisely. As she walked down the path through the front garden and down the side of the house, she found that she was humming. Clutching her branches of leaves in one hand, she delved in the pocket of her Barbour for the back-door key. She was looking down, and did not at first see the figure sitting, motionless, on the doorstep. Her fingers closed round the familiar smooth metal, and she raised her head, only to freeze into immobility as she took in the dark shape that was made larger and more menacing by the black holdall beside him. She felt her heart thud in pure animal panic. The fingers of her right hand closed so tightly round the key that she felt the sharp edges of the wards bruise her skin, and with her left hand she held the ridiculous bundle of twiggy branches against her, as a shield or even a hiding place. A burglar? A mugger? But he did not move to stand up, only lifting his head.

His hair, dark but with reddish glints where the sun caught it, was trimmed – shaved? – close at the back of his head, up to about half-way. Above that it was long and thick, pulled back into a small ponytail held by a rubber band. A pale face, she realised dimly, with a nose that would one day, in age, become aggressively beak-like but which still had the softness of youth. Strong dark eyebrows, uncompromisingly straight and pulled to meet in the middle by a small frown, over hazel eyes. Glowing, brownish hazel eyes that were narrowed against the sun. Edward's eyes. Surely. Edward's eyes, lacking only Edward's affectionate look.

Laura's hands relaxed their grip.

'Mark?' Through dry lips, her voice came out as a whisper. She swallowed. 'Mark? Are you Mark?'

'Yeah.' His voice was husky, surprisingly deep for fourteen. His eyes dropped, and his head, so that the tuft of ponytail jutted upward, revealing the area of short hair, close cut and smooth as moleskin. The step was low; he sat with his legs bent up and forearms resting on the lifted knees, so that his hands dangled between them. They were large hands, but young-looking, soft and almost plump, the skin pale. He seemed to be looking at them. Laura studied him.

It was difficult, since he was sitting, to judge his height, but from the width of his shoulders and the length of his legs, bent up like a crane-fly's, he must be fairly large for his age. His black jeans were worn but clean, and above them was a black leather jacket over the kind of black sweatshirt that Daisy often wore. A rim of white at the neck indicated a T-shirt beneath. Teenage boy, standard issue, she thought. Well, he's here. I'd better get him inside.

'Shall we go in? I'm Laura, by the way. Your, um, your father's wife. Well, you must have guessed that. Anyway, do please call me Laura – Mrs Melville sounds ridiculous, and I don't believe in all that "Auntie" stuff – unless one is really an aunt, of course.'

She brought the key out of her pocket. For a moment she thought he wasn't going to move, that she would have to step over or round him to reach the door, but then he stood up, picking up the holdall and standing awkwardly. His head was still lowered, his shoulders slightly hunched so that he looked, she thought, like a young bullock that might turn out to be aggressive, but hasn't quite made up its mind how it feels.

Laura unlocked the door and stood aside. 'Go through to the kitchen. I've just got to take off my boots.'

Alone in the lobby she put the branches down on the freezer and pulled off her boots, hung up her Barbour, moving slowly like someone swimming in treacle, to gain herself a breathing space. Edward's eyes, she thought again. He's got Edward's eyes. Carefully she gathered up the branches, went through the kitchen to the hall for the copper jug, filled it with water at the sink in the utility room, and dumped the branches in. Typically they fell into a graceful shape, as if arranged with consummate care. She carried the jug back to the hall, set it on the carved oak dresser where the light from the windows shone through the delicate green of the leaves.

Only then did she return to the kitchen where Mark stood, washed up like flotsam against the Aga where he leaned, as everyone always did, against the rail. She noticed that he had removed his heavy black army boots – out of the corner of her eye she could see their massive ugliness lined neatly up with her wellingtons and gardening shoes. She thought of things Jane had told her about visiting boys. At least his feet don't smell, she thought. What a relief.

'Let me show you to your room,' she said, cross with herself the minute the words were out of her mouth. How stupid I sound, like an amateur production of a fifties comedy. She glanced at him, wondering if she would see a derisive expression on his face, but he was bending to pick up his holdall.

A childless couple has, necessarily, more bedrooms than they need. This house, with its five bedrooms, had been bought at a time when Laura still hoped to use two or even three of them for her children. For some years she had left three of the rooms as they had been when they bought the house, with visions of redecorating in nursery colours. In the end, gradually, the rooms had taken on their own identities. One Edward had quietly taken over, installing a desk and lighting. There he could work on the plans and drawings for projects he had undertaken, as he sometimes did, more for his own amusement than for profit.

The fifth room, being rather small, had for a while been used for ironing and for sewing, when Laura did an evening class in dressmaking. She had not liked the clothes she so painstakingly made, however, and found that ironing was less tedious in the kitchen, with the television and the cats for company. In the end, since it lay between the spare bedroom and the other, unused room, Edward had split it down the middle and created two shower rooms, with arched doorways to the bedrooms that echoed the rounded arches of the windows. Then, at last, Laura had furnished and

59

decorated the remaining bedroom. Since the main spare room had been done in soft pink and green, it had seemed right to her to move away from the ultra-feminine colours. It was a corner room, with windows to the south and west, and Laura had decorated it very simply, in soft yellow and slate blue. It had seemed the natural choice, therefore, for Mark.

'Shower room through there – or if you don't like showers, there's a bathroom across the way. Cupboard here for your things. All right? I'll go and see about lunch. Come down when you're ready.'

As she left the room he was still standing in the middle of it, much as he had stood in the kitchen. He did not, at least, immediately shut the bedroom door behind her, which seemed promising. As she walked downstairs she spared a moment of regret for the fact that Edward, perfectionist that he was, had made sure that no such thing as a creaky board existed in their house. He could be dancing round the room for all she knew. Then she heard the flush of the lavatory, and the sound of water moving through pipes as he ran the basin taps. He was human, then. And clean. Another plus.

'Lunch,' she muttered to herself, opening the door of the refrigerator and surveying its pristine bareness. 'What on earth do I do about lunch?' On her own, she rarely bothered with more than a corner of cheese and an apple, but for a hungry boy? 'Soup.' She went to the freezer. 'Thank God for microwaves. Cheese. Bread – no, toast. Butter and jam. The rest of the fruit cake. Fruit. And something to drink. Tea, coffee, squash?'

A distracted cat, surprised by all this activity in the middle of the day, twined round her legs. 'For heaven's sake,' she said crossly, 'don't expect to be fed now. You know perfectly well that you don't get fed until four at the earliest. You're just being greedy. Go out and catch something if you're desperate.'

She heard a small sound above the hum of the microwave as it defrosted the soup, and looked round to see Mark hovering in the doorway, watching her warily.

'Not you!' She tried to laugh naturally. 'I was talking to the cat. Do you like cats? I hope you're not allergic to them, or anything?'

'Dunno. Don't think so.'

It was the longest sentence he had so far spoken. She noticed with some relief – and was ashamed of it – that though his speech was slovenly, the vowels, at least, were pure. You revolting snob, she chastised herself.

'Well, you probably aren't, then. Come and sit down. Are you hungry?'

'Yeah.' For the first time a trace of enthusiasm appeared on the stillness of his face, like a trickle of sunlight breaking through heavy cloud-cover.

'Good. There's not much, I'm afraid, only soup and cheese and things. We usually have our main meal in the evening. And, of course, I didn't know you were arriving today . . . ?'

He sat at the table, where she had indicated. 'Yeah. Sorry.'

'Well, I don't mind, Mark. In fact, it's rather a nice surprise. Getting it over with, if you know what I mean.' She stirred the soup in its bowl, prodding at frozen lumps, put it back in the microwave. 'I was rather dreading meeting you for the first time. I expect you were too. It's all a bit, well, strange, isn't it?' He grunted, which she thought was probably agreement. 'Is that why you came down today? To get it over?'

'Sort of.' She sliced bread and put it in the toaster, carefully refraining from looking at him.

'Does anyone know you're here? Your . . . your mother?'

'Suppose so. It's where she was sending me, after all.' Was that resentment in his voice? 'She was fixing it all up, and I thought, why wait for the weekend? So I packed my things and came.'

On his own terms, Laura thought. Poor kid, I can't say I blame him for that. Everyone arranging his life for him, telling him he was going to stay with an unknown father and his still more unknown wife. Terrifying, really. The microwave ding-ed, and she took out the soup and poured it into bowls. She waited until she was sitting opposite him, the soup steaming in front of them, before speaking.

'Do you think you should give her a ring? Tell her you're here? She'll think you're at school, won't she?'

He glanced up from his soup, which he was stirring round and round but had not, so far, tasted. Was that a gleam of amusement in his eyes?

'Not by now, she won't.'

Laura, who wasn't used to schools, thought about it. 'You mean, they'll have been in touch with her? Because you're not there? After only one day?' Another look. One straight dark eyebrow lifted, and it was definitely amusement in the hazel eyes. 'Oh, I see. Not just one day. All the more reason to ring her, then.' She stood up and fetched the cordless phone from its perch by the door. 'The soup's too hot to eat yet. You might as well get this over with as well. I'll give you five minutes. OK?'

He shrugged. 'OK.'

Laura went out of the room and pulled the door shut behind her. Feeling rather guilty she stayed within earshot, however, and was relieved to hear the indeterminate grumble of his voice a few moments later. There was a pause, quite a long one. Then his voice again, louder and higher. Laura retreated upstairs. She didn't want to risk being caught eavesdropping.

On the landing she hesitated, but when she walked forward she saw that his bedroom door was open. The holdall lay in the middle of the floor, unzipped. A tangle of clothes bulged out of it, and nothing had been unpacked even – she peered into the bathroom – no, not even a washbag. The only thing he had taken out was a Walkman, complete with earphones, and a pile of cassettes that lay neatly aligned on the bedside table. Did that, she wondered, count as settling in? For a fourteen-year-old, perhaps it did.

Laura went slowly back downstairs. The kitchen door was still closed, but no sound of his voice came through it. She hesitated for a minute, two minutes, then opened the door. The phone was back on its hook and Mark sat as before, stirring his soup. His face, what she could see of it, was unreadable. Laura sat down, buttered her toast briskly, tasted the soup, which had cooled to a reasonable temperature.

'Just about right now,' she said, a vague and unthreatening conversational gambit. She longed to ask, How was it? Was she angry? Is everything all right? but past experience with Daisy and Ben had taught her wisdom. 'Cheese?'

'Thanks.' He cut a chunk. 'What's in the soup?'

Not a fussy eater, please God, she thought. Aloud, she said cheerfully: 'Chicken, potatoes, onions, and a couple of leeks from the garden. We've got hundreds of them so I put them into almost everything. Leek soup, leek casserole, leek mousse, leek pie, leek pudding, leek ice cream . . .' His face, which had been growing alarmed, cleared.

'With chocolate sauce?'

'Of course.'

He grinned at her and, picking up his spoon, ate with appetite. Goodness, thought Laura, startled into immobility, he's beautiful. The smile burned itself on her retina. Startlingly perfect teeth – oh, the good fortune of today's young with the benefits of fissure sealing, fluoride, orthodontistry – and the eyes warming into honey gold, the outer corners crinkling so that they became oddly and attractively triangular beneath the winging brows. She realised that she was sitting with her spoon dripping half-way to her mouth, and lifted it self-consciously. She need not have worried. He was eating with the uninhibited absorption of a small child, or an animal. Neatly, she noticed with some relief, and with his mouth closed.

They ate in a silence that, though at first it seemed natural, grew increasingly uncomfortable. Laura felt exhausted. I'm too tired for this, she thought. What can I say to him? Any question I ask is going to sound intrusive, inquisitive. Home, school, friends – all taboo, between them. For a while, at least.

In the end she turned on the small television that was perched on a stand so that she could watch it from the table, the sink, or the working area. The lunchtime news flowed round the kitchen, filling the spaces between them. The weather. Trails for evening programmes. A familiar tune, and Laura's hand automatically went to the remote control but stopped, arrested by his face that was turned, sunflower to the sun, to the cheerful colours of the screen. *Neighbours*. His expression, even through the opening sequence, was absorbed, interested, relaxed. But I hate *Neighbours*, she thought. Oh, well. If you can't beat 'em, and all that.

Peace, of a kind, descended on the kitchen.

Round one, she thought. And if I haven't won it, at least I haven't lost it either.

Chapter 6

'Jane, it's Anna. You OK?'

Long usage enabled Jane to interpret this inquiry, correctly, as relating not to her general well-being but rather to her availability for a chat. Reaching behind her without looking, she hooked her foot round a kitchen chair and dragged it, with a protesting screech, near to the wide-open garden door beside the telephone.

'Yes, fine. Candy's gone into town with some friends to buy something crucial, like a belt or some earrings; Ben's gone for a walk, and Toby's been invited to London for the day – someone's birthday treat. Lady of leisure, that's me.'

'Yes, I can imagine. So you're going to spend the morning having a manicure and pedicure, reading magazines, drinking coffee . . . ?'

'Yes, of course. All of that. After, that is, I've done the ironing, found Toby's missing school pullover, defrosted the freezer, and concocted something so incredibly nourishing for lunch that even if Ben only eats two tiny spoonfuls he will still be getting his full complement of vitamins, minerals, protein and roughage.'

'Oh, dear. Is he still not eating?'

'Not really. Oh, he eats something when he's at home. A small portion, and leaves half of it. But I hardly dare to watch. He's getting – well – clever about it.'

'Oh, lord. And when it comes to being clever . . .'

'Ben beats us all hands down. Yes, I know. Oh, Anna, I wish I knew what to do! I used to worry about Candy being plump, and I was always terrified she'd take it into her head to diet and go anorexic or bulimic or something, but I never thought Ben . . . I mean, he never gives a damn what he looks like! Not that that's what it's about, of course, in his case, but I ask you!'

'Poor you.' Anna's voice was warmly sympathetic. 'And poor Ben, too. You can't talk about it?'

'He won't. Or can't. I don't know.' Jane reached up to the windowsill and picked a browning leaf off the scented geranium that was beginning, Toby said, to colonise the whole room. Absently she rubbed it between her fingers. It crumbled dryly, but the scent that rose from it was fresh. She closed her eyes, breathed in. 'I'm so frightened,' she said.

'I know. The eternal problem with teenagers. If you don't say anything, do they think you don't care? And if you do, are you interfering, and will you just make things worse? I do know,' said Anna with feeling, 'what it's like.'

'Of course you do. Oh, Anna, I never thought it would be like this, did you? When they were babies, I mean?'

'No, of course not. Nobody does. People don't warn you – or they do, but you don't believe them. Just as well, I suppose, or the human race would have died out long since.'

'Conspiracy theory.'

'Yes. What about slimming biscuits?'

'Slimming biscuits?' Jane was fairly used to the way Anna's mind tended to dart off at a tangent, but this one threw her. 'Part of the conspiracy?' she hazarded.

'No, for Ben.'

'But that's the last thing I want . . .'

'No, listen, I read about it somewhere. Those biscuits they sell where you eat two or three to replace a meal. They're fortified, or something, added protein and vitamins and all that, so the misguided creatures can have a nice sweet snack instead of a meal, which is what most of the young prefer to do anyway. So, if you just eat those instead of proper meals, I suppose you're bound to lose weight. But if you eat them as well as ordinary food, you're actually upping your intake. Get it?'

'Goodness! How machiavellian! Do they taste different?'

'No idea, I've never tried them. Of course, you'd have to hide all the packaging, just fill the biscuit tin with them as if they were ordinary chocolate digestives or something. It means the others will eat them too, and it will cost a bomb, but it's worth thinking about.'

'Goodness, yes. Anna, that's brilliant! I'll go and get some straight away!'

'What, and miss the manicure? I'm going into town later on, and I've got to go to Boots, so I'll stock up for you, if you like. Any particular kind? Chocolate?'

'Oh, bless you. Are you sure? Tell you what, do you think they do any with coconut?'

'Haven't a clue, but I'll try. Is that what he likes?'

'Yes, adores it, and the really beautiful thing about it is that the others loathe it, so I can put them in with the ordinary biscuits and they won't touch them. Neat, eh?'

'Brilliant, if they do them. I'll check it out. Anyway, what I really rang you about was Laura. Have you spoken to her?'

'Not for a couple of days. She was running around like a headless hen, hoovering the cats and polishing the ceilings. It's funny, isn't it, how you feel compelled to have the house looking nice for someone you don't much like? Or at least, someone you're not sure about. I mean, what fourteen-year-old boy is ever going to notice whether the brass has been polished, or if the linen cupboard is untidy?'

'I know. But I'd do exactly the same, wouldn't you?'

'I suppose so. Though I have to admit my standards aren't quite as high as Laura's.'

'You do have rather more to do. And a much bigger house. But that still isn't what I wanted to tell you. He's arrived!'

'Who's arrived? Guy?' Jane, who had glanced defensively round her kitchen and noticed a large cobweb gathering dust in a corner, felt she had lost her grip on the conversation.

'No, don't be dotty! The boy! Whatever his name is. Edward's son!'

'Good heavens! Already? But I thought he wasn't getting down until tomorrow! It is still Saturday, isn't it?'

'Yes, all day. I know, that's what she told me as well. But it seems that he turned up, unexpectedly, yesterday lunchtime. She went out for a walk, came back, and there he was, sitting on the doorstep.'

'Good God! Heavens, I mean!' Jane, irrationally, had reservations about what was, and was not, proper to say in a rectory. Swearing seldom bothered her, but using the word 'God' as an exclamation gave her an uncomfortable feeling of a disapproving, purse-lipped presence standing at her shoulder, lowering. 'How do you know? Did she ring you?'

'No. I met them. Yesterday, late afternoon, in Sainsbury's. I tried to ring you last evening, but you were out and then I thought I'd leave it, wait till you'd be more likely to be on your own.'

'Goodness.' Jane settled back in her chair, her own problems forgotten. 'What's he like?'

'Silent, mostly. Rather sulky-looking, I thought, but then the whole situation's a bit fraught, isn't it? For him too, I mean. And they're not often very chatty at that age, are they?'

'No. Heavens, poor Laura, coming back and finding him there, it must have been such a shock!'

67

'No, actually she said it was rather good. A surprise, of course, but she said she'd been so keyed up waiting for him to arrive, she was glad to get it over with and miss out two more days of waiting and panicking.'

'I suppose there is that. What about Edward?'

'Oh, she rang him at the office to warn him, but he was out on site somewhere and his portable phone was on the blink, so he did the same – came home and found him there.'

'It must have been an extraordinary meeting.'

'Yes. Laura wasn't very forthcoming about that, not surprisingly, but she said it was all right. A nasty little part of me would have loved to be a fly on the wall, wouldn't you? I mean, a son of fourteen you've never set eyes on! And Edward, of all people!'

'I know, that's what got to me, too. I mean, *Edward*! Anyone else and I mightn't have been so surprised, but I always thought they were such a devoted couple!'

'That's what we used to think about you and Bill,' Anna pointed out.

'I know. I thought it myself. So why should I have been surprised by Edward? Most men, now, I wouldn't trust further than I could spit them. But Edward . . .'

They each fell silent, contemplating feet of clay.

'You don't think, maybe – ' Jane's voice was tentative – 'it's a . . . well, a mistake?'

'I should say it most certainly is,' said Anna, rather grimly.

'No, I mean . . . is this boy really Edward's? Or is Edward being taken for a ride? What does he look like?'

Anna thought back. 'Rather nice-looking, in a sulky sort of way. Big, for fourteen.'

'Well, Edward's tall, but I wouldn't call that conclusive. Come on, Anna, wasn't there anything? What about his hair?'

'Dreadful!' Anna's voice was decisive. 'Shaved at the back, and the top in a ponytail. But not curly like Edward's. Dark. Oh, I don't know, Jane. He hardly looked at me, and then Laura told him to go and choose some ice cream, so I didn't get much of a look at him. You'll have to judge for yourself tomorrow.'

'Why tomorrow? I was going to pop over and say hello and good luck to Laura this afternoon, but of course I can't do that now. Isn't it better to leave them alone for the weekend, give them a chance to get to know one another?'

'Presumably not. That's the other reason I rang. Laura wants us all to go for lunch tomorrow. Your young especially, so that this boy can meet them before school on Monday. And Daisy – I've fixed her a Sunday leave. Her housemistress thought it was a bit odd, the first weekend of term, but I said it was a special party her godmother was giving, and she gave in. I suspect she's only too pleased to have Daisy off the premises at weekends. One less day for her to be getting into trouble. Daisy, of course, is thrilled to bits. She was most put out to think that we would be seeing the little bastard, as she so fragrantly calls him, before she did.'

'Goodness.' Jane inspected her fingernails, frowning to see them short and stained from gardening. 'It's a major event, then. Tiara? Twinset and pearls?'

'Jeans and sweatshirt, I'd say. Laura's planning a barbecue. I think we're only invited along as extras; it's the children she wants. And for moral support, I suppose. She's going to ask Cassandra, too.'

'The coven, Bill used to call it. And now he isn't around, poor old Edward has to face us women all by himself.'

'Poor old Edward nothing,' said Anna robustly. 'After all, if he hadn't been fucking around he wouldn't have been facing us anyway.' Sometimes it amused Anna to shock people, and it was one of the few benefits of her widowed state, she often said, that people made allowances for occasional lapses of language. 'Don't forget that, when you start wondering whether this boy is really Edward's or not. Even if he isn't, he could have been. Anyway, Edward won't be the only man. My Friend the Widow is coming.'

'Oh, good. I like him. And he gets on well with Ben. On an intellectual level, that is,' Jane finished, rather defensively. Anna's Friend the Widow was an elderly man of unequivocally homosexual tendencies whose boyfriend had bought a small house in the village more than twenty years earlier to use as a weekend retreat. The village worthies, fearing they knew not what, had been prepared for the worst, whatever that might have been. Vague and hideous fears of a succession of rent boys, or transvestites, or merely men in raincoats who would accost their sons in bus shelters, had drifted like dry-ice vapour through the community, but were soon realised to be unfounded.

James and Tod – short, as he loved to tell everyone, for Bartholomew – soon proved themselves to be ideal members of the village. James had inherited wealth, enough so that neither of them needed to work, although Tod, the younger of the two, ran a small and exclusive art gallery to which he would drift, exquisitely, late on Tuesday morning until early Thursday afternoon. On Thursday evening he would load the car, an elderly Bristol, with wine and whatever gastronomic delights James had garnered

69

while haunting his favourite store, Harrods, then they would drive sedately down to Ashingly.

Their house, a little Georgian gem like a full-sized doll's house, was crammed with antiques, the walls encrusted with paintings. They spent many an enjoyable hour rearranging these, bickering happily over juxtapositions, and driving their cleaning lady into near hysteria by the endlessly finicking and contradictory instructions they left her. Artistic, gossipy, inquisitive and generous, they flung themselves into village affairs with the joyful abandon of berserkers going into battle, and with much the same effect. Meetings of the Village Hall Committee, the School Fête Committee, the Stoolball Club and even the Thursday Club (a social club for the elderly women of the village that was strong on bingo sessions and cream teas) emerged from their rural tranquillity and found themselves, battered and bleeding but excited, rising to new and unheard-of heights.

All that, however, had come to a end five years earlier when James, without any warning, since he had always seemed to be in what he referred to as '*rude* health, darling,' had suffered a massive heart attack in the middle of a stoolball match, and died. All those present testified to Tod's anguish, citing his frantic attempts to resuscitate his friend, and his disbelief when told by a doctor, who had fortunately been part of the visiting team, that James was indeed dead and beyond the reach of medical skill.

The village mourned with Tod, and mourned no less sincerely when it was found that all James's favourite interests had been generously remembered in his will. The church had seldom been so full of people as it was for his funeral, which featured among other things a Victorian hearse – glittering with silver decorations, so that one child was heard to mention, piercingly, Cinderella's coach – pulled by four black horses with nodding ostrich plumes. It was, everyone agreed, the best funeral they had ever attended, and those few whose personal commitments or infirmity had meant they were unable to attend were much pitied, though they received from well-meaning friends a detailed description of the service, the lavish displays of flowers, and the even more lavish buffet lunch in the village hall where all James's favourite foods were served. This, since James's favourites included caviar, lobster, beef wellington and sausage and mash, turned out to be an epicurean fantasy against which everything for the next five years was judged and found wanting. Doting mothers planning their daughters' weddings had been known to curse James's memory.

Tod, however, who had kept himself going during the first few weeks by carrying out this and all the other extravagant gestures James had ever mentioned, then suffered a nervous collapse. The art gallery was sold, as was their Mayfair flat, and he retreated like a salted snail into the little Georgian house. The clubs and societies saw him no more; visitors were left rejected on the doorstep; the telephone was answered, macabrely, by James's voice on the answerphone, and messages left thereon brought no response.

The village, on the whole, was both warmly sympathetic and profoundly approving. Such extravagant grief was, they felt, right and proper under the circumstances, and where a woman left widowed at a similar age would be exhorted to get on with living, Tod was permitted, and even expected, to give way to his feelings. 'He'll never get over it,' was the phrase much bandied about in village shop and pub. 'Lost, he'll be, without James. Go out like a light, he will. Wouldn't give him more than two months at the most.' A sigh, a shake of the head, added to the relish.

Tod, however, proved more resilient than anyone had guessed. For six months he kept to himself, seeing no one, shopping in the anonymity of town supermarkets, his sole communications the elegantly penned replies to the various letters of condolence he received. Then, one morning, the quicker-eyed of his neighbours noticed that neither the milkman nor the paper-boy had delivered, and that the curtains stayed closed all day. It was soon discovered that the cleaning lady was to resume her duties and that her son, who made a good living cutting the grass of those affluent enough to afford him, was to keep the garden tidy. Tod had gone abroad, no one knew where or for how long, but the house was to be properly looked after in his absence.

Six months later, with as little warning, Tod returned. Returned to a house where every painting had been meticulously dusted, every beloved antique polished to a mile-deep shine, and where three attempted burglaries had been foiled by the complex alarm system, and by the strength of the metal grilles that had been installed at every window, however tiny.

The following morning the grilles were pushed back, curtains recklessly opened to allow the June sunshine to fall on cherished furniture and carpets, and Tod himself stood at the open front door like the little man in the weather house emerging to foretell fine weather. His small, rotund frame was as exquisitely dressed as ever, his beautifully shaved face was tanned to light mahogany, and his smile was wide and welcoming. Tod was back.

Since then he had become, once again, one of the king-pins of village life. Where before he had deferred to James, always, now he brought his not inconsiderable intelligence and energy to bear on the never-ending problems of fund-raising. In an increasingly depressed economy that everyone knew was heading for recession because the government denied it so strenuously, his ingenuity and drive ensured that the Village Hall Fund, the Church Fabric Fund, and the Pensioners' Christmas Party Fund had never been so healthy.

When Anna's husband, Michael, had become ill, she had found to her surprise that it was Tod, of all the people she knew apart from Laura, who was of most help to her. There was no lack of offers, of course – to look after Daisy, to shop, to cook, to visit, to listen – but somehow it was Tod, with his acerbic wit and complete lack of sentiment, to whom she often turned. Even more, after Michael's painful and protracted death, she found his brisk, even brusque, ways tremendously comforting. He seemed to know what she needed, whether it was sympathy, a joke, a gin, or a metaphorical slap in the face. Later, when she was able to thank him, she did so.

'Think nothing of it, dear,' he said, sitting neat as a cat in the corner of her sofa and eyeing, complacently, the shine on a new pair of hand-made brogues. 'I knew I was the best person for you. After all, I'm a widow too.'

The phrase had been too good to keep to herself, and Anna knew in any case that he would not expect her to. Tod's *bons mots* were always for public consumption. The name was soon universal, and 'the Widow Tod' or, in Anna's case, 'my Friend the Widow' passed into common parlance among her friends.

For Anna, though she enjoyed his absurdities as much as anyone, he had become a friend second only in importance to her old schoolfriend, Laura. Artistic and knowledgeable, he had introduced her to the world of theatre and the arts that she had always found interesting, but as a wife and mother had never found the time to explore. Now, once the first raw anguish had worn off, she found herself being taken to exhibitions; to plays in strange, out-of-the-way theatres and even pubs; and to concerts of all kinds from classical to jazz to, once, the Rolling Stones at Wembley. Events she would have hesitated to attend as a woman on her own became possible in Tod's company. Missing Michael fiercely, but unable to contemplate the idea of replacing him in her heart or in her bed, Tod supplied a masculine, but asexual, element in her life and filled a need she had scarcely been aware of.

Her father, who might have been expected to supply some of the male support his generation would assume a young widow would need, had been affronted and disgusted at finding 'that bloody pansy', as he termed

Tod, haunting his daughter's house. Anna being his only child, he had resented even Michael's presence in her life, and had been inclined to view his early death as expressly designed by a sensible providence to return his daughter to his exclusive care. Himself a widower – Anna's timid mother had quietly died, with a look of relief on her face, several years earlier – he assumed that his daughter would naturally return to live under his roof and, incidentally, provide him with the care that a rapid succession of expensive housekeepers had failed to provide.

Unused to being crossed, he had been appalled to find that Anna had no intention of selling her house (far too big for her now), or of returning, with her children, to her childhood home. The fact that the inclusion of a lively and argumentative fourteen-year-old, as Daisy then was, into the staid surroundings of his Harrogate house would have torn the even tenor of his existence into shreds, never weighed with him. Daisy needed discipline, that was all. Her father, even before he fell ill, had spoiled her ridiculously. He, her grandfather, would soon put that right.

Where before he had been able to blame what he considered to be Anna's recalcitrance on Michael, now he found in Tod an equally convenient scapegoat. Over a stormy weekend visit he had made his feelings clear, and had signified his unwillingness to have any further dealings with his daughter until she had, in his terms, come back to her senses. Anna, her gentle temper roused, had told him roundly that, while he was her father and nothing could change that, she was not prepared to give up her friends and her own life to please him. Since then he had not visited, although Anna telephoned him every weekend, and regularly invited him to come for Christmas, or Easter, or a week in the summer.

Even Daisy, generally scornful of her mother's friends (except Laura, Jane and Cassandra) was surprisingly tolerant of Tod. She treated him as a cross between a grandfather, a contemporary, and a maiden aunt. Tod, for his part, took a serious interest in even the most bizarre of her outfits, was prepared to join in long and scurrilous discussions on the shortcomings of her teachers and friends, and best of all was always good for the loan of five pounds in times of dire emergency.

'Jane? Are you still there?' Anna's voice recalled Jane from her thoughts.

'Yes, sorry. Thinking.'

'I know. It does rather have that effect, doesn't it? All this drama, that is. Somehow, though I've had it, and you've had it, and dear old Cassie never seems to have anything else, I'd got so used to Laura and Edward sailing through life like a couple of yachts, all gentle breezes and blue sea and white billowing sails, that I find it hard to accept them having crises, like everyone else.'

'Even harder for them,' said Jane grimly. 'But Laura will cope. She always does.'

'Yes, of course she will.' Anna, her voice reassuring, answered the subtext.

After she had put the telephone down, Jane, knowing that she should be starting the ironing before it got any later, still stood by the door, picking moodily at the geranium plant until her left hand was full of leaves, dry as cornflakes, and she was surrounded by the flowery scent of them.

'Careful, Ma, you'll disappear into that plant one of these days, and we'll have to send a search party with machetes to find you.' Ben's voice, behind her, made her jump.

'Oh, Ben! I didn't hear you come in!'

'Well, I wasn't exactly creeping, but you were in a different universe, I think. You OK?'

He was bending to pick up some leaves that had fallen, his face averted. Of her three children, he was the one who worried about her most. Since he was also the one who was the most sensitive to her emotional temperature, it was difficult, sometimes, not to confide in him. Thank goodness, she thought, that at least this time I was thinking about something different.

'Yes, fine. I've just had Anna on the phone. She tells me Edward's son has arrived already – yesterday. Laura wants us all to go there for lunch tomorrow to meet him. She's doing a barbecue.'

'Oh.'

'I know it's a bit of a drag,' she said, answering the reservations in his tone, 'but I don't think she expects more from you than from any of the rest. I know he's about your age, or a bit younger, but nobody expects you to do more than show him round a bit at school, keep a vague eye on him.'

'Yeah.' Ben was notoriously fussy about his friends, preferring to have a few that measured up to his exacting standards of intellect, interest, and that elusive attribute that his generation, emulating her own, still referred to as 'cool'. 'Well, I'm sorry for the kid . . .' To Ben, who had considered himself a short adult at the age of eight, most people his own age seemed childish. '. . . but it's all a bit bizarre, isn't it?'

'Just a bit. But then . . . things are, don't you think? More than I used to realise, anyway.'

He grinned. 'Good, isn't it?'

He was, she was pleased to see, rather elated than otherwise by the strangeness of the world. But she suspected that to him, always, the world had seemed peculiarly inexplicable in its refusal to conform to his own personal standards of logic. School rules, by and large, had generally struck him as at worst pointless and at best irrelevant to him. This, which his teachers were inclined to see as arrogance, Jane believed was symptomatic of the kind of other-worldly, absent-minded-professor character that she discerned within his youthful exterior.

'Stupendous. Where's the dog? You didn't leave her behind in a wood somewhere, did you?' Ben was notorious in the family for his forgetfulness, and lost items of uniform and other clothes were a regular occurrence – the only thing immune from this being his books.

'Dog? What dog?'

'Ha ha. She'll need drying off before she comes in again.'

'I know, O Houseproud One. I left her in the garden and came in for a towel, her old one's vanished.'

'Yes, sorry, I put it in the wash, not before time. I meant to get a new one out, but I didn't expect you back so soon.'

It was, rather carefully, not a question.

'Well, Slops had a good race round, so I think she got enough exercise. I had thought of going up to the forest, but I felt a bit tired, so I didn't bother. Why, have I interrupted a tryst with the milkman or something?'

'No, the paper-boy. I like them young.'

'I'll warn my friends. Where's the towel?'

Jane went to fetch it. Returning with it, she found Ben perched against the Aga. It struck her, again, how painfully thin he was. His jeans hung from his hip-bones, held up only by a frayed leather belt, and the baggy sweatshirt only emphasised the bony wrists and neck that emerged from it. The lack of energy, of strength, was something else.

'Tired after a walk that short?' she said cheerfully. 'I'd better get you some vitamins.'

'You already did,' he pointed out kindly. 'And I even remember to take them, occasionally.'

'Oh, Ben . . .'

'Don't fuss, Ma. It's all right.' He took the towel and vanished.

Chapter 7

Sunday night. Laura went through her nightly ritual: alarm on, lipsalve on, light off, punch pillow, stretch out, sigh with pleasure. Her body was tired, her legs aching, her head faintly muzzy with wine in spite of the two glasses of water she had just drunk, but she still felt stimulated rather than sleepy, her mind alert. Beside her Edward lay silent, too still to be asleep.

'I think that went well, don't you?'

The stillness of his body gave off waves of tension, like a thundercloud. If he moves, thought Laura, the bedclothes will crackle and spark, like nylon underwear full of static.

'Very well. It was a good day. Thanks.'

A vast no-go area of unspoken thoughts lay between them. Laura reached out her hand, feeling as though her arm would need the reach of a seven-league boot to cross the space, and touched him. His arm lay inert along the side of his body. Her fingers smoothed down it, the hairs thick and ticklish sliding beneath her touch, until she reached his hand. She took it firmly into her own, and after an infinitesimal hesitation it curled round hers, the grasp tentative rather than firm.

'Everyone enjoyed it,' she said, not without satisfaction. 'I think Mark enjoyed it.'

'Yes, I think he did.'

'He's . . . I like him.'

'Yes. Good. Thanks.'

'For Christ's sake, don't keep thanking me!' Her voice was calmer than her words, and she gave his hand a little squeeze in further mitigation.

'No. Sorry.' He drew in a breath, made an effort. 'The lunch was great. One of my better efforts, really – nothing burnt, nothing raw – a triumph, in fact.'

'And such classic barbecuing weather . . .'

'Yeah . . .'

The fine weather of Friday had continued through Saturday and into

Sunday morning. On Friday, not knowing what to do with Mark, Laura had decided to carry on as if he hadn't arrived, and had gone off to shop, taking Mark with her.

'That way, you can tell me what you like. And don't like,' she said comfortably. 'I need to stock up with boring things like cat food and washing powder anyway, so if you don't mind pushing the trolley . . .'

'No, I don't mind.' Silent in the car, he sat hunched in the front seat, scarcely glancing out of the window when Laura pointed out her friends' houses, the pond, the haunted oak. When she had found herself on the verge of saying, 'Oh look, sheep!' she stopped. In Sainsbury's, however, he was unexpectedly helpful, and she once or twice caught him standing on the back of the trolley and pushing off to whirl unsteadily between the aisles. The first time he looked rather sheepish, but she grinned and admitted that she had frequently wanted to do the same. After a moment's pause he smiled back, if warily.

'I've never done this before,' he volunteered.

'What, helped with the shopping? Shame on you.'

'No, I mean the trolley. Sainsbury's. Big shops like this.'

'Oh.' Laura was unsure what he meant. 'Don't they have them near you?' She thought vaguely about Camden, could only visualise the zoo, Primrose Hill, and a Belgian restaurant she had once visited. 'I suppose they don't.'

'Yes, they do.' Mark seemed to feel that she might despise an area so deficient in modern amenities. 'But George doesn't approve of them.'

'George . . . ?'

'My mum. Her name's Georgia, but she's always called George.'

'Ah. Well, I expect she's quite right. I do try to shop in the smaller shops as well, but parking is so hard, and this is so convenient. Just born lazy, I guess.'

'I think it's great.' Leaning on the handle of the trolley he pushed off again, flying down the crowded aisle and missing a harassed mother with two toddlers by a matter of inches. Laura followed more sedately and found him transfixed by a display of crisps. Laughing, she let him choose some, egging him on to try some of the more outlandish flavours.

Laura had known from long experience that it was impossible to go round Sainsbury's without meeting someone she knew, and she was glad when the first familiar face she saw was Anna's. Introducing Mark in as neutral a tone as she could command, she sent him off to choose some ice cream.

'Any kind?' He looked faintly alarmed.

'Yes, whatever you think looks nice. Three or four kinds, so we've got plenty of choice.'

'Uh,' he grunted, a sound she had already learned meant assent and qualified pleasure, and set off purposefully to the freezers.

'How's it going?' asked Anna in a swift whisper.

'All right, I think.' Laura rapidly told her how she had found Mark on the back doorstep. 'I'm rather dreading Edward's homecoming,' she concluded. 'I tried to get hold of him, but his phone's on the blink or something, so he's going to get a shock. And what on earth am I going to do with them all weekend?'

'Take him shopping,' said Anna decisively. 'Buy him a present. Didn't you tell me that his mother had never let Edward give him anything for birthdays or Christmas? Well then. Something special. A computer and some games. A ghetto-blaster.'

'What on earth's a ghetto-blaster?'

'A Brixton briefcase? No? Oh, you know, one of those enormous radio-and-cassette players that produce great volumes of noise, that the young carry round with them polluting the environment. They do them with CD players on, too.'

'Oh, those. You don't think that's a bit like, well, like trying to buy him?'

'Of course it is,' said Anna robustly. 'That,' she explained kindly, 'is how it works. And it does work, believe me. At least, usually it does. And I think, under the circumstances, a bit of bribery is quite justifiable.'

'Yes . . .' Laura was dubious. She could see Mark coming back with the trolley. 'Will you come to lunch on Sunday? Bring Tod, and Daisy? And I'll ask Jane and her lot, and perhaps Cassandra as well . . . do a barbecue; or something . . .'

'Safety in numbers?'

Laura smiled ruefully. 'Something like that. Can you fix it?'

'Don't see why not. It might be a bit tricky with Daisy. They're supposed to be revising furiously for these last few weeks, but I expect I can do something. I've a good line in moral blackmail. There aren't many advantages to being a widow, so I might as well make the most of the few that there are.'

'Bless you. I'll ring. 'Bye.'

Edward arrived home early, summoned by the network of messages Laura had left spread out between office and sites. Laura, putting away mountains of shopping, failed to hear his car and he walked into the kitchen to find his wife burrowing like a squirrel after nuts through a pile of bulging plastic carriers, while Mark stood watching her, balancing a pile of boxes of cereal that pushed his chin up in the air.

Awkwardly, they all stood looking at one another. Laura straightened up, dropping a box of eggs on to the table with an ominous crunching sound.

'Hello, darling!' Impossible, in that moment, not to sound artificial, acting a game of happy families as if they were the incarnation of some television commercial. 'You're home early! You got my message? Mark's arrived.'

'Yes, I see.' Mark, still clutching the cereals, neither moved nor spoke. 'Does his mother know?'

As soon as the words left his lips Edward knew they had been disastrously wrong. To speak of the boy in front of him, to ask Laura instead of Mark himself, it was the kind of thing he wouldn't dream of doing with Daisy or Ben.

'Sorry, Mark.' He tried to retrieve himself, smiled at the boy. 'That was crass.'

'I don't know what that means.' Mark's voice was muffled by the angle of his jaw. Laura reached out to take away the packets but he clung to them as a shield. 'I'll put them away.'

Between them they stacked the packets in the cupboard, while Edward stood watching them.

'There,' said Laura briskly. 'Well, there's no prescribed way of doing this, so Edward, this is Mark. Mark, this is Edward.'

They looked at one another. Mark's head was lowered again so that he looked up from beneath the straight dark brows, shoulders raised. Edward, realising from Laura's meaningful look that he must take the initiative, held out his hand. After a moment's hesitation, Mark put out his own without moving any closer. Solemnly, they shook hands.

'Very English,' said Laura, trying rather desperately to lighten the atmosphere. 'Now, how about some tea?'

Somehow the evening was passed. The television, as might have been predicted, was less than useless, showing nothing but game shows, reruns of old sitcoms, and earnest gardening programmes that Laura always found depressing because they made her feel inadequate. Questions from Edward, grudgingly answered, interspersed with chats and anecdotes from Laura, nibbled at the aching void of the unspoken. Acquainted with teenage habits, she was relieved when, at ten o'clock, Mark shuffled to his feet and announced that he would go to bed. Edward stood up.

'Shall I . . . ?'

Mark shied away to the door. 'No, it's all right. 'Night.'

'Goodnight, Mark. Give me a shout if there's anything you need.'

'Uh.' He was gone. Laura, feeling as though she had done ten rounds with Frank Bruno, leaned back in her chair.

'Do you think he'll be all right? I mean, he won't be homesick, will he?'

'At fourteen? I shouldn't think so.' Edward looked so calm that Laura was amazed. 'I'm tired, too. D'you want another drink, or shall we go up?'

'No, no more.' They went upstairs. Mark's door was closed, no sound came from beyond it.

They went to bed in silence. Later, when the light was out, Edward reached out to Laura with a tentative caress that was almost humble. When she responded he pulled her fiercely to him, and they made love for the first time in several days, Edward with a kind of desperate urgency that Laura found both touching and exciting. Their lovemaking had, during the years, become something familiar and comforting: a sharing of love rather than the passionate battles of the early years. It had never occurred to Laura to question or to regret this, but now she found herself responding with raw nerve-endings, as if a layer of skin had been sloughed away, leaving her vulnerable to sensations that seemed almost newly discovered.

Afterwards they lay whispering to one another, like teenagers lying together in secret in a parental home.

'Goodness,' said Laura. 'That was rather dramatic.'

'Too dramatic?' Edward's question was smug; he already knew the answer.

'No, just an Oscar-winning performance.'

'I would like,' intoned Edward nasally, 'to thank all the *wunnerful, doorling* people who made this possible: my director, my producer, my agent, my parents, and of course my *faaaabulous* wife . . .'

Laura giggled. 'I didn't say it was you getting the Oscar . . .'

'You can have the next one.'

'Now you're talking . . . Edward?'

'Hmmm?' He was half-way into sleep.

'It's all right, isn't it? Us, I mean?'

'I think it's me that should be asking that. I did wonder, for a while . . . I was afraid . . . You know.'

'I know. I wondered, too. But it's so long ago. If I'd known then – I don't know. I would have found it difficult to bear. But now . . . well, he's here, and . . . and he's got your eyes.'

'Has he? So you think he's definitely . . . ?'

Laura was shocked. 'Of course he is! And even if he hadn't been, we'd have had to pretend he was after all this time. But I'm positive. The eyes, and other things, little things – expressions, something in the shape of his face. There's no question of it. He's your son.'

'Yes.' It was impossible to tell from Edward's voice whether he was pleased or otherwise. 'How strange.'

'Strange or not, tomorrow you take him out and buy him something, or several somethings, to make up for all the Christmases and birthdays you've had to miss. And if his mother doesn't like it,' she added firmly, forestalling any possible objections, 'it's too bad. She shouldn't have sent him down here if she didn't want him to have anything from you.'

'Yes.' He sighed. 'We can't really afford it.'

'We have to. We can economise some more, do without Christmas and birthday presents for us, things like that. No take-aways.'

The bed shook as he clicked his bare heels and saluted. '*Ja, Obersturmbahnführer*!'

'Oh, go to sleep.'

'Don't you want your Oscar?'

'What, already?'

'Actually, no. Give me an hour or so? Feed me oysters?'

'Can't afford them. But I'll set the alarm if you like.'

'On second thoughts, two performances in one night is rather taxing for artistic types like me. I'll settle for an early matinée, tomorrow morning.'

'Don't call us, we'll call you. But I think I can say that's a firm booking, Mr Melville.'

The following day, claiming to be too busy to shop, Laura sent Edward and Mark off to town after a late and leisurely breakfast. They both, getting into the car, cast slightly desperate glances in her direction, but she waved them off cheerfully, calling after them to have lunch there if it got late. Then she set about telephoning Jane, who had already heard from Anna, and Cassandra.

'Lunch on Sunday? Oh, I don't know. Stephen said he'd probably be free this evening, and he might even be able to stay the night, so . . .'

'And if he doesn't? Come on, Caz, I was counting on you. We need a few more adults to counterbalance the young, and Edward always enjoys your company.'

'Well . . .' Cassandra was torn. Laura waited, and refrained from pointing out how often Stephen said he would be free and wasn't, and how, even when he did stay the night, he invariably disappeared first thing the following morning.

'Please, Caz. Now is the time for all good men . . .'

'If it's good men you're after, you'll need more than twenty-four hours to track any down,' said Cassandra sourly. 'Oh, all right. But if Stephen turns up . . .'

'. . . you'll abandon me to my fate, I know. Thanks, Caz.'

'Oh, Laura, I know I'm awful. I don't mean to be, it's just . . .'

'I know. It's all right.'

'Is it men that make life so hellishly difficult?'

'Well, I suppose they're often the cause. But most of the time I rather fear we do it for ourselves.'

Edward and Mark returned, in the middle of the afternoon, with the back of the hatchback loaded with cardboard boxes.

'A computer,' Edward puffed as he carried the largest one in, 'and a desk to stand it on, and do his homework on or whatever they call it now. Ongoing personal study development project, or something.' He rested the edge of the box on the kitchen table. Mark clattered past him, his face intent, carrying two bags and another large box. 'And some games. And one of those eardrum-busters, or whatever they're called.'

'Ghetto-blasters. Well done, and especially for thinking of the desk, I'd never thought about where we'd put it.'

'We aim to please,' said Edward modestly. 'It has bookshelves above it, too. And I bought a lamp.'

'Wonderful. Um, shall I have to offer my body for sale on the village green, or can the overdraft stand it?'

'We'll get by,' he said lightly. Laura felt the familiar sick twist in her stomach, and banished the thought by brute force, as if she were drowning a rat in a bucket. She glanced towards the doorway.

'How was he? Was it all right? Did he seem pleased?' She lowered her voice but tried not to sound too conspiratorial.

'I think so. A bit silent at first. A bit suspicious, too. His mother's taught him not to take gifts from strange men.'

His tone was ambiguous, but Mark's return prevented Laura from asking any more.

'You did have lunch, didn't you?'

'Yes.' Mark's gruff voice was equally difficult to interpret.

'Good. What did you have? Fish and chips? The Italian?'

'Indian.' Mark was hovering, waiting to fetch the rest of the things from the car. 'Shall I take that one?'

'No, it's all right.' Edward straightened up, careful to show no effort. 'Mark doesn't like fish,' he amplified to Laura, 'so we went to the Taj.'

He lumbered off, soon to be followed by Mark with more boxes. They spent the rest of the afternoon setting things up. Edward, producer of meticulous architectural drawings and plans, was in a frenzy of irritation trying to decipher the instructions for putting together the flat-pack desk and bookshelves. Laura, going upstairs with a tray of tea and a packet of chocolate biscuits, found the room covered with discarded packaging and liberally strewn with discs, instruction manuals, cassettes, and four empty crisp packets.

'Very homely,' she said, approvingly. 'Would it help if I cleared up the boxes and the polystyrene?'

'Don't throw any of it away,' mumbled Edward, on his knees with his head under the half-completed desk. 'If any of it's defective, it's got to go back in the same packaging. And judging by the state of this bloody thing, it's all sodding well defective. Ouch! Shit!' He emerged, sucking a thumb which, when he withdrew it from his mouth, had blood welling from beneath the nail. 'Can't see what I'm doing in there,' he complained in a muffled voice, round the reinserted thumb.

'For goodness sake stop and have a cup of tea. Mark, there's a torch in the lobby, where the wellingtons are.'

'You'd think,' said Edward bitterly when he had drunk a mug of tea, 'that someone like me, a practical man, ought to be able to put a thing like this together with his eyes closed. I don't know why they don't just print the instructions in Chinese, and have done. It wouldn't make any difference. And the drawings they give are even worse – they don't seem to bear any relationship to the real thing at all, even if you reverse them.'

'Then I should abandon them altogether, and just put the bits together as they seem to fit,' said Laura equably, holding out the packet of biscuits to Mark.

'That's what I usually do,' agreed Mark rather gruffly. 'Instructions are stupid.'

Laura smiled at him. 'Then I should do it your way.'

By suppertime the desk was set up, and the computer on it. After they had eaten they went back upstairs. Laura and Edward watched while Mark, without bothering to consult the manual at all, connected the keyboard, monitor and processor, fed in discs and, miraculously, summoned up on the screen a busy little figure that hopped, ran and flew through a brightly coloured landscape peopled with monsters, warriors and, obscurely, birds that behaved like bombers.

'That was quick! Have you got one of these at home?'

'No. But someone I know has one. And they're mostly the same, really. Do you want to have a go?' It was the longest sentence Laura had ever heard him speak, and she responded with suitable gratitude. The evening passed surprisingly quickly, and Laura felt quite optimistic about the lunch on Sunday.

She was even more hopeful when she woke to bright sunshine on Sunday morning. Even the weather, it seemed, was in her favour. They could almost eat outside, she thought as she lay in bed sipping her early-morning tea. If it was as warm as yesterday, it would be quite warm enough.

'Are you going to church this morning?' Edward, who went on sufferance even to weddings and funerals, was tolerant of what he regarded as Laura's superstitions.

'I'd have liked to, but I don't think I've got time. I did puddings yesterday, and there's plenty of ice cream, but I want to make garlic bread which is fiddly, and then there's the potatoes and the salads. And I must wash down the garden furniture – unless you'd do that for me?'

'Of course. The forecast's not very good, though.'

'Nonsense, look out of the window. It's a beautiful day.'

The beautiful day lasted until eleven, when heavy clouds rolled over the blue sky and the temperature dropped. By twelve o'clock there had already been two or three showers, and Laura had abandoned any hope of being outside. Fortunately she invariably pre-cooked chicken and sausages in the Aga, mistrusting Edward's ability to make sure it was cooked through to the middle. Ever optimistic, she had lit the charcoal, assisted by Mark.

'I'll do it for you, if you like.' He sounded quite enthusiastic, and she reflected in amusement on the age-old pleasure that men seemed to find in setting fire to things – Edward was never happier than when pottering around a bonfire.

'That would be lovely. Although I'm not sure we'll get a chance to use it.'

'Oh.' It was spoken on a long, rising inflection, indicative of disappointment.

'But Mark, it's raining!'

'Yeah.'

'You like barbecues, then?'

'Dunno.'

'You've never had one before? That's different, then. You must definitely have your chance to try Edward's incinerated sausages. You watch the fire, and I'll look out the big golfing umbrella.'

The guests, fortunately, brought umbrellas of their own. Edward, staunchly cooking in a heavy downpour, was sheltered by Mark who held the large umbrella over barbecue and cook and was getting more and more wet himself.

'Mark needs an umbrella too. I'll go and hold one for him,' volunteered Candida, who had a strongly developed instinct for mothering.

'Then you'll get wet,' Ben pointed out. Edward had offered him a lager which he had accepted without really thinking about it, still young enough to be flattered. 'I'd better hold one for you.'

'And I'll hold one for you,' broke in Toby happily. 'And when Daisy gets here . . .'

'We can all stand in a circle and pretend to be a fairy ring.'

'Ben!' Toby exploded into embarrassed giggles, casting his eyes towards the portly form of Tod, who had just arrived.

'Tod doesn't mind things like that, do you, Tod?'

'My shoulders are broad, dear boy. Like my mind,' said Tod suavely. Toby blushed scarlet, having hoped Tod hadn't heard. Ben grinned.

'Come on, then, Rosebud. Umbrellas on parade.'

Laura, pouring drinks in Edward's absence and reminding herself periodically to check the potatoes and the garlic bread in the oven, glanced out of the window from time to time. The little group of umbrellas, standing stiffly at first, seemed to coalesce after a little while, the older three shifting and moving slowly while Toby, bumping their heads when he forgot to lift his umbrella high enough, circled round them like a satellite, or like a sheepdog with some particularly somnolent sheep.

Daisy arrived, bubbling with pleasure and curiosity, and at once commandeered another umbrella, a bottle of wine and several cans of lager. The group opened to receive her, closing and regrouping so that she took her place, as of right, in the middle.

'So that's Edward's boy.' Tod's voice, urbane, puffed at her shoulder. He always sounded slightly breathless, and although everyone knew that this was caused by a combination of asthma and being overweight, the effect was always one of hurry and busyness.

'Yes,' said Laura. 'That's Mark.'

'Any trouble so far?'

'No, of course not.' Laura felt rather defensive.

'Good.' There was a suggestion in the breathy voice of something hanging unspoken. Laura turned to look him in the eye – they were the same height. He raised his eyebrows. 'Nothing sinister, my dear. But the situation has its – potential – does it not? For problems, I mean. Boys of that age can be difficult. I'm sure I was.'

'Oh, no,' said Laura brightly. 'It's been a bit tense, of course, but he's settling in all right, I think. Let me get you some more wine, your glass is nearly empty.'

When Edward returned among his throng of umbrella-wielding assistants, they squashed themselves round the table in the dining room: adults at one end, young at the other. Laura, who had made sure that she was sitting on the boundary, conversed absently with her ears tuned into conversation on the other side of her. Ben and Candida, aided by Toby when he could insert his high voice between theirs, were giving Mark an introductory run-through of the staff, teaching and otherwise, at the comprehensive. Daisy, who knew them by name if not by sight, sat at the end and adjudicated.

'. . . and there's Mr Atkinson, teaches maths, he's called Viper . . .'

'Because he's an adder . . .' put in Daisy.

'. . . and he's a real knob,' said Ben.

Laura, distracted for a moment, visualised a viper in a top hat, going to Ascot. But it was 'knob', not 'nob', she remembered, and was a term of derision.

'Yes, he's a turd,' said Toby with relish. 'He gave me a detention last week *just* because I was a few minutes late!'

'How few?' Candida reached out to tweak his hair. 'Ten few? Twenty few?'

'Well . . .' Toby was notoriously unreliable about time.

'And you need to watch out for Mrs Ponsonby. She's a right cow, and she has BO.'

'And she only likes girls.'

'She's not a lesbian or anything,' put in Candida fairly, 'she just doesn't like boys. At least, only the little ones. If they're not too noisy.'

'And don't forget Loopy Cooper . . .'

'Oh, yah! Loopy Cooper, how could I forget! Droopy Loopy! He teaches physics and he's just *so* sad! He's got this long bit of hair at the side of his head, and brushes it up over the top, and then he keeps his head really still so it doesn't come unstuck . . .'

'. . . so we all ask him questions, and call out to him, and try to get him to turn round quickly . . .' Toby's voice rose with excitement.

'. . . and open the windows when there's a good breeze.'

'. . . and it always comes down, and flops round his ear and on his collar . . .'

'. . . and he goes absolutely ape-shit . . .'

'Don't take any notice, Mark,' said Candida. 'He's a bit of a nerd, but he's quite a good teacher even if he does teach physics which is the dreariest thing . . . and he can't help being bald.'

'Oh Candy, don't be so *good*!'

'Not bald, angelic one,' said Ben acidly. 'That's a very unkind phrase. And not politically correct, surely?'

'Well, he isn't that bad. And what should I say, anyway?'

'Egghead? Coot-like? Follicly challenged?'

'What're follicles?' Toby's quest for new and rude phrases made him eager. It sounded promising, he thought; like a cross between bollocks and testicles.

'Follicles, dear little brother, are the balls of stupid men. Fools' testicles, you see? It's called elision, when you run two words together. It's rather interesting, really . . .' He was well launched, sounding like Robert Robinson on a bad day. Toby, leaning forward absorbed, was swallowing it whole, while Candy, who might have stopped him, was prevented by Daisy's hand gripping her arm. Mark, his eyes going from one to the other, looked mystified until his glance came round to Daisy's face, which was lit up with mischief and laughter. Then the little frown cleared from between his brows, and he leaned back in his chair and laughed.

The sound was so open and spontaneous that the others stopped their teasing. Toby, catching on at once, simply said, 'Ben, you pig' in resigned tones, being too used to such treatment to make much of it. The others, except Ben who merely looked sardonic, laughed with Mark. Satisfied, Laura brought her attention back to Cassandra, who was sitting next to her.

After lunch, when the young ones under Candida's capable management had washed up, Daisy suggested a swim in their pool.

'A swim!' Mark was appalled. 'But it's raining. And freezing cold!'

'No, it's all right, the pool's in a sort of greenhouse, and it's heated. At least, it's not very warm yet, but not bad. I went in last week. Come on, don't be wimps. After all, it is a barbecue.'

In the end, they all went except Tod, who was catlike in his dislike of water and preferred to stay and read the arts section of the paper. Edward, who was always complaining he didn't get enough exercise, swam, and so did Cassandra who thought she might as well show off her figure while she still had one. Laura, Jane and Anna went along to watch, picking up a couple of cakes from Jane's freezer on the way. The swimmers were playing a game of Edward's invention when they arrived – 'Silent Swimming', a kind of blind-man's buff in the water, where the seeker had to rely on the bubbles and splashes made by the others to be able to catch them.

The swimming-pool building was big enough to hold a table and chairs. Laura set down the tray of teacups she had brought from Anna's kitchen, and sat down to watch. The two girls were, she thought, equally beautiful in different ways. The softly rounded flesh that Candida thought of as fat was smooth and sweet, still honey-gold from last summer's holiday. Her dark hair sleek as a seal, she swam elegantly, relying on stillness rather than speed to keep her out of trouble.

Daisy, in contrast, was silver and ivory, her slim smallness cutting through the water like a minnow. Even when wet, her hair retained its pale fairness. Laura saw that Jane's eyes were following Ben, and noticed how Daisy's slenderness contrasted with his thinness. Where she was fine-drawn, he was bony. Her pale skin and slight body were still well muscled and full of wiry energy; he was wasted and lethargic.

It's worse than I realised, thought Laura and, passing over Toby, who frolicked with all the unselfconscious abandon of a puppy, her eyes found Mark and rested on him thankfully. He had the broad shoulders and strong legs of an athlete, the muscles even at his age quite clearly defined, his neck strong and adult-looking. Though less tall than Ben he looked older, and the tufts of dark hair revealed as he lifted his arms to dive, with scarcely any splash, over the head of Edward who was the blind man, were an unnecessary indication that physically, at least, he had reached manhood.

Watching him Laura felt a gentle glow of pride and pleasure. He had been caught, and with closed eyes was lunging across the pool after a splashing sound that Toby had initiated by throwing a handful of water. She saw the childishness of his hands, the softness of nose and chin and the skin of his cheeks that had yet to coarsen into their adult state, and felt a sudden fierce yearning to know how he had looked as a baby. Already, even at this age, the man he would become could be seen more clearly than the infant he had been, and she mourned for the knowledge she would never have.

The moment passed. Mark dived splashily and with a shout of triumph grabbed Toby, who had taken one risk too many and left his escape too late. Not so very grown up yet, after all, she told herself.

That evening, after everyone had gone and they were eating leftovers round the kitchen table, Laura finished her piece of chicken and pushed her plate away.

'Couldn't eat another mouthful,' she said, lifting her glass of wine.

'Can I have the last sausage?' Mark's fork was already reaching out.

'Of course.' Laura did not even look to see if Edward would have liked it, she was so pleased to see him enjoying his meal. Mark took the sausage and ate it. He had a glass of white wine from an unfinished bottle, which he was not much enjoying but was drinking anyway. Now, awkwardly, he lifted his glass to Laura.

'It was a great barbecue,' he said gruffly. Laura leaned forward to clink her glass against his.

'Thank you, Mark.'

For once his eyes met hers as he smiled. Laura felt her throat tighten. He looks happy, she thought. Relaxed and happy. It did not occur to her, as it did to Edward watching them, that the relaxation was due more to the wine than anything else. That's how he should look, Laura thought. That smile! He's happy. I made him happy.

Chapter 8

Later, looking back, it seemed to several people that the barbecue, innocuous and even dull as it might have been at the time, marked a kind of turning point; when at the throw of the dice they set their feet on the bottom of fortune's ladder, or the head of a snake.

Anna, driving a reluctant Daisy back to school, cursed the Sunday traffic – where had all these people *been*? – and her own lack of willpower that had given in to Daisy's pleading for 'just a bit longer, Mums, *please*'. It had been that 'Mums' that had softened her: the childhood name so rarely used in the last year. She was unable to resist it. Now, she thought, Daisy rarely called her anything. To outsiders she was 'my mother' in tones of resignation, despair or even loathing. To her face it was invariably 'you', or at best 'mum', which she disliked but dared not say so, any more than she dared to complain at the glottal stops, the slovenly vowels, and the general overlay of Estuary-speak that Daisy so often used. It was, she supposed, a kind of inverted snobbery on Daisy's part, and perhaps a protection against the derision that the idea of public school so often aroused among the idealistic young. Candy, Ben and Toby, at the comprehensive, seemed to feel no need to alter the way they spoke.

Daisy was slumped in the front passenger seat. In the flashes of light from the headlamps of passing cars her face appeared and vanished, a glitter of eyes and a gleam of smooth skin stretched over the fine bones of the face. For once she had forgotten to bring a tape – usually these journeys were rendered hideous, to Anna, by the mindless clamour of some heavy metal band. This time, with nothing on the radio and with only the swish of tyres on the wet road and the purr of the heater, it was possible to talk.

'What did you think of him?' Direct questions were usually rather risky, but Anna really wanted to know the answer.

'Of who?'

Daisy was being deliberately awkward, but Anna gritted her metaphorical teeth and answered mildly, 'Of the boy. Mark. Edward's son.'

91

Daisy shrugged. It was a swift hunching of the shoulders that had no gallic charm whatsoever about it. It was, she knew, a gesture that her mother found particularly grating. 'He's all right.'

Anna suppressed a sigh. She had a sudden, overwhelming memory of a little Daisy, at ten just promoted to the much-longed-for honour of sitting in the front of the car, chattering like a magpie about anything and everything. Then it had been, at times, distracting and even irritating, but looking back Anna thought she would give anything to have that voluble child back again. A gust of wind shook a spatter of heavy drops from a tree overhead, and they clattered on the windscreen like pebbles. Both of them flinched, then laughed at themselves. 'Actually,' Daisy continued in a more friendly voice, 'I thought he was rather sweet. I liked him.'

Anna remembered how Mark's eyes had followed Daisy, how he had manoeuvred to sit next to her at lunch. 'Cradle-snatcher,' she murmured.

'Mummy!' The old name slipped out into the dark interior of the car, warming it. 'I didn't mean that sort of like. Though he is going to be very attractive in a few years,' she added thoughtfully.

'In five years' time, the age difference won't seem so much,' Anna suggested.

'You naughty old matchmaker! I'm not Rachel!'

'?' Anna sought through Daisy's friends to find a Rachel, and failed. 'Rachel who?'

'Rachel in the Bible. Or do I mean Rebecca? The one that Jacob served seven years for, and then got palmed off with the wrong one. Anyway, it would be incest, practically.'

Daisy's conversation had always had this grasshopper quality, Anna thought happily, and quite failed to realise that her own was much the same.

'Incest for who? Whom?'

'Me and Mark. I worked it out. He's my step-god-brother.'

'I don't *think* you need a dispensation for that one. Not,' Anna added hastily, 'that I want you to fall for Mark. Or vice versa. I just thought it would be nice if you could be friendly. It would help Laura, for one thing. And Mark himself, of course. It can't be easy for any of them.'

'No.' Daisy wriggled in her seat. There was a silence, and Anna wondered if that was it. The first conversation for months that hadn't become a row. Yet. So . . .

'How did he get on with the others? With Ben?' Then she waited, not hoping for too much. So often a question like that provoked a furious tirade about privacy. There was another pause.

92

'Well . . .' Daisy, miraculously, seemed only to be pondering her reply. 'He was a bit quiet at first, which wasn't very surprising. And Ben can be rather intimidating, even when you've known him for years. You know.'

'I know,' said Anna with feeling. 'I adore Ben, but sometimes he makes me feel a complete idiot. Not that he means to, of course,' she amended quickly, 'but the words he uses! I don't understand half of them.'

'Nor does anyone. I think he must spend half an hour a day foraging through the dictionary. Unless he makes them up. But he didn't do that with Mark. I think he quite liked him. I don't know why, really, because Mark obviously never reads anything unless he has to, but they seemed to find something in common. And then Mark,' she turned sideways in her seat, hooking one leg up so that her knee was dangerously close to the gear lever, 'just upped and asked him if he was anorexic!'

'Good heavens!'

'I know! It was after we'd been for our swim – and I must say I was horrified when I saw Ben in his swimming things, he looks *awful* – and we were up in Mark's room trying out his new computer and playing music. Toby and Candy were playing a game, and Ben and Mark and I were sitting around, half watching and half chatting, and Mark asked him. Just like that, "Are you anorexic?" I mean, we've all noticed how thin he is, and how he hardly eats anything, but I wouldn't dare . . .'

'Or me. What did he say? Ben, I mean?'

'He just said, "No, of course not." And Mark gave a little shrug like – well, you know, like we do – and grunted. Uh. Like that. And then it was our turn with the computer, so nobody said anything else.'

I must tell Jane, thought Anna. In case the other two don't. She knew how protective the young were of each other, and also how careful Candy and Ben were not to worry their mother. She had been envious of that, sometimes.

'How extraordinary.' Anna thought of Mark, visualising the face that seemed, whenever she saw it, so carefully wiped free of all expression. 'So is he just incredibly tactless and thick-skinned, or is he clever?'

'I don't know,' said Daisy soberly. 'How do you tell?'

'By what happens next, I suppose.'

After the swim Cassandra had hesitated about going home, but everyone else was returning to Laura and Edward's so that the children could try out Mark's new computer, so she went along with them. She had been surprised to find how much she had enjoyed the lunch and the swim. The flow of chat, erupting now and then into a volcano of laughter; the teasing and the small in-jokes; the relaxation of being with people who liked her for herself, not because she was slim or elegant or well-off; all of these had been surprisingly pleasurable. She felt herself relaxing, in mind and body, from a tension and perhaps a kind of loneliness she had not been altogether aware of until now, when it eased.

At eight o'clock, Anna and Daisy left to drive back to school by nine, and this galvanised everyone else into going home.

'I didn't realise it was so late,' said Jane, kissing Laura. 'Come on, Toby. School tomorrow, and I've still got your games things to sort out, and you've got that project to finish, too.'

'Sod the project,' said Toby, flying high from new computer games and a can of lager he had managed to appropriate.

'Try saying that to Mr Duncan tomorrow. Come on, you two. Is Mark travelling in with you tomorrow?'

Laura had thought she should drive him in, and opened her mouth to say so, then caught Jane's eye and thought better of it.

'Yeah, it's all fixed. See you, Mark.'

They were gone in a flurry of wind and rain, leaving a memory of the warmth of Candida's kiss, a grin from Ben, a low mutter of 'Mr Duncan's an arsehole' from a rebellious Toby. Cassandra peered dubiously through the open front door at the driving rain. Her umbrella, while decorative, was neither robust nor large enough to provide much shelter from anything more than a light shower.

'I'll get the car out and run you back,' said Edward, correctly interpreting her body language.

'Oh no, of course not,' Cassandra protested feebly and insincerely. 'It's not worth it for so short a distance.'

'Of course it is . . .'

'Nonsense, dear boy.' Tod's voice came from the sitting room, each breath edged with a wheeze. 'I've got my car here, I'll take Cassandra on my way. Not,' he amended fussily, 'that it is on my way precisely, but what difference does it make? Once I am in the car and driving, a few extra minutes are nugatory. Come along, my dear.' He put his beautifully manicured hand through her arm. 'We shall shelter beneath my *huge* brolly, and take ourselves off. People like us, all alone in the world,' his voice oozed self-pity, 'must *cherish* one another.'

'Of course you must. Goodbye, you poor, lonely old creature,' said Laura warmly, kissing them both. She knew as they all did that Tod, once he had recovered from the shock of James's death, had re-established his place among the huge circle of friends the couple had always had. It was rare for him to spend more than one evening a week by himself, and what with the theatre, concerts, private views and the many village committees he sat on, his life was passed in a pleasurable bustle of activity.

At Cassandra's gate he gallantly came to the passenger door with his umbrella, squiring her solicitously down the brick path so that she wondered, for a suspicious moment, whether he had somehow heard a rumour about her condition. He was not called the 'Ashingly Gazette' for nothing, she thought wryly.

Still, he was never malicious, she thought, and he was being very kind to her now. For once her little house felt, if not cold (the heating was roaring), at least rather empty and dead.

'Come in and have a drink,' she offered suddenly. He looked surprised – they had never been more than acquaintances, friends of friends. His eyes peeped inquisitively into the hall, and she was fairly sure he would not be able to resist coming in to see what she had done with the rest of the house. She could sympathise with that – she always loved to see other people's homes.

'Well . . .' It was no more than a pretence of hesitation; already he was putting down the umbrella and shaking it. 'Just a quickie. Leave this here? My dear, what a *witty* hall! And this is the sitting room?' His eyes darted round, probing with such uninhibited pleasure that it could not be resented. '*What* a clever girl! I wouldn't have believed it could work, but it does. And how audacious! *Such* a refreshing change from dainty florals and pine and that *dreadful* pot-pourri with coloured wood shavings in that always, my dear, makes me think of lavatories in a second-rate restaurant where frankly, darling, I sometimes think I would prefer just to smell good, old-fashioned piss.'

As he spoke he sat down neatly in the corner of her white sofa, watching in approval while she set a match to the fire.

'Already laid,' he murmured. 'How *organised*.'

Cassandra, who lived in the constant hope and expectation of Stephen's arrival, and who knew that Tod was aware of it, did not respond but fetched a bowl of ice from the freezer, and asked what he would like to drink.

'I'll have a pink gin, my dear, if it's not *too* much trouble. Such a *naughty* drink, I always feel, unless one was in the Navy which, sadly, I never was.' He paused for a thoughtful moment to regret, presumably, a life on the ocean wave, then brightened. 'And the colour will go *perfectly* with my shirt!'

Cassandra laughed.

'That's better,' he said with satisfaction.

'Really, Tod, you are getting appallingly camp.' Cassandra poured gin over the ice in the glass, shook in angostura. 'One of these days you'll shock someone.'

'Oh, do you think so? What fun. I find everyone so very *un*shockable these days, don't you?'

Cassandra poured herself a plain tonic water, adding a shake of bitters as an afterthought.

'Not always,' she said, a shade grimly.

'That's because you're so young,' he said kindly. 'People make allowances for the old, I find. Especially old poofs, like me. They're all so tolerant, sometimes it makes me quite cross.'

Cassandra blinked at him, a bit shocked herself. 'Better than being beaten up by queer-bashers,' she offered. 'You aim to shock, then?'

'Well, it does make life more *stimulating*, if you know what I mean. Off with the humdrum and the workaday, you know.'

'And fiddle-de-dee to you, too.' They grinned at one another. 'Although I'm beginning to wonder whether humdrum and workaday don't have something to be said for them, after all.'

'Oh, my dear. A little hiccup in the romance department?' he suggested delicately.

'More like acute indigestion,' she answered gloomily.

'Ah. Heartburn,' he diagnosed smugly. 'And you, no doubt, have been trying metaphorical antacids and bicarb?' She nodded. 'And they're not working. Well, what I would recommend,' he put his fingertips together, judge-like, and looked at her over the top of non-existent bifocals, 'is a counter-irritant.'

'Pickled onions? Curry? A mustard footbath?'

'Precisely.'

Cassandra wondered whether to tell him that the prescribed counter-irritant, in the shape of an unplanned pregnancy, was already in place. She drew in breath to speak, but was interrupted by a thunderous knock at the door. Her heart gave a thud. She knew that knock.

'Stephen!' She opened the door wide. 'What a lovely surprise.' She could already see he was in a vile temper, and from the scotch on his breath and the waft of stale beer and cigarette smoke that affronted her nostrils as he leaned towards her, he had been fuelling his temper in the pub. 'Come in out of this horrible rain. I was just having a drink with . . .'

'Where the *hell* have you been?' he interrupted, stepping into the hall and dropping his keys, as of habit, on the table. 'I've been phoning you all bloody *day* to say I was free to come, and when there was *still* no answer I got worried and came over, and here you are all the time. Don't you answer your bloody phone any more?'

'Oh Stephen, I am sorry!' Cassandra remembered belatedly that she hadn't switched on the answerphone before leaving. 'If I'd known . . . but when you didn't ring last night, I thought . . . Anyway, you're here now. Come and have a drink,' she repeated soothingly. Stephen, still looking aggrieved, had marched to the sitting room and was halted in the doorway glaring at Tod, who smiled beatifically at him from the sofa.

'Well, *hello*!' he fluted, lifting his pink gin so that it glowed in the lamplight. 'I would get up, but this *beautiful* sofa is so *soft*, and rather *low* for my poor old joints!' He made it sound as if he had been luxuriating there, dubiously, for hours. 'I'm *Tod*,' he said cosily, holding out a limp-wristed hand.

'How do you do,' said Stephen frostily, ignoring the hand and crossing to the drinks tray where he poured himself half a glass of Famous Grouse and added, as an afterthought, two ice cubes.

'Nicely, thank you,' simpered Tod. 'And you must be *Stephen*. How *lovely*! I've heard *all* about you!'

'Have you, by God!' Stephen turned a threatening look on Cassandra, who hurried forward.

'Of course he hasn't. He's just teasing. Tod, you're a dreadful old man.'

'Oh, don't mind me, dear!' burbled Tod. 'I'm just going to finish my lovely drink and be off. I can see you two have got *so* much to talk about, you don't want me hanging around, do you?' Stephen watched him in disgust while Tod composedly sipped down the rest of his drink and stood up. His short, tubby figure looked dapper next to Stephen's weekend dishevelled appearance. He smiled guilelessly up into Stephen's face.

'My word, you *are* a big boy, aren't you?' he chirruped breathlessly.

Cassandra, appalled, gave a gasp of horrified laughter at the expression on Stephen's face. Tod bounced jauntily to the door. 'I'll see myself out, Cassandra dear. *Such* a lovely name, and so deliciously *ominous*! Now don't mind me, darlings. Just think of me as a mustard footbath.' He winked at Cassandra and was gone, the front door closing with a tactfully decisive snap behind him.

'Good God, Cassie! Who the hell was that appalling little queer?'

Cassandra, who was cross with Tod but still struggling with a mad inclination to giggle, found herself transferring her anger to Stephen.

'That appalling little queer,' she said coldly, 'was a good friend of mine. Do you have a problem with that?'

'Well you obviously don't!' They glared at one another, then Stephen sucked in a breath, pulled back his shoulders, and smiled thinly.

'Look, I'm sorry,' he said more moderately. 'I suppose I was just disappointed. Sarah had to go to her sister unexpectedly, some kind of crisis, and she took the kids to keep their cousins entertained, so I'd thought we could have the day together. Go out to lunch or something. Then I rang and rang, and when there was no answer all afternoon, I started to get worried about you.'

His voice became maudlin. He was, she realised, rather drunk, which was unusual. He liked to be in control of situations, and therefore of himself. Obviously he had spent longer in the pub than he had intended.

'I was here all yesterday evening,' Cassandra pointed out, not very warmly. 'You had said—'

'I know, I know.' He dismissed it with a gesture. 'It was all this business with her sister; they were on the phone half the evening. And this morning, too, until she decided to go. I couldn't ring you until she left. But where were you?'

He still sounded aggrieved. Does he think, wondered Cassandra, that I have no life at all, apart from the small bit of it I share with him? I suppose he does, and I've only myself to blame, because that's more or less how I felt, and how I made it seem to him.

'I went to lunch with friends,' she said calmly. 'Here in the village. Laura and Edward's house. We had a barbecue. Anna and Jane were there, with their kids. And Tod.'

'Oh dear, poor you.' His voice was warmly sympathetic, which annoyed her again.

'Why "poor me"?'

'Well, a load of kids, a bunch of middle-aged women, an old queer and one poor beleaguered man . . . it's not exactly the social Mecca, is it?'

'Perhaps not. But I enjoyed it. It was,' said Cassandra crisply, 'the best day I've had for ages. I wouldn't have missed it for the world.'

She still had not sat down, but remained stiffly by the door to the hall. Stephen, aware that he had overstepped the mark, held out his hand. He had always had tremendous charm, that elusive quality that seems to work almost independently of the owner's will. Why was it that now, for the first time, she saw it only as manipulation?

'Come on, darling, don't let's quarrel.' His voice coaxed her. 'I'm glad you had a happy day. I only wish I'd been able to share it with you.' He managed to sound both plaintive and whimsical.

'Not your sort of thing, though, is it? And you've never wanted to meet my friends.' Cassandra ignored his hand, and he let it drop to his side, looking rather foolish.

'It's not that I don't *want* to,' he said peevishly, 'it's just not sensible, is it? I mean, under the circumstances. I have to be discreet, for Sarah's sake. And the children's.'

'And mine?'

'And yours too, of course, darling. Don't want to upset all the old dears in the village, do we?' Stephen, who lived in Sheen, persisted in regarding himself as a London sophisticate, while considering that anyone who lived in the country must necessarily be a bumpkin. 'Now, it's not very late. Sarah's going to stay as late as she can at her sister's, so I told her I'd probably go out. How about we go and have dinner somewhere? That little restaurant in the pub, for instance? I thought that was remarkably good, for the sticks. And reasonable, too.'

Cassandra looked at him moodily. She had enjoyed her day. It seemed a pity, she found herself thinking, that Stephen had turned up like this and spoiled it.

'No, thank you,' she answered curtly. 'I'm not very hungry.'

'Well, I am,' he cajoled, smiling. 'Won't you come along anyway? You can toy with a starter or something while I eat. I know I let you down last night, and I was just as disappointed as you, but I'm here now, so can't we just make the most of it?'

His face was smoothly handsome above the expensive shirt, the silk cravat knotted with such careful carelessness in the open neck. I've always hated cravats, she thought. He ran his fingers boyishly through his hair, a gesture she had always found adorable, though this time she saw how careful he was not to disarrange it, artfully cut and styled as it was to conceal, as far as possible, the thinning patch on his scalp. Folicly challenged, she thought, echoes in her head of lunchtime conversation. Well, follicles to you, too.

'No, I don't think so. It is a bit late now, and that pub is a good ten miles away. I'll do you some sandwiches if you like, or you could go there on your way back.'

'Oh, for God's sake, Cassie. It's not like you to sulk.'

'I'm not sulking.' She was surprised. 'I'm just tired, that's all.'

He drained his glass, looking at her over the rim. She saw his eyes narrow in suspicion, and realised to her dismay that by some ageless instinct she had lifted her hand and laid it, protectively, over her abdomen. Slowly he lowered the empty glass.

'Tired? That's not like you. Come to think of it, you do look a bit pale. Under the weather, are you?'

'A bit.' Her voice shook. She saw the suspicion harden.

'For Christ's *sake*!' he exploded. 'You're not bloody well pregnant again, are you?'

Unable to lie she looked at him dumbly. He read the answer in her face.

'Oh *hell*,' he said viciously. 'Hell and bloody damnation. Not again. We're not going through all that rigmarole again, are we? What is it with you? Are you being deliberately bloody-minded, or are you just so thick that you can't get it into your head that I'm not going to mess up my kids' lives, and Sarah's, just because you've got yourself in the club?'

His deliberate coarseness grated on her nerves like sand between the teeth, but she held on to the shreds of her composure.

'It's not something I planned,' she said quietly. 'It's just bad luck. An accident.'

He poured himself another drink, sloshing the whisky into the glass. 'So you say.'

'It's true, though I suppose I can't prove it. These things happen, even when you're careful. And – ' she knew it was unwise, but she had to say it – 'it takes two, you know. To make a baby. And this wasn't precisely the immaculate conception.'

'Oh yes, I knew you'd get that one in soon. Of course, it's all my fault, isn't it?' He sat down, nursing his glass morosely. 'Well, I'll pay, of course. Though it's not cheap, you know. Not that I grudged it last time, but it did come to several thousand with the nursing home and anaesthetist and everything. Amanda's school fees have rocketed now she's at boarding school, and it isn't all that easy to lay my hands on that kind of money without Sarah noticing. We'll have to miss out on the nursing home, find somewhere cheaper, and you'll have to come home straight away. I'm sure one of your friends here will look after you.' The whisky was doing its work, and he now sounded more aggrieved than angry.

Cassandra, on the other hand, was icy with rage. Never, in all their time together, had she seen this side of him. Previous quarrels had been no more than lovers' tiffs, their bitterness sweetened by the certainty of a joyful making-up. Remembering how charming he had been, how amusing, how full of ideas for small surprises and romantic gestures, she found it hard to believe that this was the same man. Only his firmness, when he had made her choose between ending her previous pregnancy and ending their relationship, might have given her warning; but she had given in almost at once, and he had been quick to wrap his own wishes up in a tinsel of concern for her. Never before, she realised, had she held out against his wishes. At every turn they had taken the path he chose, and it was a revelation to her now to see how he reacted when crossed. I never knew him, she thought.

'Aren't you taking rather a lot for granted?'

'What do you mean, for granted? I'd have said it was you taking things for granted, expecting me to pay out for you again.'

'I haven't asked you to pay out.'

He frowned. 'You're surely not going to do it on the National Health?' He made it sound as though she were proposing to call in the village witch. 'No, come on now, Cassie, I wouldn't want you to do that. Nothing but the best for my girl, eh?' He smiled at her blearily.

'I don't mind using the National Health, if it comes to it. But what I'm saying is, I'm not sure I want to have an abortion. Another abortion.'

He took a mouthful of whisky and choked. 'You what? But then . . . but then you'd have the baby!'

'Exactly. Other women have babies, why shouldn't I? I'm not getting any younger.'

'Oh God.' He groaned the words, dragging them out. 'Don't tell me you've gone broody. Not the bloody biological clock. For Christ's sake, Cassie, it's just your hormones. Go to the doctor, get some pills or something. What would you do with a baby?'

'Love it? I believe that's the accepted practice. Look after it. Play with it. Bring it up. The usual sort of thing.'

'Here?' He looked round the small, immaculate room.

'Yes, why not? I can change the house. Or I could move if it doesn't work. None of that matters.'

'It does when you have to pay for it. And I tell you now, I can't afford it. Not another one to feed and clothe and educate.'

'I have not,' she said distinctly and loudly, 'asked you for money. I have not asked you for anything at all. Or at least, nothing that you would know how to give.'

He slammed his empty glass down on a small table beside him. Being made of metal, it emitted a loud clang and the glass broke.

'Oh *shit*!' He looked at his hand. A small cut oozed sluggishly; he put it in his mouth. 'If you think you can blackmail me,' he said indistinctly, sucking, 'then you can think again. You won't use that kind of pressure on me. And if you think you can go running to Sarah with your great revelation, then don't bother. She already knows about you, and it doesn't bother her one bit.'

'What a wonderful, warm marriage yours must be.' Her voice was steady, and she made no move to clear up the broken glass or find him a plaster. He wound his handkerchief round his finger, and looked at her resentfully.

'She knows she doesn't need to worry about *you*,' he said spitefully. 'She doesn't see *you* as a threat.'

Cassandra looked at him as if she had never seen him before. Where were the good looks she had once loved so much? The grey eyes that had once been able to make her melt inside with a look now were sharp and hard. And had he always had that small, mean little mouth with its pouting lower lip, like a spoiled baby? Was this really the man for whom she had given up so much, and so willingly?

'I must have been mad.' She spoke her thought aloud, wonderingly. 'I think you'd better go.' She felt quite calm.

'Don't worry, I'm going. And don't think I'm going to come crawling back, either.'

'I wouldn't want you back,' she said judiciously, 'even if you came wriggling on your belly, in sackcloth. I don't need you. *We* don't need you. Not you, or your money. Particularly not your money.'

'That's what you say now.' He was on his feet, edging past her to the door. 'But how do I know you won't be suing me later for maintenance? You don't know what an expensive business it is, bringing up a child.'

'We'll manage,' she said shortly. She found herself thinking of Edward, who had unquestioningly paid for a child he thought might be his, and had done his best to be as much of a father as he had been allowed to be. But I am not a nineteen-year-old, she thought. I am a woman of thirty-seven, with a house and a shop. And, she thought with elation, a child.

'Shut the door as you go,' she said. The last thing he heard before he slammed the door was the sound of her laughter, clear and ringing and joyous.

Chapter 9

'I must have been mad! I don't want to finish it like this! I don't want to finish it at all! What am I going to do without him? He was drunk, that's all, and I gave him such a shock that it made him behave like that! That's not really how he is. It can't be. It was just some kind of nightmare. Oh, Laura, I want things to be the way they were!' Cassandra wept.

After a sleepless night, during which she had gone over and over her quarrel with Stephen in her mind, she was unable to contemplate a future without him – without, that is, the kind of man she had thought he was. The baby seemed no more than an unreal imagining. Stephen, and the relationship they had shared, was familiar, even safe, part of a well-known pattern of living. She had almost succeeded in persuading herself that last night had been all her own fault, and she was trying hard to suppress the little voice of common sense that told her otherwise.

Cassandra was sitting at her kitchen table. Laura, opposite her, thought that it was just as well she had inveigled her out of the sitting room, where she had been reclining on the sofa in floods of tears. It might be easier, in the more bracing atmosphere of the kitchen, if not to damp down entirely, at least to steer this outburst of drama into more practical channels. Laura, whose feelings about illegitimate children had undergone a drastic sea-change, was hoping to encourage and support this new turn in her friend's life.

She had always felt that Cassandra's affair with Stephen was potentially a disaster. Fond though she was of the younger woman, it was difficult for someone in her position to sympathise with any great warmth with a relationship with a married man. Nor, though she had never met him, could she think of Stephen as anything but selfish, dishonest, and self-centred. While she would never have dreamed of pushing Cassandra into finishing with him, now that the breach had come she would do her best to see that it was not healed. Now, she thought, Cassandra could have the best of all worlds: an ending of a self-destructive love affair, and a new beginning with someone worth loving – a child of her own.

Physically tired from the effects of the last few days, Laura felt full of mental energy this morning. She had drifted off to sleep the night before in a warm cloud of happiness which had still been there, insulating and uplifting, this morning. Neither Edward's uncustomary Monday-morning gloom – he enjoyed his work and was seldom reluctant to go to the office – nor Mark's silent exit to meet Ben on the corner where the school bus would pick them up, had been enough to dim her pleasure in life. Business would pick up; Edward would soon get a new commission; it was unthinkable that his small practice which had been so successful for so much of her married life should suddenly fail.

As for Mark, she had already learned that he was not at his best in the morning. This, she knew, was normal for his age when, with a strictly enforced bedtime a thing of the past, the young tended to stay up later than was sensible to listen to music or watch videos. Then, too, he had to face a new school, which even with Ben and Candida around was enough to make anyone a bit silent.

Not more than ten minutes after the school bus left the green – watched by Laura from her bedroom window where she had, by carefully timing the bed-making, happened to be – the telephone rang. Laura, on her way downstairs and guessing it would be one of yesterday's guests, ran the rest of the way so that she could settle in comfort in the kitchen for a gossip. She was longing to talk of Mark, and to hear what her friends would say about him.

'Laura! Thanks so much for yesterday. It went really well, they all came home raving about it.'

Jane's voice sounded more cheerful than it had done for a long time.

'Well, I'm glad you all had a good time. I think they got on all right, don't you? Your lot were great with Mark. And Daisy too, of course. Will you thank them from me?'

'No need. They liked him. Ben in particular, for a wonder. You know how choosy he is over his friends. And of course one's parents' friends' children are usually a disaster, socially speaking. Remember Anthea?' Anthea, the daughter of one of Jane's mother's friends, had bullied Jane unmercifully in her childhood. When she had appeared, years later, at a wedding in the village, Jane had at first been thrown straight back into her childish awe of her, but surrounded by her friends had suddenly seen how ridiculous it was to be afraid of this elderly, badly dressed woman who was trying so hard to patronise her. She had snubbed her without compunction, to everyone's amazement.

'Anthea!' said Laura now. 'As if I could ever forget her. The Hamdens

104

always say that it was her interfering that broke up their son's marriage, and it wouldn't surprise me in the least. You didn't hear from her again, did you?'

'No, never. Though I must admit I was a bit wary of picking up the phone for a few days after that wedding. But I think she got the message.'

'I should think she might. You know, at the time I was amazed by you standing up to her like that. Now, of course, I wouldn't be. I know how strong you are. But then, I always thought you were so gentle – too gentle, really. A bit of a doormat, in the nicest possible way.'

'I know. With "Welcome" printed on it. I was, wasn't I? It's funny, I was always so anxious about hurting anyone's feelings that I would put up with almost anything rather than speak out. Pathetic, really.'

'You know,' said Laura slowly, 'if it weren't for the children, you might almost be grateful to Bill. You've changed so much – at least, not changed, but developed new sides to yourself. New horizons, new boundaries, all that. I really think you could do anything, achieve anything, now.'

'I don't know about anything, but in a funny sort of way I know what you mean. I was always living in his shadow. It was where I wanted to be. But now he's taken that shelter away, I've learned that there's something to be said for braving the elements. But you know that, don't you? You've always been strong, always coped with things.'

'I suppose I have,' said Laura. 'But maybe I've not had all that much to cope with. In everything except having children, I've always been lucky. Things have always gone well for me.' She knew it was true, but at the same time she also felt that yes, she had coped with the bad things life had sent her. It was, secretly, something she prided herself on and, believing it was a gift, had always tried to use it to make her own strength available to help her friends in their own troubles. She spoke modestly of luck, but did not believe it, not knowing how much of her life had been passed in the sunshine of fortune's smiles.

'Anyway, I really rang to tell you how grateful I am to Mark,' said Jane, who was overflowing with her news.

'To Mark? Why?'

'He had a go at Ben about being anorexic!'

'Good grief! And you're grateful? What happened?'

'Well, the first I heard of it was a call from Anna last evening, when she got home from taking Daisy back to school. She was over the moon, because Daisy had talked to her in the car. Not about anything personal, but just about the lunch and everything. And she told Anna, who told me, that Mark had asked Ben if he was anorexic. Anna was a bit worried about it, thought she'd better let me know, though she said Daisy didn't think Ben had been particularly worried about it.

'Well, I thought about it, and then I went upstairs, and Ben's door wasn't closed – it was only about ten, and you know he has trouble getting to sleep, he's usually reading until at least midnight. So I went and sat on his bed, and asked him about it.'

'Oh, Jane. I'm so glad. And it was all right?'

Jane gave a sniff, and her voice was husky. 'I think so. He said he hadn't really thought about anorexia – they all tend to think it only happens to girls, you know – but that he never seemed to be hungry at the moment. He said he had been pleased when he got thinner, lost his pot-belly and his bottom, and that he didn't want to have them back. So I told him that he wasn't eating enough to maintain even the weight he is now. Thank goodness I lost all that weight myself, and I've read up quite well on nutrition and calories and things, so I was able to explain to him roughly how much he needed as a maintenance diet, and that he was now too thin to be healthy. He admitted, then, that he felt tired most of the time, and fed up, and I hope I persuaded him that this was all, or mostly, a side-effect from not eating enough. Anyway, he says he'll take the vitamins I got for him, and cod-liver-oil capsules, and that he'll try to eat more.'

Jane sniffed again, her voice wobbling upwards. 'And I made him some hot chocolate with milk, and he drank it!' she concluded, tearfully triumphant. 'If you only knew how hard I'd tried to get him to eat something that wasn't low-fat, or low-calorie, or just a lettuce leaf! Not that I want him to live on junk food and chocolate, of course, but I don't want to see him denying himself the occasional sweet treat just because he thinks it's fattening. And I want him to see that, at his age, things like potatoes and pasta, and even chips, are what his body needs.'

'That's wonderful, Jane! I'm so happy for you. I must say, when I saw him in the pool yesterday . . .'

Jane gave a shaky laugh. 'I know, awful, wasn't it! I suppose that's why Mark spoke up, bless him. I'm so grateful, I can't tell you. Anna said she and Daisy couldn't decide whether he was actually being rather clever, or just not very sensitive, but I don't care. As far as I'm concerned, he's a genius and probably a saint.'

'Well, I shan't tell him that!' said Laura, smiling nonetheless with pleasure at praise of Mark. 'He probably didn't have any idea what he was doing, but I'm so glad it's turned out well. Ben's so very bright, once's he's accepted that there's a problem I'm sure you can trust him to work it out.'

'I hope so. And I can well believe Ben didn't really know what he was doing to himself. I mean, bright is one thing, but he's hopelessly impractical in every other respect. He sometimes behaves like a sort of youthful mad professor, living in an ivory-tower world of his own.'

'Well, there're worse things than that. Oh, Jane, I do hope you're over the worst now. It sounds very hopeful. But did he say anything about his father?'

'No, nothing, and I didn't ask. I didn't really want the two things to be connected in his mind, though I suppose they must be. Anyway, if I can get the eating thing sorted out I shall be thankful, and we'll tackle the business with Bill when we have to.'

Laura had scarcely finished clearing up the breakfast things when she had Cassandra's tearful phone call. She was thankful that Jane had rung first; the warm feeling of pleasure from Jane's praise of Mark still wrapped her round as she promised, soothingly, to go to Cassandra's cottage as soon as she had finished sorting out the house.

It was an exhausting morning. Cassandra's mood swung wildly between abject misery and self-blame – which Laura discouraged – and fury at Stephen's behaviour – which seemed a healthier feeling. Laura encouraged her to recount, several times, exactly what had been said and done between them the previous evening. It seemed to her that nothing she could say would be more telling than Stephen's own words and attitude, which she considered disgusting. By lunchtime Cassandra was calmer, and had recovered to the extent that she was thinking of going back to the shop where the faithful Jenny was, as ever, holding the fort.

'After all, it's our livelihood,' she said gloomily. 'I can't afford to let it go wrong now, can I?'

'One morning in Jenny's hands is scarcely going to drive you into bankruptcy,' Laura said bracingly. 'And it's not as if Stephen's ever contributed anything to your expenses anyway, has he?'

'Certainly not! I'm not someone's kept woman!'

'Of course you aren't. We've all admired what a success you've made of that little shop. You don't need him, Caz.'

Cassandra, agreeing, carefully repaired her make-up (a good sign, Laura thought), and went to the shop. Laura went home, meaning to catch up on some letters and perhaps do some gardening, but ended up fiddling with supper and making a cake and some home-made biscuits for tea.

By the time Mark came home from school, Laura was in a fever of anticipation. Her eager, 'How was it?' was met, dauntingly, by a curt, 'All right.' Laura blinked and readjusted her perceptions. She had spent so much time during the day thinking about Mark, about what he had said to Ben and about his apparent pleasure in yesterday, that she had begun to feel closer to him, more in touch with him than she actually was.

'Good. Cup of tea? And there's some cake if you're hungry,' she offered casually.

'Uh.'

'Dump your things upstairs, then. I'll put the kettle on.'

By the time he came down again, changed out of uniform, the cake and the biscuits were on the table and the television was on. Laura poured two mugs of tea and handed him one, but did not sit down with him, not wanting him to feel too threatened. Instead she said, 'Help yourself', indicating the cake and the biscuit tin, and from her place by the Aga pressed the button on the remote control of the pre-set video. A familiar jingle rang round the room, and he looked up frowning from cutting himself a slice of cake.

'*Neighbours*? It's not half past five already, is it?'

'No, I recorded it for you. I thought you might like to watch it now, with your tea. Then,' she added with a mock sternness, 'you can get on with your homework without interruptions.'

'Uh.' The opening credits rolled by; laughing faces, tanned and healthy, exuding strong family values and the generally optimistic feeling that Friday's crisis would, inevitably, be happily resolved by Monday or, at the latest, Tuesday. 'A cunning plan?' His eyes met hers fleetingly.

She smiled. 'A cunning plan,' she agreed. 'Have some more cake.'

'Thanks.' He cut a large slice and leaned back, his legs stretching out beneath the table, relaxed. Laura happily sipped her tea, and set herself to learn, without asking questions that would disrupt his viewing, who was who in Ramsay Street. If you can't beat 'em, she told herself again. At least it's a point of contact, something we can talk about.

The days slipped into weeks, and a routine was established. Mark's life, and Laura's also, revolved around school, homework, television and, increasingly, friends. Laura was pleased when, a few weeks after his arrival, the telephone rang with an invitation to go to someone's house on Saturday evening.

'Can I go? Ben's going.' Laura was quite surprised to hear that, for she knew that Ben tended to be solitary, though Candida, Toby and Daisy were for ever going to friends' houses, or having friends over for the night.

'Of course. So long as I know where you are, and when you're coming and going. Doesn't your . . . don't you do this sort of thing in London?'

'Not much.' His head was down again. They were in the car, Laura having collected him from school after a late-afternoon swimming session. Laura flicked a glance at him and said nothing. After a moment he said, with difficulty, 'She doesn't like my friends. She says they're a bad influence.'

'And are they?' Laura's voice expressed no more than mild interest.

'Not really. The other way round, probably.'

'Oh.' Laura digested this. '"A" for honesty, anyway. Do you really behave that badly?'

'Sometimes. Not always. But they expect me to. The teachers. They all hate me.' He spoke with a gloomy acceptance that bordered on pride.

'Got yourself a bad reputation, have you?' He nodded. 'Then why not try to prove them wrong?'

He grinned. 'Mustn't disappoint my public, must I?'

'Oh, Mark.' She could not help warming to the honesty, the rueful humour. 'And what about here? Are you a bad influence? Should I be warning Jane to protect Ben from your evil ways?'

'Ben's OK. He's clever. He does what he wants.'

'So you couldn't influence him? But I think you already did. Jane says it's thanks to you that he's eating more. She's very grateful to you.'

He grunted, but she thought he was pleased.

'Would your mother mind you going to visit Simon this weekend?'

'Dunno.' His chin was up, his nose looking beakier than usual, and he was looking down it like a recalcitrant camel. 'It's nothing to do with her.'

'We are responsible to her, Mark. We can't go against the way she chooses to bring you up.'

'It's not her,' he burst out, 'she's all right. It's Fran. She's always on at her about me; that I need discipline, that I must be kept in, not allowed to mix with unsuitable people, all that shit.' His shoulders hunched. 'She's a pain.'

'Who,' asked Laura with foreboding, 'is Fran? I thought . . . I thought your mother lived on her own. With you, that is.'

'She does. Fran's her mother. My gran, really, but she won't let me call her that. Says she's too young to be a grandmother. She doesn't live with us, but she comes to stay a lot. Weekends, holiday times. On and on, smoking, drugs, bad language, staying out late – as if it was anything to do with her!'

'Where does she live?'

'In Hertfordshire. She's a civil servant.' Mark spoke the words as another might have said: she's pimp, she's a drug-dealer. Laura, who had formed an image in her mind of Mark's mother with which a civil-service mother did not at all fit in, was stunned.

'Oh. How very . . . very respectable. And are they very close? Oh dear, I suppose I shouldn't ask you that.'

'Why not? Yes, I suppose they are. At least, they fight quite a lot, but she still keeps hanging around, laying down the law. She's an arsehole.'

Laura thought, secretly, that she agreed with him, but: 'Well, that's nothing to do with me. Anyway, I can hardly ring your mother in California to clear it with her every time you get invited somewhere, so I'll work on the premise that if it's OK for Ben, it's all right for you too. And that's only because I don't know any of the kids or their parents yet, so I have to follow Jane's judgement. Once I've met them myself, I'll make up my own mind. Is that fair?'

'Yeah.'

'Good. Chilli for supper, and jacket potatoes. All right?'

'Great.' He was quiet for a moment, staring apparently out of the windscreen, although Laura had learned from previous journeys that he was taking in nothing of what he saw, merely allowing the world to pass in front of him, as irrelevant as a moving image on a screen.

'Laura?' It was the first time he had used her name.

'Yes?'

'Thanks.'

Oh, my dear, she thought.

'You're welcome,' she said lightly, slowing as they came to the village. 'All part of the service.'

After that, Laura made a point of driving Mark as often as possible. Used to village life, she was accustomed to hearing her friends complain, semi-seriously, that they were no more than a glorified taxi service. To her, however, it was something new, and she was always happy to take or collect him from school or friends. For Mark, too, it was unaccustomed, but if he felt the loss of freedom, and having to arrange meeting times instead of just turning up when it suited him, he showed no resentment. And it was, Laura discovered, the ideal place to talk.

The weather for much of May was cold and wet, so that the little taste of spring they had had in late April seemed like no more than a mirage.

110

Isolated in the warmth of the car, the heater purring and the windscreen wipers performing their hypnotic hiss-click-hiss-click, Laura soon found that Mark was far more forthcoming than he ever seemed at home. It was, perhaps, the privacy, the sense of being in a little universe of their own bounded by the clammily misted windows. Or possibly it was merely the boredom engendered by car journeys in a child accustomed to almost constant on-screen entertainment. The fact that she was driving, with her eyes and at least some of her attention directed at the road ahead, probably helped as well. Whatever the reason, she found that as well as responding to the openings that she carefully thought out and initiated, he would even at times raise some topic of his own.

She learned, gradually and always trying not to ask questions, more about his home life. Of his mother, whom he invariably referred to as 'George', he spoke with guarded affection. She was, it appeared, deeply involved in the women's movement, was often at meetings and, although she had a teaching job at a nearby school (not his own), she appeared to regard that as of secondary importance. The meetings, Laura gathered, were generally in the evening, but from Mark's garbled accounts it was clear that she always made meticulous arrangements for his care. Now, having left him for the first time for longer than a few days, she did not telephone him (to Laura's secret relief), but sent letters and particularly postcards, which seemed to please him more for the pictures than for the messages on the back, two or three times a week.

Of her work and her interests, so far as they impinged on his own life, Mark was relatively well informed. But her character, her personality, her hates and loves and feelings, seemed to be something he had never noticed or thought to speculate on. It seemed that it had never occurred to him that she might be of interest as a human being in her own right. Was it, Laura wondered, simply because he was still in many ways a child, and thought of adults as a race apart who had nothing to do with him except as providers of basic necessities and, sometimes, aggravation? That his mother might have hopes and fears and wishes, that she might feel happiness or misery as he did, was something that seemed never to have crossed his mind. The impression she gained was of a person so controlled, so repressed even, that none of the normal human emotions were allowed to appear.

'Happy? I don't know. I suppose she is,' he answered vaguely when Laura asked him. 'She gets cross sometimes,' he added, making it clear that he thought this most unreasonable.

'Well, so do all parents. So do you, surely?'

'Yes, but . . . only because things happen . . . other people . . .' He struggled to find the words. Laura had noticed that his vocabulary was narrow, that he frequently found it difficult to express what he thought, even though he was, she was convinced, quite bright.

'Do you think your mother is wrong to get cross with you?'

'No. I make her cross.' He was, she had also noticed, scrupulously honest to the point of presenting his faults and misdemeanours laid out, like smorgasbord on a tray, for inspection. Laura suspected that this was one reason he was so often in trouble at school – if there was anything going on, it was always Mark who was caught. Then, too, he kept rigidly to the code of loyalty that protected his fellow transgressors, even at his own expense. Like a latter-day martyr, he would burn at the stake rather than name even his worst enemy to authority.

His world was, Laura perceived, run by laws and customs as powerful as that of any primitive tribe, which in some ways it resembled. Narrow, it excluded anyone older than about nineteen or younger than twelve. Above or below that boundary, other people were not so much a sub-culture as actually non-human: at worst dangerous aliens, at best approached as warily as a trained tiger, which might appear friendly but was not to be trusted.

With no one was this more apparent than with Edward. That, of course, was a far more difficult relationship – if such a word could even be used to describe their behaviour with one another. Mark, of course, was accustomed to live with women. To be in a house where there was a man was different enough, and when that man was the father he knew only from letters it must have been even stranger. The written word was not, in any case, a medium in which he was at home, and Laura wondered how much good those carefully penned messages had done. Edward, she thought, had certainly done his best then, but, knowing him as she did, she could see that he was finding the actuality of Mark's presence very hard to come to terms with.

At ease as he was with her friends' children, it had never occurred to Laura – or perhaps to Edward himself – that he would be uncomfortable with his own son; but so it was. Conversation between them was so strained that it seemed, sometimes, as though each were wilfully misunderstanding the other's words. The harder Edward tried to communicate with Mark, the more a barrier seemed to come down between them.

Laura could not tell how much Edward minded about this. Mark seemed to feel no need to make friends with his father. It seemed as though he neither liked nor disliked him, but regarded him as an irrelevance. If Edward felt the rejection he did not show it. Was he, perhaps, relieved, Laura wondered? She tried to make opportunities for them to do things together, even going so far as to feign a headache on two occasions when they had planned to go somewhere together, so that the two of them would be forced into each other's company. They would return as they went out, in a silence that was not resentful or antagonistic, but arose merely because they did not have anything much to say to one another.

'You do *like* Mark, don't you?' she asked Edward in some exasperation after the second such expedition had taken place. They had been to Brighton, to see a film and have supper on the pier, an outing that Laura had given up reluctantly and with a strong sense of self-immolation.

'Of course I do!' Edward had sounded surprised. 'He's a nice enough kid. I think he enjoyed himself today. He certainly ate enough candyfloss to make most people sick as a dog, and as for those rides – just watching them makes me feel quite peculiar. Still, that's what they seem to like.'

'But did you enjoy yourself?'

He hesitated. 'Well, you know . . . it wasn't really my kind of film, and nothing in the world will get me on one of those infernal Whiplash rides, or whatever they're called. It was good to get some sea air, though. I just wish—'

'What?' asked Laura, hardly knowing what she hoped to hear.

'That you'd been there too. It would have been much more fun.'

So much for martyrdom, thought Laura, sighing. She saw, unwillingly, that Edward, who would have responded wholeheartedly to any attempt by Mark to make a father of him, was finding it hard to feel anything but a sense of duty and responsibility towards the boy. If only, she thought sadly, Mark were more outgoing. If only he could trust Edward, as Daisy did, or ask his advice, as even Ben had sometimes been known to do. But to Mark, Edward was one of Them, and Edward was unable to get beyond this divide.

With the zeal of a nineteenth-century missionary, Laura set herself to change this world view. Mark would be tamed, by love and kindness, by food and treats and attention, like an animal captured in the wild. And she would teach him that adults were not the enemy, but were human beings like himself.

Protected and cherished by her parents, by Edward, by her childlessness and by her own inclinations towards optimism and happy endings, Laura had no doubt that if you loved enough all things were possible, and that by giving love you would gain it. It never occurred to her that it might not be wanted.

Chapter 10

Everyone agreed how fortunate it was that Daisy's half-term coincided exactly with that of the Comprehensive.

'I really don't know what I'd do,' said Anna to Laura over coffee. 'That's the trouble with boarding schools: all their friends seem to live miles away, and then in holiday time they want to go blinding off round the country to parties, and you never know if they're really staying with the people they say they are, or whether they've pulled a fast one.'

'Surely Guy didn't . . .'

'Oh no, not Guy. I never had to worry about him,' said Guy's mother dubiously. 'That was what I worried about.'

Laura laughed. 'Never satisfied, are you? But I know what you mean. One expects boys to be, well, naughty at times. Mark was in trouble again yesterday.' She could not keep an edge of pride out of her voice.

'What for? Smoking again?'

'No, going out of school during the lunch-break.'

'Surely they're allowed to do that, aren't they? It's not like Abbotsford, where they can't go into town on their own in case they get beaten up.'

'They are allowed. Only not if they've been gated.'

'Ah. Oh well, boys will be boys.'

'Yes. Oh, it's all harmless enough, he went out to get a birthday card. Only he did it for someone else, who was also gated. I ask you! Mark seems to think he's invisible or something. At least, he never seems to think he'll get caught, and when he does he behaves as though he's being persecuted.'

'He'll grow out of it. At least it's open mischief. It's the ones that don't get caught that you really need to worry about.'

'What, like it's only the nice girls who get themselves pregnant, because the clever ones know how not to?'

'Don't! If you only knew how much I worry about it! I even wondered whether to suggest she went to the doctor to be put on the pill, but I didn't dare. She'd only say I was interfering, and besides, I don't want to encourage her to go to bed with someone, do I?'

'Is there anyone around, do you know?'

'No idea. Well, hundreds of them, of course, at school. All bursting with hormones. No one in particular that she's "going out with", at least not that I know of. Do you? Oh dear, I shouldn't ask.'

Laura, who took her duties as a godmother seriously, wrote to Daisy from time to time, and had an occasional telephone call (reversed charges) in return. She understood, therefore, that in Abbotsford parlance 'going out' implied a formal relationship requiring a degree of fidelity, everyone else being 'just a friend'.

'I don't see why not. Daisy knows we talk to one another. She probably wouldn't tell me anything she didn't want me to tell you, or at least she'd ask me not to. And then I suppose I wouldn't, though it might be difficult if it were something I really felt you ought to know about. Thank goodness that hasn't happened yet, anyway.'

Anna fished in the biscuit tin, noting vaguely that there was more choice than usual, and far more chocolate ones. 'Let's hope it never does. I have the same problem with things Daisy tells me about school, or I used to have in the days when she told me things. Sometimes there were things I really thought the housemistress ought to know about, but then it might get the girl into trouble and that, in turn, would come back on Daisy's head, and they'd all give her hell. You know how they protect one another.'

'I'm learning. Did you ever do it?'

'Only once, because I thought the girl was doing something rather dangerous – she was planning an exeat to go to an all-night party with some boys she'd met only once in the town. Even Daisy said she thought she was potty.'

'Insane, more like. I thought they had to have parents' permission for an exeat?'

'They do, but apparently her parents' marriage had split up and her mother had just acquired a boyfriend ten years younger than herself and wasn't taking much interest in anything else.'

'What happened?'

'I had a quiet word with the housemistress. I must say she handled it very well. She had a long talk with the girl, told her she'd heard about the party and that under no circumstances was she to go. There were floods of tears, and all the usual sulks and scenes, but a few days later they heard the party had been raided and several of the kids found with drugs – not just pot, either – and one of the boys was later charged with dealing.

It gave all the girls a fright, and the girl involved even admitted she was relieved she hadn't been there.'

'And they didn't know it was you?'

'No, thank goodness. For heaven's sake take these biscuits away from me. This skirt's too tight at the waist already. I've only had it a few months, and it's got an elasticated waist.'

Laura looked at her friend. Even now she got a shock, sometimes, when she looked at Anna properly. In her mind's eye, when they spoke on the telephone, she still saw her as the slightly plump size fourteen she had been until three years ago. Now she was – what? Size eighteen, at least. Laura still saw, within the blurred planes of the plump face, the attractive girl and woman she had once been. If Anna didn't do something about it soon, she thought, it would be too late. Not only would the fat have settled in for good, but if she did succeed in losing it, her skin, without the elasticity of youth, would be left deflated and wrinkled. As so often before, Laura wished she could say something, but what?

'Is it . . . do you still miss Michael very badly?'

'Yes,' said Anna immediately and, 'No,' she denied at once. She looked down into the dregs of her coffee, swirling them round the mug, and thought about what she had just said. 'I suppose that about sums it up, doesn't it? I do, a lot of the time. I still find myself thinking, I must remember to tell Michael that, I must ask him about the other. Or I wake up in the night and reach out for him . . . you know. And the rest of the time I just get on with things. I've got used, mostly, to being on my own. No rushing around in the morning, getting him off to the office. No worrying about a proper supper when I'm tired and all I want is a boiled egg. It's not agony, like it was. There are times when it comes back and I could curl up and howl, but they're not so frequent and quite often, now, I can distract myself and fend them off.' She pushed the biscuit tin away decisively. 'The eating is just a habit. I know I should stop, and I do mean to, but it's always next week, isn't it?'

'Food is very comforting,' agreed Laura.

'Yes, but look at Jane – when she was miserable she lost two stone. I was miserable and put on four.'

'Not that much!' Laura protested.

'Well, three then. More than two, anyway. Daisy's always nagging me about it. Tells me I should go on a diet, join Weight Watchers, go to aerobics classes. I ask you! Can you see me, in lycra, lumbering around a gym? I'd be a laughing stock. Sumo wrestling, now—'

'You could swim. Now it's summer – well, sort of summer – you could swim in your pool, nice and private, wonderful exercise.'

'You healthy types are all the same. It's enough to drive a person to, well, if not drink, at least to chocolate bars. Do I look dreadful? Is Daisy ashamed of me?'

'No, of course not, to both,' said Laura warmly and in distress. 'It's just that it's such a shame. You were so pretty.'

'And I'll never get another husband looking like this? But I'm not very sure I want one.'

'I don't suppose you do. Michael was special.'

'He was, wasn't he?' Anna smiled mistily. 'I can't imagine finding anyone else like him.'

'It's nothing to do with that. But for your own sake. Wouldn't you feel better?'

'Perhaps. Eventually. But think how many months of feeling awful I'd have to go through first!' She drained her mug. 'I'll do it one day. But not yet. Now, tell me, how's Edward? I haven't seen him for ages, but the last time I did I thought he looked a bit worried. I expect he was tired.'

Laura, who had been afraid she had already overstepped the limit, accepted the change of subject.

'Oh, he's fine,' she said automatically, then stopped. How was Edward? She thought back over the last week, the last two weeks. He had been quiet. Too quiet. Not that he was ever precisely noisy, but it occurred to her that they had scarcely had a conversation about anything less trivial than the meal they were eating, or what was on the news. She had talked to him, told him about her day and, what was now more important, Mark's day. She would relay, almost verbatim, conversations they had had in the car, analysing them for evidence of his thoughts and feelings. And Edward had listened with apparent interest, but contributed almost nothing.

Business, she knew, was still bad. Edward never spoke of it, and she seldom asked. Partly out of cowardice, and partly because when she did he gave her no more than the quiet smile that failed, now, to reach his eyes, and a gentle assurance that everything was all right. Knowing him as she did, she knew very well that it was far from all right. She also knew that he wanted, even needed, to protect and reassure her, and that she was glad to let him do so. In the moments when she did think about what they would do and how they would manage if the business failed, she felt her insides twist themselves into knots, her heart pound, and her breath become rapid and shallow with fear. Then, because it could do no possible good for her to panic, she would push the thought away from her, bury it in the trivia of day-to-day living and hide, ostrich-like, in the sand of more cheerful preoccupations. Like, for instance, Mark.

She did what she could, in small ways. Her own income, from the share of her parents' capital, went towards paying for their food and some of the household bills. She shopped as economically as possible, hunting for bargains, never buying convenience foods, and making things like soup and sauces. When her cleaning lady had moved house and left her six months earlier, she had not replaced her.

Now, guiltily, she wondered whether she had been unfair to Edward. A good wife, surely, should be supporting and encouraging her husband, not wilfully shutting her eyes to his problems? For better, for worse, and all that. For richer, and for definitely poorer. She was ashamed that Anna, who seldom saw him, had noticed that Edward was worried, while she who shared his bed and his breakfast and dinner table continued blithely to collude in the fiction that everything was as it had always been.

Should she, perhaps, look for a job? She realised ruefully that it wouldn't be easy. The secretarial course she had done on leaving school was half forgotten, the skills superseded by modern technology. For the first few years of their marriage she had worked, happily, for an elderly author, to whom she had been a combination of secretary and nanny. When he had died she had not bothered to seek another job, so sure was she that she would soon be involved in pregnancy and motherhood. Now, she thought, the most she could hope for would be shop work, or perhaps work in the home where she already helped on a voluntary basis.

'He's fine,' Laura repeated slowly, 'but you're right, he's not sleeping very well. I'm afraid business isn't exactly booming at the moment.'

Anna, who, having been married to an architect for so many years, still kept an interest in that world, nodded sympathetically.

'I know, the recession and all that. It's always hard on people like Edward, running their own show. But he's hanging on in there?'

'Oh yes, of course,' said Laura loyally, hoping it was true. 'You know Edward.'

Tonight, she thought. I'll talk to him tonight. While Mark's doing his homework.

'I'm glad Daisy's going to be home at half-term,' Laura went on brightly. 'Mark's mentioned her several times. I think he rather fancies her.' Her tone of voice was congratulatory. If Anna was aware of this, or of the sudden change of subject, she gave no sign of it. She was not, herself, altogether sure about Mark, though Jane was very much in his favour since he had helped Ben (inadvertently?) to confront his eating problem. Laura, of course, was as besotted as a hen with one chick, but that too was probably a good thing now that Cassandra . . . A perfunctory knock at the door interrupted her musings, and she gave a startled blink to see Cassandra walk in.

'Caz!' Laura was already reaching for the kettle. 'Coffee – no, of course not – tea? You all right?'

'Radiant,' said Cassandra dismally as she dropped into a chair. 'Hi, Anna. Did you feel like death when you were pregnant? Jane says she did, but I think she only said it to humour me.'

'Yes, awful,' said Anna cheerfully. It was, fortunately, true, though she knew Jane had in general never felt better than when she was pregnant, and had scarcely known the meaning of the word nausea until her pregnancy with Toby. 'I know it's hard to believe, but it does pass, and it shouldn't be much longer. How far are you now?'

'Eleven weeks,' said Cassandra. 'Are *all* your biscuits chocolate ones or ginger nuts, Laura?'

'Mark's favourites,' explained Laura. 'If you dig down I think there are a few Rich Teas at the bottom. But you're all right really?'

'Yes,' said Cassandra, sounding rather surprised. 'Yes, I am.'

'Have you heard from Stephen again?' After a silence of two weeks, Stephen had telephoned, full of bluster and making it clear that he was ready to accept the climb-down which he clearly felt was his due. Cassandra, in spite of the discomfort of morning sickness, was becoming daily more excited by the prospect of motherhood, and dismissed him with a brisk, unsentimental kindness that was more convincing than anger or tears.

'No,' said Cassandra, with a giggle. 'He really couldn't believe that I meant it, you know. So bloody arrogant! And to think after all these years I've only just noticed it. It's extraordinary. I feel quite liberated.'

'That's wonderful. I always thought he wasn't good enough for you.' Laura put a mug of weak tea down in front of Cassandra.

'God, you sound just like my mother.' For once, mentioning her parents, Cassandra sounded wryly amused rather than resentful.

'Mother knows best.'

'That's almost the worst thing about all this, having to admit that the old bat was right.'

'Not that you have . . .'

'No, of course not. Well, not in so many words, but, you know. I told you so, and all that. Only,' said Cassandra, with the air of one making a discovery, 'she hasn't actually said that. In fact, she's been rather sweet, really.'

Laura and Anna gazed at her. Accustomed as they were to sympathising with Cassandra after her parents' frequent telephone calls (Cassandra had forbidden them to visit without an invitation, which she rarely gave), this change of heart was startling.

'They'd be pleased about Stephen, of course.' Laura had met them once, and though she felt they were far too possessive of their only child, she had sympathised with their feelings about the married man who was keeping Cassandra at his beck and call with little hope of any future. 'But . . . ?'

'The baby?' Cassandra wrinkled her brow. 'As a matter of fact, they're delighted. Thrilled to bits. At least my mother is, and even Pa didn't say anything dreadful. He just patted my hand and humphed, and said I wasn't to worry and they'd stand by me.' She gave a slightly watery sniff. 'It was all a bit Victorian. I felt a bit like a maidservant who might have been turned out in the snow without a reference, but actually he meant it nicely, I think. And as for Ma, she's over the moon!'

'That's lovely. Let's face it, Caz, you're going to need all the help you can get. I mean, I know you've got us and the others, but, well, family is family, isn't it? And it's nice for babies to have doting grandparents, too.'

'And even nicer for their mothers. I wonder,' said Anna pensively, 'whether that was why your mother was so against Stephen? Not just the fact that he was married, I mean, but because, since he was, you wouldn't be likely to settle down with him and have a family. Doing her out of her grandchildren, if you like.'

'I wonder. She never said anything, but . . . yes, it could be. I know she was disappointed that I was the only one: she always wanted to have a large family. I suppose that's why she always made such a fuss over me.' Cassandra spoke with the casual acceptance of an indulged only child. 'Anyway, she's wildly excited now. She was all for rushing out to buy baby things straight away. Not just your basic Mothercare, either. She wanted us to go to London, Harrods, The White House, all the works. It's mad, of course, because with the shop I have contacts with all the suppliers, I can get everything at cost. But that wouldn't do for her. She wants the name on the label, the right sort of wrapping paper, all that stuff.'

She was beginning to sound irritated.

'She wants the best for you,' said Laura gently.

'Yes, I know, I know. But she went on and on about it, and in the end the only way I could get out of it was by saying I wasn't well enough to go up to London.'

'Well, you're not really, are you? You need to be feeling fit for London, it's no good feeling queasy in the middle of Harrods. And it is a bit soon, too. I don't want to sound like the village witch, but I always felt a bit superstitious about that sort of thing.'

Laura and Cassandra gazed at Anna in amazement. She coloured, the pink flowing up beneath the fine, fair skin of her plump face.

'Don't look at me like that! Do you walk under ladders?'

'Yes, of course!' said Cassandra firmly. 'But I cross my fingers first,' she added seriously, so that they were all laughing when the telephone rang.

Anna was the first to hear it.

'Phone,' she said, waving her hand to attract Laura's attention. Laura listened, then stood up quickly to go and answer. As she did so she sagged, her knees giving way and her face suddenly paling to the colour of lard. She reached blindly for the chair back. Anna and Cassandra were beside her in a moment. Anna, large and capable, slipped an arm round Laura's waist to support her.

'I've got her. You answer the phone, will you? Just in case.' In case of what she was not sure, but it was another of her unacknowledged superstitions that any call should, if humanly possible, be answered. Laura's head lolled on to her shoulder, and she felt the drag of her weight increase on her arm. Carefully Anna lowered her back into the chair, keeping her arm round her, and with her other hand pushing Laura's head down towards her knees. Dimly, behind her, she heard Cassandra's voice.

'Edward! Yes, it's Caz, I was here having coffee with Laura and Anna. No, she just stepped out for a moment, she wanted something from the shop, so I thought I'd better answer it . . . yes, fine. Well, a bit sick, really, but they keep telling me it's normal. Oh, thank you, yes, I'd love to. Yes, I'll tell her when she comes back . . . not until eight. Right. Poor you, but I suppose it's all business, isn't it? OK. Bye!'

She hung up, then rushed back.

'Is she all right? I didn't want to worry Edward, he sounded a bit stressed out, and it was only to say he'd be late back this evening.'

Laura stirred, mumbled a muffled protest and tried to sit up.

Anna kept her hand firmly at the back of her neck. 'It's all right,' she said calmly. 'Keep your head down a moment.' After Michael, she had no difficulty in keeping her feelings hidden, putting on a reassuring front. Inside she was filled with irrational alarm, as she always was when illness, however trivial, threatened anyone she was fond of. And Laura of all people. Laura, who all through her adolescence, when girls at school fainted readily – in chapel, in class, at games – had never so much as felt giddy. Laura, who so seldom had a cold, even, that when she did she regarded it as a personal affront. Aware that she over-reacted, Anna banked the emotion down.

Laura heard her, but it was as though her ears and even her whole head had been stuffed with damp wool. When she tried to sit up she felt her head begin to whirl again. She knew it was again, although she could not concentrate well enough to remember when it had done it before.

'Anna?' Her tongue felt huge and numb, as if she had just had an injection at the dentist, and her lips stuck gummily together.

'Yes, I'm here. You've had a bit of a dizzy turn, that's all. Take some deep breaths if you can.'

'Feel sick.'

'Don't worry. It doesn't matter.' Anna looked up at Cassandra, who went to the sink and fetched the empty washing-up bowl. Then, with memories of her own spells of nausea, she fetched a glass of cold water, and damped a clean tea-towel under the tap at the same time.

Laura breathed in, concentrating on filling her lungs, which was surprisingly difficult in that position; concentrating also on not swallowing, in case the movement of the throat muscles should make her vomit. Her head was clearing, thank God. The grey buzzing, shot with nasty little flashes of light, was receding. She sat up slowly, and this time Anna did not stop her. Once she was leaning back in the chair, she pulled in a long breath.

'Better,' she said, and opened her eyes. She ran her tongue stickily over her lips, and Cassandra offered her the glass of water. She drank, enjoying the cool feel of the water over tongue and gums, slipping down her throat. 'Lovely. Thank you.' Her hands felt icy. She lifted them to her face and, finding it hot and clammy, took the cloth from Cassandra and wiped it, slowly. The cool dampness felt wonderful, clearing away the fluffy remains of the damp wool that had invaded her thought-processes.

'Goodness, I'm sorry,' she said, her voice much firmer. 'What a ridiculously dramatic thing to do. I'm fine now.'

'You don't look it.' Cassandra, typically, said what Anna was only thinking.

'Well, I am. Or, if I'm not, I will be in a moment. Honestly. It's like Anna said, it's only a dizzy spell.'

'But you never have dizzy spells.' For once Anna was glad of Cassandra's tenacity. 'You know you don't.'

'Has this happened before?' Against her will Anna was joining the interrogation. Laura's face gave her the answer. 'It has, hasn't it? How many times?'

'Only once or twice. Well, perhaps three times. But not as bad as that usually. It's nothing, really.'

'Not as bad as that means that it's getting worse. You're not dieting or anything?'

'No, of course not. Wouldn't you know if I were? Everyone gets dizzy spells at times.'

'Not you. At least, you never have in all the years I've known you.'

'Time of the month?' Cassandra, frequently coarse in her general speech, was invariably delicate when speaking of what Laura and Anna would always refer to as 'The Curse'.

'No, but . . . it might be something to do with that. I've been a bit irregular recently. Perhaps I'm getting to a Certain Age. Perhaps that was a kind of hot flush.'

'That wasn't a hot flush,' said Anna firmly. 'Not anything like one. And you're too young for that, anyway.'

'You're only saying that because we're the same age,' said Laura, sounding more like herself with every word. 'It's not all that unusual for women my age. Just because you're not—'

'Don't drivel. Have you seen the doctor?'

'No, ma'am.'

'Then you're going to.'

Laura protested, but Anna stood over her until she had telephoned the surgery and made an appointment for late that afternoon.

'I've a good mind to come with you,' she said, eyeing Laura dubiously. 'You will go, won't you?'

'Of course I will. It's a lot of fuss about nothing, but now I've made the appointment, I'll go. All right?'

'And I shall want to know what he says,' said Anna grimly.

'Bossyboots,' retorted Laura childishly. She was secretly rather relieved. These dizzy spells seemed to be getting worse, and on top of that she seemed to feel more tired than usual, too. Don't let it be anything bad, please, she said, a silent order inside her head.

The doctor, not her own but a locum filling in while he was away, asked brisk, impersonal questions, took samples of blood and urine, told her not to worry and to come back in a week. Laura found this rather daunting, and was glad when the following week her own doctor was back. They knew one another well; she had registered with him on first moving to the village. He had seen her through all the anguish of those earlier years, comforted her and encouraged her as the tests for which she went became more uncomfortable, more undignified. Now he leaned back in his chair, his hands loosely on his knees but his eyes intelligent and sharp as he looked at her.

'I'm wasting your time coming back here again,' said Laura easily. 'It was only a few dizzy spells, and I haven't had one since just before I came last week. It was probably just a virus or something. Or is it My Age?'

'Is that what you thought?' He consulted the notes the locum had taken, though Laura had never known him not to have all the facts ready in his head before.

'Well, I wondered. I don't take much notice of my periods, really, and I have been rather busy – did you know Edward's son is staying with us? Mark?'

'Of course I knew. We may only have a surgery here in the village twice a week, but we get all the gossip.'

'So, you see, it's nothing, is it? Surely the tests didn't show anything up, did they?'

He looked at her and smiled. 'As a matter of fact, they did. The chap last week had his suspicions, but he didn't want to say anything until the results of all the tests were through.'

'Suspicions? What have I got? Not . . . not anything dreadful?'

'Depends how you look at it. No, my dear Laura. It is neither a virus, nor are you menopausal. In fact, very much the reverse.' His face blazed with delight. 'I'm happy to inform you, Mrs Melville, that you're pregnant.'

Chapter 11

It was not until many years later that Laura was able to acknowledge even to herself that her first instinctive feeling on hearing the doctor's words was of dismay, even horror. She suppressed it at once, so quickly that she was almost certain she had not given herself time to notice it, and transformed it into the kind of astonished disbelief that makes one query something that seems to be too good to be true, like winning the Pools or finding buried treasure in the garden.

'But . . . but I can't be! At my age, after all those years . . . surely I couldn't . . . Are you quite certain it's not a mistake?'

'Absolutely certain.' The doctor leaned back in his chair, enjoying what he knew would be the high point of his week, if not the month. 'My locum last week was fairly sure, in fact, and did a quick urine test there and then, but he had the sense to check your notes, and thought he'd better get a lab. test done and let me handle it on my return. And I must say, I'm grateful to him! My dear, it makes me very happy to be the first to congratulate you. Of course,' the wary manner of the professional returned for a moment, 'there are risks, as you know. It's too early at this stage for any tests, but you're going to have to take great care of yourself and, of course, be prepared for all the tests we'll want to do.'

'Down's Syndrome. I know.' Laura felt numb. She had rejected the idea of adopting such a child, but one she had carried and borne . . .

'That, of course, and other congenital problems . . . It would be wrong to deny the risks, but it would be even more wrong not to hope and believe that the baby will be normal and healthy. Forty-two is nothing, nowadays, even for a first baby. And who knows, now you've done it once, it might even happen again! It's by no means unheard of. Now, we'll just check your blood pressure, shall we? No need for anything else today, though I shall want to see you regularly, and you'll be getting an appointment at the hospital shortly. Shall you be thinking of going privately, like you did for the other tests? There would be no medical advantages,' he added quickly, aware that many of his better-off patients were feeling the pinch at the moment. 'I'm afraid the insurance doesn't cover childbirth, unless there is some problem.'

Laura, still reeling, tried to pull her mind back into the practical. 'No, I know . . . I don't really mind. At least, I've never had much experience of hospitals, I've always been so healthy . . .' Until now, her mind added. 'It's the treatment that matters, after all, isn't it? And you don't stay in the hospital long, I believe, so it's hardly worth worrying about being in a ward. It might be rather fun – like being back at school.'

'There's a lot of hanging around,' he warned her. 'Sitting about on clinic days waiting to be seen. That's one of the big advantages of private treatment.'

'Oh, I shouldn't mind that. I can always read a book, or knit. That would be appropriate, wouldn't it, knitting? Bootees, or something. Not,' she pulled herself up, 'that they wear bootees these days, but still . . . No, a new baby will be expensive enough already for poor Edward, I don't want him to have all that extra expense. He'll want to insist, of course. I shall rely on you,' she said firmly, sounding more like herself, 'to persuade him that I – we – will do just as well with the National Health.'

'If that's what you want. Now, is there anything you want to ask about? Any worries? I should try to lead a normal life, don't cosset yourself too much. Nothing risky, of course – no horse riding or mountaineering, and keep the alcohol intake to a minimum. Just common sense, really. And you can ring me any time, day or night, if you have any worries. All right?'

Laura knew that there ought to be hundreds of things she should ask about, but as usual on such occasions her mind was blank. All she could think was that she didn't want to leave this room. The Health Centre was a new building, purpose-built and as impersonal as only fresh paintwork, new furniture and bright posters can be. In spite of an overlay of homely clutter – photographs of the doctor's family, drawings of box-like houses and stick-men presented by young patients, a collection of toys to distract the recalcitrant toddlers – there was a clinical lack of personality that was very institutional and, to Laura at this moment, profoundly reassuring.

'I don't think I shall tell anyone yet,' she said, rather shyly. 'Edward, of course, but . . . it's not as if I have close family, my mother, say, who'd be hurt if I didn't tell them.'

He nodded. 'Not a bad idea. You know, of course, that the first twelve weeks carry the highest risk of miscarriage. I often recommend that the news shouldn't be too widely broadcast until at least the end of that time. It can be easier in the long run.'

Laura drove home slowly and carefully. She thought that she hardly knew how she felt, yet. Amazed, of course. Delighted. So many times, in the past, she had imagined this moment, had felt the pale shadows of the emotions – joy, exultation, triumph – that should now be filling and surrounding her with glory. They would come, of course. It was the shock, the unexpectedness. If only, she thought, it could have been *then*. Was it not, perhaps, too late? Was she too set in her way of life to adapt to the demands of a baby, a toddler, a growing child?

Edward would be pleased, surely, but it would be a worry, too. Another financial burden, another hostage to fortune. And Mark: how could she tell him? Already he had made himself a place in her world. For the first time she was experiencing the subtle pleasures of motherhood: must she give up all that; would it be taken from her? He would be embarrassed, she thought. Disgusted, probably. Not jealous, of course, but resentful perhaps of the time and attention transferred to the baby.

She let herself into the house. Its daytime emptiness, which she had always taken for granted in the past, was suddenly overwhelming. Even the cats had disappeared, curled up no doubt in their favourite corners of the garden. In the kitchen the warmth of the Aga seemed sterile and impersonal, the gleaming clean worktops and sink looked cold and unfriendly. It's too tidy, she thought. Too clean.

Unable to settle, she wandered from room to room, feeling like an intruder. Upstairs, Mark's room was as always littered with discarded clothes, tapes without boxes and boxes without tapes, magazines, a few books from school. Automatically she gathered up clothes for the wash, straightened the pillow and duvet, picked up a damp towel and put it on the bathroom rail, then stood in the middle of the floor transfixed by a sudden thought. Which room would be given over to the baby? The spare bedroom was somehow so very definitely a guest room that she couldn't imagine losing that, but Edward's work room . . . if things went wrong and he had to give up the office building in the town he would need his space here all the more. This one, before, would have been the obvious, the only choice, but now? Now it was Mark's room. She felt a spasm of possessive anger on his behalf.

'Mark's room,' she said aloud, staring defiantly at the blue and yellow curtains that she had chosen long before Mark himself had come into her life. But Mark will go back, she told herself. Back to London, to Primrose Hill. Back . . . home. There, she had said it. Mark would go home. This, to him, was no more than an interlude. It might be pleasant, even enjoyable now that he had settled in, but it was not his home. Still clutching the bundle of washing, she sat on the side of the bed and put out one hand to smooth the pillow case.

'He might be happier here.' The words, spoken only in her head, were insidious. Laura felt like a character in a cartoon film. If I turn my head, she thought, I'll see a little devil-me, with horns and a tail and a pitchfork, all red and black. And on the other side an angel-me, in a white nightie, with wings and a halo. Get thee behind me, and all that.

Laura shook her head, sat up straighter, banished the cartoons. Mark may well be happy here, and of course I hope he is, she told herself. And maybe, if he is, it will help him to be happier at home, too. And then, of course, he will come back and see us. For weekends, holidays, things like that. We are, after all, family. And, with any luck, friends? And instead of sitting here maundering, you'd be far better employed in the kitchen, making something really nice for supper which is, though they won't know it, a kind of celebration, after all. Her spirits suddenly rocketed and she went to drop the clothes in the laundry basket before heading purposefully for the freezer where there were some pork ribs she had been saving. Mark was extremely fond of her Chinese-style spare ribs.

The meal was a great success. There were some chicken breasts in the freezer, too, that Laura had forgotten about, so she made chicken with almonds as well. They all got rather hilarious trying to eat the spare ribs with chopsticks, and pick up the almonds that had a tendency to shoot like missiles across the room. Laura produced a bottle of white wine, even though it wasn't strictly a weekend. and Edward raised his eyebrows a little at the extravagance. She suddenly remembered she shouldn't be drinking, but with Mark's enthusiastic assistance the bottle was soon empty anyway.

Edward leaned back in his chair, the last glass of wine tilting gently in his hand, and watched his wife and his son. Mark was finishing the last of the ribs, holding the bones in his fingers. He and Laura were bickering amicably about *Neighbours*, to Edward's secret amusement. Laura had always, in the past, been scathing about Australian soap operas.

'Well, I think Brad might be better off with Lauren,' she said earnestly. 'She's more lively, more of an outdoor type. I mean, Beth never wants to go surfing with him or anything.'

'But Lauren's rude . . . she's got a fat face. And Beth's really horny.'

'She's certainly very pretty, but horny? I thought she was supposed to

130

have hang-ups about sex? All that business with her mother's boyfriend and things?'

Mark picked up the final rib. 'That's different. Horny means sexy.'

'Oh.' Laura, and Edward too, stored away this fragment of adolescent vocabulary, their eyes meeting in a shared moment of amusement.

'Anyway, I'm not sure she's right for Brad,' pursued Laura. 'I like Brad, he's so sweet.'

'Brad's not *sweet*!' Mark was disgusted. 'Brad's wicked. He's a Boy.'

'Translation, please,' murmured Edward. 'And who's Brad?'

'Brad's Doug and Pam's son,' said Laura, as if that explained everything, as it probably did. 'He's, um, let's see, he's wicked, that means he's great, and a Boy . . . well, the same thing, really.'

'You spicka da lingo?'

Laura grinned at him. 'I'm learning. Have you finished, Mark?'

'Yeah. I'm stuffed.' The corners of his mouth were sticky and brown from the spare-rib sauce. Laura leaned over, put one hand on his head to hold him still, and wiped his mouth with the other, a process to which he submitted with surprising docility. Mark, Laura had noticed, disliked being touched. 'What's for pudding?' he asked as soon as he could. Laura tapped him gently on the cheek.

'Banana ice cream. And I made some more butterscotch sauce.'

'Cool.'

'Wicked,' amended Edward.

At the end of the meal, Mark went reluctantly upstairs to finish off some homework to get it out of the way before the weekend. Anything written, Laura had noticed, seemed to take him a long time and involve a great deal of scribbling out.

'Shouldn't he be helping with the washing up?' Edward asked mildly as he helped clear the table.

'Yes, but during term-time I don't mind letting him off. I think he's struggling a bit with the work.'

'Yes.' Edward scraped the chewed bones into the bin. 'His mother did say he's a bit dyslexic.'

'Dyslexic? Poor Mark, does the school know? Should he have any special lessons? Why didn't you tell me?'

'To start with, because I thought it was difficult enough having an unknown child wished on you, let alone one with educational problems. And later . . . well, I didn't want you to fuss, I suppose. The school know, they're coping with it. At least, I assume they are. I thought I might go and see his form master, or whatever they have, some time next week.

He'll have been there just about half a term by then.'

'Tutor,' corrected Laura absently. 'Yes, I think you should. Should I . . . ? No, you're right. I mustn't fuss. Only we must make sure everything's all right.'

'What does he say?'

'Nothing much,' Laura admitted. 'He doesn't talk about school, at least not about the work.'

'Well, I shouldn't worry. He seems happy enough, if his appetite's anything to go by.'

'Yes, it's lovely to see him enjoying his food.'

'Well, he'd have to be a bit strange if he didn't enjoy a meal like that. Er, was there any reason for it? I mean, it's not some kind of anniversary that I've forgotten, or anything like that?'

Laura tipped the washing-up water out of the bowl.

'Too clever, that's your problem. No, it's something I found out today.' She glanced towards the door. The sound of Mark's music, or at least the rhythmic thud of the bass, came dimly from upstairs. 'Something very special, but I don't want to tell anyone else yet.'

Edward frowned thoughtfully, turning the bowl he was drying round and round in his hands.

'You've got a job?' he hazarded, with a little lilt of hope.

Laura laughed. 'No, not that. At least, I have in a way, but not the way you mean.'

She felt awkward, even nervous. What a ridiculous situation to find myself in, she thought. Frightened of telling my husband that we're going to have a baby. At least, not frightened exactly, but . . . Once I've told him, it'll be real. Why should that bother me? If only it were fifty years ago, I could go all coy, and simper out some trite little phrase.

Edward was watching her. Seeing that it was something important, and that she was having difficulty in telling him, he laid aside the tea-towel and came to the sink. Standing behind her he put his arms round her waist, tightening them as she leaned back into his embrace. Her hands still warm and damp from the hot water, she took hold of his wrists and moved them so that his hands lay against her stomach. He felt the firmness of her well-exercised stomach muscles tense and then soften again as she moved her hands to cover his, pressing them to her.

'I'm pregnant,' she said simply.

His hands gave one convulsive jolt, then held her again. He drew in a deep breath.

'Oh, my dear . . .' His hands were infinitely gentle as he held her, but

Laura frowned. She hardly knew what she had expected – excitement? Amazement? Even disbelief would not have been surprising. But not sorrow, and certainly not pity. She turned herself round, putting her hands up to his shoulders and leaning away a little to look up into his face. His hazel eyes, so like Mark's, looked down at her with sad, kindly sympathy. He doesn't believe me, she realised with relief. He thinks I'm having some kind of menopausal breakdown, a phantom pregnancy or something. Oh, poor Edward!

'It's true,' she said. 'I went to the doctor last week because I hadn't been feeling too good. It was a locum, not Alan, and he didn't say anything, just sent off blood samples and things. I went to see Alan today, and he told me. I didn't believe it at first, but he wouldn't make a mistake about something like this. We're going to have a baby.'

Laura watched his face change. That face that she knew almost better than her own, that she had seen in joy and anger, in laughter and misery and the withdrawn concentration of orgasm, was suddenly transfigured by a mixture of emotions so powerful that for a moment it was utterly a stranger's. Transfiguration, she thought, and felt her own suppressed emotions erupt to meet his.

'Laura! Oh, Laura! Oh, my darling, darling girl! Oh, Laura!' His voice was hoarse, the tears he was not aware of brimmed over his lower lids and ran down his cheeks. She put up her hand to wipe them away. At that moment it seemed impossible that she could ever love anyone, even a baby, as much as she loved this man. Her own eyes filled with tears, and they clung together.

They went to bed early, to be private. Laura, calling good-night to Mark through his door, wondered whether he would be surprised that they had come upstairs at only half past nine. She had yet to learn that Mark was supremely uninterested in what adults did, unless it affected him directly, and thought no more than that, if he was quiet, he could go back down to the kitchen later and watch the late-night horror film.

Laura and Edward lay closely twined together in the warm darkness of their bed, whispering to one another. With the kind of tacit understanding that the long-married sometimes achieve, they spoke little of the future. The harsh realities of life with a small child, the thoughts of money and schools had no place here. The present, extraordinary as it was, was enough for them.

'I don't want to tell anyone yet. Except Mark.'

Edward, who had expected to hear 'Except Anna', was vaguely surprised.

'Mark? Are you sure?. What about Anna and Jane? And Cassandra? After all, you'll be going through it all together. She'll be delighted.'

'Mmn. Maybe.' Laura, knowing Cassandra better than he did, thought that she might be more inclined to be resentful, to feel that her thunder had been stolen. 'Mark is family, I must tell him, but nobody else. I'm going to wait until the first twelve weeks is over. You know. And until we know that everything's . . . all right.'

'Yes.' He was silent. 'And if it's not?'

He felt her shake her head. 'I don't know. I really don't. What do you want?'

'No, it has to be your decision. You're the one doing all the work, and all the looking-after later on. Whatever you want, that's what I want.'

'And if I don't know?'

'I think, if it comes to it, you will know. We won't worry about it for now. If it happens – which God forbid – we'll do what seems right to us then. OK?'

'OK.' Laura yawned, then giggled. 'That's what I should have asked Alan.'

'What?'

'Whether we're allowed to bonk.'

'You have such a refined vocabulary. Better not, I'm afraid. Just in case. Don't want to disturb young Oscar, knocking on the door.'

'Oscar?' Laura yawned again. 'Oh, that night.' She was silent, and he could feel the slight movement of her fingers as she counted. 'Yes,' she agreed with cheerful satisfaction. 'Quite probably. Oscar.' She gave a snuffle of laughter, and fell abruptly into sleep.

Thank goodness it's Saturday, thought Laura the next day, and I'll get a chance to talk to Mark. Edward had continued to seem surprised and perhaps a little put out that she intended to tell Mark about the baby, but Laura was insistent.

'I think it's important that he should feel part of the family,' she said earnestly. 'I'm sure he needs a father. Boys do, surely? And with something like this he could so easily feel excluded. It would be different if we'd already got other children, but as it is he's used to being an only child.'

'If you say so. Does that mean you want me to tell him?'

'Oh, no,' said Laura immediately. The opportunity of a heart to heart with Mark was, she felt, too precious to hand over. It was so difficult to communicate with him sometimes. Surely I'll learn more about him from his reaction, she thought. And he will see that I trust him, that's important. He doesn't seem to trust anybody, not really.

It seemed a heaven-sent opportunity that Mark had been invited to visit a school friend who lived several miles away, on the other side of the town, right at the far edge of the school's catchment area. Not only would they have to negotiate the heavy Saturday morning traffic in and out of town, but Laura knew that the road on the far side was being dug up for the laying of a new gas main. They would have plenty of time, and Mark would by then have overcome his first-thing-in-the-morning gloom.

He was silent as they set off, and though it was a relaxed silence on his side – Mark rarely initiated a conversation – Laura felt almost as tense as she had done the night before. She began to hunt for phrases in her mind, rejecting each one as she did so, and with every passing mile her ability to begin speaking seemed to recede. Perversely the roads seemed almost empty, every traffic light was green. I must start, she told herself. She glanced sideways. Mark stared ahead of him. His arms were no longer defensively crossed, she noticed, but relaxed in front of him, the hands palm down on his thighs. Get on with it, she told herself. Now. You've got to start before we get to the next junction. Now.

Like a swimmer plunging into a cold sea she gasped in a breath. 'Mark.'

'Uh.' His familiar grunt.

'I've got something to tell you. It's a bit of a secret, actually. I'd rather you didn't mention it to anyone else – except Edward, of course.'

'OK.' He seemed uninterested, and why not? Adult secrets, she thought, were not often very interesting to the young, however important they might seem to us.

'I've not been feeling very well recently. Nothing serious,' she added quickly, as he frowned slightly. What did the frown mean? Concern? Anxiety? Irritation?

'Sorry,' he muttered, lowering his head. Laura, not quite sure whether he was commiserating or, for some reason, apologising, thought it best to continue.

'I went to the doctor, just for a check-up, and he told me something rather amazing. I'm . . . well, I'm going to have a baby.'

Silence. Laura flicked her eyes to the left, keeping her head still so that he would not be aware of her glance. He had not moved, his face was as withdrawn and unreadable as ever.

'I know it's rather extraordinary,' said Laura as lightly as she could.

'Are you sure?' Goodness, thought Laura, he sounds just like Edward.

'Yes, perfectly sure. I didn't believe it at first, either, but the doctor said it was quite definite. I hope you don't find the idea too appalling, or embarrassing?'

He glanced at her, surprised. 'No, of course not. Only, I thought . . . George said . . . George said you couldn't.'

'Did she?' How dare she, thought Laura furiously. How dare that woman say anything about me? And how did she know? 'How did she know?' The question came out abruptly.

'I don't know. From . . . from – him?' He brought the words out with difficulty. Laura had noticed that he never called Edward anything but 'you' or 'him'.

'Edward wouldn't discuss me with your mother. Not anything like that, anyway.'

'Uh.'

Laura's anger subsided abruptly. Edward had, after all, tried to adopt Mark; perhaps something had been said then. Or perhaps she had simply guessed, when his letters told all about his life but never mentioned any children. What did it matter now anyway? It was no longer true.

'Well, never mind. It's true we had thought we'd never have a baby of our own. And of course we're very happy about it. But it doesn't make any difference, you know. To you, I mean.'

Mark frowned again. His face, for once, was easy to interpret. It was quite obvious that it had never occurred to him that the coming of a baby would affect him one way or another. It was silly, Laura told herself, to feel that twinge of sadness. She should be pleased that he didn't mind.

'It won't be born for a long time yet, anyway,' she said. 'Not until February, probably. That's why I don't want to tell anyone yet. There are sometimes problems with the baby when old ladies like me get pregnant. If anything goes wrong, or anything . . . well, it's easier not to have everyone fussing around. You know.'

Mark nodded. He knew.

'But I wanted to tell you,' said Laura a shade wistfully. 'Because you're family.'

'Am I?' He sounded surprised.

'Oh Mark, of course you are! You're Edward's son! His oldest son, his first child! Nothing can change that! I don't tend to think of myself as a "stepmother" – it sounds like some old bat out of a fairy tale – but of course you're family.'

'Uh.' It was hard to tell, but she thought he sounded pleased.

'And nobody else is to know,' she reiterated. 'Not even Anna, so don't tell Ben, please.'

'All right.' Knowing his taciturn nature, she thought he would be unlikely to be indiscreet.

They were through the roadworks now, and would be at the house in only a few minutes. Laura said nothing, checking back over the conversation. She wasn't sure what she had expected – had it been this? She thought she was fairly satisfied with the way things had gone. We're a little bit nearer to understanding one another, she thought hopefully. Perhaps, soon, I can tackle him about Edward. At least persuade him to call him something, for a start.

They drove up to the house in silence. When she had pulled up, Laura waited while Mark reached into the back of the car for his overnight bag. He did not immediately get out of the car, but sat holding it on his knees.

'Have a good time,' said Laura cheerfully. 'I'll come and fetch you at about eleven, is that all right? You can bring Jay back with you if you want.'

'Uh.' Still he did not get out of the car. The door of the house opened, and Jay came out. Mark clutched his bag, his shoulders hunched. He opened the car door, and hesitated again.

'Drive carefully,' he said at last, his voice gruff. Laura felt a rush of warmth run through her. It's like a kind of code, she thought.

'Thank you, Mark.' Oh, thank you, she repeated inside. Thank you. She did not know whether she spoke to God, or to Mark, or to the baby. All three, perhaps. She drove home carefully, and sang all the way.

Chapter 12

'Have you seen Laura recently?'

Anna stirred a sprinkle of green – parsley? – into her soup. The weather was disappointing for late June, grey and chilly, and she was thankful to see that Jane was giving her more than the salad that women often give other women at lunch-time.

'Laura? No, I haven't.' Jane checked the table before sitting down. I really ought to have proper table napkins, like Anna does, she thought vaguely. The paper ones, from a half-used packet she had found at the back of a drawer, looked rather crumpled. 'She's all right, isn't she? I thought she was just rather tied up with Mark. She's not used to having a child around, and she's enjoying fussing over him. It'll wear off.' She offered bread.

'Thanks. It's just that she had that fainting fit the other week, and since then she's seemed rather withdrawn, I thought. But I probably only imagined it.'

'Well, I know she went to the doctor, and she said there was nothing wrong, so I suppose it was just a bug or something. Do you want butter, or low-fat spread?'

'Oh, butter please,' said Anna after the smallest hesitation. 'I know I shouldn't, but I do like it.'

Jane, who ate her bread dry, said nothing. She watched while Anna tasted the soup.

'Oh, coriander! I thought it was parsley! How delicious.' She took another spoonful, fishing in the bowl for pieces of fish and mushroom. 'You are clever. Is that crab or prawn?'

'One of those Ocean Sticks – you know, the fake things with bright pink outsides. They taste quite good, and they don't disintegrate or turn into rubber if you let the stock boil.'

'And it's not fattening either, I suppose? How sickening of you.'

'Don't worry. I've got a disgustingly rich chocolate cake for pudding. All part of my feeding up Ben campaign, really, but it looks less obvious

139

if some of it's already been eaten. If I keep putting new cakes on the table when he gets home from school, he gives me funny looks.'

'Looks like I'll just have to help out by eating some, then, doesn't it? How is he? Are you still getting the diet biscuits.'

'Yes, I am. I think he's really making an effort to eat more, only of course his appetite's not very good. I don't think he's put on much weight, but at least he's stopped getting thinner, so I'm not nearly so worried. For the moment, that is.'

'Why, what's happened?' Anna, who had rather wanted to talk about Laura, realised that Jane had invited her because she needed to talk about something. How often, in the past, she had done the same, even when all she wanted was not to get advice or unburden herself, but simply to refresh her spirit by spending an hour or two in the emotionally undemanding company of her women friends.

'Oh, Bill of course, what else? Having messed me around for a year saying he wasn't sure whether or not he wanted a divorce, now that he's finally decided he does, he's being perfectly bloody about it. For a start, he's trying to make out that the delay is because I refused to agree to a divorce, when I told him, right at the start, that though of course I didn't want one, I wouldn't say no if that was what he wanted.'

Anna made the sort of indeterminate noise that indicates sympathy and agreement.

'Obviously it's too late to patch things up – though I did hope for a while . . . all those cryptic remarks he kept making, you remember? Anyway, since he's definitely not intending to come back, surely it's better for all of us to get it sorted out properly? When Ben and I had that heart to heart a few weeks ago, he actually said he was glad the divorce was happening because it was all the up and down that got to him, and that the little patches of hope made the bad bits even worse.' She sniffed and blinked hard.

'At least he felt able to talk to you about it,' said Anna. 'That's a big step forward.'

'Yes, I think so. Anyway, the solicitors have been instructed, and of course I know things like this are never that simple, but I had a letter from my solicitor yesterday with the most awful bundle of stuff, including Bill's preliminary affidavit, or whatever the thing's called.'

'Horrid for you.' Anna remembered the protracted business of winding up Michael's estate. She, at least, had received the sympathy and kindness due to a young widow, but even so the paperwork had seemed at times more than she could cope with, a mindless juggernaut of bureaucracy.

'How do you get on with your solicitor? It's very important that you should feel comfortable with her. I know she's very high powered, but is she easy to talk to?'

'Yes, very, but you know how it is – I hesitate to ring her because it's so expensive. Whenever we talk I have this little clock ticking away in my head, notching up the pound signs. Oh, she warned me that it would be upsetting, that his solicitors would dredge up everything they possibly could. I know it's a negotiating tactic, but . . . I just couldn't believe some of the things he said.' She paused, stirring her soup as if she could see pictures in it.

Anna smoothed the butter on her bread as precisely as if she were icing a wedding cake.

'Don't tell me, unless you really want to.'

'No, I don't mind. I'm so angry, really, and I just want to get it off my chest a bit, if you can bear it?' She glanced at Anna, who nodded.

'One of the things that really upset me was that he said our marriage had been over for years before he went, that he'd told me he was unhappy and we had frequently discussed the possibility of a separation. That's how it was put. Frequently discussed! I ask you, Anna! We had our rows, like any couple, and in the heat of the moment one of us might say that we hated the other, and wished we'd never married, but it never *meant* anything! As far as I was concerned, we were a normal, happy couple.'

'Of course you were. Why else would we all be so astonished when he went?'

'Precisely. And he said – this was the thing that really got to me – that we hadn't slept together for six months before he left. That we had separate beds. And it's just not true! How could we have hidden something like that from the children? Not that I'd dream of asking them to say so. It's so unfair!'

'Stupid, too,' said Anna. 'After all, you still had Mrs Evans coming three mornings a week then, didn't you? And in my experience, cleaning ladies are far harder to hide things from than children. There's no way you could have been sleeping in separate beds without her noticing. And while it may be distasteful to have to ask your cleaning lady to give evidence, or whatever it's called, it's better than involving the children.'

Jane gave her a grateful look. 'Of course. I should have thought of that! That'll get the bastard! Not that it makes any difference in the long run, I suppose, but it's quite good to catch him out on a lie because, as far as the money's concerned, he's claiming to be very hard up, which I'm certain isn't the case. I know he came into a fair bit from that family trust when it was wound up, but he seems to have squirrelled that away somewhere, and the bonus he got last year. Says he didn't get one, but I don't believe it. He always does, and they had a fairly good year, so there'd be no reason for them not to, and that's a fairly hefty sum.'

'Surely all that can be checked? Your solicitor should be dealing with that.'

'She is. But the worst thing of all, the thing that really frightens me, is that he's pushing for the house to be sold. Says it's too big, and he needs his half of the equity. But he's got the London flat, which is worth a lot, and the trust money; and whatever his salary is, it won't have gone down, you can bet your life on that. It's just spite, because he always loved this house, and if he can't have it, he doesn't want me to – but can't he see what it'll do to the children? We've been here since before Toby was born, for God's sake! If it didn't make me so bloody angry, I'd almost be sorry for him, because if it happens they'll never forgive him. He's already taken away half their security, but if they lose their home as well it would be a complete betrayal. Bastard!'

'Yes.' Anna' s brow was creased with thought. 'I can't believe he'd get away with it, but if by any chance he does, would you be able to buy out his half?' She knew the answer before she asked, but she was clutching at straws. 'I could . . . I could help out, if you'd let me. I'd hate to see you go.'

Jane's lips trembled, and she firmed them for a moment, her eyes filling again. 'I know. Thank you, it's so sweet of you . . . if the worst came to the worst, I might be tempted, but I don't think I could let you. As you say, he probably hasn't got a leg to stand on, it may be just a try-on to rattle me. So I mustn't give him the satisfaction of letting him think it's worked.' She smiled, albeit shakily. 'Now, that's enough of my problems. Thanks for letting me go on at you.'

'No problem.' Anna put on a fake American accent to hide her feelings. 'Any time, babe.'

'I know. I feel better. It makes such a difference being able to talk about it. Now, let's forget Bill and his machinations, and talk about what really matters. What about Daisy? How's she coping with GCSEs?'

Anna accepted the change of subject. 'All right, I think. At least, she rings me up after every exam and gives me a blow-by-blow account of all the things she thinks she's done wrong, then when she's got me into a complete panic she says, "Oh, well, I think it went quite well, really", and rings off, leaving me a quivering jelly. Then she goes off to have a giggle with her friends, because they all feel it's very important to relax and not to overdo the last minute revising, and I have a sleepless night. What about Candida?'

'Oh, you know my dear old pudding,' said her loving mother fondly. 'She just goes off and does them without any fuss, and says she thinks she did fairly all right. She's worked hard, thank goodness, and I keep telling her that all that matters is that she should have done her best. At least she's older than Ben, so she hasn't got to live up to him. I'm always thankful for that. And I just hope there's a big enough gap between him and Toby that he won't feel pressured either. I'm afraid he's going to be another "fairly good all-rounder", like Candy.'

'Well, Ben's a difficult act to follow. But I'm sure she'll have done well. She's so sensible, and that makes all the difference. At least she's not likely to have answered the wrong questions, or spent all her time on one essay, or something.'

'Daisy hasn't done that, has she?'

''No, thank goodness, though she nearly answered questions in the wrong section in something – History, I think. Anyway, it'll soon be over now, thank goodness.'

'Yes, and then the holidays will be upon us. Will you have some more soup? There's plenty, I was hoping that Laura would come as well.'

'Yes, please.' Anna passed her bowl to be refilled. 'That's just what I mean. She always used to be free for lunch when either of us asked her. And it's not as if Mark's home during the day, after all. She can't be making butterscotch sauce and home-made ice cream every day, surely?'

'Home-made ice cream? Goodness, she'd better stop that before the summer holidays, or we'll never see any of our children again. Or, worse still, they'll expect us to make it too.' She paused, stirring her soup without attempting to eat it. 'She has gone a bit overboard about Mark, hasn't she?'

Anna glanced at her. 'You thought so too? I thought he was the bee's knees with you, too, since he said to Ben about being anorexic.'

'Well, it was very helpful,' said Jane, a bit defensively. 'I was really very grateful to him, and I still am. But . . .'

'Exactly. But. I've got nothing against Mark, he seems a nice enough boy. A bit sulky-looking, sometimes. Or perhaps I mean sullen, but that's understandable enough at his age and under the circumstances. In fact, I'd say he was coping rather well, all things considered. But Laura seems to be besotted with him! As far as she's concerned, he's perfect, the sun shines out of him, she's running her whole life round his whims. They never eat fish any more, which she and Edward used to love, because

Mark doesn't like it, and the same with mushrooms and all sorts of things. It's not good for him, and I'm not really sure it's good for her either.'

Jane finished her soup and cleared the bowls away.

'Salad,' she said unnecessarily, pushing it towards Anna. 'Is it really so bad?' she asked. 'For her, I mean? Or even for him, come to that? I suppose she is spoiling him rather, but Laura thinks it's good for him, and he does seem to have blossomed in the last few weeks. I know you think he's sullen, but you haven't seen him much, except at the end of half-term. He's here quite a bit, after school and at weekends, and he's certainly rather keen on Daisy. He could scarcely take his eyes off her, and did you notice how he always tried to sit next to her?'

'No, because I hardly saw her at half-term. If she wasn't here, she was at Laura's.'

'Jealous?' It was a gentle tease.

Anna laughed. 'Hardly! You know I don't expect her to stay at home, though of course she's always welcome to invite her friends. I didn't really even want her to do any revision, either. The school said it was better for them to relax. But what I mean is, Laura kept asking her over – as if she was serving her up on a plate for Mark, like a *petit-four*.'

'She didn't have to go. And Candy and Ben were usually there too. She's surely not in danger from a fourteen-year-old, surrounded as she is by sixth-form boys? Though I must admit, Mark is attractive. That brooding, devil-may-care look, you know.'

Anna was beginning to feel rather foolish.

'I'm not worried about Daisy! At least, I worry about her constantly, but not where Mark's concerned. He's far too young, and in any case she looks on him as a kind of relative – a step-god-brother, if you please! As far as she's concerned the whole situation is rather romantic and exciting, and she's very fond of Laura, of course. Wants to make it all work out happily for her. It's not her, it's Laura I'm worried about.'

'I know. But I thought, when we all had that meal together at half-term, that I'd never seen her looking so happy.'

Anna buttered another slice of bread.

'That's what I mean.' She looked earnestly at Jane, her blue eyes large with worry. 'Not that I don't want her to be happy – darling Laura, my oldest and best friend in the world, I'd do anything for her – but I'm afraid she's building too much on Mark. It's understandable enough, God knows. All those years trying for a baby. Watching me and you, and now even Cassandra, getting pregnant. Seeing us with our babies, and our children, being a godmother, a friend, a baby-sitter, but never a mother.

144

And now here he is, out of the blue, a child. Not just any child, but Edward's son. Suddenly she's a mother. Well, a stepmother, but still . . . You see what I mean?'

Jane chewed a mouthful of salad and swallowed. 'Mmm. I hadn't really thought about it. I suppose you're right. But he *is* her stepson. Why shouldn't she be happy making a fuss of him, if it gives her pleasure?'

'Because he's not a proper stepson. Fourteen years old, and this is the first time she's ever heard of him, let alone set eyes on him. Once that mother of his gets back to England, he'll be off. And then what? Supposing she says he can't come down again?'

'Why would she do that?'

Anna shrugged. 'How do I know? Why would anyone take maintenance money from the father all these years, and refuse to allow him to meet the child, or even send him a photograph or tell him anything about him? Only someone as gentle as Edward would put up with it. And if she says, "Right, thanks a lot, that's it for the next fourteen years", will Edward fight it? He might complain, but I don't see him going to court, and with people like that the threat of a legal case is the only thing they're likely to take any notice of.'

'But what about Mark himself? He seems happy enough here, you said so yourself. She can't stop him from keeping in touch at his age.'

'No, but once he gets home again, involved in school and all his old friends, will he really bother? If his mother puts pressure on him – and I get the feeling that he's used to being pretty strictly controlled, don't you? – I'm not sure if he'll think it's really worth all the hassle. He'll just disappear into the blue, and Laura . . . Laura will break her heart.'

Jane pushed away her plate. The dog, who had been lying in her basket with her nose on her paws, lifted her head alertly and then came over to raise melting eyes to Jane's face. When people pushed away their plates with that decisive gesture there were often scraps to be disposed of.

'Don't be silly, Slops. You don't like salad,' said Jane absently. 'You know you're not allowed to beg at the table.' She pushed the nudging head away, and the dog sighed, returning to her basket with a well-simulated air of dejection. A medium-sized animal of indeterminate breed, she was toffee brown with eyes to match. A loving and extrovert nature was allied, in the silky dome of her pretty head, with a sharp intelligence, and it was generally agreed that she had spent her time in the Dog Rescue Centre, where they had got her, in closely observing all the various tricks of the canine trade. In her more impecunious moments Jane had even toyed with the idea of registering her to work on television, since she was capable of startling feats of learning. Now, however, Jane's eyes followed her without seeing her. 'Oh dear,' she said anxiously, 'I have to admit, I hadn't really thought of it like that. But don't you think you're being just a bit pessimistic? I suppose it is a mistake for Laura to get too involved with Mark, under the circumstances, but I can't believe he'll just disappear once his mother gets back. I know teenagers are a bit "out of sight, out of mind", but surely even basic self-interest would make him keep in touch?'

'Perhaps. It's just that I get the feeling that Laura is almost ignoring the fact that he's only visiting. Things she's said – about Christmas, in particular – worried me a bit. But I expect I'm over-reacting. After all, Laura's so sensible. After all those years of her looking after me, perhaps I just wanted to redress the balance and worry about her for a change. And, as you say, she seems very happy. I suppose it's selfish of me to wish that she wasn't cutting herself off from us all quite so much.'

'I must admit, I have almost felt that she was avoiding me the last few weeks or so. Ever since that time she fainted, actually. You don't think . . . No, she'd tell us if she were ill, surely? Wouldn't she?'

Anna stood up, remembering not to catch her tights on the wooden legs of the battered chair.

'Of course she would,' she said firmly, pushing that nightmare memory back into its box. 'Laura knows very well how wrong it would be to keep something like that secret. No, whatever it is, she'll sort it out. Now, where's that chocolate cake you were talking about? And then we could salve our consciences by taking the dog for a—'

'Careful!' cried Jane, for Slops had already leaped from her basket.

'A perambulation?' suggested Anna carefully.

'Right,' said Jane, relieved. 'Coffee, or tea?'

The sun struggled through while they were out in the forest, and as a result they were later getting back than they had intended.

'Sorry,' said Anna as they crossed the stile that took them back into farmland. 'It's my fault we're so late; you can blame it on me if the kids complain.'

'Complain?' Jane laughed. 'They prefer it if I'm out when they get home. They go on and on about being latchkey kids, but secretly they love it. I think they feel happier to think I'm not just sitting waiting for them to come home, with nothing else to do but cluck over them. I should probably get a job: that would teach them. Look, isn't that Cassandra's car?'

Anna, who was a bit short-sighted, peered at the distant road. 'Is it? I haven't got my glasses, and I'm not very good at cars, anyway.'

'Yes, look, she's waving at us. Goodness, I hope nothing's wrong.'

They lengthened their stride and the dog, still full of energy, raced ahead to where Cassandra, who had climbed over the gate in spite of being unsuitably dressed in a slim skirt and good shoes, was coming to meet them.

'She'll break her ankle, trying to hurry over this rough grass,' puffed Anna anxiously. 'Whatever can be the matter? It surely can't be a problem with the baby, or she wouldn't be galloping about like this. Oh dear, you go on. I've got a stitch.'

By the time Jane reached Cassandra she was standing still, trying ineffectually to fend off the joyful overtures of the muddy dog.

'Get *down*! No! Down, I said! Keep your paws off me, wretched creature! Oh, Jane, do call off the Hound of the Baskervilles! This skirt is quite new, and I want to wear it while I can still get into it.'

'Then you probably shouldn't climb over gates into fields in it,' said Jane reasonably. 'Come *here*, Slops. Sit. No, not in that, don't be so damned literal. Bloody hell, Cassie, whatever's the matter? It's not the baby, is it?'

'No, of course not. I wouldn't be here if it were. No, it's Laura.'

'Laura? What's happened to her?' Anna, clutching her side, reached them and stood half bent, catching her breath.

'Well, I don't know! That's the trouble!'

'For heaven's sake, Cassie, pull yourself together and *tell* us!' Jane glanced at Anna's face, concerned. 'Anna's been worried about Laura anyway, and you're frightening her half to death.'

'Oh, Anna, I'm sorry. Laura's fine. At least, I suppose she is. Only I went to the maternity clinic, and she was there! I was just driving away, and I saw her walk in! I would have gone back and spoken to her, but you know what it's like, there's never a parking space to be found, and someone had already taken mine. I drove round once, then abandoned my car on the bit for ambulances, and ran back to Reception. She was sitting in the area where you wait when you're going to see the consultant! Chatting away to the woman beside her. I was just wondering whether to go and ask her what was going on when an ambulance came in, and I had to run back and move the car. I was so shaken I couldn't face going straight back to the shop, and I'd said to Jenny I might not anyway, so I came home to tell one of you, and see if you knew what was going on. Only you were both out, and Toby said you'd probably taken the dog up to the forest, so I came here on the off-chance I might find you. I'd more or less given up, then I saw you in the field and stopped. And here I am.'

A loud and impatient hooting from the lane made them all turn.

'You can't park there, woman!'

'Bloody Range Rover drivers,' fumed Cassandra. 'You own that bit of road, do you?' she shouted back.

'Yes!' came the succinct reply.

'You are blocking the entire lane,' pointed out Jane, rather amused. This, she surmised, was another of Cassie's storms in a teacup.

'But he doesn't need to be so impatient,' said Cassandra crossly. 'Still, I suppose I'll have to move. I'd offer you a lift, but . . .' She looked dubiously at the dog, sitting with an expression of extreme virtue in a cow-pat.

'There isn't room, anyway,' said Anna firmly. 'I'm not squashing in the back of that, and I don't suppose Jane wants to either. We'll cut across on the footpath, and see you back at the village in a few minutes. Come to me. You know where the key is, you can put the kettle on for us.'

Cassandra clambered back over the gate, watched derisively by the man in the Range Rover, who wore a tweed jacket of a peculiarly aggressive check, with a cap to match that did little for his florid face. Anna and Jane ignored him, and took the footpath that was a short-cut to the village.

They arrived at Anna's to find Cassandra pacing round the kitchen. 'I'm sorry to make such a fuss, but it seemed so peculiar! What on earth could she have been doing there? Unless she was looking for me? But she didn't know I was going . . . and she looked so settled, as if she thought she belonged there!'

'Calm down,' said Anna, almost pushing her into a chair. 'You'll frighten the baby. You know Laura and her good works, she was probably just giving someone a lift. Though I must admit she usually steers clear of anything to do with babies.'

'Exactly! And I don't know about you, but she's been a bit funny lately, don't you think? I thought perhaps it was just me, and that she was upset about me being pregnant or something. I mean, it would be very understandable, wouldn't it? You don't think – ' she gulped – 'you don't think she's gone a bit *funny*, or something, do you?'

'We'll soon get the chance to find out,' said Jane drily from the window. 'She's just driven up the drive.'

'Where?' Cassandra leaped from her chair. 'Oh God, yes, she's coming in.'

When Laura came in a few moments later, she looked round the three of them standing in self-consciously relaxed attitudes in the kitchen. Her lips twitched.

'You look terribly guilty. Is this some kind of conspiracy or something?'

Anna relaxed. She knew Laura too well not to recognise this exuberant mood, though it was one she had rarely seen since their schooldays.

'Yes, it is,' she said cheerfully. 'We're just wondering whether we should call the men in white coats to haul you off, or whether it's just Cassandra's fevered imagination at work.'

Laura laughed. 'So you did see me! I thought it was your car, but I only saw it out of the corner of my eye. Yes, I was there, and no, you won't need to be visiting me in the loony bin and encouraging me to do basket work on Fridays. Is that kettle boiling for tea? It ought to be champagne, really, but I'd prefer tea, I'm so thirsty after all that hanging around at the hospital.' Seeing that they were all stunned into immobility, she went briskly to the kettle and made the tea, as at home in this kitchen as her own. It was easier, anyway, to have something to do.

'I'm afraid I owe you all a bit of an apology for holding out on you,' she said, setting out cups and saucers – Anna disliked mugs. She spoke into a silence that was as brittle as thin glass. 'The fact is, my dears, that after all this time something wonderful has happened. I'm pregnant. Oh, dear, I feel like one of those women in the Bible. Sarah, was it, or Rachel? I should be saying "I am with child", and bursting into song. Probably with timbrels, whatever they are.' She turned round. Her face was radiant. 'I kept it a secret because I could hardly believe it myself, and it seemed sensible to get over the first twelve weeks. Well, I'm up to ten weeks, and at the clinic today the consultant said everything's fine. I rather thought my guilty secret was peering out of the bag – idiotic of me not to realise that Cassandra might be at the hospital too! – so here I am!'

She looked round the room. 'I wish you could see your faces,' she said with a giggle.

Anna was the first to move. She came over to Laura and put her arms round her.

'I'm so happy,' she said simply. 'It's – oh, so wonderful I don't know what to say! Oh, Laura!'

'Well, don't cry about it,' said Laura, hugging her.

'I'm sorry! It's just that I'm so happy!' Anna wept. Jane and Cassandra joined them, and they all clung together for a moment in a tearful huddle.

'Oh dear, how ridiculous,' sniffed Jane. 'The best news I've heard for years, and here we are crying about it! Where's that cup of tea? This calls for a toast!'

149

Thank God, she thought. Thank God for the happy things that come out of the blue. All the problems with Bill, and the worry over Ben and Toby, and even darling Candida, all of a sudden they seem almost irrelevant compared to this. And to think that we were worried about her getting too involved with Mark! With a baby of her own, everything will be in proportion. Maybe there are happy endings, after all.

Chapter 13

The following weeks were, for Laura, a time of such happiness that it was as if she had entered some kind of parallel universe modelled perhaps on a cartoon film, or the idealised world of advertising. Colours seemed brighter, objects and even objectives more clearly defined, simple and satisfying. It was unusual, too, in that she was acutely aware of her own happiness, instead – as so often seemed to be the case in adult life – of only becoming aware in retrospect that she had been happy, usually in contrast to a present feeling of despondency.

Out of a superstitious need to propitiate jealous gods, she found herself attending church more regularly than before, and also visiting the old people's home more often. Outside the village and at the end of a long private drive, it was oddly named St Barbara's Hospice – St Barbara was, as far as Laura knew, the patron saint of miners and a singularly inappropriate protector for its elderly inhabitants.

The building had previously been a private house, and the village had breathed a collective sigh of relief when it had been bought by a charity for its present use. The Victorian house, inconveniently large for a modern family, was too small to be of interest to investors (there were strict planning restrictions on building on the park and woodland), and had the added drawback of being almost startlingly ugly. There had been disquieting rumours about the advent of a commune, and even more worrying ones about housing disturbed adolescents, so a private nursing home had been welcomed by all, particularly some of the older residents, who could imagine a time when they might need to make use of it, and who would be happy to stay in the village.

The house had converted fairly well, however: the ground floor into communal sitting, dining and television rooms, the large first- and second-floor bedrooms (accessible by lift) to suites and rooms to which inmates could bring their own furniture and treasures, while the addition of two ground-floor wings, though they did nothing to improve the appearance of the place, gave additional (and less expensive) units which included specially fitted hospital-style rooms where the chronically ill could be cared for. In cases of need, these rooms were subsidised by the income from the private suites and rooms.

Laura, reluctantly searching for somewhere for her mother, had been put off at first by the hideous building. Its aggressive red brick that was so inappropriate to the gentle Sussex countryside was made nightmarish, rather than enlivened, by fiddly carving and pointless, overlarge turrets, but since it offered excellent facilities and was near enough to walk to, it had been the only choice. Her mother had been content, even happy there, and in time the overlay of pleasant memories made Laura see it quite differently, its ugliness endearing rather than daunting. After her mother's death she had continued to visit, partly as a link with the past, and partly because she had made many friends there among the residents.

Leaving St Barbara's one afternoon in late July, she was surprised to encounter Tod in the hall, standing bemused in front of a large fireplace constructed, apparently, out of decaying liver. Jane's dog, Slops, left Laura's side and trotted over to greet him. Tod was usually a soft touch for a biscuit, and had been known to carry bars of chocolate about his person.

'Tod! Don't tell me you're moving in?'

'My dear, *no!* I'm on the *committee*, so I thought I'd pay a surprise visit! Catch them out, you know – matron on the gin, patients locked in cupboards, that sort of thing.'

'And were they?'

'No, it was all quite dismally proper. Tell me,' he lowered his breathy voice to a confidential whisper, 'you don't think this sort of thing has an unhealthy effect, do you?' His eyes, round as buttons, indicated the fireplace, which he turned away from with a shudder. 'I mean, some of the poor old dears here are *definitely* rather *Parthenon . . .*'

'Parthenon?' Laura was confused.

'Lost their marbles, darling. And when you consider the positively *surreal* outside – I mean, I'd be gaga in a week if I had to look at it all day! It can't be good for them!'

His concern was genuine, and Laura stifled her amused indignation.

'It is *very* ugly,' she agreed seriously. 'Edward always says the architect must have been raised in a workhouse on a diet of opium. But don't forget that, apart from a gentle saunter in the garden on a warm day, most of the people here never see the building from the outside. It's warm, and comfortable, and you must admit that the rooms are very pleasant, if a bit bland. And I'm afraid,' she added with genuine regret, 'that not everyone minds as much as you, or even I, about beauty.'

'No, one realises that. Of course, the educational system is *much* at fault in that respect.'

'Oh, I don't know. Mark says they have a lot of prints of famous paintings hanging at school – there's a kind of library, they can change them round every so often – and posters of cathedrals and castles and so on. I'm afraid he calls them boring, but then Mark takes much the same view of culture as Goebbels did, unfortunately.'

'Copies!' Tod waved a dismissive hand. 'Better than nothing, I suppose, but then look at the *buildings* they're in! How can their poor little souls not be stunted by spending their days in something that looks like the offspring of a multi-storey car park mated to an aluminium greenhouse?'

In his indignation he allowed his voice to rise, and his arms gyrated. Slops, who had been sitting lovingly on his foot, took this as an invitation to play some kind of throwing and fetching game, and jumped up with a bark.

'Quiet, Slops,' said Laura firmly. 'Come on, Tod, you're getting her over-excited. Are you going back? We could walk together, or did you come by car?'

'Walked,' said Tod lugubriously. 'The doctor told me I should take more exercise. Me! Can you imagine? Shall I take up *jogging*, I asked him, or *squash*, or just go to aerobics in one of those *deliciously* revealing leotards? But he said no, just gentle exercise. It sounds quite pleasant, doesn't it – gentle exercise, pale pink and fluffy. The reality, however, is less appealing. My feet, you know,' he added confidentially, 'are not what they were.'

Laura laughed. 'You should come swimming with me and Cassandra. That's gentle exercise, and it wouldn't hurt your feet.'

'Oh, wouldn't it?' he answered darkly. 'I've heard you can *catch* very nasty things in those changing rooms, verrucas – or should one say *verrucae*? – and athlete's foot which sounds so *virile* but I believe can be quite painful. Besides, look what's happened to you swimmers, all so wonderfully *fecund!* Not that I'm not delighted for you both, as you know, but really, where might it all end?'

'The imagination boggles,' agreed Laura. 'Come on, then, let's get going. Mark's coming back with some friends at six, and they're bound to be starving.'

They walked towards the steep brick steps outside the grandiose front door. A ramp, twice as long because of the height of the steps, had been built on one side of it, and Tod, wincing, picked his way down it.

'Oh dear, Tod, you do look uncomfortable. I'm sure the doctor didn't mean you to suffer like this. Why don't you sit here, and I'll come back for you with the car? It wouldn't be very long.'

'Lovely of you, but no. Just between the two of us these new shoes are a *fraction* tight. Once we're just a little further – round this bend – I shall undo the laces and tie them loosely. *Fatal* to have bought them, but the colour was exquisite and I just couldn't *resist*.'

'I know,' agreed Laura cosily. 'I've done it myself. One always hopes they'll *give* a little, but of course they never do.' Goodness, she thought, I'm beginning to sound like Tod. It must be catching.

'Aah, that's better!' Tod sighed with relief and rose, pink-faced, from the tree stump where he had sat. 'Here you are, then, you creature you. Fetch!' He threw a piece of branch with surprising vigour, and Slops raced happily to fetch it. 'I'm being stupid, I know, but Jane hasn't gone away without telling me, has she?'

'No, of course not. Why? Oh, you mean Slops? No, I bring her along sometimes if the weather's dry. The old dears love her, and she's very well behaved with them. They say it's good for you, don't they, being with an animal? Lowers the blood pressure or something. Slops adores it, they make a frightful fuss of her, and if I didn't keep an eye on them she'd be absolutely bloated with the treats they give her. One of them keeps a packet of those doggy chocolates – Choccywoofs or Woofychocs – especially for her, and I caught another one giving her a chop bone she'd saved from lunch.'

'All these Good Works,' sighed Tod. 'You don't think it's too tiring, in Your Condition?'

Laura laughed. 'No, of course not! I wouldn't do it if I didn't enjoy it, I'm afraid. And it seems . . . appropriate, somehow. To give something back, I mean. I suppose that sounds rather silly.'

'No, sensible,' said Tod, surprising her. 'Life's a tightrope, my dear,' he said, soberly for him. 'You have to keep your balance.'

'Yes, that's what I meant, I suppose.' Laura, pleased, felt a rush of affection for Tod. 'Is it wrong, do you think,' she asked rather shyly, 'to feel so happy? When I think of Anna and Jane, I feel quite guilty about it.'

'Don't,' he said, taking her hand and patting it. 'Just enjoy it while it lasts. You don't have to worry about Anna, she's so happy for you, it's the best thing that's happened to her for a long time, and it's doing her a power of good. I can't speak for Jane, of course, not knowing her so well, but I'd say much the same thing applies.'

He spoke soberly, for Tod, and Laura was touched.

'You are kind, Tod. Of course, I knew that already, from Anna. And all the things you do for people here, committees and things – I like the way you talk about *my* Good Works, by the way! I knew you were kind, but I didn't know you could be like this. I'm sorry, I'm not making much sense, am I?'

He stooped to tug the stick out of Slops' mouth, and perhaps to hide his face. When he was upright again, he looked rather pink.

'I can be serious, you know. I can even be sensible. In fact, inside, that's what I am. Sensible, rather dull, what my old Granny would have called "a proper sobersides". But it doesn't get you anywhere, does it? At least, it never did for me. And because I love the Arts, and loathe football, and because I prefer the company of women to that of men, people categorise me. What a dreadful word!' For a moment the usual Tod came through. 'So American! One does rather wonder whether the French aren't right, and we should all make their dreadful jargon illegal!'

'What are you saying, then, Tod?' Laura wanted to keep him talking. 'That it's all an act?'

'Oh, that!' He waved dismissively, forgetful of the stick in his hand. Slops barked, and made little encouraging dashes ahead and back, then crouched, front legs extended and her hinder end wriggling with the violent movement of her tail. Tod looked at her as if he'd never seen her before, then followed her gaze to the stick. He pulled back his arm and threw it, high and far, watching the piece of wood tumble end over end against the sky. 'We all do that, don't we? Anna acts the brave widow, Jane the wronged wife, Cassandra the other woman or the single mother. We have to, it's the only way to get by. And so do I. People need to be able to label you – that's a better word, thank goodness. You're easy to label, so are most of the people one meets. And me? Perhaps I find life is easier if I'm labelled "The Widow Tod"; that fantastic old queen, over-the-top camp, sit-com stereotype Tod. Then everyone knows where they are, what to expect. I give them a good show, make them laugh, everyone's happy.'

'But you? Are you happy? Don't you want to be like you are?'

'Does anyone, truly? But yes, of course I am. Don't look so anxious, silly girl! I send the image up a bit, but where's the harm in that? I get a great deal of amusement out of it. and so do other people. Even the ones that think I'm dreadful – think how much they enjoy being shocked! All that lovely self-satisfaction – "thank God *I'm* not like that" – gives them a nice, warm glow. No, I'm very happy. I've had a good life, and though of course I miss James, I'm thankful he died as he did, and thankful too for all my good friends. The only thing . . .' He paused, and for the first time in her life Laura saw him looking self-conscious.

'The only thing?' she prompted. 'Something you regret?'

'I should have liked to be a father,' he said, not looking at her.

Laura stopped, frozen in her tracks. 'Oh, Tod!' She was stricken. 'Oh, I *know*! How you feel, I mean. How could I not, after all those years! I'm so sorry!'

He shook his head. 'I don't mind any more. Or not much and not often. Just sometimes, now, I think I could have had grandchildren to play with . . .'

'But Tod, couldn't you have . . . I mean, people do, get together, just to have a baby . . . wouldn't it have been worth it?'

He was silent, and she wondered if she had said too much.

'I did think of it,' he said at last. 'But there was James, and . . . oh, it never seemed right, or possible. Now, of course, it might have been possible for us to adopt, or foster a child, but I don't know . . . would it have been fair to the child?'

'You'd have been a wonderful parent,' said Laura warmly.

'Who's to say? Nobody knows until they've tried it. It's hard enough, sometimes, for natural parents to get on with their children. It could be ten times harder with someone else's.'

'I get on with Mark . . .' Laura could not help smiling. She loved to speak of him, to hear her voice saying his name and feel its shape in the movement of her lips.

'Oh, well, Mark . . .'

'Don't you like him?' She could hear the defensive note creeping into her voice, tried again. 'He's difficult sometimes, I know. But when you get to know him . . .'

They were almost at Laura's gate. Tod slowed down.

'I've nothing against Mark, dear heart, and if he makes you happy then I'll think him perfect, like you do.'

'I see it more as me making him happy,' said Laura wistfully.

'Ah, that's a very different thing. Seductive, I grant you, but . . . not always as easy as it seems, and not always possible.'

'Is that a warning?'

'My *dear*!' Tod's eyebrows shot up. He transformed himself, instantly, back into the Tod she knew. 'You make me sound like some ghastly old *sibyl*, all cryptic and sinister. You mustn't listen to me. I've had so little to do with *boys*, thank heaven – not my cup of tea at *all*, which is a blessing in its way because what could be more embarrassing than knowing one's friends dare not leave their children in the same room with you – or should I say, with one? So difficult, and how the dear Royal Family *ever* cope with all that "one" business, I can't imagine!'

Laura saw that the moment for confidences was past.

'Will you come and have a cup of tea with one?' she asked lightly. 'And a piece of chocolate cake? You deserve it after all this exercise.'

He shook his head. 'Tempting, but no. I must go home and remove these *beastly* shoes before I get a corn, or a bunion, or whatever it is that makes people have to go round in *ghastly* tartan slippers all the time.'

He trotted off across the green, and Laura stood at the gate to watch him go. How strange, she thought, and how fascinating people were. For all these years she had taken Tod at his face value, and had even wondered, with perhaps a tinge of hurt feeling, why Anna had sometimes found him more helpful and comforting than Laura, who had been her friend since early childhood. Now she thought she understood. There was a great deal more to Tod than met the eye. I suppose that's true of everyone, really, she told herself. Even me? The idea made her smile. Her own character seemed so simple and straightforward to herself that she couldn't imagine anyone finding hidden depths in it.

The weather stayed changeable, sunny days interspersed with days of cloud that were grey but dry, so that vegetable gardens had to be watered. Busy and happy, Laura scarcely noticed the clouds, and her mind garnered memories of sun-filled days and warm evenings. Mark and his friends came and went; Laura heard herself making jokes about being a taxi service, while she quietly revelled in the pleasure of driving them to and from the station for trips to Brighton, to the town for cinema and shopping, or to each other's houses.

In early August, Jane and Anna went to Turkey with their various offspring, plus a friend of Toby's.

'It is a pity,' said Laura to Cassandra. They were sitting in Laura's garden one Saturday, one of the rare sunny days, their loungers set up in the dappled shade of a willow tree, a tray of cold fruit juice on the grass between them. 'Of course, those sort of holidays have to be booked months in advance, in fact I think they sorted it all out back in January, but if only they'd known, Jane said they'd happily have taken Mark with them. The villa's easily big enough, and it looks like a beautiful village. He gets on well with Ben; they would have been company for one another.'

'Mm,' said Cassandra, half asleep. 'Wouldn't have minded going myself, really. It looked idyllic in the brochure, and I've never been to Turkey. Still, Turkey in August would be terribly hot. I'm beginning to feel the heat now, even in England, so I don't think it would be a very good idea for me just now. And, of course, there's always a health risk in a hot climate. One does need to be careful what one eats.'

At twenty-three weeks, Cassandra was beginning to show her pregnancy. Rather to everyone's surprise, instead of hiding her bulge under the kind of beautifully cut maternity clothes she stocked in her shop, she had at an early stage moved into floating smocks that emphasised it. She might just as well, as Tod had remarked acidly, hang a fluorescent sign round her neck announcing 'I am pregnant'. She was inclined to patronise Laura, in the kindest possible way, and from a vantage point of at least seven weeks' more experience tended to offer advice as if she had been a veteran matron with half a dozen confinements to her credit.

'Oh, I wouldn't have gone,' said Laura. 'Edward couldn't get away at the moment, and I wouldn't want to go without him. No, it was just Mark. Daisy and Cassandra will share a room, of course, and Toby's got his friend Nick, Jane and Anna have a room each, but Ben's on his own. Jane did ask him if he wanted to take anyone else, but he couldn't think of anyone he wanted to invite at the time. Of course, he's quite a solitary boy, and always happy if he's got a book to read, but he and Mark do get on well, and it would have got him doing things more.'

'I don't think Ben really wants to do things much. Oh!' She jumped. 'Not like this little person here!' She laid her hand on her stomach. 'Obviously a born swimmer,' she said proudly. 'She's already practising her breast-stroke kick. Or is it the butterfly? It feels violent enough. Is yours kicking much yet? I suppose it's a bit soon.'

Laura smiled at the complacent tone. During the past week she had, in fact, experienced the first faint butterfly flutters she had been waiting for. So tentative, at first, that if she had not been on the watch for them she would have thought they were no more than the normal stirrings of her digestive system. She had found the tiny movements slightly unnerving. Thrilled though she was – and what woman could fail to be thrilled by the evidence of this new life, she asked herself – it was also a disquieting reminder that this was not just some part of herself, but a separate being. Someone who would have ideas, wishes, a will of his own. Mark had brought home a video of the film *Aliens* and she had watched it with him, then worked hard at not remembering how the alien creatures had burst forth from their host bodies . . . It seemed so ungrateful, almost wicked to fear the child she was carrying, but she did, perhaps because she was older and could see so clearly how their lives must be changed by him. Changed for the better, she told herself firmly. Meanwhile, she rested her mind on the thought of Mark, who was familiar and dear.

As if thinking of him had conjured his physical presence, Mark appeared at the door of the house and came towards them. He walked slowly, his habitual walk with the slightly bent knees and turned out feet that he cultivated, Laura thought fondly, because it looked tough. His head was down and his shoulders slightly hunched. He reached them, nodded a greeting to Cassandra, and collapsed into an ungainly sprawl on the grass between them, reaching automatically for a biscuit from the tray.

'Hullo, Mark. You look a bit down, darling. What's the matter?' Laura poured him some fruit juice into her own glass.

'Bored,' he growled.

'Poor old thing,' Laura sympathised. 'We were just saying it's a pity you couldn't have gone to Turkey with Ben and the others. What about Jay, isn't he around? You could give him a ring, ask him over. You know Anna said you could use the pool whenever you liked. We could go and pick him up if his mother's busy.'

'No thanks. Jay's a loser.'

'Oh?' Obviously Mark had fallen out with Jay. 'Had a row, have you? Is it worth it?'

He shrugged. 'No, not a row. He's just completely mateless.'

Laura refrained from further inquiry, knowing that it would be pointless. In Mark's world, all was black and white. There were friends, and there were not-friends. A friend was to be stood by, in adversity, to the utmost, but if he should in any way transgress Mark's own inflexible rules of behaviour, he would be excised from Mark's life.

'Anyone else? Or is everyone away at the moment?'

'Dunno.' He lapsed into silence, frowning at the grass. 'There's Tom,' he said in a more animated tone. 'He might be back by now.'

'Give him a ring, then. His mother works at weekends, doesn't she? He might like to come over, perhaps stay the night. We could do a barbecue, and you could have a day in Brighton tomorrow, if you like.'

'Ace. Thanks, Laura.' His smile flashed out, gilding the sunshine, and he loped back to the house.

'You spoil that boy,' said Cassandra lazily.

'Yes, I know. But I think it's good for him,' answered Laura cosily. 'I like to make a fuss of him, and he needs to know he's loved.'

'He's got a mother to love him.'

'I know he has. Of course,' said Laura earnestly. 'But she's not here, is she? And doesn't everyone need all the love they can get? Especially teenagers.'

159

'I suppose. What about Edward?'

'What do you mean, what about Edward?' Laura knew she sounded rather defensive; she was feeling a bit guilty about Edward.

'I mean, what does he think about Mark, what does he think about you spending your time clucking over him, and how is he anyway? He doesn't say much, of course, but I rather gathered that business isn't wonderful, still.'

'No, it isn't.' Laura felt the familiar cold wrenching in the pit of her stomach, and stifled it. 'As a matter of fact, it's appalling. That's why he's working on a Saturday. Of course, it's not just Edward,' she added. 'It's the same with everyone, and not just architects. Builders, plumbers, electricians, estate agents, conveyancers – they're all struggling, and some of them have gone to the wall. The big firms have cut their staff, but for the small firms and the one-man bands, like Edward, it's a bit dicey. Of course, he can cut his overheads as far as possible, and has done, but there's a limit . . .'

'Poor you.' Cassandra's voice was warm; she knew all about the problems of running a small business in a recession, although her own shop continued to do well. 'Could he work from home? Get rid of the expense of the office building? It must be far bigger than he needs.'

'It is, but it's not rented, he owns it. He bought it some years ago. It was a good investment, and after he'd done it up the profit seemed so good that he bought some other places – not big office blocks, just small places to do up – and let them, like he let the rest of his own building. It was great.' Laura fell silent, remembering that time when everything seemed so simple and secure. 'Now, of course, the tenants are going bankrupt one by one, the buildings are empty, and we're stuck with paying rates on them on top of the repayments for what we borrowed . . . No, I think you could say that business isn't wonderful.'

'Oh, Laura!' Cassandra sat up, appalled. 'I had no idea! I'm so sorry!'

'It's all right. I suppose I shouldn't really have told you, but that's how it is. The trouble is, Edward's so busy protecting me that he doesn't tell me, half the time, what's going on – I only found out by accident that our main tenants had done a bunk last month – and so we keep on pretending to one another that everything's all right. And maybe it will be,' she added optimistically. 'This recession can't go on for ever, surely. And the bank manager has been very good. Thank goodness he's been there for years, knows Edward well and knows he can trust him.'

'It's got to improve some time,' agreed Cassandra. 'You've hung on this long . . .'

'Yes. Anyway, you can see that Edward doesn't worry too much about Mark, and whether I spoil him or not.'

'I didn't mean . . .'

'No, but I do. I know I do. And yes, perhaps sometimes Edward does find it a bit irritating, though I can't believe he'd be jealous of his own son. But it's such a comfort, somehow. To feel that I can make him happy, even help him to learn to deal with the things he finds difficult, teach him to trust people . . .' Unaccountably, her eyes filled with tears, and she stopped speaking.

'Laura . . .' Cassandra got up, forgetting for once to heave herself carefully out of the lounger as if she were in the final stages of carrying triplets. She knelt at Laura's side and hugged her clumsily.

'It's all right.' Laura sniffed, blinked hard. 'I'm all right, love. To be honest, I try not to think of it, because I can't do anything to change how things are, and it seems to me the best way I can help Edward is by being cheerful and hoping for the best.'

'And spoiling Mark.' Cassandra gave her a little shake and a watery smile. 'Don't forget that.'

'As if I could! Darling Mark, what would I do without him to love?' Laura saw Cassandra's shocked face. 'Oh, there's the baby, of course,' she added quickly. 'And we're both thrilled to bits about him. But that's all in the future. I mean, it's lovely to think about him, but it's so unreal, so far ahead. Whereas Mark's here, and now.'

'He certainly is.' Cassandra withdrew her arms and stood up. Mark came across the lawn.

'Tom says he can come, and stay for two nights. If . . . if that's all right?'

'Of course it is! That's wonderful!' Laura put her feet to the ground. Mark shifted his feet, looking sideways at her pink eyes.

'Are you sure?'

Laura couldn't help glancing at Cassandra, inviting her to share her pleasure.

'Of course I'm sure. Lie down again and have a doze,' she said to Cassandra. 'I'll be back in half an hour, and if you're here I needn't bother to lock up.'

'OK. If I hear anything suspicious, I'll bark.' Cassandra lowered herself back on to the lounger, and closed her eyes.

'Good dog,' said Laura. 'Come on, Mark. Let's go and get Tom.'

161

Chapter 14

Laura had looked forward to the return of Anna, Jane and their children from Turkey, both for herself and on Mark's behalf. When it happened, however, it was a mixed blessing. The end of the summer holidays suddenly seemed, instead of remote beyond the horizon, to be only just round the corner. And just before the end of the holidays was the date set for Mark's mother to return to England, and for Mark himself to go back to London.

It seemed hardly possible, remembering how Laura had dreaded his arrival, that the thought of his departure should be so terrible to her, but it was. Mark himself seemed unmoved by the prospect of seeing his mother again – though naturally this was a subject Laura felt unable to broach with him. While he was easily downcast or cheered by small things, he showed nothing when confronted by major changes. Laura still found herself unable to decide whether his invariable lack of reaction to the things that happened to him was the result of control and the hiding of his feelings, or whether in fact the outside world simply washed over him like waves over a rock, and was less ignored than simply not noticed.

'It's going to be strange when Mark goes back,' she said to Daisy, who had had a row with Anna and was taking refuge and seeking sympathy in Laura's kitchen. Her black clothes, more bizarre than ever and featuring a satin corset trimmed with fronds of black lace, looked even less appropriate against the clear blue sky and brilliant sunshine outside. She was perched on her usual stool, scowling, while Laura sat at the table, working her way through preparing a huge pile of runner beans from the garden.

'Yeah,' she said, grumpily.

Laura worked on in silence. Daisy swung her booted feet, kicking them against the leg of the stool.

'Would you like anything to eat or drink?' Laura was tired of waiting for Daisy to say something.

'No. No, thanks,' she amended, as Laura raised her eyebrows. 'Oh, sorry, Laura.' Daisy tried a smile.

'That's all right. I'm in training for sulky teenagers,' said Laura mildly.

'I'm not sulky! At least,' Daisy was nothing if not fair, 'I don't mean to be. Not with you. Shall I help you with those?'

'Yes please. You know where the knives are. I'll do the fiddly strings down the sides, and you can do the slicing. It'll be therapeutic for you.'

Daisy fetched a knife and chopping board and sat down opposite Laura. 'Chunks, or little slivers?'

'Chunks, please. I think they have more flavour, especially if they're frozen, like these are going to be.' Laura sighed. The beans would be eaten during the winter, at meals where there would be no Mark to cook for. 'So, what's the matter?'

Daisy lined up a row of beans on the board, and hacked at them vindictively but, Laura was relieved to see, neatly.

'Oh, the usual,' she said gloomily. 'School, and all that.' She scooped up the pieces into a bowl, and lined up another row. 'We're both a bit twitchy about the results,' she admitted.

'GCSEs? That's next week, isn't it? I thought you were fairly confident about them?'

'Well, I was. But you know how it is – the nearer they come, the more I keep remembering the things I did wrong. I started off thinking I'd get fairly good grades, but now I'm beginning to wonder whether I'll even pass them.'

'Of course you will. You did well in your mocks, didn't you? And they always make those a bit more difficult, I've heard. It'll be fine, and even if you've done less well on one or two, you know you did your best.'

'Yes, I did,' said Daisy emphatically. 'I really did. Only nobody believes me.'

'Why not?' asked Laura, who knew the answer.

'Well . . . my report wasn't very good, if you remember. In fact, it was pretty crap. All that "doesn't try hard enough" and "could do better" and . . .' She paused, looking sideways at Laura.

'And "playing around in class"?' Laura finished for her. Daisy grinned.

'And that, too. I thought you'd know about it, you sneaky godmother, you.'

'And do you? Play around, I mean?'

'A bit. Um, quite a lot. But not all the time, and not in every subject.'

'So was the report fair?'

'I suppose so.' Daisy was grudging. 'I was a bit disappointed with it,' she added honestly. 'But it isn't really the report that matters just now, is it? It's the results that count. Only, if they're bad . . .'

164

'They'll be proved right?'

'Yes. It's hell, isn't it?'

'Just a bit. But it'll be all right, you'll see.'

'Yeah. I do think so, really, but . . . my bloody housemistress said it was touch-and-go whether I'd make it through the sixth form. That's what Mummy's started niggling on about. The nearer we are to going back to school, the worse she gets.'

'Are you surprised? There's not much point in going back at all if you're going to get yourself thrown out.'

'But I'm not! Anyone would think I *wanted* to be expelled!'

Her tone was aggrieved.

'Of course nobody thinks that. They just want to be sure you won't be. If you ask me, your housemistress just wants to give you a little jolt, now, to remind you that they really do mean what they say with all those rules about smoking and drinking and so on. After all, you get quite a lot more freedom in the sixth form, don't you?'

'Yes, but I'm going to be sensible. I really am.'

'Great, then you've got nothing to worry about.' Laura handed over the last few beans for slicing.

'You make it all sound so easy,' said Daisy, between irritation and relief. 'Would you be this calm about it if I were yours?'

'Well, Mark's report was pretty appalling,' said Laura cheerfully. 'It does worry me, but I don't see much future in nagging him about it. Luckily, it's much more difficult to be expelled from a state school.'

'And he won't be at this school next term anyway, will he?'

'No.' Laura didn't like being reminded of that. 'I wish he were a bit less paranoid about school,' she said. 'I mean, you seem to be able to admit that some of the things your report said were not completely unfair, but he regards anything remotely resembling a criticism as some kind of unprovoked attack. He just says "Oh, they all hate me", but quite casually, as if it didn't really matter.'

'He doesn't really expect to be liked by teachers. Or want to be. Well, who does, really?'

'Except it's surely better to have them on your side. I sometimes think Mark actually sets out to antagonise them. Then it all becomes a kind of circular issue, doesn't it? The teachers hate me, therefore I don't get good grades. I don't get good grades, so the teachers hate me. And then, of course, it's not worth even trying to work, because he thinks it won't get him anywhere. And that gives him a good let-out, none of it is his fault, and he can go on telling himself that he could have done well, only they wouldn't let him. I think he's frightened of finding that he actually can't do it, and it's easier not to try than to have a go and fail.'

Daisy, who liked Mark for Laura's sake and also in the way an older girl is pleased by the admiration of an attractive younger boy, was impressed.

'You've put a lot of thought into this, haven't you? I expect you're right, but what's the answer?'

'If I only knew!' Laura tipped the bean parings into a bowl for the chickens. 'He seems to find it so difficult to relate to adults. Well, not so much difficult as unthinkable, really. I'm not sure that he thinks of adults as people at all.'

'Oh, surely . . . he likes you, anyway. And Edward. And he gets on all right with Mummy and Jane and even Caz. Doesn't he talk to you?'

'Yes, a bit,' admitted Laura. 'In the car, sometimes. He can be quite chatty. I think he's improved while he's been here, don't you? He seems more open and friendly than when he arrived. A bit less suspicious.'

'Yes, I think so. He's had a good time, and you've certainly been good to him.'

'It's like trying to tame a wild animal,' admitted Laura with a laugh. 'It's all done by kindness. But it's a long, slow job.'

The day approached. Laura planned the last meals, and had a barbecue at the weekend for all his friends. She also invited everyone else who had come to the barbecue she had given the first weekend of his stay. It seemed fitting that they, her closest friends, should be there at the end as well as at the beginning, and she needed the distraction they provided. The evening turned into a proper celebration, as Daisy's and Candida's GCSE results had come two days earlier. To everyone's pleasure and, perhaps, surprise, they both did well, Daisy getting five As and four Bs, and Candida the other way round. A few days later, Laura took Mark shopping to buy clothes for the coming winter. She knew she should be economising – Edward had taken to tucking bank statements, unopened, into his briefcase to open at the office, and he was sleeping badly – but her mood was reckless.

In the car coming home, Mark was unusually talkative, pleased with his clothes and with the computer game Laura had bought him. There were so many things that Laura wanted to say to him, many of them things she knew she would be unable or unwise to say, that her head seemed to be jammed with them. Was he conscious of this? she wondered, and was his chattering designed to prevent her from saying anything intrusive or embarrassing? She found it hard to believe that he could be so empathic, and told herself that she should just enjoy his openness without worrying about its cause.

'. . . just like Arnie in *Kindergarten Cop*,' concluded Mark with relish, and Laura realised with a guilty start that she had not been listening to him.

'Who is?'

'The teacher at my little school. When I was small.'

'But I thought you liked Arnie?'

'Yes, but she was a *woman*. Anyway, Arnie was wet in that. He should have blown them all away – d-d-d-d-d-d-.' He mimed a Kalashnikov. 'They were the pits.'

'I thought they were rather sweet. Don't you like children, Mark?'

'Ner.' He drew out the word in disgust.

'You were little, once.'

'Yes, well, I didn't know any better, did I?'

'You'll feel differently when you have children of your own.'

'I won't. I'm never going to have children.'

'People your age always feel like that, but you'll feel differently when you're older.'

'No.' He spoke abruptly and with complete conviction.

'Why not?'

'I don't . . . I wouldn't want my children to go through that.'

'Oh, Mark. Was it as bad as that?' Laura was appalled, and rather scared. Was he implying that he had been . . . what was the current word . . . abused? And if so, what should she do about it?

He shrugged. 'I dunno. It wasn't so bad, but . . . I didn't enjoy it.'

Laura was torn between relief and sadness. 'But it doesn't have to be like that, Mark. That's what it's all about. We try to give our children something better than we had ourselves.'

'Uh.' She could see that he was not convinced.

'Childhood doesn't have to be dismal,' she said firmly, 'and children don't have to be obnoxious.'

'Well, some of them are all right,' he admitted grudgingly. 'I like Toby, he's cool, but when they're little all they do is cry and dribble and smell.'

'Oh dear! You should have warned me sooner!' Laura patted her tummy. It was beginning to round out now that she was into her eighteenth week.

'Oh, well . . . that one will be all right, I expect.' He still sounded dubious.

'I certainly hope so. I wouldn't want you not to come and see us because we had a screaming, smelly baby.'

He hunched his shoulders. 'Can I?'

'What, come and see us? Oh Mark, of course. You can come here any time. Give us a ring, or just turn up if you want to. I shall miss you when you go.'

'Will you?' He sounded surprised.

'Of course I will! And so will Edward.' Careful, she thought. Don't get too emotional.

'Oh. Well, I'll come, then. If I can.'

His tone was faintly smug, and Laura smiled. 'Oh Mark, you *are* kind. How *very* good of you.'

He grinned, and they reached the house in good spirits. Mark dashed off to fetch Ben to come and try out the new computer game. Laura set about preparing supper, a rather more elaborate meal than usual in honour of Mark's imminent departure. She had onions, garlic and ginger frying to make her version of satay sauce, and was busy threading chunks of marinaded beef on to skewers when the phone rang. Giving her hands a cursory rinse, she picked up the receiver.

'Hello?' Anxiously she reached out and pushed the browning onions around. There was a short silence, then: 'Hello? Is that . . . is that Mrs Melville?'

'Yes, it is.' The voice was well bred, quite high-pitched, a strange combination of the forceful and the hesitant.

'This is . . . I'm Georgia Alcantara. Mark's mother,' she added, unnecessarily.

'Oh. Oh, goodness, yes! You're back today, aren't you? I expect you'd like to speak to Mark, wouldn't you? I'm afraid he's just gone to a friend's house, but he should be back in a few minutes. Shall I ask him to phone you?'

'No, it's all right. I'll see him tomorrow.' How strange, thought Laura. If I'd been parted from Mark for all these months, I wouldn't be able to wait to speak to him. 'It's about tomorrow I was ringing, really. I gather Mark's got rather a lot of luggage.'

'Yes, I'm afraid he has.' Laura found herself sounding apologetic. 'I hope you don't disapprove of him having a computer – Edward wanted to give him something, a proper present, it's been a good ice-breaker with the other kids at school and it's quite educational, really . . .'

'No, of course. It's very kind of you both.' Her voice was calmly polite, devoid of real gratitude. 'It just makes the journey more difficult.'

168

'No, he can't very well go by train,' agreed Laura. 'I think Edward is expecting to drive him up on Sunday. Tomorrow.' Goodness, she thought, I must pull myself together. I sound like a complete half-wit.

'Yes, I know. It's very kind of him, but . . .'

But you don't want him to visit your house, and with me in tow too, probably, looking around and criticising . . . I suppose I don't really blame you for that.

'I'm afraid Mark would be disappointed if he had to leave things behind,' Laura pointed out. 'Perhaps we could send them to you – some kind of special delivery—'

'Oh no, I wouldn't dream of it.' The high, light voice was firm. 'I just wondered whether it would be better if I came to fetch him.'

And have a look at *my* house, thought Laura with a flash of amusement. Why didn't I think of that one? I suppose she'd like to see where her son's been all this time. You'd think she'd have checked it out before he arrived, rather than now when it's too late. I wonder what he told her in his letters? At Edward's and her insistence, Mark had written every week to his mother, with much groaning and sighing and chewing of his pen. Well, I've got nothing to hide.

'Of course! I should have suggested it, only I thought you'd be too tired after all your travelling.'

'If you're sure it's all right? I can understand that you might not want to meet me.' The words were stiff, without apology.

'After all this time?' Laura forced a smile on to her face, knowing that it would come through to her voice. 'That seems a bit silly, don't you think?' You may be younger than me, but I don't fear you! she thought. Not as a rival for Edward, at any rate, though as Mark's mother . . . 'It's Mark who matters now, isn't it? And now that he's got to know us, wouldn't it perhaps be better for him if we could all, well, get along, as it were?'

'Thank you. It probably would.' Georgia spoke with an assumption, at least, of civilised gratitude. 'I hope he's behaved all right with you?'

'Oh yes, he's been great,' said Laura. 'No trouble at all. We've enjoyed having him.' Careful, she thought. Mustn't rub her nose in it. It won't do to antagonise her. 'Of course, they always behave better in other people's houses than they do at home, don't they?'

'One likes to think so.' There was a dry humour in her voice that Laura found not unattractive.

'Have you had a good trip?'

'Oh – yes, thank you. Successful, at least.' She sounded faintly startled by the question, and Laura wondered if she was being too matey.

169

'Good. Well, if you're sure you don't want Mark to ring you . . . ?'

'No, he hates talking on the phone. He just grunts, so it's never very satisfactory.'

'Well . . . we'll see you tomorrow, then. Do you want directions? The village is quite well signed, and the house is on the green. It's the cream one, with arched windows.'

'Thanks, I'll find it.' She was brusque again, in control. 'I'll be with you at about eleven, if that's all right.'

'Yes, of course. Er, see you then.'

'Yes. Bye.'

She had rung off. I could have invited her to stay for lunch, thought Laura. Better not, though. Mustn't push her too hard, and I expect Edward would have hated it. And Mark might have been embarrassed. She looked round the room, mentally reviewing the rest of the house. I'll get some fresh flowers for the hall, she decided, and perhaps a few more for the sitting room? She went for the secateurs.

When the knock came at the door on Sunday morning, Edward and Mark were upstairs packing up the computer in its box. They had meant to do it the night before, but the meal had finished late – they had all been reluctant for it to end, and had sat over it for a long time. Every time Laura thought of saying goodbye to Mark her throat tightened, and she cursed the hormonal imbalances of pregnancy that made her even more weepy than usual.

Laura opened the door. On the step was a tall, rather thin woman, with Mark's dark hair, but without the strong eyebrows that gave his face its forceful look. What she had in full measure, however, was his air of withdrawing, a rather prickly separateness that the demonstrative Laura instinctively found chilling. Though under the circumstances, she thought, it was hardly surprising that she – Mark's mother – should seem distant. She stuck out her hand abruptly.

'Hello,' she said in her tight, high voice. 'I'm Georgia Alcantara. They call me George.'

Who were they? Laura wondered. Don't be silly, she scolded herself, it's just a manner of speaking. She took the large, bony hand and shook it.

'Laura Melville,' she said simply. 'Come in. Mark's upstairs, just finishing his packing. I'll call him.'

'Thank you.' Georgia came in. Her dark hair was cut short in a style that was more tidy than attractive, and she wore a man's checked shirt over her jeans. Her tanned face was free of make-up, her lips dry and slightly chapped. Laura, who hated her lips to be dry and who had Lypsyls in every handbag and Barbour pocket, longed to present her with one and beg her to use it.

'Would you like a cup of coffee after the drive? And perhaps . . .' She indicated the cloakroom.

'No, I'm fine. But I'd love the coffee, thank you.' She followed Laura into the kitchen. 'You have a beautiful house,' she said politely, though Laura had seen how carefully she had refrained from turning her head to look properly.

'Thank you. Milk? Sugar?'

'No sugar, thanks.' At Laura's gesture she went to the table but did not sit down. Her eyes kept sliding sideways to Laura, and down. Laura suddenly realised what she was looking at, but hesitated to ask.

'Mark didn't tell you, then?' She laid a hand on her bulge.

'No. Mark's letters – and I'm sure I have you and . . . and your husband to thank for those – weren't very informative. He only told me about school, though not much. And there was quite a bit about Ben, and Daisy, and all of them. So, you're . . . ?'

'Yes, I'm expecting a baby. In January.' Laura found that she was obscurely pleased that Mark had written nothing about her and Edward. She liked to think that whatever relationship they had achieved had been a private thing. 'After all these years,' she said, with a proud lilt in her voice. 'Mark must have brought us luck.'

'That's nice.' The trite words fell flat, like tossed pancakes uncaught.

'Yes. We're very happy about it,' said Laura primly, pouring boiling water into the coffeepot. 'Here they are,' she added, unnecessarily but with relief.

Mark and Edward came into the room.

'Hi, Mum.'

'Hello, Mark darling.' The endearment seemed slightly unnatural, and they made no move to embrace or even to approach one another. Laura, rather shocked, quickly poured out coffee and handed the mugs round. Edward and Georgia exchanged stiff 'Hellos', and Edward came to stand next to Laura by the Aga. She had the feeling that he would have liked to clutch at her hand, and she smiled at him. Perhaps he thought they had been talking about him – comparing notes, she thought with a little amusement. Not very likely, somehow, at least not with someone like Georgia. Laura couldn't imagine her having the kind of giggling, female gossip that she sometimes enjoyed with Jane, Anna or Cassandra.

The car – a Citroën Deux Chevaux – was loaded with Mark's new

171

possessions. In his room the desk stood forlorn and empty, and there were faint sticky marks on the walls where his posters had been stuck. He had offered, rather touchingly, to strip the bed for her, but Laura had said no. She would do it tomorrow, or the next day, when the sight of those bare pillows and mattress and duvet might seem less final, more like an ordinary washing day.

Tactfully, Georgia made her goodbyes and got into the car. Mark stood looking at them. His usual stance when he felt uncomfortable was so dear and familiar that Laura longed to take him in her arms and soothe away the defensively crossed arms, the raised shoulders and lowered head, and the frowning blank face that hid – what? Sadness, relief, or nothing at all but the discomfort of not knowing what to say? As a compromise she put her hands lightly on his shoulders.

'Safe journey, Mark, and have a good term at school. Come back and see us whenever you like, won't you? We'll keep in touch.'

'Yeah. Uh, thank you, Laura. It's been great. Really.' For Laura, used to his inarticulate struggles to express himself, it was the equivalent of ten minutes of flowery speech. She stretched her eyes wide and forced herself to keep smiling.

'Brace yourself, Mark,' she said cheerfully, 'I'm going to kiss you.' She had never before dared to attempt such a caress, and half expected him to recoil, but when she touched her lips to his cheek – still almost childishly smooth – he turned his face a little and she felt the movement of his lips against her own cheek as he kissed her also.

Unable to speak, but still smiling, she moved back to give place to Edward. Solemnly the two shook hands, then Edward, to Laura's relief and pleasure, did what she had not been able to do and hugged him.

'Goodbye, Mark. Let us know how you're getting on – you know you can always ring and reverse the charges. And come back, if you can . . . if you have time, I mean. You know. Whenever.'

'Yeah. Thanks, Edward.'

The husky voice was low, the words spoken as Mark was already turning away. She looked at Edward, almost unbearably moved. At last, she thought. Not Dad – that would have been too difficult, perhaps, but Edward. Like the others – like Ben, and Daisy, and all of them. At last.

They stood side by side as the car drove away, then went back indoors. In the house Laura wept in Edward's arms, and he comforted her.

'He called you Edward! You don't mind – that it wasn't Dad, I mean?'

'No. Edward's better. I'm not sure that I really feel like his father, after all these years, and I don't suppose he really feels like my son. But at least I have a name. I'm – a person.'

'A friend. And what's more important than that? Oh dear Mark, I shall miss him so much!'

'I know you will, darling. You've been sweet to him, I'm so grateful . . .'

'Was he happy here, do you think?'

'Of course he was. Why wouldn't he be? You did so much, and there was Ben, and Daisy, and all the others. He'll come back, don't worry.'

'If she'll let him.'

'She will, of course she will. He'll be back.' He seemed more relaxed than he had been for a long time. Was he relieved, Laura wondered, that Mark had gone? She could not deny that it had always seemed to her that Edward endured, rather than enjoyed, Mark's presence in their house. Perhaps now, she hoped, things would be different. Next time Mark comes . . . 'And meanwhile,' said Edward firmly, 'we've got our own little Oscar to look forward to.'

As if recognising his name, the baby moved inside her; nothing vigorous enough to be called a kick, but a stirring definite enough for Edward to feel it too. He laughed.

'There you are! Oscar's telling you he'll look after you. Come on, love. I'll make the lunch – as long as it's soup and you've already made it.'

Laura mopped her eyes and blew her nose.

'Strangely enough it is, and I have. Come on, then, you can make the toast.'

'It's a deal.'

Chapter 15

It seemed to Laura that she began to feel less than well as soon as Mark had left.

'You've been overdoing it,' scolded Jane, who called round one sunny September afternoon to see if Laura would like to come and walk the dog with her, and found Laura lying pale and limp on the sofa. 'All that running around after Mark, and standing over the Aga in the heat, it was too much for you. Do you want me to call the doctor?'

'Good heavens, no!' Laura struggled to sit up. 'There's nothing wrong. No bleeding or anything, I mean, and the midwife checked my blood pressure only two days ago and it was fine. I suppose I am a bit tired, or something. But then I *am* what they call an "elderly primigravida", so I suppose I'm entitled to be.'

'What nonsense. Forty-two is no age at all. I was nearly that when I had Toby, and don't give me all that rubbish about first babies – it's much harder work being pregnant when you've got a four-year-old and a six-year-old both demanding constant attention as well! For heaven's sake lie down again. I'll go away if you're sleepy, but if not, Slops can perfectly well wait for her walk, and I'll stay and chat.'

'Oh yes,' said Laura, who for the first time in her life had been conscious of feeling lonely, 'that would be lovely. Are you sure, though? Poor old Slops, it seems a bit unfair.'

'Nonsense. One of the kids will take her out after school. I was only going because it's such a lovely day, and I knew I should be doing some weeding. Talking to you will be much nicer, it seems ages since we've had a proper heart to heart, without any of the kids around.'

'Yes,' said Laura rather forlornly.

'You look very peaky,' said Jane critically, surveying her. 'Did you have any lunch?'

'No,' admitted Laura guiltily. 'I wasn't very hungry, and I couldn't be bothered.'

'Silly girl! I'll go and do you a boiled egg, if you could eat it? You ought to have something.' Her managing tone betrayed her anxiety. Laura smiled wanly.

'Thank you, Nanny,' she said primly. 'With soldiers?'

'If you're good,' was the austere response.

Laura had to admit that when she had eaten the egg, dipping the strips of lightly buttered toast into the runny yolk with all the enjoyment of a five-year-old, she did feel rather better. Still on her sofa, she sipped a cup of tea and said so.

'Good,' said Jane, kicking off her shoes and curling up in an armchair. 'You must take proper care of yourself. Surely they've told you all that, haven't they?'

'Yes, but I feel so limp, and I just can't be bothered to cook when it's only for me.'

'I know it's a bore, but you must make the effort,' said Jane, making a mental note to make some individual portions of soup and put them in Laura's freezer. 'I don't want to be worrying about your eating habits when I'm only just over worrying about Ben's.'

Laura seized on the change of subject.

'Yes, how is he? Did he eat well in Turkey? I thought he was looking much better when they last went swimming, not nearly so bony.'

'No, isn't it a relief! You know, he really had more or less to force himself to eat at first. His appetite was quite gone and he felt full after two mouthfuls. Turkey was good, though – he liked the kebabs, and all the different starters, and in spite of the heat he ate much more. And there were ice creams, of course, on the beach, and a glass or two of beer with the evening meal. I suppose he's a bit young for it, really, but it did seem to help him relax, and most of them seem to be drinking by now. I'd rather he did it under my eye than going off and getting plastered – though he's done that once or twice as well.' Jane paused. She wasn't sure whether Laura knew that both those episodes had been in Mark's company. Although she still felt a residue of gratitude to Mark for shocking Ben into awareness of what he was doing to himself, she was far from sure that Mark was altogether a good influence.

Laura, who did know, was inclined to take the incidents lightly. The effect on Mark had been to send him into a profound sleep, from which he had woken the following morning heavy-eyed and silent. He had obviously hoped that his late return from what had been supposed to be an evening at Ben's house might pass unnoticed, though Laura had, in fact, removed his boots when she found him snoring face-down on his bed, fully clothed and reeking of beer and cigarette smoke. She had also put a towel beneath his head, and left a plastic bowl strategically positioned on the floor beside him.

He had appeared, rather sheepishly, late the following day, and thanked her gruffly for looking after him.

'I did think you were going to Ben's for the evening,' said Laura mildly.

'I did!' His face was exaggeratedly innocent, and Laura laughed.

'Oh, come on, Mark! Don't tell me you sat there smoking and drinking in Ben's room, with Toby snooping around and Jane wondering who was setting off the smoke alarms! Listen, love,' she said more seriously, 'I don't mind you having a fling, within reason, as long as you're not doing anything illegal that's likely to get you or Ben into trouble, but I'd rather know where you are than have you lie to me.'

'I'm not lying! I did go to Ben's. We'd bought some cans of beer in town in the afternoon, and we went up to the forest. Jane said we could take some sausages, and cook them up there on a camp fire, so we did.'

'It sounds fun,' said Laura. 'Did Ben get back all right?'

'Yes. He was sick. I made sure he got home,' said Mark virtuously. 'I wasn't sick,' he added, rather proudly. 'I'm hard, me.'

Laura had discussed it with Edward, who had been inclined to dismiss the whole thing.

'Better not to make too much of a fuss about it,' he said. 'All boys do things like this sooner or later. After all, we let him have the odd beer at home, so we can hardly complain if he does a bit of experimenting. A few evenings being sick as a dog, and mornings of hangovers, will teach them both more than any lecture on the evils of drink. Within reason, of course. Beer is one thing, but if you start finding empty vodka bottles we'd better crack down hard.'

'Ben was all right, wasn't he?' Laura asked now. 'I didn't talk to you about it at the time, but I discussed it with Edward and he seemed to think it was a fairly normal part of growing up.'

'He was very sick,' grimaced Jane. 'I wasn't really worried about it, except that I did wonder whether it was another manifestation of being upset over Bill. I tried to ask him, but he just clammed up and more or less told me to mind my own business.'

'Oh dear. But he didn't drink too much in Turkey?'

'No, and I stopped worrying then, because it's all so cheap out there, he could have got absolutely plastered every evening if he'd wanted, for not much more than the cost of a couple of Cornettos.'

'And does he seem any happier in himself? How does he feel about Bill?'

Jane sighed. 'He's still refusing to see him. Candy and Toby went to London twice during the holidays to have a day with him, but when it came to it Ben refused to go, and even to speak to him on the phone. He's terribly bitter and resentful. He admired his father so much – they all did, but Ben in particular because Bill was clever, like him, and their minds worked in the same way. He can't understand why his father won't explain things to him.'

'What's to explain?' asked Laura cynically. 'I mean, how can you justify it?'

'I know, going off with someone from the office after eighteen years of marriage does take a certain amount of explaining to one's children. But you know Ben. In many ways he's very adult. I truly believe that if Bill had said to him, quite honestly, "Look, Ben, I've fallen madly in love with this woman, I know it's hard to understand but I just can't live without her, it doesn't mean I love you children any less, I'm not happy about the way things are but I hope you'll try to understand and we can work things out between us", something like that, I think he could have learned to accept it. He wouldn't have liked it, but he would have made an effort to understand. But instead, all Bill says is that things had been bad between us for years – which they *hadn't* been, and you know you can't hide a thing like that from your children – and that he can't understand why Ben is making such a fuss about it. As far as he's concerned it's happened, he's got what he wanted, and nothing else matters. The others have accepted it, more or less, but Ben's never been able to accept anything just like that, on someone's say-so. Remember how he was as a little boy, with that business of the colours?'

Laura laughed. 'As if I could ever forget! He talked about it for weeks, and about a year later he suddenly turned to me one day, and said he'd thought of another way of testing it! I had the devil's own job persuading him it still wouldn't work!'

Ben, at the age of five, had somehow latched on to the idea that when other people saw colours, they might not be seeing the same colours as he did, that their perception of 'red' might be what he called 'blue'. The problem had niggled at his mind like an aching tooth: he had devised endless methods of testing this theory, always coming up against the barrier of never being able to get inside someone else's head to see what they saw, as they saw it. At the time they had all thought he might become a scientist, but now it seemed that it was the philosophical rather than the physical implications that had fascinated him.

'Poor Ben,' said Laura. 'He must be missing his father.'

'Yes, he is. But he's missing the father he used to have, not the one he has now. And no one,' said Jane sadly, 'can give that father back to him. Did he even exist, Laura? I find myself wondering, sometimes. That man I was married to all those years, was he real? Is he still there inside the awful person he is now? I have this image of him, trapped inside a strange shell, fighting to get out, calling to me to help him . . . I dream about it, sometimes.' She stopped, and swallowed. 'I suppose it's just that people change,' she resumed, more steadily.

'Of course they do,' said Laura, who couldn't imagine Edward ever changing.

'Only . . . what if he changes back?'

Laura looked at her helplessly. She knew, of course, that husbands in their early fifties who went off with someone else frequently did return a few years later and want to be readmitted to the nest.

Jane shook her head, and laughed. 'Sorry – getting too deep, I'm afraid! The truth is that however well you know somebody, or think you do, there must always be aspects of them that you haven't discovered, for one reason or another. I ought to know that by now – I'm continually discovering things about my children that astonish me, and I thought I knew them inside out.'

'Maybe the things are always there, but hidden, and then something triggers them. I mean, if Bill hadn't gone off, you wouldn't have been the way you are now, would you? But all that strength and independence was there all the same. You just didn't need to bring them out. Oh!' Laura felt suddenly exhausted, and yawned widely. 'Oh, I'm sorry! It must be the food or something, making me feel so sleepy.'

Jane looked pleased. 'Well, a little doze will be good for you. I'll go and take Slops for her walk now. And for goodness' sake take care of yourself!'

Laura promised that she would. It seemed to her that, apart from her occasional lapses with regard to eating at lunch-time, she could scarcely be more careful. Edward cherished her almost to the point of distraction, trying with some success to anticipate her every move, and doing so much for her that she laughingly said she was in danger of losing the use of her limbs.

The weeks drifted by, with little to mark their passing except the routines of clinics and visits by the midwife and the doctor, who frequently dropped in as a friend at the end of the day. Laura admitted to him that she felt lethargic, full of minor aches and pains, and was frequently a bit nauseous, all of which he nodded over and dismissed with a wave of his hand, confident that all the necessary tests and checks had been done,. What she did not tell him, because it made her obscurely ashamed, was that she also felt low, depressed and filled with intangible forebodings, which were much more difficult to bear than the physical problems because she felt unable to acknowledge them even to Edward.

A short visit by Mark at half-term cheered her. Remembering what his mother had said about the telephone, she had chosen to keep in touch with him by letter, knowing that he would not reply, but feeling that at least she could communicate in this way better than she could to a silent telephone receiver.

Mark was able to stay only one night, and Jane insisted on cooking supper for all of them to save Laura from extra effort. Laura was grateful, of course, and naturally she realised that Mark would want to see Daisy, Ben and Candida, but she found the evening exhausting, and she regretted that she scarcely had a chance to speak to Mark at all. She thought he had grown taller, and he seemed both more grown-up and more silent. When he left for the station the following day she kissed him goodbye as a matter of course, and was happy that he appeared not only to accept, but even to expect, that she should do so.

The last days of October were grey and dismal. It did not rain but the skies were often so heavily overcast that the day seemed darker than the night. Laura, wandering desultorily round the house, felt from time to time a feeling that was neither a pain nor an ache, but a tightening across her stomach that was strong enough to make her stop and breathe until the discomfort had passed.

'Braxton Hicks,' she told herself wisely. 'Nothing to worry about.' Cassandra, who was going to weekly ante-natal classes with the National Childbirth Trust, had passed on these gems to Laura, who had not felt well enough to go yet, and she knew that such practice contractions were to be expected. Nevertheless, when a second one came an hour or two later, she thought it best to lie down for a while.

During the afternoon it happened twice more, but by the time Edward came home, at seven o'clock, several hours had passed without anything happening. He looked pale and anxious, and she guessed that things at the office were worse than usual. Feeling cowardly, she did not ask him, thinking that she needed to protect herself from any outside worries, and knowing that he preferred not to have the added strain of pretending to her that everything was fine. After two not very well soda-ed whiskies, some of the tension leached out of him, and over a supper of casserole and the summer's runner beans from the freezer, with jacket potatoes and a salad, he became quite chatty. Their conversation, however, was confined to the books they were currently reading, and a documentary on the television. Laura put the contractions out of her mind, fearing to bring the anxiety back into his eyes, those hazel eyes that were so like Mark's.

She slept heavily, but woke feeling tired and leaden and with faint twinges of backache, the muscles in legs and arms protesting at every movement. It had been some time since she had been to an early session at the pool, although she still went two or three times a week during the day. Perhaps I'll go this afternoon, she thought. To swim gently up and down in the warm blue water, with the unaccustomed weight of her bulge supported by it, might ease some of the aches. She knew from the past how exercise could, surprisingly, refresh tired muscles and restore energy.

During the morning she forced herself into effort, grimly pushing a trolley round Sainsbury's and stocking up with all the things she had run low on, like tins of cat food, washing-up liquid, lavatory cleaner and bin-bags. It was boring but necessary, the more so since she no longer allowed herself to buy the little treats she used to get as a reward. She did not need Edward to tell her that they could not really afford a packet of smoked trout, a pot of duck paté, or a box of dark Belgian chocolates.

The trolley had misaligned wheels and veered infuriatingly to the left. It hadn't seemed so bad at first, but by the time she had weighed it down with two dozen tins of cat food, it was exhibiting a malign wilfulness that made its very handle seem to be grinning evilly at her. Laura, wrestling furiously with it round corners, knew that she should have changed it for another, but now the prospect of bending to transfer twenty-four tins to a second trolley seemed more than she could manage.

The store, which was familiar enough to be, if not precisely friendly, at least fairly unstressful, was undergoing a reorganisation of its chilled and frozen departments. For some reason these were being moved, which meant that practically every type of commodity had been re-sited in strange and sometimes illogical places. Laura, moving automatically to the place where she had always bought washing-up liquid, found herself instead staring bemusedly at an array of tinned fish. Around her, other customers muttered irritably to themselves. They all seemed to be elderly, and the confusion made them slower and more indecisive than usual, so that every aisle was clotted with indignant groups, their trolleys sticking out at angles as they shared their annoyance or recondite information as to the whereabouts of tinned rice pudding. Laura longed for Mark to go skidding through them on the trolley like a ball in a bowling alley.

There were long queues for the checkouts. Laura, her trolley quiescent but radiating a kind of recalcitrant truculence, shifted from foot to foot and longed to sit down. Or, better still, lie down. The shiny floor was cold and hard. She began to wonder what she could use to cushion it – packets of disposable nappies, perhaps, or hundreds of bags of cotton-wool balls? She smiled at the picture, then drew in a sharp breath and bent forward slightly as a ripple of contraction spread across her stomach with the unstoppable inevitability of a tidal wave.

'You all right, love?'

Laura looked round to see the person behind her, a round woman of late middle-age, peering at her with small kind eyes. She had fawn-coloured hair that almost exactly matched her fawn-coloured face, which was liberally sprinkled with long pale whiskery hairs, giving her the look of some little creature like a hamster or a guinea-pig that was curiously reassuring. She was dressed in the kind of ageless brown wool coat, bulging at elbows and hips, that seemed not to have changed since the fifties.

'You all right, dear?' she repeated, tilting her head. Did Laura imagine that the button nose quivered and the whiskers twitched? Even her voice sounded furry.

'Yes, thank you. Just a bit of a twinge,' said Laura, smiling.

'Only you want to be careful in your condition. These nasty heavy trolleys, and all that tinned stuff. You want to get your man to fetch that in for you.' Her calm assumption, in these days of single parenthood, that any pregnant woman must have a supportive man in the background, was as cosy as a plate of hot buttered toast.

'He would, if I asked him, but he's so busy,' confided Laura. 'I shall leave it in the car when I get home, though, and get him to carry it indoors.'

'That's good, then. Baby coming soon, is he, the little love?'

'No, I'm only twenty-six weeks. Just under seven months,' amended Laura, sensing that the more old-fashioned way of calculating a pregnancy was appropriate here. 'Quite a way to go, yet.'

'Thought you were a bit small,' nodded the woman, 'though not everyone shows it, specially if they're carrying high. Keeping well, are you?'

'Oh, yes,' said Laura automatically, then, 'well, all right. It gets a bit tiring, sometimes, and it's my first, you see. Rather late in life, really,' she laughed a bit self-consciously.

'Nonsense, dear. Plenty of time, yet. Just so long as you don't do yourself a mischief with that nasty trolley.'

'It does seem to have a mind of its own,' admitted Laura ruefully as the queue shuffled forward and she tried to push the trolley up.

'Beastly thing, it only wants to go sideways.'

'Ah, been a crab in another life, I shouldn't wonder. Here, let me move it. I don't stand any nonsense from Things.' She gave the word a distinct capital letter, as if the trolley were a denizen from the planet Thing, as perhaps it was.

When they reached the till, Laura's new friend insisted on hurrying off for a different trolley. She also, with a calm imperiousness wonderful to behold, summoned a spotty youth from the mysterious offices 'out the back' to pack the shopping into bags and take it to Laura's car.

'In America,' she informed Laura chattily, 'they do that everywhere, you know. Can't hardly lift a finger for yourself in a shop, over there.'

'Did you go there on holiday?' asked Laura, with visions of a visit to Disneyworld with a gaggle of grandchildren.

'No, I lived there, dear. New York, Washington, California – you name it. Ten years, it was, and I enjoyed every minute of it. I might have stayed there for ever, only my sister took sick, so I came home. Her kids both had good jobs, and one of them was married with young ones of her own, and they just couldn't cope. Nor could her husband – but then I always thought Fred was a bit of a poor stick. Nothing *to* him, if you know what I mean. Still, Maureen never would hear a word against him, and give him his due, he was that cut up when she died you'd have thought he'd never get over it. Then he upped and married the widder next door, just like the song, which just goes to show, really, doesn't it, dear?'

Laura, fascinated, agreed that it did. 'So what did you do next?'

'Well, he offered me the house, if I'd like to rent it. Cheap, too – I think he felt badly about marrying so soon, with Maureen hardly cold in her grave as you might say, though of course she was cremated, really – but I didn't take it. Couldn't bear the thought of living there, with all the memories, and having to nod over the fence to them every time I came out the front door, or went out the back to hang the tea-towels out. I had a tidy bit put by, one way and another, so I came down here where my Gran was from, and found a nice little cottage for myself. And here I am. And here I shouldn't be, if I'm going to get that bus. If you're sure you're all right, dear?'

'Yes, I'm fine, but can't I give you a lift?' Laura was loath to part with her: she was eager to know what this enterprising woman had done for ten years in America. Certainly it did not seem that anything from that ten years had left a mark. Neither her speech nor her appearance gave any hint of transatlantic influence, though Laura had known people return, after two years of working in the States, speaking in a kind of hybrid vocabulary and with violently mutated vowels.

'Certainly not,' was the firm reply. 'You should be going straight home, and having a nice lie-down, I should say. And it wouldn't do any harm to call your doctor, either. Not that I want to worry you, dear, but you don't look too well to me. Better safe than sorry, eh?'

'Perhaps you're right,' said Laura, who was conscious of a growing ache in her back. 'But I should like to see you again. I so much want to know what you did in America?'

'I was a nanny, dear.' Now that she had said it, it seemed so obvious that Laura thought she should have recognised it straight away. 'When my Jim died, and we'd never been lucky enough to have any children, I thought I'd go back to it. Trained as a nursery nurse, I was. So you give me a call when Baby's come, if you want any help.' She rummaged in a capacious shopping bag and produced a notepad and pencil, writing swiftly. 'There you are: Hilda Davis, that's me. Now, I must run for that bus. See you do as I said, mind!'

'Yes, thank you.' Laura found she was speaking to a retreating back. She lowered herself into the car, and drove home slowly, conscious that her powers of concentration were not at their best.

Obediently, at home, she called the doctor. He was with her within an hour, scolding her gently for not having called him sooner. He examined her, listening for a long time to the baby's heart before patting her gently on the stomach.

'I wouldn't normally be worrying about this, but under the circumstances, and just as a precaution, I think we'll take you in. All right if I use the phone?'

Laura had no time to do more than nod. She lay in a stunned daze as he called the hospital, summoned an ambulance.

'Not an ambulance!' she pleaded when he had replaced the telephone. 'Can't I just call Edward? He'll drive me in. He could be here in twenty minutes.'

'It's not the speed, my dear. You'll be better lying down, if by any chance anything's started up that shouldn't have done. Too late to stop it now, anyway. It'll be an experience, you'll love it. Just lie back and enjoy the ride.'

'You might as well say "lie back and think of England",' grumbled Laura.

'You won't find *that* kind of man crewing our ambulances,' he said austerely, but with a twinkle. 'Baby kicking much?' he asked, almost as if it was an afterthought.

'Not much. Though I have felt some movement,' added Laura hastily.

'That's good. Do you want to phone Edward? Otherwise you can be sure one of the neighbours will be burning up the telephone wires when they see the ambulance coming here. I'll have a word with him, if you like. Now, we'll get you a few things together, shall we?'

'I can do that.'

'Don't be daft. I may be only a man, but I'm not completely helpless. Now, wash things, towel, nightie, just give me your orders, ma'am.'

Laura submitted, lying meekly on her bed while he packed her things up neatly. She rang Edward, and tried not very hard to persuade him not to bother coming to the hospital.

'Have a word with Alan,' she said. 'Bother, where is he? Alan? It's Edward, will you speak to him?'

'I'm downstairs,' came a distant voice. 'I'll pick it up down here.' She waited for the click, then replaced the handset, hearing the distant rumble of his voice as he spoke to Edward.

The journey passed in a blur. It seemed strange to be at the hospital when it wasn't a clinic. Laura stared at the ceiling as she was wheeled down endless corridors. The lights flickered past, and the porter's shoes squeaked on the polished floor. She was whisked off for an ultrasound scan, wired up with monitor and drip until she could not have moved even had she been allowed to.

'But I want to go to the loo!' she wailed.

'I'll bring you a bed-pan.' The staff nurse was brisk. 'But you'll have to stay lying down, mind.'

How can you pee lying down? Laura wondered. With difficulty, of course.

Edward arrived, his curly hair wild and his pale face fixed in a resolute smile.

'Poor old love, what a bore for you! Never mind, it won't be for long, and you can enjoy the rest. You said you'd been feeling tired.'

Laura lay quietly, holding his hand and watching the drip bag above her. Her arm felt cold and heavy, as though all the fluid from the drip was collecting in it, but that could only be imagination. She could not bear to tell Edward that she had not felt the baby kick for some hours. The monitor screen was turned away from her, and the faces of the doctors and nurses who checked it were unreadable.

Supper came, and went. Laura could not have eaten anything, and did not mind that she was not allowed food. Edward bought sandwiches at the canteen and ate them guiltily, ashamed of being hungry, even though he had had no lunch and knew he should have something. The minutes passed. Laura felt encased in ice. The ice had entered her heart and her mind, piercing and numbing. She thought that she should tell Edward what she believed she knew, but could not put the thought into words, in case it made it true. I won't think about it, she thought. I will think of something else. Something nice. She was unable to remember anything nice to think about, and it was a relief when at last her bed was moved into a small side ward where they were alone, and the consultant came to them.

'I'm so sorry,' he said. 'I'm so very sorry. The baby's heartbeat is very faint and erratic now. There is some kind of problem with his heart, it isn't possible to say exactly what at this stage, but we are fairly certain that he is dying.'

Laura nodded, knowing it was true, but Edward shot to his feet.

'But there must be something you can do! Deliver him by Caesarean, or some kind of operation in the womb, I've heard of that being done. I'll pay for anything . . .'

The consultant shook his head regretfully. 'We have considered all that. Delivering by Caesarean won't help. Although he's twenty-six weeks, his lungs seem to be very poorly developed, and with the additional problem of his heart . . . as for surgery *in utero*, I discussed that also. I actually rang Great Ormond Street for advice. But such intervention is only likely to be successful where the baby is, in other respects, strong and well developed. In this case . . .' He shook his head again. 'I'm so sorry,' he repeated.

Edward sat down and buried his head in his hands. Laura reached out her free hand and laid it on his clenched fingers.

'What happens next?' she asked simply, and to her relief he gave her a straightforward answer.

'We can only wait, I'm afraid. The baby's heart will be monitored continuously. If it picks up, then all well and good, we keep you as still as possible and hope for an improvement. If not . . . if the heartbeat ceases, then we disconnect the drip and allow the birth to continue naturally. It's the best way for you in the end. Not now – I know how hard it will be for you to go through the birth knowing there will be no baby at the end of it. But some people find it helps.'

'Oh yes,' said Laura. 'Yes, it's all I can do for him, now. He is a little boy, isn't he? You said he. I know you can see from the scans, though I've never asked.'

The consultant touched her shoulder. 'Yes,' he said. 'A little boy.'

Chapter 16

'How is she?'

Cassandra's voice was hushed, although since she was in Jane's kitchen even the loudest shout was unlikely to disturb Laura, who was in her own bed at home. Anna, who was also there, looked at her with a face blotchy with tears, and shrugged helplessly.

'As you would imagine. Devastated. Exhausted, too. The labour went on for quite a while, and the pain was quite bad in spite of everything they gave her. In fact, they offered her an epidural but she turned it down.'

'Oh, dear.' Jane remembered her own experiences in the labour ward. 'Doesn't she believe in them? I had one with Toby, it was wonderful, I didn't feel a thing.'

'No, I think that's just it,' sighed Anna. 'From what I can gather from Edward, she said she wanted to do it properly.'

'Do it properly?' Cassandra's voice rose to a muted shriek. 'What do you mean, do it properly?' she asked more moderately.

Anna rubbed her hands up and down the rail of the Rayburn her back was against. Jane had made coffee – tea for Cassandra – but none of them had felt able to sit down to drink it. It did not seem the moment for relaxing.

'I know what she meant,' said Anna from the depths of her own experience. 'She wanted the pain. Pain is real. It distracts you from the pain in your mind, or at least gives it a voice. When Michael was dying, I used sometimes to dig my nails in the skin of my arms, or bite the inside of my cheek. It wasn't much, but it made me feel I was sharing his suffering a bit.'

'The baby didn't suffer, did it?' Cassandra's voice wobbled.

'No. It – he – just slowed down, and stopped. Very peaceful, like going to sleep.' Anna saw that Cassandra needed protecting. She knew that this childish side of Cassandra sometimes irritated Jane, and saw the signs of it in the deepening of the little lines etched round her friend's mouth. She gave her a little smile, which Jane returned.

'One of the things people feel when this sort of thing happens to them, is guilty,' explained Anna gently. 'I felt guilty about Michael, because I was well and he wasn't, because I was going to go on living without him.' Cassandra nodded. She had already found herself wondering how on earth she was going to face seeing Laura while she still had her own triumphantly pregnant stomach or, even worse, when she had the baby in her arms.

'It's worse losing a baby,' continued Anna, 'because you feel responsible for it – that's how mothers are supposed to feel, after all. If the baby dies, from whatever cause, you feel it must be your fault.'

'It wasn't her fault, surely?' Jane had been worried about this. 'I mean, I know she had been overdoing it, but would that have made any difference? Should we have tried harder to stop her?'

'There you are, you see. We're feeling guilty, too. But we shouldn't, and nor should Laura. Edward said that it was nothing to do with that. The trouble is, they don't have any real idea why it should have happened. The baby was developing a little slowly, but not unduly so. It was perhaps less active than it might have been, but again not enough for them to be concerned. No, the general feeling is that it's just one of those inexplicable tragedies that happen for no particular reason, like being struck by lightning.'

Cassandra shivered.

'It seems so unfair. Laura, of all people. Why should it have to happen to her?' She began to cry, gasping snuffly sobs that made her tea splash over the sides of the mug she had forgotten she was holding. Jane, tight-lipped, took the mug from her and put her firmly into a chair, then went to get a cloth and some tissues, leaving Anna to do the hugging and the murmuring and the soothing. What Jane felt, more than anything, was anger. She hadn't been so burningly furious since that moment when she had first discovered that Bill, contrary to all the protestations he had made and she had believed, was cheating on her.

Such anger was, she knew, useless, but it was at least warming, and thus easier to bear than the blank misery that she knew was lurking behind it. Like Cassandra, she thought, why Laura? but unlike her she also thought, if it had to be, why not Cassandra? Not that she wished her any ill, but after all, whose need was greater? And who, ultimately, would be the better mother? Her own guilt at this thought made her put the kettle on to make a fresh cup of tea for Cassandra, who had reached the deep breaths and mopping-up stage of her crying.

'It should have been me,' said Cassandra sadly, echoing Jane's thought and making her feel even worse about it. 'Laura deserves a baby much more than I do. I didn't even *want* the first one. At least I wanted it, but not enough . . . not like I want this baby.' She put her hands on her dome of stomach, as if she thought some divine vengeance might descend and snatch the baby from her womb.

'It's not a question of deserving,' said Jane. 'Life isn't like that, you know it isn't. Just imagine, if we all deserved what we got – or got what we deserved!' She shuddered, and gave a little laugh. 'It doesn't bear thinking of.'

'But it's not fair,' repeated Cassandra with childish stubbornness. Jane tightened her lips again.

'Of course it isn't,' said Anna bracingly. 'Who ever told you life was going to be fair? Fair has nothing to do with it. It wasn't fair that Mike should die, or that Bill should go off, but it happened, and we have to deal with it. Now Laura has to deal with this. And our job is to help her to do it.'

'But how?' wailed Cassandra. 'How can I go and see her looking like this?' She gestured to her shape.

'How can you not?' Anna replied simply. 'Are you going to stop seeing her altogether? You'll have to move to another village – another county, really. Abroad. And even then she'll know you're pregnant, know you've had the baby. How will it help her for you to run away? Yes, of course it will upset her, of course she'll break her heart to hold your baby in her arms, but that won't stop her from wanting to do it. The world is full of pregnant women and newborn babies. She can't hide from all of them.'

'I'd share it with her, if I could.'

'Good idea,' said Jane briskly. 'Ask her if she would like to be a godmother. And don't tell me you're not intending to have the baby christened. You can bloody well go ahead and do it, if she says yes, and to hell with everything else.'

Cassandra looked more cheerful. 'Do you think she'd like that? I hadn't really meant . . . Stephen always said it was wrong to commit a baby to a religion when it didn't know anything about it.'

'Stephen,' said Jane firmly, 'talked a lot of crap. Having a baby baptised is your commitment, not the baby's. You'll soon find that children have very firm ideas of their own about almost anything you care to mention, and a little thing like having some water splashed on their heads isn't going to make them believe anything. Especially when they get to be teenagers. Ask the vicar. About ninety per cent of the families who bring their babies to the font only do it because Grandma expects it, or as an excuse for a party, or just to extract a few presents from people. If you do it as a way of giving Laura a little happiness, I'd say your motives were better than most people's.'

'Have you seen her yet?' Cassandra took a gulp of tea and sat up straighter.

'I have,' said Anna. 'I went round yesterday, soon after she came home.'

'Wasn't it a bit soon?' Cassandra, while deferring to Anna's experience, was dubious.

'I don't think so. If she hadn't wanted to face seeing anyone, she could have told Edward to tell me and she would have known I'd understand. But I remember with Michael how people used to shy away from me. With the best intentions in the world, I know. People are afraid of upsetting you, afraid of saying the wrong thing. But I know that for me, at least, I was so lonely, and I longed for people to talk to me, and to be able to talk about Michael. I was so grateful to the people who did phone, or come round, or who stopped me in the street instead of crossing the road or darting into a shop to avoid me. I learned then that it's better to risk saying the wrong thing than to say nothing at all.'

'I'll go tomorrow, then. Perhaps I'll phone first. Oh dear.'

Anna nodded, and so did Jane. There seemed nothing more to say.

Laura lay in bed. Flat on her back, her arms by her sides. It felt stiff and awkward, but she could not bear to have them on her stomach and feel its soft flatness with its reminder of emptiness, and her breasts were still painfully swollen with milk.

That rush of milk into her breasts had been almost the most difficult thing to bear. Irrationally, she had not expected it, feeling that once the business of the birth was completed, it would all be over. Instead her internal muscles felt bruised and aching, she was conscious of the thick pad between her legs and the stickiness of blood, and above all her breasts were enormous, hard and heavy as boulders in spite of the tablets the midwife had given her. To crown it all, she had been told to drink as little as possible until the milk had dried, so her mouth and throat felt parched. As always, the knowledge that she must not drink made thoughts of coffee, of tea, of cold fruit juice from the fridge, float endlessly and temptingly to the forefront of her mind.

'It's such a waste,' she had said tearfully to the midwife. 'All this milk . . . couldn't I give it to the premature babies?' She remembered Jane, after Toby's birth, expressing milk and taking it to the hospital.

'If you do, you'll just go on making more and more,' said the midwife gently. 'The more you take, the more you'll make. It's not good for you at the moment. I know it's uncomfortable, but in a day or two it will disappear, I promise.'

'I feel as though they're going to explode,' complained Laura. 'It just reminds me, all the time . . .'

'Of course it does, my dear. And if it carries on, it will remind you for that much longer. Now, how are you coping otherwise?'

'All right,' said Laura automatically. That had been in the morning. Edward had brought her home from the hospital the previous day, at the end of the afternoon. On reaching the house she had cried, and so had he, difficult tears and slow, aching sobs that had been withheld until they were alone and at home again. They had seen and held the baby, small as a doll and with the distant expression of one who has glimpsed the world and withdrawn from it. The little figure had felt no more real in her arms than a toy might have done, and although she knew that in the future she would be glad she had done it, the immediate experience seemed unreal, almost irrelevant, as if she were acting in some kind of play.

It had been inexpressibly reassuring to climb into her own bed. She had spent a long night in the high hospital bed, with its slippery plastic mattress and pillow covers beneath the harshly laundered sheets that were too small and never stayed tucked in, and the thin cotton blankets that were warm enough, but were so light and insubstantial that they were the very antithesis of comfort. At home she had fallen asleep almost at once, cradled gently in Edward's arms, and when she woke in the night they had clung together and cried again until they were both drained and slept once more.

Now, though her body felt exhausted, she was unable to sleep. She could hear the faint noises as Edward pottered in the kitchen. Knowing that he could not afford to neglect the business, she had begged him not to stay at home.

'I'll be all right. I'm not allowed to drink, so I won't even be needing cups of coffee, and I couldn't face eating anything. You know Jane or Anna would come round to be with me, it only needs a phone call. Or Cassie,' she added, an afterthought.

His face had twisted for a moment.

'No. I'd like to be here with you, even if it's just for today. Ellie will deal with the hordes of clients anxious to bring me their business.' Laura, guessing that he was better off finding things to do at home than staring at the silent office walls and the empty architect's desk, was glad to have him there.

Laura lay still, and wondered what to do to make the slow minutes pass. Radio and television seemed unbearably trivial, to read a book impossible, she knew that the words would pass meaninglessly before her eyes and never reach her brain. She had adopted the stratagem she had evolved long before for dealing with moments of intense misery or worry, which was not to allow herself to think about it very deeply.

I can't cope with this just now, she thought. Later, I'll be able to. Later, when I've stopped aching, when the milk has gone, when I'm stronger. Then I'll look at what has happened, work my way through it, learn to live with it. But not now. Now, I'll push it away from me.

It was effective in a limited fashion. The pain was dulled, but the effort was very great. Her feelings of misery and loss were so deep-rooted that in insulating herself from them she also cut herself off from everything else, so that she ended up cocooned in a muffling blanket of nothingness, like being marooned in a thick fog. Even her own limbs felt heavy and numb, as if she were semi-paralysed, or perhaps as though they had been amputated. She had heard that people often continued to feel the presence of a lost arm or leg for some while after it had gone.

I must think about something else, she thought. Something pleasant. Holidays, for instance. But they had not had a holiday this year, and the prospects for the future looked equally thin, unless the housing market and the building trade should improve. Mark, she thought. I'll think about Mark.

It was only too simple. Mark, after all, could so easily fill the gap, the empty space that the baby had left in her life. He was alive and real; more real than the baby had ever truly been to her. She felt, moreover, that she had the possibility of helping him. The world, to Mark, seemed to be a hostile and inexplicable place. Could she not show him, teach him, how to understand the world? Could she not, from her own experience, teach him how to look at and understand those problems within himself of which the battles he had with adults and authority were but an outer manifestation? Streetwise in his way, he was in others as innocent of an ability to deal with society as any primitive tribesman might be. Surely he needed, if not a mother, at least a guide and a friend.

Laura rested her mind against the thought of Mark, and dreamed. She thought of future conversations, of journeys in the car when she would talk, and he in his turn would open up, receptive to her words and giving vent, in time, to his own worries and perplexities. Simple at first, this dream became over the following weeks and months her lifeline. She could retreat into it whenever the realities of the life she was living became intolerable. Inevitably, over time, the Mark of her dream became more and more her own creation. His sullen brooding was transformed into thoughtfulness, his flashes of wit into subtle and intelligent humour, his inarticulate seeking for words a careful search for proper communication, and above all his acceptance of her was turned into love.

In her wiser moments, Laura knew that she was, if not wrong, at least misguided and mistaken. She knew, in her deepest thoughts, that the real Mark was nothing like the Mark with whom she conversed so often in her head. She realised that if she were actually with him she would be able to speak few of the wise remarks and cogent suggestions that flowed so persuasively from her mental tongue, and even if they did he would be unlikely to find them anything but incomprehensible or just plain embarrassing. Nevertheless, while retaining this ultimate grasp on reality, she still found the dream world she had created so comforting, almost narcotic in its ability to soothe and cheer her, that she was unable to resist using it as a crutch to help her through her days.

Her friends were amazed by her resilience. Cassandra, who in spite of all that Anna and Jane had said had found it almost impossible to face Laura at first, was soon calling in even more frequently than before. The invaluable Jenny had been promoted to manageress at the shop, and now that she was within a few weeks of giving birth, Cassandra was able to leave most of the day-to-day running to her.

'Honestly, Laura, you are amazing,' she said warmly one afternoon in late November. 'I really don't think I could have coped with what you've been through.'

Laura, who was measuring out ingredients for Christmas puddings, looked up from the raisins she was sorting and smiled across the kitchen table.

'I couldn't have done it without a lot of support. Edward, of course, he's been wonderful, but also you and Jane and Anna. And Tod, bless him. You know he's found me a job?'

'As a matter of fact, I did,' said Cassandra. 'I see quite a lot of Tod these days. It's funny, until recently I used to think he was just a funny old thing, one of those "village characters"–' her lifted hands sketched quotation marks in the air '–but not a real person, if you know what I mean.'

'I know exactly what you mean. There's a lot more to Tod than meets the eye, isn't there? I have to say I only discovered that a few months ago,' admitted Laura, thinking back to her conversation with Tod in the summer, her face clouding momentarily as she remembered his warnings about Mark.

'Mm. Well, we were having lunch together a few weeks ago, just after . . . just after you'd come out of hospital, and he told me there was a vacancy at St Barbara's, and asked me if I thought you might be interested in working there.' Cassandra's face, mobile and transparent as ever, revealed her pleasure in being so consulted. 'Of course, I said I thought it might be a wonderful idea, so he went ahead and sounded them out before mentioning it to you.'

'Yes, it's been a godsend,' said Laura, still pulling the clumps of sticky raisins apart and removing the stray pieces of stalk and pip. 'Three days a week will suit me very well: it will leave me time to do the house and the garden and so on, but it means I'll be busy and won't have too much time to brood. The money'll be handy as well.'

'Things haven't improved for Edward?' asked Cassandra tentatively.

'No, I'm afraid not. He's getting the odd thing, mostly bits and pieces like the people who wanted a new porch, and the occasional extension, and of course it all helps to keep things ticking over, but only just. At least now I'll be able to pay for things like food, and the odd trip to the cinema or something, or even buy him his Christmas present without having to feel I'm just running through his money. I'm going to try to save up a little bit, too. Nothing much, but it's a lovely feeling. I remember being just the same when I put sixpences from my pocket money into my money-box when I was little.'

The work at St Barbara's was partly administrative, partly practical. It had been decided that it would be a good thing to offer the residents rather more in the entertainment and time-filling line than daytime television and the crocheting of woollen squares for Save the Children Fund blankets, worthy though that might be. A new post, rather grandly named 'recreations manager', had been created, and it had not been difficult for Tod to persuade the managers and administrators of the home that someone local, someone above all who knew the residents and staff and was trusted by them, would be far better than some person from outside who might set them all at sixes and sevens and upset the delicate equilibrium of that enclosed society.

Laura, who had suffered all the usual doubts about whether she was up to the job, went to the home to talk to her friends there, and was encouraged. She thought that not only could she do the job, but that she would enjoy it tremendously. The elderly residents, many of them fiercely independent and equally fiercely on guard against any kind of patronising, knew Laura well enough to feel confident that she would neither push them into pointless activities for the sake of keeping them occupied, nor underestimate the skills and experience that several of them had to offer. She made it clear that this was to be their venture: she might suggest, but the ideas must be their own input. Her job would be merely to arrange and to facilitate.

As a result, although Laura would not be working officially until January, plans were already afoot to start a local-history study group, a general-knowledge quiz was being set up against the local pub team, and it was hoped that a weekly trip could be arranged to the local swimming baths, where there was a coach/physiotherapist who specialised in water exercises for the elderly, particularly arthritis sufferers. St Barbara's was buzzing with interest and excitement, for as a side effect of these plans it was necessary to raise some money, and there were to be coffee mornings, sales of work, and a sponsored wheelchair marathon that occasioned much hilarity, one man going so far as to suggest stealing some road cones to make a kind of slalom course.

The other thing that helped Laura to keep going was the prospect of Christmas. Or rather, not so much Christmas as the Christmas holidays. Laura was not expecting to do very much over the festival itself: fortunately the baby had not been due to arrive until the New Year, so she did not have to fear the poignant might-have-beens for this year, but even so the paraphernalia of the season, the decorated tree, the stockings, the general child-orientation of it all was bound to bring sadness. After Boxing Day, however, Laura hoped very much that Mark would be able to come and stay with them. She had written to tell him what had happened, and had received a well-intentioned letter from Georgia as well as an ill-written but touchingly sympathetic scrawl from Mark himself, overcoming his usual allergy to writing. Laura had wept over his letter, but had been comforted by it.

Another person Laura had been helped by was, rather surprisingly, Hilda Davis, the woman she had met in the supermarket the day she had begun to lose the baby. Somehow, in Laura's mind, Hilda had become associated with a feeling of comfort and security, and two weeks after the baby's death Laura had fished the piece of paper out of her pocket and telephoned her.

The phone call had been followed by a visit. Laura had sat in the exquisitely neat little house and poured out the story of the whole event, in more detail than she had done even to Edward or Anna. The tears that accompanied her recital had been more cathartic than any others, perhaps because to this almost stranger she felt no need to hold back her grief, no worry that she was upsetting someone else. The older woman's experience, her practical and unsentimental good sense, had been bracing and supportive, and Laura had several times telephoned for a chat at moments when her feelings of desolation seemed more than she could bear.

Now, sitting with Cassandra who was so few weeks away from the birth of her own baby, she was initiating a small private plan. 'I've got someone turning up in a moment. Someone I thought you might like to meet,' she added, seeing Cassandra about to gather herself to leave.

Cassandra subsided with some relief – Laura's kitchen was warm and friendly, the upright kitchen chair padded with cushions and surprisingly comfortable. 'Oh? Who is it?'

'Someone I met in the checkout queue at Sainsbury's.'

Cassandra laughed. 'Typical! Is this one of your lame dogs?'

'Certainly not! If anything, it's the other way round, and I'm her lame dog. No, she's a dear, I think you'll like her. She lives about three miles away. I offered to go and fetch her – she doesn't have a car, though she can drive – but she insisted she'd come on her bicycle.'

Laura said no more, feeling that to mention Hilda's previous profession might make Cassandra wary. At the moment Cassandra was perfectly determined that she could care for the baby and run the shop without any help from anyone. So she probably could, but Laura suspected that she would find the baby more of a tie than she imagined, especially if it gave her sleepless nights, and that things would be even more difficult when she had, not a baby in a travel buggy, but an active toddler to contend with. Hilda Davis would be exactly the kind of person she might need, and Laura was looking forward to seeing them meet. She had by now heard some of the tales of Hilda's life in the States, and had been amused by the sharp observations that had noted, without criticism, the foibles of her previous employers.

A few minutes later, Hilda Davis arrived. Laura, going to open the door to her, was delighted to see that she had come on an old fashioned sit-up-and-beg bicycle with a basket on the front.

'What a lovely bicycle! Though I would have been perfectly happy to come and fetch you.'

'No, I prefer to do it this way. Otherwise it's so difficult to know what to do about leaving, isn't it? You might be dying to get rid of me and not know how to say so, or I might want to go when you're having to answer the telephone, that kind of thing. And as you say, it's a good old bike. The one I had as a girl that I left here with my sister. Looked after it beautifully, she did, and when she died I was glad to have it back. I can't be doing with these modern things with the handlebars down by your knees. Makes all the blood go to my head, that does.'

As she spoke she propped the bicycle tidily against the wall and took a jar, neatly wrapped in a brown paper bag, from the basket.

'I've brought you a pot of my apple and ginger chutney. I know you make all that sort of thing yourself, but it's always nice to try someone else's, isn't it?'

'Lovely,' said Laura sincerely. 'My husband takes cheese sandwiches to work with him, he'll really enjoy some of this in them. Come on in, my friend Cassandra is here, and I'm just getting the fruit ready to mix the Christmas puddings.'

'Then I'll give you a hand,' said Hilda with evident satisfaction. She smiled cheerfully at Cassandra, taking in her imminent birth without so much as a flicker of surmise, and calling her 'Mrs Happold', saying that she was of a generation that did not use first names on first acquaintance. Cassandra, every inch the modern young woman, told her that everyone called her Cassandra, and added that she was not in any case married.

'Miss Happold it is, then,' countered Hilda serenely. 'Now, Mrs Melville, dear, if you've finished those raisins, shall I start chopping the apples? I see you've everything else ready. Then you can mix it up, and we can all have a stir and a wish. Proper treat that is for me. My poor sister was too ill to eat a Christmas meal last year, and her husband can't abide pudding, so I've not made a proper one for longer than I care to remember. It didn't seem worth making one just for me.'

She spoke not with self-pity, but as one stating an obvious fact.

'It always makes too much, doesn't it?' agreed Laura. 'You must let me give you a little one for yourself when they're done. Didn't you have Christmas pudding in the States?'

'Over there everything was bought, no one ever seemed to think of making, and they didn't have proper puddings half the time, just pumpkin pies and that. Very nice, of course, but not the same, to my way of thinking. And you can't make a wish on a pan of pumpkin mush, however much it needs stirring, can you?'

Cassandra laughed and looked interested. Laura, well satisfied, made a fresh pot of tea and got out the pudding bowls. It looked as though her little plot might work out very well.

Chapter 17

Cassandra's baby daughter was born in December, a week early, on a night of spectacularly violent storms.

Even Cassandra, not known for her propensity for self-recrimination, had to agree that it was entirely her own fault that she was on her own at the time. While her relationship with her parents, and particularly her mother, had improved tremendously since she had announced her pregnancy, she was still very much disinclined to accept her mother's help or advice. Mrs Happold had never been altogether happy, in any case, about Cassandra living as she did. For a young girl (as her mother still fondly saw her) to be alone in a little cottage that seemed to her, accustomed to the strict security precautions imposed on the expensive private estate where they lived, perilously open to outsiders, seemed to be inviting dangerous trouble.

As the expected birth date drew nearer, this anxiety became much more pronounced. Unfortunately, Cassandra was so used to discounting and ignoring her mother's fussing that she took very little notice of it now.

'I really don't think you should be here alone,' was the kind of remark that made Cassandra tighten her lips and raise her brows in exasperation.

'For heaven's sake, Mum, don't go on about it! I'm perfectly all right here. Ashingly isn't the back of beyond, you know.'

'Don't call me Mum,' said Mrs Happold automatically, but she was not to be diverted. 'I'm not saying it is the back of beyond. It would be just the same if you were in a town, or even on a nice estate. Supposing you were to feel funny in the night?'

'Then I'd have a good laugh,' said Cassandra sarcastically. 'If you mean, supposing I were to go into labour, then for goodness' sake say so. If I did, I have a telephone, I have neighbours who would rally round if necessary, but surely even in your day women didn't produce their babies that quickly? At the classes they said it's likely to start off quite slowly, especially a first baby.'

'Not necessarily. Look at all those people who have their babies in taxis.'

Cassandra giggled. 'Goodness, yes, hundreds of them. Really, Mummy! Look, if you're really worried you'd better come and stay here with me. Then you can come in the taxi and help deliver the baby.'

'Oh, I couldn't leave your father!' came the expected response. 'However would he manage?'

'Well, I'm not having him stay here for weeks on end,' said Cassandra firmly. 'You know he hates this cottage; he's always complaining the doors are too low, and the stairs too steep, and it's always too hot, or too cold, or there's too much garlic in the food, or something. So unless you can produce me a nice meek little Victorian companion who won't drive me to distraction, we'll just have to leave things as they are, won't we?'

Reluctantly, Mrs Happold had to agree.

By December, everything was ready for the baby. The little room that was to be the nursery was prettily decorated in cheerful greens and yellows. A mobile hung over the cradle, and another one in the window. Piles of baby clothes were lovingly arranged in the cupboard, the changing mat and all its attendant paraphernalia waited, only the pram was still at the shop, Cassandra having had a fit of superstition brought on by Laura's troubles, and refusing to take delivery until after the baby was born. She had spent a busy day wrapping and labelling all her Christmas presents, a job which as always took far longer than she had expected, and when she felt vague niggling pains in her back she assumed it was from standing and bending over the table – she never found it easy to wrap things neatly when sitting down, and she prided herself on her beautifully presented parcels.

Feeling rather tired, she didn't bother to watch any television but went to bed early with a milky drink, a hot-water bottle and a good book. She therefore failed to hear the weather forecast with its warning of gales and storms across the south of the country. Soothed by the warm drink, with the hot-water bottle tucked against her back, she slept through the first wild gusts of wind. Her house, after all, was old enough to have been built at a time when more thought was given to shelter from weather when choosing a site, and when wind and storms came it seemed to do no more than huddle the smooth curve of its thatch more closely to the ground.

It was not until there came a tremendous crack of thunder almost directly overhead that Cassandra opened her eyes. The darkness in her bedroom was total, so she knew at once that the electricity must be off. Since she now woke at least once a night needing to pee, she had taken to leaving a small light on in the bathroom, for although familiar, the uneven floors and low beams were hazardous when she was half asleep.

The thought made her realise that her bladder was uncomfortably full. She cursed the milk drink, shivering as she rolled to the edge of the bed and pushed back the covers. Without electricity to drive the pump, the heating was also off, and the room felt disagreeably chilly. For the first time she became conscious of the sound of driving rain hammering against the window like gravel, and heard the moaning gusts of wind. Then the room was briefly lit with the unreal brilliance of a flash of lightning, followed at once by another crash of thunder. Cassandra cowered back into the warmth of her bed. The ache in her back had increased, and now it gripped her with a kind of relentless and sullen immediacy that made her groan out loud. I must get to the loo, she thought. That's one less thing to be uncomfortable, anyway. Damn this weather. I can't even do another hot-water bottle or make a drink. I wish I'd thought to bring the torch up with me.

In the bathroom even the towel rail, which stayed on summer and winter, was no more than tepid. Cassandra ran the hot tap, relieved to find that in the well-insulated cylinder the water was still hot, and went back to the bedroom for her bottle. As she stood at the basin, filling the bottle and listening to the sound of the water to know when to stop, she felt a strange internal pop. It rang through her body so that she almost thought she had heard it, and instinctively turned off the tap in case the hot-water bottle had somehow burst. Then she felt the flood of warmth down her legs, and knew that the pop had been the membrane rupturing. Her waters had broken.

Automatically she reached for the bath towels, dropping one on to the wet carpet to stand on, and padding the other between her legs. Already her wet skin was puckering with cold; she pulled the saturated fabric of her nightie away from her, then stripped it off and dropped it into the basin. She felt very calm, and was pleased with herself that it should be so. There could be nothing, after all, to worry about. It was all perfectly normal. She would telephone the hospital, an ambulance would come, and maybe by the morning she would be holding the baby in her arms.

Shivering, she felt her way back to the bedroom, and pulled on the clothes she had discarded the evening before, glad that she had not bothered to put them away. Then, warmed as much by this further evidence of her ability to cope as by the clothes, she sat down on the edge of the bed and picked up the telephone.

It was dead.

She clamped it to her ear in horrified disbelief, then rattled futilely at the button of the receiver. Nothing. As she replaced the receiver, the ache in her back grabbed her again, reaching round to the front of her belly. She put her hands there, feeling the muscles tighten across the hard dome, and heard her own voice whimper in panic. She controlled herself.

'The breathing,' she said aloud. 'Do the breathing.' It was something positive, and as she breathed through her first proper contraction, the slow pattern of inhale, hold, exhale calmed her. When the pain ebbed she stood up at once, and went purposefully to the cupboard where her overnight bag was packed and ready. With it in her hand she felt her way cautiously downstairs, and put on a warm coat, scarf and gloves. The torch. Now where was the torch? It was in its usual place, of course, as things generally were in her cottage, but in the dark her sense of orientation deserted her, and she felt too far to the side of the shelf. Frustrated, she pulled her hand back, and felt the hard weight of the torch against her fingers for a moment before it slipped through her grasp and fell, with an ominous splintering noise, to the hall floor.

'Bugger!' she said, bending with difficulty and sweeping across the ground with her hand. 'Bugger, bugger, bugger.' The torch had rolled. By the time she found and grasped it she had cut her fingers on the pieces of broken glass. She scarcely needed to push the switch to know that the lens and the bulb were smashed.

Once again the inexorable tightening came and she breathed through it, but raggedly this time as her racing mind tried to plan. Useless to think that she might be able to drive herself. She must go and seek help. Not the couple next door: elderly and deaf, they would be no use even if she could succeed in waking them, and she knew that the house after that was empty, its owners spending December in the Bahamas. Still thinking, she took the doorkey from its hook, picked up her bag again, and let herself out of the front door.

The click as it closed was horribly final, as if her own home were rejecting her. Resolutely she fumbled the key into the lock and turned it, then turned round. The rain was sheeting down, and the lightning which might have helped her to see something had moved on. The green was wholly dark, no gleam of light from any of the houses was to be seen. The power cut, then, was a major one, and so probably was the problem with the telephone line. Huddled in the shelter of the porch, she considered her options.

She longed for her friends, for Anna or Laura or Jane. Anna, of course, was too far away down her lane, and she could not bring herself to disturb

Laura on such an errand, except as a last resort. Jane was probably the nearest in distance – the rectory was directly across the green from her cottage – but that was just it, across the green. In the dark and the rain the green, by daylight so small and innocent, assumed the proportions of a great empty plain. Cassandra imagined herself stumbling across it, going in circles like people were supposed to do in the trackless wastes of the desert; falling . . . No, she could not do it. Then—

'Tod,' she said aloud. Of course, Tod's house was nearer still, nearer even than Laura's. Tod had a car, Tod was a light sleeper and, moreover, slept in a front room, whereas Jane's bedroom was at the back of the house, far from the sound of doorbell and knocker. With a little sob of relief Cassandra plunged out into the darkness.

The garden path was slippery with moss – why had she not cleared it? – and the gate had swollen with wet and jammed, so that her wet fingers slipped across the wood, catching her nails and filling them with splinters and fragments. She tugged at it again, and it swung back and hit her stomach.

'Bloody thing,' she muttered tearfully, bending her body protectively over, though she knew that so small a bump could not disturb the baby. To punish the gate she left it swinging after she had gone through. It was a relief to feel the gritty tarmac of the footpath beneath her feet, but she was fearful of falling off the edge of the kerb, and shuffled carefully along, her free hand feeling to one side and in front of her for the hedges and walls of the houses. Just in time she remembered the row of flowering prunus trees, planted in the Jubilee year and now substantial enough to have solid trunks, and edged nearer the wall. At last, to her relief, her fingers felt the slippery hardness of knapped flint, and she knew she had reached Tod's.

Fortunately, the doorbell was not a small push-button but a substantial iron pull that was easy to find. Cassandra hung on it, hearing the distant peal, then pounded the knocker for good measure. It was not very long before the door opened a crack, with the rattle of a safety chain, and the round eye of a torch appeared round it, dazzling her. Cassandra put up her hand to shade her eyes, realising for the first time that her hair was clinging to her skin and dripping down on to her face.

'Cassandra! My *dear*! What*ever* . . . ? Is it the baby?' Tod's voice changed in mid-question, all the affectations suddenly abandoned as he took in the gravity of the situation. The door jerked wide. 'Come in, Cassandra. Good God, you're soaked. Take off that coat and sit down.'

The powerful torch flashed round the hall. Cassandra's wet coat was gently removed and a dry one of his own put round her shoulders, and she was carefully pushed into a priceless porter's chair.

'I'm dripping . . . I'll ruin it . . .' she raised distracted hands to her hair, tried to get up, but at that moment another contraction made her subside with a gasp. There was the rasp of a match, and a candle was lit. Its glowing flame, reflected in a mirror, made the room seem safe and familiar, and Cassandra relaxed into her breathing. Tod, in what seemed to be the most exotic Noel Coward silk dressing-gown, was already bounding up the stairs.

'I'll be dressed in two ticks, then we'll go. No point in hanging round for an ambulance . . .'

It was such a relief to have him take over. Cassandra felt her eyelids drooping as she sat, smelling the faint dry scent of Tod's aftershave on the smooth cashmere of his coat. It seemed the most comforting garment she had ever known. Tod reappeared, pulling on a Barbour and reaching for an enormous umbrella.

'Stay right there,' he ordered. 'I'll bring the car to the front for you.'

Moments later, Cassandra found herself tenderly put into the car beneath the umbrella's shelter. The inside of the car smelled luxuriously of the lovingly tended leather of the seats; she closed her eyes and felt the surge of the engine as Tod accelerated out of the village.

At the hospital, it seemed extraordinary that there should be electric light, telephones, all the bustle of modern living. Cassandra blinked in the brightness as she stood helplessly in the foyer, and it was Tod who went to the desk and summoned a wheelchair, a porter, and a nurse. It was all very brisk and efficient, but the very efficiency made Cassandra suddenly frightened. She looked at the gleaming white corridor that would take her to the delivery suite, visited once with her ante-natal class, which she remembered now as a Frankenstein's lair of shining instruments, and reached out to grasp at Tod's sleeve.

'Stay with me,' she begged. 'Please stay and keep me company, Tod. Just for a little while?' she pleaded.

'That's all right, dear,' said the nurse brightly. 'Your dad can stay as long as you like.'

Cassandra met Tod's eyes in a moment of shared amusement.

'I'm afraid he's not my father,' she said.

'Oh – sorry, dear,' said the nurse, glancing at him. 'He's the father, then? The baby's father?' she pursued, seeing their questioning faces.

'No, not that either,' said Tod, straight-faced. 'Just a friend.'

'A close friend,' emended Cassandra, smiling at him.

'Well, he can be the King of Wallamalloo for all it matters,' said the nurse cheerfully. 'If you want him, he can stay as long as he likes.'

'Thank you,' said Tod. 'Thank you very much.' The words were simple, but they spoke volumes, and they were not addressed to the nurse.

'Right,' said Cassandra briskly, to hide her sudden emotion, 'where's this gooseberry bush, then? Let's go and check it out.'

Tod sat patiently in the waiting room while Cassandra was examined and put through what would in other circumstances have been the humiliating routine of preparation. He was thankful to find he was alone, not feeling sure that he could sustain his side of a discussion with any prospective father who might wonder what on earth he was doing there. He rather wondered himself, and he was strongly tempted to leave a message of good luck to Cassandra, telephone her parents and perhaps Anna, and scuttle back to the safety of his home. Only the memory of Cassandra's clinging hand and pleading face stopped him, but he was relieved when Cassandra herself came to find him.

'Was it a false alarm, then?' he asked, not noticing that she was clad only in a hospital gown with her own dressing-gown over the top. 'Shall I take you home?'

'No, of course it isn't, not when my waters have broken,' said Cassandra with what he felt to be a brutal disregard for his sensibilities. 'I'm just not very far on yet, that's all.'

He eyed her dubiously. 'Shouldn't you be, er, lying down, or something?' he inquired nervously.

'No, only if I want to, but I don't. It's not very painful, but too uncomfortable to let me go back to sleep, and besides, I'm far too excited. I haven't felt like this since I was six years old, and wide awake on Christmas Eve. Oh, here we go.' She leaned her hands on the table, controlling her breathing. Tod shot out of his chair.

'Shall I call the doctor?'

Speechlessly, counting under her breath, she shook her head, smiling. 'No, I'm fine,' she said when the contraction ebbed. 'It's really better if I walk around a bit. It's distracting, and it will keep things moving, as they say. I want to get on with this!'

Nervous though he might be, it was not in Tod to desert her. With a courtly bow he offered his arm.

'Then shall we promenade?' he asked grandly.

'Yes, let's,' said Cassandra less elegantly. She tucked her hand into the crook of his arm. 'Oh Tod, it's such a comfort to have you here,' she confided.

205

'Is it?' He was surprised. 'I don't know the first thing about what's happening, I'm afraid.'

'I know, that's what's so nice. There are plenty of experts here – the place is stuffed with them, after all. I feel like the new girl starting late at school. But you're even more of a new girl than I am, if you know what I mean.' She cast him a quick glance, as if fearing she might have offended him.

'Maisie of the Upper Fourth, that's me,' Tod agreed. 'The one who loses her lacrosse stick, and comes into tea wearing the wrong coloured socks.'

Cassandra giggled. 'You see! This is meant to be fun, after all!'

'Is it?' he asked dubiously, remembering the stage births he had seen on television, with a lot of groaning and gasping and even the odd scream. 'If you say so.'

'I might never do this again, but I'm going to make the most of it,' announced Cassandra. 'Look out, here's another one. Check the time for me, would you?'

Obediently he drew out his fob-watch, which he had not taken time to thread on its chain but had thrust into his pocket when dressing, not feeling complete without it.

'That's right, ducky, keep breathing,' he said, remembering the television again. 'Good girl.'

For three hours they paced up and down the corridor. It was, for both of them, a time that was extraordinarily immediate and yet strangely unreal. Once, from the delivery suite, they heard the protesting wail of a newborn child, and smiled at one another. By the time Cassandra was ready to go there herself, Tod was so involved with what was happening that he thought he would have strenuously resisted any attempt to remove him, though before he had longed to disappear.

'Don't stay if you don't want to,' said Cassandra. Her voice was calm but the contractions by now were very close together, and almost as she spoke her face contorted again. He waited, gripping her hand and unconsciously copying her breathing, until it was over.

'I'll go, if that's what you want. I could wait in the corridor. But I'd like to stay, if that's all right. If you wouldn't find it . . . embarrassing.'

Cassandra laughed, her old uninhibited peal.

'Embarrassed! If you knew how many strange men have peered at my bits in the last nine months, and stuck things like salad servers in to have a better look, you'd know that I've nothing left to be embarrassed about! But I thought you might find it, not embarrassing exactly, but perhaps a bit revolting. Still, you can always concentrate on my top end.'

He laughed. 'So I can! Don't worry, I shan't pass out on the floor. I don't want to miss a moment of this, any more than you do. "Lead on, Mac—" oh no, that won't do. Mustn't quote the Scottish piece. "Once more unto the breach, dear friends . . ."' he declaimed. The midwife, who had sensibly been ignoring their peculiar conversation, turned from the tray of instruments she had been checking.

'Breech? It's not a breech birth, dear. A perfectly normal presentation, and coming along very nicely.'

And so, laughing, Cassandra went into the next contraction.

Secretly, Tod had wondered whether his squeamish nature was going to be up to whatever might lie ahead, but in the event he became so fascinated that he never gave it a second thought. Between contractions he held her hand, or wiped her face carefully with a damp cloth, whispering encouragement. When she strained to push, he felt his own muscles tighten in sympathy, and unconsciously he echoed the midwife's words.

'Come on, Cassie, push! Push! It's coming! I can see the head! I can see it, Cassie! Nearly there, love, nearly there!'

'Lift me up,' panted Cassandra. 'Want to see.'

At the midwife's nod, he lifted and supported her shoulders and head, propping her against his own shoulder.

'Now,' said the midwife. 'Deep breath, chin down, and PUSH! Yes, that's lovely, lovely. Pant, now. Just pant.'

'Good God, Cassie! It's talking already!' exclaimed Tod, as the baby made a little mewling protest, quite unlike the cry they had heard earlier. Cassandra gave a little gasp of laughter, gazing at the round head that was turning as the midwife rotated the baby to free its shoulders. As she did so there was a slithering sensation, and the baby slipped sweetly and easily from the birth canal and into the midwife's waiting hands. Swiftly she checked the child, clearing mouth and nostrils, and when the baby gave a cry she laid her on Cassandra's stomach.

'There,' she said, proudly. 'A lovely little girl, my dear.'

The baby lay quiet against the warm skin, her crying stilled, and Cassandra reached to stroke her. After a few minutes the cord was cut, and Cassandra held her daughter in her arms. She was still sitting against Tod, who gazed down in awed amazement as she held the child awkwardly to her breast. At the touch of her nipple on her cheek, the little head, with its thatch of dark hair, turned to her, mouth already opening. The baby sucked, her eyes open and gazing up at Cassandra.

'Hello,' whispered Cassandra. 'Hello, baby. Hello. Oh, Tod, she's so perfect. And so clever, look, she knows how to suck and everything. Isn't that the cleverest baby you've ever seen?'

Tod blinked. 'She's wonderful. Amazing. She's . . . I can't find the words. So new. So alive. I feel . . . I feel like God.'

'Yes.' Cassandra knew just what he meant. 'It's the ultimate creation, isn't it? A whole new world. That's what she is. That's what I'll call her. Eve. No, Eva. Do you hear, darling? Your name's Eva.' Her fingers stroked the perfect curve of her skull. 'Hello, Eva. Say hello to Tod, Eva.'

Tod leaned forward over Cassandra's shoulder. For a moment, he was afterwards to swear, the baby's eyes moved up to rest consideringly on him. She had stopped sucking, and now the nipple left her moist lips with a little pop. For one long instant she gazed at him, then her look wandered back to Cassandra's face. Quite suddenly, she sneezed.

'Bless you!' exclaimed Cassandra. 'Oh, how clever! She knows how to sneeze, too.'

'She is, without a doubt, the most intelligent baby I've ever seen,' he agreed, perfectly seriously, and forgetting how few babies he had ever had to do with in his life. 'And the most beautiful. Oh, Cassandra, thank you. You've given me something I never thought I'd have, and it's probably the most wonderful thing I've ever been given. I'll never forget tonight.'

'Today,' corrected Cassandra, glancing at the window. 'Look, it's dawn.'

'Thank goodness it didn't come any sooner, you'd have been calling her Aurora, or Dawnie, or something,' he joked to relieve his emotion. 'Had you not decided on a name for her? You seemed to have been doing nothing but talk about names for months. I'd lost track of all the things you'd chosen and rejected.'

'No, I gave up in the end. I just couldn't choose, so I decided I'd wait until I saw her, and then I'd *know* what her name was. And I did, didn't I?'

The midwife came back into the room. She had left this extremely odd couple to their moment of privacy, as she always did so long as the baby was healthy, but there were still things to be done and she wanted to be finished up before the end of her shift, if possible. It was always irritating to go off duty and leave a job half done.

'I've brought you a nice cup of tea,' she said briskly. 'I'm sure you can both do with it, and Baby must be weighed and checked. I'll bring her back very soon. We'll get you all cleaned up and back in bed shortly.'

'Her name's Eva,' said Cassandra. 'Eva Mary, for my mother.'

'Very nice too,' approved the midwife, pleased to have something normal happening. She had gathered from the nurse that the elderly gentleman was neither the baby's father, nor the patient's, and she found it bothersome that he didn't fit in with any of the usual scenarios. These things were all very peculiar now, she thought, with mothers bringing goodness-knew-who to be with them. Time was, she thought nostalgically, when even fathers weren't welcome until all the business of the birth was safely out of the way. Still, she had to admit he had been helpful, and certainly hadn't made more work for her by fainting, or crying, or being sick, so she smiled at him forgivingly and offered him more tea.

'I suppose I'd better be going,' Tod said reluctantly. 'You'll be able to telephone your parents, of course, and the others – unless you'd like me to do it?'

'No, it had better be me,' said Cassandra, 'Oh, Tod, thank you for coming and holding my hand. You were marvellous, really. You know, I'm quite glad the telephone was off! It must have been Meant!'

'Yes,' he agreed. 'If I'd known how it would be, I'd have disconnected it myself, just to be on the safe side! Now, is there anything you want? Anything I can bring you? And can I come back and see you soon? Your parents will want to visit today, but tomorrow, perhaps?'

'Oh, I'll probably be home by tomorrow,' said Cassandra blithely. 'I don't suppose . . . ?'

'Of course I will! I'd love to! How exciting!'

'I'll ring you, let you know what's happening. Oh, Tod, isn't it all wonderful?'

'It is. It really is.'

Chapter 18

Christmas Day itself passed by Laura in a blur of self-induced amnesia. Right up to the last few days she had been unable to decide what she wanted to do. Edward had offered to take her away – to France, perhaps, or Italy – any place where there would be no memories, no reminders, nothing to disturb the still, oily surface of her pool of grief. Knowing that they could not afford it, she had refused, as she had also refused invitations from her sister, from Jane and Anna, even, tentatively, from Cassandra. In the end it had seemed best to her to stay at home, to retreat into the cosy shell of familiarity where she could be private with her misery.

At the midnight service on Christmas Eve the church was packed, so that Laura and Edward, who had only to walk over the green and were therefore later than most, had to sit on extra chairs borrowed from the Parish Room. Laura was grateful and touched that Edward should accompany her. She knew that church services affected him almost physically, making him fidget with discomfort like a child in scratchy woollen clothes. He would make no pretence of joining in, remaining stubbornly erect during the prayers, only lowering his eyes more from embarrassment than from anything else, and clamping his lips together during the carols, although Laura knew he had a good baritone voice. Still, he was there, and squashed together as they were she could feel the solid warmth of him beside her, a touch that was almost as immediate as if they had been holding hands. For once she was thankful for the modern form of the service, feeling that the beauty of the old words and their echoes of past and childhood days might have been more than she could bear.

Only during the carols did her throat tighten, so that though she continued to mouth the words, no sound came out. Around her the church seemed to swell with the unaccustomed pressure of voices; the air was heavy with perfume, and with gusts of alcohol-laden breath from those who had dined rather too well, and were carried away in the throes of belting out an old and familiar tune. Laura looked at the Crib, with its stiffly carved wooden figures that were brought out each year, at the manger of real hay in which the doll-like image of Christ had now been placed, and found she could make no connection either with the God in whom she thought she believed, or with the child whose soul, she wanted to hope, was in his care.

Afterwards, carried through the door on a stream of people cheerfully greeting one another and smugly conscious that this attendance freed them from the inconvenience of church on Christmas morning, when there was the turkey to be cherished, the presents to be opened and the over-excited children to be pacified, Laura found herself next to Tod.

'My *dears*! The Compliments of the Season,' he exclaimed in theatrical tones. 'I will *not* say Happy Christmas,' he confided breathily. 'Too like a cheap Christmas card.'

'Yes, compliments of the season is definitely more of a big, glossy number with your name printed on it,' agreed Laura. 'Like the lovely one you sent us, in fact.'

'You liked it? I'm so glad. I had wondered whether it wasn't just a shade *outré* – but then your taste is so sophisticated.'

'Flatterer,' laughed Laura. 'I did like it, but I didn't understand it. Should I have?'

'My dear,' he confided, 'how can I possibly say? With modern art, it either speaks to you or it doesn't. To me it conveyed emotion, but if to you it was merely a collection of harmonious colours attractively arranged, does it matter? On a Christmas card, in any case?'

'You must come and explain it to me one day soon. Where's Edward? Oh, there he is, talking to Jane and Candida – oh, and Daisy too. Merry Christmas, Jane, Candy. And you, darling.' She kissed them all in turn. Jane and Candida returned her greeting, but Daisy had had several glasses of wine during the evening and was feeling rather emotional. Christmas, in any event, always made her feel tearfully sentimental, and now she gazed at Laura with wide, tragic eyes, then hugged her convulsively.

'Dear, darling Laura,' she said. 'How can you be so brave?'

'Well, I can't be, if you say things like that,' said Laura. 'Please, Daisy.'

Daisy blinked hard. 'I'm sorry,' she said. 'It's just . . .' Her lower lip trembled.

'It's just that you've only been back from school a few days, and you've scarcely got used to seeing us yet,' said Edward, putting an arm round her shoulders and giving her a little shake. 'Everything's all right, Daisy. Where's Anna? I saw her in church, I thought.'

'Yes, she's here,' said Daisy, rubbing her head against his shoulder

212

and finding comfort in the rough friction of his woollen coat. 'Over there, with Guy, talking to the Blackmans. Or should it be the Blackmen?' She gave a watery giggle at this rather poor joke. 'I wish you were coming to us tomorrow,' she said wistfully. 'It would be much more fun.'

'Well, we'll see you all on Boxing Day. And have you seen Eva yet?' Edward judged it better to get all the awkward things over with in one go. Daisy started, and turned her eyes anxiously towards Laura again.

'Isn't she a poppet?' asked Laura with firm cheerfulness. 'I'm so thrilled, Caz has asked me to be godmother, and you too, I believe? And Tod as godfather, which is only right seeing he practically delivered her single-handed.'

Jane, who had been talking to Tod, gave a sudden jaw-cracking yawn. 'Oh, I'm sorry!' she exclaimed. 'But we really must get back. Sophisticated Ben may be, but he still wants a stocking, and so of course does Toby, and I haven't finished wrapping all the bits yet. It's so much more difficult to find things for a fourteen-year-old boy, too old for toys and too young for socks.'

'I should think so!' said Daisy, shocked. 'Socks! How drab!'

'It depends on the socks,' said Jane, who knew that Anna had found a particularly resplendent pair that played 'Jingle Bells' for Daisy's own stocking. 'Come on, Candy. 'Night, everyone.'

Laura leaned against Edward as they walked home through the cold night air. 'I wish . . .' she said softly.

Edward tightened the grip of his arm. 'I know. I wish, too.'

But Laura knew that his wish had not been hers. The knowledge kept her guiltily silent. He wished, simply, that they still had a baby whose stocking, over the years, would become increasingly difficult to fill. So, of course, did she. But, at the same time, the subject of her immediate wish had been that she could have been filling a stocking for Mark, that very night.

Laura had invited everyone to lunch on Boxing Day. She had not bothered with a turkey for herself and Edward, and as she had sometimes done before had bought a pheasant, which was a treat but did not commit them to endless meals of leftovers. For Boxing Day, to give everyone a change, she had prepared a large piece of spiced beef and a fish terrine, which with jacket potatoes and several different salads she hoped would provide a good contrast to the rich meals they would all have eaten the previous day.

The party was, unusually, a bit stiff at first, with everyone trying to be careful not to say the wrong thing, but surprisingly the atmosphere lightened after Cassandra arrived with Eva. It might have been because she was escorted by Tod, who had no truck with watching his words, but tended rather to give voice to the one thing that everyone else was avoiding.

'Here we are, then,' he trumpeted. 'One Cassandra, one baby, one Wise Man . . .'

'Which one? Gold, frankincense, or myrrh?' asked Edward, eyeing the box that Tod was clasping to him. 'Gold, I hope. I'm not sure what to do with the others.'

'Liquid gold, at any rate,' said Tod, puffing as he bent to put down the box and producing from it several bottles of champagne. 'Ready chilled, if you want to use them. I meant to be here first, but her majesty needed changing just as we were leaving the house.'

'Champagne! Wonderful! I had some sparkling white, but this is much better – luckily I'd only opened one bottle so far. Thanks, Tod, it's very generous of you. Come and let me pour you a glass. And you too, of course, Caz – bring Eva with you, why not? Better get her used to a busy social life right from the start.'

Soon, under the influence of the champagne, conversation was flowing in a cheerful babble, and by the time they ate the initial tension had vanished, to be replaced by the kind of happy uninhibitedness engendered by champagne among a group of people who knew one another well. Laura had moved an extra table through to the dining room, so that it was possible for all eleven of them to sit comfortably, leaving her guests to seat themselves as they willed. As usual, this meant that the younger members sat at the far end, with only Guy joining the adults, the buffer zone between the two generations being provided by Cassandra and Tod.

Daisy and Candida had their heads together, with Ben listening and throwing in a remark from time to time, which the girls appeared not to resent. Toby, rather flown with the sips of champagne he had sneaked while helping or, as he called it, buttling, was describing his new computer game to Cassandra, who was putting on a very creditable show of interest, and Tod had embarked on one of his long and involved stories which, since it was almost certainly slanderous, Laura very much hoped was apocryphal. Of the adults, only Guy looked a bit lost. Why was it that he found it so difficult to fit in? wondered Laura. She leaned forward and asked him a question about his work, knowing that he could prose on for hours about it, and that she need do no more than smile and nod and make the occasional murmur of appreciation.

It's going well, thought Laura. I wish Mark were here, he enjoys these get-togethers, and I'm sure they're good for him. He needs to see that different generations can be together and still enjoy themselves. Dear Mark, I hope he's having a happy Christmas. She fell into a brief reverie, and when Guy asked her a question she jumped, and looked guilty, which made him worry a bit.

The afternoon was fine, one of those soft mid-winter days when the air smells as sweet as if spring were already stirring. Even Tod consented to leave the fireside and come for a walk, along with the ecstatic Slops who foresaw numerous victims for her stick-fetching game. They ended up at Anna's for tea and Christmas cake, and Edward started a noisy game of Pictionary, whilst a quiet but vicious game of Scrabble between Tod and Ben carried on concurrently at the side. Laura was very thankful, on getting home at nine o'clock, that her protests about allowing her guests to clear up had been overruled. Anna and Jane had dragooned the reluctant young into the washing-up, and had themselves seen to the putting-away, the tidying, and the wiping-down, so that apart from moving the extra table out from the dining room, nothing remained to be done. Laura undressed, putting on the old velour dressing-gown that she still adored because it was so warm and comfortable, and joined Edward in the sitting room.

When the telephone rang she sighed, because she had made herself so cosy on the sofa with her feet tucked up under a fold of dressing-gown, and had begun the new Dick Francis paperback that Edward had given her and she had put off starting until now because she knew that she would be unable to put it down. She and Edward had agreed to give one another only small, relatively useful things this year, and she had rather enjoyed hunting for them. She heard Edward pick up the phone in the kitchen.

'Hello? Oh, hello, Mark. Happy Christmas.'

Mark! Laura cast the cherished book from her, disentangled her feet, and pattered through to the kitchen without bothering to put on her slippers. She resisted the urge to snatch the telephone from Edward's hand, but stood close, hoping to hear what Mark said, only to be frustrated by his usual mumble.

'Good, I'm glad you liked it,' Edward was saying. 'Sorry it wasn't more, but . . . yes, I know. School OK? Ish? Well, yes, I know that, but . . . Yes.'

Laura leaned on the Aga rail, putting first one foot and then the other against the hot side, and finding it too hot, as always, for bare skin. Edward raised his eyebrows in a question and she nodded.

'Right, then, it's good to hear from you. Here's Laura. Bye now, see you soon.'

Laura took the receiver.

'Mark! How lovely that you rang. How are you?'

'All right,' he said dismally.

'Oh dear, as bad as that? Boxing Day can be a bit drab, can't it – but how was Christmas? Did you have a nice day?'

'No.' His voice was low, but explosive. 'It was the pits. The worst Christmas ever.'

'Oh dear,' said Laura inadequately. 'What a shame, I am sorry, Mark. You're the wrong age for it now, I suppose.'

'I hate Christmas.' His tone was uncompromising. 'I wasn't allowed out at all, just stuck here with them. I'd rather be at school. At least I can be with my friends there.'

'Poor old thing.' Laura thought sadly of her own day, and wished once again that he had been there to share it. 'What about the New Year? Will you be able to see your friends then?'

'Shouldn't think so. Fran'll be coming over again, and I won't be allowed to go anywhere.'

Laura thought, not for the first time, that this kind of thing was scarcely going to encourage Mark to be fond of his grandmother, though naturally she could not say so.

'Well, if you've spent Christmas with her,' she said tentatively, 'would you perhaps be allowed to come here for the New Year? If you'd like to, that is.'

'Shouldn't think they'll let me.' His gloomy tone was not encouraging.

'I'll fix it for you if I can. If you want me to.'

'Can you?' The hope in his voice gave her the answer she wanted.

'I'll do my best. Perhaps Edward can do it. But if they say no, try to make the best of it, it's not for very long. Just remember that they want you to be there because they love you.'

'Uh.' His grunt was noncommittal.

Laura replaced the telephone gently, and went to look for Edward. 'Poor old Mark,' she said. 'He did sound depressed, didn't he? A bit desperate, even. I know I shouldn't criticise, but I do think if they gave him a bit more freedom, he'd be so much happier.'

Edward looked up from the book on Venice, his abiding passion, that had been one of Laura's presents to him.

'It's a risky business, giving freedom to fourteen-year-old boys. Particularly when you live in a city, and he's already been in trouble at school. But I know what you mean. He does sound a bit like a volcano ready to blow.'

Laura sat on the arm of his chair, and trailed her fingers through his curling mop of hair. 'I said I'd try to fix it for him to come down here for the New Year. Well, in fact I said you'd try to fix it.'

'Same thing,' he said peacefully. 'Would he want to, though? I'd have thought he'd have been going to some kind of party with his friends.'

'No, that's just it, he's not. He thinks he won't be allowed out at all, just like at Christmas. That's why he was so desperate. He said he'd like to come, and I'm sure he could be included in whatever Ben has planned. Will you have a go? Please?'

'If that's what you want.' He was already pulling himself up from the chair.

'You don't mind, do you? I mean, he is your son.'

'Mind? Of course I don't mind. I'm always happy to have Mark here, and as long as it doesn't make too much work for you . . .'

'No, it doesn't, not at all.' Laura knew there was no point in trying to explain to Edward, still so protective of her, that the extra work involved in having Mark to stay was actually a pleasure, a positive thing. She waited, sitting in the chair Edward had left, and listening to his voice as it spoke, calmly and reasonably, to Georgia. She knew before he came back smiling that he had succeeded.

'All arranged. She wasn't terribly keen, but it's not very easy for her to refuse now that he's stayed with us and got to know us a bit. And I think she's glad to know he'll be away from some of his more dubious friends. It's bad enough in the towns round here, but when you hear what goes on in city schools, you wonder how any of these kids grow up without becoming drug addicts or joy riders. He'll come down on the train on the morning of the thirtieth, and he can stay until the second – but no longer, because of going back to school.'

'Lovely,' said Laura, counting on her fingers. 'I'll go and ring Ben straight away.'

'Hang on!' Edward was amused by her eagerness. 'It's after ten o'clock. I know Ben won't have gone to bed, but I should think Jane certainly will, and I think you should too. It won't hurt to leave it until the morning.'

Reluctantly, Laura agreed with him.

The few days of Mark's visit passed by in a flash. He seemed pleased to be there, his face splitting into a wide grin as he came out of the station and saw Laura waiting for him. As he got into the car he leaned across quite spontaneously for her kiss of greeting.

Ben's New Year's Eve party turned out to be rather a grand affair, run for people from fourteen to eighteen in aid of the local hospice. Anna, fortunately, was on the committee organising it, and was able to produce a ticket, as well as digging out an old dinner jacket that had once been Guy's.

'It was secondhand then,' she said, 'but he went to several of these charity balls at that age, and when I found how expensive it was to hire, I went round all the Oxfam shops until I found one the right size. It had the most unbelievable flared trousers, but I had them taken in and it looks all right, I think. At least it should be more or less the right size, and you'll never find anywhere to hire one now, everything's closed or emptied out.'

'It's fine,' said Laura gratefully. 'I've managed to get him a shirt, and he can borrow Edward's tie and cummerbund.'

Laura – knowing that, although the ticket said that food would be provided, what was on offer was likely to be tepid pizza and crisps – invited as many of Ben's and Daisy's friends as were free to come and have supper before the ball. Rightly suspecting that they wouldn't want to eat too much, she made a good selection of finger foods, carefully omitting anything with garlic, or anything messy that might stain. As they began to arrive she was tying Mark's tie.

'Stand still,' she scolded. 'Bow ties are such monstrous things, but I can't bear the ready-done ones . . . there, let me just tighten it and get it straight . . . good, that's it.'

He had grown since the summer. Now he stood looking slightly down at her, smiling self-consciously as she evened the wing collar of his shirt and straightened his jacket. With her hands on his shoulders, she leaned back to survey him.

'Goodness, Mark, I'm not sure if we dare let you loose on the world,' she said admiringly. 'You look so handsome, you probably should carry some kind of government health warning.' He grinned sheepishly. 'Get out there and slay them,' she said, touching his freshly shaved cheek with her fingertips. About to turn away, she remembered the warning she had received from one of the other mothers. 'Um, you haven't got any bottles of vodka hidden in your pockets, have you? Only it's strictly forbidden to take drink in with you, and I believe they sometimes frisk you at the door at some of these dos. They've had too much trouble with people adding strange things to the fruit cup, and people throwing up and collapsing all over the place.'

His eyes widened in the candid look she did not altogether trust. 'Nothing,' he said earnestly, patting his pockets. 'You can check if you like.'

'I wouldn't dream of it,' she said. 'I know I can trust you, Mark.'

He tilted his head, considering her. 'We were thinking of having a few beers before going,' he offered tentatively.

Goodness, thought Laura, it works! How extraordinary.

'Well,' she said carefully, 'I should think one, or maybe two, before you go to get you in the party mood wouldn't be such a bad idea. But why not save the rest until afterwards, when you're all at Ben's? You're intending to sit up half the night watching videos, I know. You'd all enjoy the beers far more then. I know you're probably all aiming to get as pissed as nudes, as a friend of mine's mother puts it, but if you overdo it, I can assure you that girls are deeply unimpressed by people throwing up all over the place, or passing out. And for another, the people who are running this shindig are mostly friends of mine, or at least acquaintances. It would be nice not to have them ringing me up tomorrow to tell me things they really feel I ought to know. What do you think, is that fair?'

He thought about it. 'Yes, I suppose so,' he admitted. 'I'll put it to the others. Don't worry,' he added kindly. 'I'm really very sensible, you know.'

Looking at him, Laura saw that he really believed what he said. 'I know you are, Mark,' she said, hoping that, if they both believed it, it would have to be true.

Laura went to the rectory late the following morning. The house was heavy with the silence of sleeping people, and Jane was stirring a large pan of soup.

'Happy New Year, Jane,' said Laura.

'And to you too, Laura,' said Jane, coming to kiss her. 'A happier one than last, anyway.'

'Oh, it's sure to be,' said Laura blithely. 'It couldn't possibly be worse, could it? I'm sure things are going to improve this year, for all of us. How did last night go? Did you get any sleep?'

'Not much,' admitted Jane. 'They did their best to be quiet, but you know what this house is like. Every floorboard creaks, every door bangs, and when anyone flushes the loo the pipes sound like a small, healthy tsunami. They were still going strong at five o'clock, heaven only knows what time they'll wake up. Come and see the sitting room: I saved it for you.'

Together they surveyed the large room. All the furniture capable of being sat on had been pulled into a tight circle round the television, and within it all the available cushions were arranged into little nests on the floor. Every flat surface was covered with empty glasses, plates and mugs, and the bare carpet outside the circle was littered with empty crisp packets, so that their feet rustled as they walked as if it had been an autumn wood.

'It looks like a *laager*,' said Laura, amused.

'It looks like rather a lot of lagers,' responded Jane rather grimly.

'No, I mean like a camp,' explained Laura. 'You know, all the wagons pulled into a defensive circle round the fire.'

'Disgusting little brutes,' said Jane without rancour. 'I suppose I should leave it for them to clear up, but how long can I live with it? I don't suppose any of them will be awake for hours, and when they do they'll only be half human. You know they had a cache of beers?'

'Yes, Mark told me.' Laura's calm voice tried to conceal her pride. 'I suggested they should have one or two, and keep the rest for after the ball.'

'Well done. I rather gathered someone had put that to them. At least they were all sober when they arrived there, and pretty much all right when they came home. Oh Laura, this sort of thing is so much more difficult without Bill! How on earth am I supposed to know how much I should let Ben experiment, and how strict I should be about things like drinking? I asked Anna, but of course she never had any of that sort of thing with Guy, he was always so sensible.'

Laura thought of Mark, who thought he was sensible too.

'I know, it is a worry. Edward seemed to think it was all right that they should have a few beers, and I think the great thing is that they should be open about it. They're bound to try things out at this age, and of course they'll overdo it sometimes. But better six beers that we know about, or even eight, than a secret nip of vodka somewhere else, don't you think?'

'It's just that I worry about Ben. He does tend to take things to extremes. Look at that problem I had over his not eating. Suppose he gets it into his head to try to get his father's attention back by drinking too much?'

'I honestly don't think he would. At least, there's no sign of it so far, is there?'

'I suppose not. At least if they're here, I can sort things out if there's a problem. And come to think of it, Bill used to get absolutely paralytic every New Year's Eve, so he wouldn't have been much help anyway. He'd either have encouraged them to drink too much, or forbidden it altogether. One extreme or the other, that's my Bill. Or was. It must be where Ben gets it from.'

'Exactly. If you ask me, you're doing a great job, with or without Bill.'

Jane gave a watery smile. 'Thanks for that. And while we're handing out compliments, I reckon you're doing a pretty good job on Mark, too. He was really quite chatty last night, and asked me several times if there was anything he could do to help, which is more than I can say for the rest of them.'

Laura felt a glow of pleasure. She loved to hear Mark praised. The warmth of it stayed with her, and carried her through the ordeal of seeing Mark go back to London, and into the cold darkness of January and February.

Chapter 19

By the time Easter came round, Laura felt that she had her life back in control once more. January had been bad, partly because of the cold and the lowering clouds that shed sleety rain in unending quantities, but mostly because the baby should have been born during the last week of the month. During that week, Laura withdrew once more into herself. Jane and Anna telephoned her every day, and Cassandra took Eva to stay with her parents for the whole of the week, an act of such delicacy and self-immolation that Laura was moved to tears.

The idea for this, though Laura did not know it, had come from Hilda Davis. As Laura had rather hoped, Cassandra had taken to Hilda at once, and although nothing formal had been arranged between them, Cassandra had developed the habit of asking Hilda, on one or two afternoons a week, to look after Eva. Hilda was delighted to use her skills, and to earn a little extra cash, and Cassandra gained as much from Hilda's experience and calm good-humour as she did from the few hours of freedom.

Cassandra, who knew to a day when Laura's baby should have been born, had discussed with Hilda what, if anything, she should do at that time. They were sitting in Cassandra's ultra-modern sitting room, with Eva kicking on a brightly coloured blanket on the floor between them. Cassandra had spent the afternoon in London, doing the rounds of the suppliers and making choices for summer and autumn stock. On returning home she had shed her beautifully cut wool suit, her high-heeled shoes and her sheer tights with a relief that two years ago she would have been horrified to feel, and she was now curled up on the sofa in velour leggings and an enormous bright pink mohair sweater.

'You have no idea how liberating it is to be able to loll about dressed like this,' said Cassandra, who had wasted no time in telling Hilda all about her previous commitment to Stephen. 'Stephen hated leggings. He said they were common.'

'Common is as common does,' said Hilda firmly. 'If you've got the figure for them – which you certainly have – then what's the harm?

223

Comfortable and practical, though I couldn't see myself wearing them.'

Cassandra eyed her roundabout shape, in its usual sensible tweed skirt and hand-knitted jumper. Her lips twitched.

'No, I don't think they're quite you . . .' Eva gave a little squawk, and Cassandra bent to pick her up.

'There's a precious girl, then,' she said idiotically. Eva nuzzled at her, and she slipped one arm out of her sweater. She had expressed some milk before going out, and left it for Hilda to give Eva if she seemed to need it, but now her breasts were hard and tight, and she was glad to feed her again. She winced slightly as the baby's lips clamped on to her nipple, then drew in a breath as the milk flowed. Without being asked, Hilda fetched a glass of water from the kitchen, knowing that Cassandra always felt violently thirsty when she fed Eva.

'Thanks, Hilda,' said Cassandra, shifting to support Eva with her arm so she could take the glass. 'I do want it, in spite of just having drunk three cups of tea. It's funny, isn't it?' She put the empty glass down on the floor, and looked down at Eva. 'I can't help thinking of Laura at times like this,' she said softly. 'Her baby would have been born next week, if things had gone right. I know she must be thinking of it, and I just don't know whether to ring her, or what.'

'Ring her, by all means,' said Hilda sensibly, 'but I should try to make sure you haven't got Eva with you when you do, in case she cries or makes a noise. In her place, I don't think I could bear the sight or sound of another baby, however fond of it I was, during that time. You wouldn't consider . . .' She paused, her head tilted inquiringly on one side. Cassandra thought she looked like Mrs Tiggywinkle.

'Consider what? I did think of going on holiday for a week, but I don't really want to spend that sort of money, and Eva's a bit little to go abroad, even if I could afford it.'

'Oh, I wasn't thinking of that. But what about your family? I know they come over to see her, but what about spending a few days with them? They'd like that, surely, wouldn't they?'

'Well, they would,' said Cassandra. 'In fact, my mother's suggested it once or twice. But . . . you know.'

Hilda wisely said no more. Cassandra sat frowning down at Eva without seeing her, then came back to herself in time to change the baby to the other side before she herself became hopelessly lopsided.

'I suppose I could,' she concluded reluctantly. 'Just for a week,' she added hastily. 'And of course I'd have to drive back to the shop for two of those days.'

'Do half a day, if you can, and leave Eva with your mother like you do with me. She'd like that more than anything.'

'Yes . . .' Cassandra's face brightened. 'She would enjoy that. And if it helps Laura . . .'

Hilda Davis, satisfied, nodded approvingly.

As the days began, almost imperceptibly, to lengthen, Laura felt her spirits lift, as she had hoped they would. Always in the past she had been more inclined to get depressed during those dark months of the year when winter seemed as if it had been going on for ever and would never stop. The first snowdrops in the garden, which she usually picked in triumph and set in little jugs round the house, were this year left to bloom in the garden. Somehow their smallness and whiteness was too much of a reminder of the baby that was gone. The robust yellow of the crocuses, however, was more cheering, and with the little early daffodils came a promise of spring and even summer. They grew almost wild in the borders and round the old apple trees of the orchard, their fat buds bursting into extravagantly frilled double flowers in shades of yellow and primrose, very different from the aggressive brightness of their bigger, cultivated cousins.

To Laura these flowers, more than any others, meant Easter. One of her favourite festivals, she sometimes thought she preferred it to Christmas; what it lacked in glitter and spurious excitement it made up for with the joy of its promise. The triumphant Easter hymns moved her, not more, but more pleasurably, than the sentimental and child-orientated carols.

As he had done for several years, Tod organised an enormous Easter egg hunt, which was meant to be for the children in the choir and the Sunday School, but which in effect attracted most of the children in the village. The younger ones followed a trail of brightly coloured pieces of paper streamer, tied to twigs and fences and plants, and hunted for their eggs along the way. As usual, Anna and Daisy took charge of this, leaving Tod to rack his own brain, and everyone else's, for clues for the older children.

'There are only so many landmarks I can use,' he complained to Laura two weeks before Easter. They had met at St Barbara's, and as once before were walking home together. 'Of course, most of them will have forgotten last year's hunt, but there's always the odd one or two really bright ones, who've been doing the hunt for years and know all my old tricks.'

'What have you done so far?'

225

'Mostly old faithfuls, I'm afraid. The lychgate, and the war memorial, and the shop. And I have found rather a good stand of hornbeams up on the forest, three trees all twisted together, quite startlingly Rackhamesque.'

'How on earth will they find them? One of those "the number of the disciples multiplied by the age of Methuselah paces west" jobs? I'd have thought the counting would be a bit tricky.'

'Heavens, wouldn't it just! No, the one before is the stile on the footpath, and from there it's not so bad – just the number of days Jesus spent in the wilderness north, and the Gospels times the Tribes of Israel east. Guy's said he'll come down and help, so he can do the distant bits, save my poor old legs.'

'What about the children's poor young legs?'

'Poor young legs nothing. You know they will run the entire course, given half a chance. I have to make the clues difficult to give the adults a chance to catch up with them. It's no good if they finish too quickly, and we want them nice and tired by tea-time, so that they're not too rowdy.'

'What about the new people at North Lodge?' suggested Laura. 'They've put up a wishing well in the front garden.'

Tod shuddered. 'Don't *remind* me! Too twee for words, and with a couple of stone doves on the roof, as well as a stone cat sitting on the wall. Too vomit-making.'

'Well, it is a bit twee, but the kids won't mind that, and it would make a new place for a clue. You could put it in the bucket. I expect they'd love to be asked, and they might give something for the tea, too. They're longing to join in what they call Village Life. I don't think they realise that most villages don't really have such a thing any more, now that half the houses belong to weekenders.'

'You can't say that about Ashingly!' Tod was seriously put out. 'We have a very strong sense of community spirit. Look at the summer fête. And the stoolball team. And the drama group, and the bridge club, and—'

'What you mean is that *you* have a very strong sense of community spirit,' interrupted Laura. 'Most of those things only keep going because you put sticks of dynamite under them regularly.'

It was true, but Tod did not want to believe it. He, as much as the new owners of North Lodge, needed to feel that Rural England was alive and kicking, and not merely reduced to pretty photographs in glossy magazines.

'Poppycock. Anyway, what's their name?'

'Who? The North Lodge couple? Sharpe, I think.'

'Ah.' Tod walked on, absently twirling the silver-topped stick that was his latest affectation. 'Nature,' he murmured to himself. 'Crature. A bit

226

Irish. I know.' He mouthed silently to himself, then stood still and raised his stick with a declamatory gesture.

'Try this one for size,' he said in a normal voice, then struck an attitude.

> 'Ding dong bell,
> The clue is in the well,
> With any luck it
> Will be in the bucket
> But really you never can tell.'

'Wonderful,' said Laura politely. 'But how are they to know which well? There are at least five or six round the green. Cassandra has one, I know, though it's covered over.'

'I hadn't finished,' he informed her stiffly. 'I was coming to that bit.'

'Sorry,' said Laura meekly.

> 'Don't shout, just talk [continued Tod],
> Don't run, just walk,
> Go carefully, then they won't hate yer,
> They're Sharpe by name, but not by nature.'

His look of triumph was ludicrous. Laura giggled helplessly.

'Oh, Tod, you've excelled yourself! What a dreadful rhyme!'

'It is bad, isn't it?' he agreed with satisfaction. 'Well, that's another one done. I must scurry home and write it down before I forget it.'

Making up for Christmas, Laura decided to invite as many people as possible to lunch on Easter Sunday. Her sister, who had been away at Christmas time, promised to come, and all her usual friends, as well as a girl from Daisy's school, who was spending a week with her, and Cassandra's parents. The week Cassandra and Eva had spent with them in January had been so successful that it had been repeated in March, and Cassandra was amazed how genial her father could be, and how he appeared to dote on his grand-daughter.

'He's been staying for two days,' she whispered to Laura as she arrived, 'and he hasn't once complained about the height of the doorways, or about the furniture! I can't believe it!'

On the strength of the party, Laura had managed to persuade Edward to put pressure, once again, on Georgia to allow Mark to come and stay for a few days. Permission was reluctantly given, and Laura was greatly relieved, since she had, without admitting it even to Edward, planned the whole party as an excuse to get Mark down from London.

Delighted with her success, Laura ordered a huge turkey and prepared all the usual trimmings. She decided on a seafood salad as a starter, although Mark didn't like fish, but made up for it by making his favourite chocolate mousse for dessert, with brandysnaps, as well as a Simnel cake and ices made like half hard-boiled eggs, with lemon sorbet for the white and apricot sorbet for the yolk.

Once again Laura had moved an extra table through to the dining room so that it was possible for all sixteen of them to sit comfortably. As before, the younger ones stayed down at the far end, but this time Mark was next to Ben, with the three girls opposite them. Laura, bored as always with the food she had prepared, picked at her own plate while keeping a watchful eye on everyone else's, and let the various strands of conversation weave their way past her ears. She noticed that Daisy's friend, Sarah, seemed fascinated by Mark and kept talking to him across the table. Mark's smile, once so rare, flashed out with the regularity of a lighthouse beacon.

'So I said, "Get a life" . . .' Toby's piercing treble rose effortlessly above the noise.

'and the salesman offered him a car for £500, beautiful condition, only drawback was it didn't have an engine . . .' Tod, embarking on one of his stories for the benefit of anyone who might be listening.

'Mark! Mark! Don't you think that . . .'

'. . . the President of Estonia . . .' Anna, to Edward.

'. . . so the salesman said "That's all right, sir, you just say 'Thank God', and it goes". So he took it for a test drive . . .'

'"Our politics is the politics of survival, as it was between 1918 and 1920 . . ."'

'but if you consider it ontologically . . .' Ontologically? thought Laura. Ben is really getting difficult to understand.

'Mark! . . .'

'. . . but how do you stop it? And the salesman told him "Just say, 'Amen'", so he did, and it stopped at once . . .'

'". . . whereas Western politics is the politics of what sort of car a person can afford."' Anna's quotation blended neatly with Tod's story, noticed only by Laura.

'. . . his wife said, "You stupid bastard, buying a car with no engine." So he took her for a test drive too . . .'

'"British politics is about clubs, not democracy,"' Edward quoted back to Anna.

'. . . said "Thank God", and off it went, and "Amen", and it stopped, and she was really impressed, so he told his mother-in-law about it, and she said . . .'

'I do rather wonder about mussels . . .' Ben was peering at one he had found on his plate.

'. . . took her with them for a drive, "Thank God" and off they went, thought he'd go to Beachy Head . . .'

'They look so very *rude* . . .' Ben was glimmering a naughty look at his mother.

'. . . waited till the last minute, and when they were right at the edge of the cliff, said "Amen", and the car stopped . . .'

'. . . and I mean that quite clitorally.'

'Ben! Really!' Jane laughed helplessly, wondering whether her son might be more sexually sophisticated than she had thought.

'. . . and his mother-in-law said, "Thank God"!' concluded Tod, to a burst of laughter.

It's going well, thought Laura. I'm so glad Mark's here. He looks happy. Tod's joke was clean, thank heaven, though as for Ben . . . Surely Ben hasn't . . . no. And if he has, it's none of my business. They all seem to know everything these days. I wonder what my mother would have thought . . . ? Or whether she'd have understood what he was saying. Which generation was it discovered the clitoris? When Guy asked her a question she jumped, and looked guilty, which made him wonder about her as she'd done that to him before.

In the afternoon they went out to help Tod set out the clues for the egg hunt the following day. Each was written on brightly coloured card in indelible pen, then put in a plastic bag secured at the top by a rubber band. Tod handed the clues one by one to Toby, who had decided he would rather go round today than join the large crowd on Monday. With some erratic help from Daisy and Candida, and a bit of tactful nudging from Ben, he solved each clue and ran ahead to fasten it in the appropriate place, making sure it was hidden from all but a determined search.

Laura, managing to get Anna and Jane to herself, broached the subject she had been mulling over in her mind since before Christmas.

'Have you made any plans for the summer? To go away, I mean?'

Jane shrugged.

'Not really. You know how it is, I'm never too sure whether Bill will pay up, though of course he's supposed to. Last year we left it pretty much until the last moment, and I expect we'll do the same.'

'I'll go along with everyone else's plans,' said Anna equably. 'I don't think Daisy has anything planned, and she may not want to come away with me. She's getting a bit grown-up for family holidays.'

'If you offer her somewhere nice in the sun, all paid for, she'll be there like a shot,' said Jane cynically. 'Did you have anything in mind?'

'I was looking at that brochure of yours from last year, There's a big house in it, it looks absolutely beautiful, you know the one in traditional Turkish style with the courtyard in the middle, and all that wood? I wondered about all of us going together. Toby could take a friend, like last year, so he's not left out, then Candy and Daisy have each other, and Ben and Mark, so they've all got someone to do things with.'

'You don't think Edward would mind, being the only man?' asked Anna. 'And – forgive me – but what about the money? Turkey's very cheap when you get there, but getting there isn't.'

'Oh, you know Edward. He's so easy-going, bless his heart, and as long as he can fish, and perhaps do some boat trips, he'll be perfectly happy. And I think it would be good for both of them for him and Mark to spend some time together, don't you? I think the money will be OK – I've been saving as much as I could out of my money from St Barbara's, and I've got a bit put by from the money my mother left me. I shouldn't need to ask Edward for anything.'

'Well, it sounds good to me,' said Jane. 'It would be lovely to have more adult company, and a man, too. Shall I ring the company and see if the house is free? We saw the outside last year, it looks lovely, but I don't think they get many lets for it, it's so big.'

'I'd better check whether Mark will be allowed to go with us,' said Laura. This time, she thought, I'll ring Georgia myself. I won't mention it to Edward until I've sounded her out, then it can be a *fait accompli*. She examined her own thought, and wondered. Would Edward, then, not want this holiday? He was singularly free, Laura knew, of the dislike many men felt at having things paid for them by women, having no problems with feelings of inadequacy. If she, Laura, were by some miracle to get a job that paid ten times more than he could ever hope to earn, he would be proud and delighted, she knew, with never a shred of envy in his pleasure.

No, the uneasiness she was conscious of was more to do with Mark. Specifically, with Edward's attitude to Mark. Somehow, though he would listen to her when she talked about him, and even make remarks of his own, there was still an underlying tension. It was as if Edward was jealous of her involvement with Mark. Not, rather surprisingly, because he felt possessive about his son and envied her for being able to spend more time with him, for being able to talk to him. Rather, he seemed in some unacknowledged way to resent the fact that she was so fond of Mark. Men, she knew, often felt this way after the birth of a first baby, when the new mother was so tied up with the child that she had little time for its father, but could that apply here? Laura resolved to try to bring them closer together. And surely this holiday, if she could manage it, would do just that?

Rather nervously, during the following week, she telephoned Georgia at a time when she knew Mark would be at school. Listening to the ringing tone she almost longed for it to continue, for Georgia to be out, but on the sixth ring it was answered. Laura felt a lurch in her stomach.

'Hello?'

Laura cleared her throat. 'Hello.' Her voice was too high. She tried again. 'Hello, um, Georgia. It's Laura. Laura Melville. Edward's . . . um . . .'

'Hello, Laura.' Georgia's voice was cool and controlled. 'Is everything all right?'

'All right? Yes, yes, of course it is. Everything's fine. Perfectly all right.' God, I'm babbling, she thought.

'Only you've never rung before, only Edward.'

'Yes, of course. You don't mind, do you?'

'Should I?' Her voice was amused. Laura felt her skin go hot with embarrassment, prickle with sweat.

'Well, I hope not. I wanted to ask you something, and I thought I'd mention it to you first, before saying anything to Edward.'

'Ask away.'

'I'm thinking, that is we're thinking, of organising a holiday in Turkey this summer. That's my friend Jane, who's got a son, Ben, who's the same age as Mark. And Anna. Her daughter Daisy is—'

'I've heard of Daisy. And Ben, but mostly Daisy.'

'Yes, she's a poppet, but there's nothing . . . I mean, she's two years older than Mark . . . but she's great friends with Ben's sister Candy, and then there's Toby, he's ten so he'd probably take a friend, and between them all there would be ten of us, and there's a large house Jane and Anna know of in the village where they went last year, they said it was lovely; not a lot of night-life, but bars with music and things where the kids could go in the evening and be quite safe, and of course we'd pay Mark's fare, naturally . . .' Aware that she was babbling again, Laura's voice ran down like a clockwork toy.

'It's very kind of you.' Georgia's voice was unreadable. 'Mark's never been to Turkey. In fact, he hasn't had many holidays abroad. I'd need to think about it.'

'Yes, of course. Of course you must. And ask Mark, too, I suppose.'

'No need. I know exactly what he'll say. He'll be delighted. He likes coming to stay with you.'

Was there just a tinge of bitterness in that light voice?

'We certainly enjoy having him,' said Laura. 'And don't you think it's good for him being with Edward?' she added, rather boldly.

'I suppose so. He doesn't say much, but he likes your cooking, and he seems keen on the other kids.'

'They all like him,' said Laura eagerly, 'and they're all nice kids, I've known them all their lives, almost. They're not . . . not a bad influence, or anything.'

'No, I should have thought it would have been rather the other way round,' said Georgia drily.

'Oh, no!' Laura was immediately stung into defence of her pet. 'Not at all! In fact, Jane's so grateful to him for helping Ben to get over his anorexia!'

'I hadn't heard about that.' For the first time there was a shade of interest, even of warmth, in her voice. 'Mark as a therapist – I don't see it, somehow.'

'Well, I'm not sure he was really aware of what he'd done,' admitted Laura. 'It was when he first came here and met Ben. He – Ben – was going through a bad time over his father, and wasn't eating properly. He'd got very thin, and we were all very worried about him, but he's difficult to deal with. Not difficult in himself, you understand, not aggressive or rebellious exactly, but very bright. Too bright, really, in some ways. He's so far ahead of the others intellectually, one forgets that emotionally he's still more or less a child.'

'You're obviously very fond of him.' Was that surprise Laura heard in Georgia's voice? Was it strange, then, to be fond of one's friends' children?

'Yes, I am, very. Anyway, we were all pussyfooting around, nobody daring to say anything to Ben in case it pushed him over the edge, and Mark came right out and asked him if he was anorexic. Ben was so shocked it made him look at what he was doing to himself, and he started eating again. He's fine now. A bit thin, perhaps, but not that awful bony look he had before. And all thanks to Mark!'

'It sounds more like complete tactlessness than anything else.'

Georgia's voice was uncompromising, and Laura was chilled.

232

'Oh, no,' she said weakly. 'Not tactless, exactly. Direct, I thought. Straightforward.'

'He's all of that.'

'Well . . . anyway, it did the trick. And Ben really likes Mark, and he's pretty choosy about his friends.'

'Mm. Mark doesn't have any problem about making friends. Keeping them, though, that's another matter.'

'He was very popular with the people at the school here.' Laura heard herself sounding defensive again.

'Oh yes, that's not the problem. But it's all black and white with Mark. Uncompromising is the word, I think. If he doesn't like something anyone says or does, that's it. He won't have anything to do with them any more.'

Laura thought, reluctantly, that she recognised an element of truth in this, though she did not want to admit it.

'It's his age,' she said, rather weakly. 'They all see things in black and white at his age, don't they?' Her own words comforted her – she thought of Daisy, and Ben, and how little they were prepared, ever, to compromise over the things they felt strongly about.

'Perhaps. Anyway, I'll let you know. About the holiday, I mean. When would it be?'

'I don't know. Late July or August, I suppose. To fit in with the school holidays. It'll be terribly hot, I'm afraid, but there's the sea, and a river, too, that they said was very clean and good for swimming.'

'It sounds lovely. Well, thanks for the invitation, Laura. I'll ring you in a day or two at the latest. I know you'll need to get on with the bookings. All right?'

Laura thought as she put down the telephone that surely the answer must be yes. How could Georgia turn down this chance for Mark to have a holiday, with his friends and, more importantly, with his father? She felt happy, really happy for the first time in months.

Chapter 20

It was not until early July that cracks began to appear in Laura's carefully constructed and safe little world.

The holiday in Turkey was now only three weeks away. Laura was in the kitchen, ironing and watching *Neighbours*. To her defiant shame, she had become completely hooked by the programme, to the extent of recording it on the video if she was going to be out all day. Doing the ironing while it was on at least justified the waste of time, and when the news came on at six she would stop ironing and start thinking about supper for her and Edward. She preferred to watch the five thirty-five programme. That, she knew, was when Mark would be watching it, and knowing that she was sharing it with him made it more enjoyable.

The day had been overcast and cool, so that the combined heat of ironing and Aga was no hardship. Laura seldom found it necessary to switch off the cooker during the summer; the vagaries of English weather meant that the warmth was often comforting on cool evenings and mornings, and on very hot days she could open doors and windows and get the air through. It was one of Laura's non-working days and, feeling cheerful and energetic, she had cleaned the house thoroughly, done two loads of washing, and was now dealing with the garden-dried results.

The kitchen looked fresh and shining, the pile of Edward's crisply ironed shirts had grown to satisfying proportions, and now, as if to crown the day, the clouds were breaking up and gleams of sunshine came in through the open windows. When Edward came home they could sit in the garden, thought Laura happily. Perhaps even have supper outside. The images on the screen flickered across her mind: boys with golden tans and tousled, shiny hair; beautiful girls with perfect figures and pouting swollen lips in a world where problems, however severe, would almost certainly be solved in a few days, even if a crisis on Friday kept everyone wondering through the weekend.

When she heard Edward's car drive in, and the bang of the garage doors as he closed them, she was pleased. It was unusual for Edward to be home so early, and now they could enjoy this summer evening together. 'Nay-ay-bours' sang the television as the credits rolled, and she switched off the iron and emptied the water out of it. They could ring Anna and go round for a swim, even, and see if she would like to come back and have supper with them. She could do a big *salade niçoise*, eking out the small tin of tuna with plenty of hard-boiled eggs from the hens, and a sprinkling of capers would add a kick and make up for the small number of olives left in the jar in the fridge.

When Edward came in she was about to put away the ironing board, and the sound of his entrance was drowned by the protesting shriek of its legs as she folded it. It was an old one, a wedding present, and Laura liked it for its size and sturdiness, although it was heavy to carry. She was so used to Edward looking after her that she never gave it a second thought, and when he did not come to carry the ironing board through to its cupboard in the hall, she balanced it against the worktop, assuming that he had gone through to the cloakroom in a hurry after too many cups of tea during the afternoon. When she glanced round, however, he was sitting at the kitchen table. Edward, always active, always busy, was sitting there motionless, his hands lying on the flat surface before him like things he had brought in by mistake and subsequently abandoned.

His face was blank, the skin that was already brown had faded underneath the tan to a livid beige. He looked like a stranger, and she noticed the grey hairs, shining in the late afternoon sunlight, at his temples. They were far thicker than before, almost a complete patch of grey rather than the sprinkling she had been in the habit of teasing him about.

I've been here before, thought Laura, and found herself glancing instinctively at the stool where Daisy had been sitting more than a year earlier when Edward had come home early to tell her about Mark. I'm not going to worry. It was all right last time, it will be all right again. And if it's another Mark? The thought was almost amusing. She balanced the ironing board more securely, and went to Edward.

'What is it, love?' His head did not move, even the hazel eyes stayed fixed at some spot half-way across the table, beyond his hands. Laura put her arms round him. He was jacketless, and the cotton of his shirt was smooth against her bare arms, familiar as the ones she had just ironed. She could still just smell the faint fragrance of the fabric softener she used rising from it. Beneath the shirt his flesh felt soft and doughy, the muscles slack over the rigidly locked bones of his skeleton.

She stroked his back and shoulders, and it was like caressing a still-warm dead body. She tightened her grip, pulling him towards her, and was glad when he resisted because even that rejection was better than this terrible nothingness.

'What is it? Tell me, Edward. Please, please tell me. Whatever it is, it can't be any worse than the things I'll start imagining. You've come home early, haven't you, to tell me? So don't put it off any longer. Waiting won't make it any better.'

'Oh, Laura!' It was like the mumble of a drunkard, or an old and senile man. 'Laura, I'm sorry. I'm so sorry.'

'What is it? What' s happened?'

'The house,' he said helplessly. 'It's the house. The bank are going to . . . it's going to be . . . we're going to lose the house.'

'What house?' asked Laura stupidly. 'You mean here? Our own house? The bank are going to take our house? But why?'

Already her mind was racing ahead. It must be a mistake. Things were bad, she knew that, but surely they were still just within the limits of the overdraft the bank had set? The bank manager had been supportive, even helpful. Why, he had given Edward the job, last year, of designing a new porch for his house. Not a very big job, certainly, but still work, still a sign that he had faith in him.

'It's a mistake,' she soothed. 'A misunderstanding. Graham wouldn't do that to you.'

'He didn't.'

He was still resisting her embrace. She took away her arms and stood helplessly next to him. She was sure, so sure, that it could not be true. People like them, ordinary, hard-working people who paid their bills on time, did not have their homes repossessed. They had always had their mortgage repayments on a standing order, and in any case the house was practically paid for by now – the twenty-five-year term would be up in three or four years. She felt nothing but the need to comfort Edward, to help him back from this state of blank hopelessness to his usual optimism. She sat down opposite him and stretched her hands across the table to clasp his.

'Come on, love. Tell me what's happened.'

He drew in a deep breath, and shook his head like a fighter who has had a punch on the jaw and is struggling against unconsciousness.

'It's so awful. I just don't know how to tell you. I sent Ellie home. I've been sitting in the office trying to think of some way out, some way to get round it, but . . . I can't see anything.'

For the first time, Laura felt the chill of reality.

'Just tell it from the beginning. There must be something we can do. Anyway, I've got to know.'

'Yes.'

Laura waited. There was no point in pushing him any more. He would tell her when he could find the words, and for the first time she wondered if she could bear to hear what he was going to say. She longed for a drink, something strong and alcoholic to numb her, but sensed that this was not the moment to move, and distract Edward from his painful reaching after words.

'It's the VAT,' he said at last. 'I work it out at the end of each quarter, you know?' Laura nodded. She knew about that. They had twice been inspected by VAT officers, once at the office and once here, at the house, since Edward did quite a bit of his paperwork at home and it was more convenient. The second time had been, coincidentally, the day when Anna's husband Michael had been dying, and it had stayed in Laura's memory as a nightmare day of making cups of tea and coffee for two polite, grey men who had shuffled their way through boxes of receipts, and ended up with a discrepancy of seven pounds. Locked in her own anguish for Anna, who had telephoned the night before to say that Michael could not last another twenty-four hours, the visitation had seemed irrelevant and bizarre, its outcome ludicrous.

'Seven pounds!' she had said to them. 'Two men working a whole day to find seven pounds! It's insane!'

'We have to check, Mrs Erm,' had said the elder of the grey men seriously. 'Of course it's the big frauds we're really after, the people who cook the books and get away with millions of the government's money.'

It had seemed to Laura then, as it seemed now, a waste of the government's money to harass innocent people with small businesses, whose turnover was never likely to run above the thousands. The incident had stayed with her, and some of the bitterness of Michael's death had, unfairly, been absorbed by the VAT office, so that it remained a kind of bogey-man in her mind.

'You get an extra month,' Edward said now, heavily. 'To work the VAT out in. The quarter ends on the last day of June, and you have to get the form in by the end of July. And the cheque, of course. I generally leave it as long as possible, but this time I thought I'd better get it out of the way because of going to Turkey. They come down on you like a ton of bricks if you're late, and I was afraid of forgetting it. So I did it, and sent it off.'

He sighed, and Laura squeezed his hands encouragingly, pleased

238

to feel the return pressure of his fingers.

'It was stupid,' he said, more forcefully. 'I could have post-dated the cheque. In fact, I meant to. Why the hell didn't I? It might have made all the difference. But I didn't. I had some other bills to settle, and I was writing out cheques like a zombie, and wrote that one out the same, with the actual date. It was quite high, too, because we had that payment in early April. I was glad to get it at the time, because it paid the tax bill and those bloody rates, but there's no VAT on either of those to offset against what I had to pay out. The cheque went off, and it bounced.'

'It bounced!' Laura had never known such a thing to happen, even when they had been over the limit of the overdraft.

'Yes. With anyone else, it might not have mattered. They would have got in touch with me, and re-presented it, and I could have sorted it out somehow. But the VAT people aren't like that. You don't get any second chances.'

'But why would it bounce? I thought you said it's not Graham's fault?'

'No, it isn't. That's just the trouble. He's on holiday. I didn't know that, of course, and I suppose even if I had known I wouldn't have realised it would make any difference. The under-manager, whatever his title is, was in charge. I don't know him from Adam, he's not been at the bank very long, and of course he doesn't know me either. So he just went by the book. The cheque was big enough to take us over the limit . . . so . . .' Edward shook his head, as if bothered by midges.

'But surely . . . when you explain to them . . .'

'It's too late for explanations. I rang the bank, of course, straight away, and spoke to this little jumped-up Hitler, but all he could say was that it was out of his hands, there was nothing he could do. He was so bloody *smug* about it, I could have wrung his scrawny little neck. He more or less told me that I had no one but myself to blame. He implied that I was totally incompetent, that it was only a matter of time before the business went down the pan anyway, and he even seemed to think he'd done me a favour by not letting me carry on any longer. If he had even shown one shred of sympathy, or given a suggestion of an apology, it wouldn't have been so awful, but he just went on and on about the overdraft limit and how it couldn't be exceeded, and how even Graham couldn't have allowed me to go above it – though I know he would, really, because it's happened once or twice in the past and never for more than a day or two. It's just so unbelievable. I've been sitting in the office trying to see a way out of it. I'd sell everything, sell the office building and find somewhere to rent, or even work from home, but it's been on the market for more than a year, and there's just no interest in it at all. The bank wants its money, and it doesn't want to wait, and the only thing that would sell easily is this place.'

'I've got the money from mother: that can pay the VAT . . .' Laura was clutching at straws. She knew it was nowhere near enough to save the house. 'And I could sell her ring, and the brooch. You know I never wear them. Hardly ever.'

He was shaking his head before she had finished, the expression on his face more miserable still, and she knew that for all her good intentions she had done no more than twist the knife in the wound of his self-esteem.

'Not enough, I'm afraid. Now things have gone this far, I have to pay off the whole of the overdraft or declare myself bankrupt. I even considered that, but of course the end result would be the same, only I'd have no chequebook, no credit cards, and it would be virtually impossible for me to go on working for myself, like now. I suppose I could try for a job with someone . . . Mike's old firm, perhaps. But I've still got to pay the money. I'd do anything to spare you this, but . . . I can't think. I just can't think what to do.'

She could hear, in the huskiness of his voice, how his throat was closing with distress. All her deep instincts to protect and to cherish were roused, and she felt a surge of strength that was like a rush of adrenalin.

'It's all right,' she said, and was amazed by the sincerity in her voice. 'It doesn't matter. It's only a house. We'll be all right. We can pay the VAT tomorrow.'

He clung to her hands. 'I could kill him,' he said viciously, in a voice she had never heard him use before. 'Self-satisfied little shit.'

Anger, she thought, was better than despair.

'Horrible little man,' she agreed. 'Graham will be furious with him.'

'He can't undo it, though,' Edward warned her. 'It's too late for that. And, besides . . .'

'What?'

'Oh, it sounds rather paranoid. But I did start to wonder whether it was some kind of put-up job.'

'Put-up job? By Graham, you mean? He wouldn't. Would he?'

Edward freed one hand and scrubbed at his face, pulling at the skin round his eyes. 'I don't know. I told you it was paranoid. But suppose he had been told that he couldn't allow us the overdraft facility any longer? He may be the manager of his own branch, but he's still got to take orders from upstairs. If they say, no more borrowing for Melville, he can't do anything about it. And it's not easy for him, because as you said, we know one another well, we're friends. So . . .'

'So he gets someone else to do it. Slimeball.' There were times, Laura found, when Mark's vocabulary came in handy.

'Well. Better not to think about it. We'll never know, and it's probably too far-fetched. After all, I've got to go on dealing with Graham . . . I hope.'

'Of course you will.' Laura pushed as much warmth and encouragement as she could into her voice. 'This is just a blip. Things will pick up again, and he'll be inviting you out to lunch again. We'll buy back the house, and everything will be just like it was before.'

It wouldn't be, of course. Laura knew that, and so did Edward.

'Of course it will,' he agreed cheerfully.

Laura stood up. 'Tea, coffee, or strong liquor?'

Edward gave a wry smile. 'Strong liquor, please. Scotch, if there is any.' The bottle was half empty, but Laura poured with reckless generosity, dropping in some ice cubes and adding only a splash of water. She poured one for herself, disliking the taste but feeling the need, for once, for something stronger than coffee. This time, when she came back, she sat down next to Edward and leaned against him until he put his arm round her. Fighting the urge to swallow her whisky in one go, she sipped it. It tasted bitter on her tongue, like medicine.

'So . . . what do we do, then?' A nasty thought struck her. 'We won't have to cancel the holiday, will we? I mean, it's all paid for, and I don't think we can get the money back, unless one of us is ill.' She stopped, more appalled by the short-term prospect of having to cancel the holiday than by the loss of the house, which still seemed unbelievable.

'I think the best thing we can do is to go to Turkey,' said Edward. 'As you say, we won't get the money back and, quite honestly, I think a break will be good for us both. I thought . . .' He paused, looking at her anxiously.

'What?'

'Well, we're going to have to get on with this. Prove to the bank that we're doing something about it, kind of thing. I thought that if I were to get in touch with an agent, we could give him a key and he could be getting on with trying to sell the house while we're away.'

Laura wrinkled her nose.

'I hate the idea of strangers going round our house while we're away.'

Edward gave her a little hug. 'I know, I know how you feel. But they'd be with the agent, they wouldn't be peering into cupboards or anything . . . and I thought it might be easier for you than having to show them round yourself. But if you don't like it, we can leave it until we get back.'

Laura thought. 'No,' she said reluctantly. 'No, you're right, it would be better. It would be even worse having to come back to it.'

'With any luck someone will like it, and it can all be fixed up by the time we get back. We won't need to meet them at all.'

'Will it sell all that quickly?' Laura had been secretly hoping that the house would be on the market for months, and that something would turn up in the meanwhile to save it. 'I thought the market was dreadful at the moment. Isn't that why business is so bad for you too?'

'Yes, it is. I keep in touch with the town agents, as you know, and they're all feeling the pinch.' He saw the hope in her face, hating himself for having to kill even that, but knowing that it was kinder in the long run. 'But good houses, not too big or too small, in a village, in good condition and competitively priced . . . they'll sell easily. That's what they said. Sorry, darling.'

'Of course.' Laura took another gulp of her drink, feeling it burn its way down her throat that felt swollen inside, so that the sound of her swallow echoed in her ears.

It was a strange evening. In years to come Laura would look back and find herself convinced that it had been winter-time, so clearly did the memory of cold come through to her. When she stood up, and lost the comforting warmth of Edward's arm, she found herself shivering, and went by old instinct to the Aga, where she stood clinging to the familiar comfort of the rail. Salad, obviously, was out of the question for supper, she thought helplessly. Something hot was what they needed. There was casserole in the freezer, she remembered, made for Mark's Easter visit – Mark loved her beef casserole, as long as it had no mushrooms in it.

As it defrosted in the microwave, she mixed up some dumplings, with the confused feeling that she needed something solid and comforting. They watched television as they ate it, each finding it easier than trying to make conversation, and Edward opened a bottle of wine, as if it had been a celebration. This, on top of the whisky, made Laura so sleepy that by ten o'clock she was yawning widely. Tonight, at least, she thought, she would not need to be lying in bed thinking about the future. She would concentrate on the holiday, she decided. Enjoy that, and as far as possible put out of her mind what must come afterwards.

It was difficult, going upstairs and starting the familiar routine of preparing for bed, not to look round at each room, each corner, each known and loved arrangement of furniture and fabrics, and see them with the eyes of one bidding each farewell. She could not help seeing them with the eyes of a stranger, and never had the colour schemes looked more attractive, or the furniture seemed so well positioned, so that it was impossible to imagine how it could ever look right anywhere else.

In bed she and Edward clung together. Laura felt her body was dull and dead, the sensitive nerve-endings dulled by alcohol and anxiety. Aware of his need, she forced a response from sluggish flesh, receiving comfort from her ability to give it, more than from the physical act. Afterwards she listened to Edward's heavy breathing, just short of a snore but enough to show that he was deep in oblivion, and let tears as thick as glycerine creep their slimy way down the sides of her face and into her ears, where they lay like cold slugs. Her nose was solid, she opened her mouth and breathed deeply and slowly. For a few minutes she allowed herself to explore her anger and despair. After all these years the house was so much a part of her that it was practically an extension of her personality, and of her marriage.

She felt as if the walls, over the years, had soaked up the emanations of all that she had felt. Away from the house, would she still exist? It seemed to her that in leaving it she would also lose her past, that so much of her would stay trapped in its shell that she would be intangible and invisible anywhere else, blown about the world like a dropped plastic bag while her spirit continued to exist, incorporate but living, in its familiar place.

And Mark, too, would have to be told. Would he mind? He liked the house, certainly. He liked its size; liked the room that was always, now, referred to as his; liked, above all, its proximity to Ben's house, and to Daisy's. Laura always referred to it, when speaking to him, as 'home', wanting him to think of it as such and hoping that constant repetition would reinforce the feeling. When he was there she made sure that the house was clean and polished, the bunches of flowers and leaves from the garden fresh, and the larder full of his favourite food.

Surely, she thought, they could find something in the village, even if it had only two bedrooms. She closed her mind to the knowledge that village properties still commanded a higher price, that it would be sensible to find something in the town near Edward's office, and above all that there was nothing, at present, for sale in the village anyway.

I'm not going to think about that, she thought firmly. Once it gets hold of my brain it'll go round and round like a mouse on a wheel, and I'll be awake all night. In the morning things will look better, they always do. I'll think of pleasant things. Turkey. Beach, and hot sun, and evening meals in little restaurants, and Mark. Mark, diving off rocks into a blue-green sea; Mark laughing with Ben; Mark chatting at the table, smiling,

243

enjoying himself. That the holiday must come to an end was something she would ignore. The two weeks of happiness was, she thought, assured.

The following morning Edward went off to work as usual. With the heartless inappropriateness of English weather, the sun shone brilliantly from a sky made even more blue by its scattering of small fluffy clouds that sailed on the wings of a light breeze that stirred the warm air and kept the temperature deliciously moderate. It was a perfect summer day like the ones that are remembered from childhood, and Laura found the sight of her house and her garden unbearably beautiful. She grabbed her bag and the car keys, and went off to the supermarket.

Once there, she realised that in her hurry to leave she had forgotten her list.

'Bother it,' she muttered to herself. 'I'm not going back. I'll do it from memory.' A young woman, with a baby strapped to her front and a toddler in the seat of the trolley, eyed her sideways, and Laura gave her a wide, mad grin. 'Talking to myself,' she explained, rather too loudly. 'Practising to be a dotty old lady,' she added.

'Oh, yes,' said the girl nervously, edging away and turning her body slightly, as if to shield the baby. She obviously thought that Laura didn't need much practice. Laura didn't know whether to giggle or sigh.

She pushed the trolley through the fruit and vegetable section, heading purposefully for biscuits. In her head she ran through what she could remember of the careful list she had made of things she wanted to buy for the holiday. Sun cream, in varying strengths, she had already bought, as well as plasters, upset-tummy pills, mosquito repellent, and all the other panaceas the traveller burdens himself with. Now, however, she was intent on stocking up with all the extras in the way of sweets, biscuits, tea and coffee that ten people would be likely to want. She knew from past experience how surprisingly welcome a cup of tea and some ginger biscuits could be after a day spent on the beach.

Her shopping finished, she decided to go and call on Cassandra at the shop. It was not one of the days when Hilda looked after Eva, so the baby would be there too, sitting in her baby chair and receiving homage from all comers. Laura thought she would like to hold that round, wriggling body on her knee and tell Cassandra her woes.

Cassandra was, in fact, so upset on Laura's behalf that Laura ended up comforting her rather than the other way around.

'That lovely house!' wailed Cassandra. 'You can't sell it, you just can't! Where will you go? You can't leave the village, it won't be the same without you. Oh, I can't bear it!'

It was all rather exhausting, and Eva was teething and was consequently tetchy, too hot and feverish to want to be cuddled, and wailing dismally much of the time. Laura, who had been rather sorry that they were not going to be in Turkey with them, found herself instead quite thankful. She escaped as soon as she could, and drove home with relief, promising herself a long, cold drink and half an hour lying in the garden.

As she let herself into the house, however, the phone was ringing. Laura dumped her carrier bags unceremoniously on to the floor, and went to answer it.

'Laura?' Anna's voice vibrated down the line. Goodness, thought Laura, she's heard already. Did Cassandra phone her, or was it perhaps Edward, summoning up the support group?

'Oh, Anna, it's so good of you to call. I was going to let you know later, when I'd got more used to it . . .'

'Used to what? Don't tell me something awful's happened to you as well. Is it Edward?'

Laura was too flustered to take in Anna's choice of words. 'Yes, in a way. The bank say we've got to sell the house,' she said baldly.

'Oh, no! Oh, Laura, I'm so sorry!' Anna, usually so calm and controlled, burst into tears. Laura couldn't believe it. Anna, who had watched her husband die, who had stood dry-eyed at his graveside, was sobbing uncontrollably.

'Anna! Anna, don't! It's only a house, Anna! We're all right, truly, it's not worth getting so upset about!'

'Oh, dear.' Anna gasped, then drew a long breath. Laura waited. 'Oh, Laura, I'm sorry. Sorry about that, I mean. And about the house. Oh dear, how awful.' Her breath caught again, and she sniffed, then blew her nose. 'Sorry,' she said again, her voice steadier. 'I should be looking after you, not howling at you. Oh, dear. It's just . . . well, never mind.'

'Never mind what? What's happened?' Laura thought back, and caught at the words Anna had spoken. 'Something awful's happened to you, too, hasn't it? What is it?'

'I don't want to worry you with anything else . . .'

'Counter-irritant,' said Laura briskly. 'You'll have to tell me some time, why not now? Is it you, or Daisy? Or Guy?' she added as an afterthought.

'Daisy, of course.' Anna's voice dropped into anxiety again.

'What's happened to her?' Not pregnant, she thought. Let it not be that, please.

'Oh, Laura, she's been expelled. I've just got back from school. We've just got back. I had to go down to the school and bring her home. She's in her room, crying. I don't know what to do.'

'Shall I come round?' Laura was ashamed at the strength of the relief she felt. Not pregnant, then. Expulsion seemed so much less awful that it was almost trivial. To her, besides, it came as a welcome distraction. It was so much easier to cope with other people's problems than with her own.

'Would you? Oh, Laura, thank you. I don't know what to say to her, I'm so angry and upset, but I'm frightened to leave her on her own up there . . . can you bear it?'

'Of course I can.' Yes, thought Laura, I can. I can bear it.

Chapter 21

Laura walked straight into Anna's kitchen, as she generally did, after only a perfunctory knock at the door. Anna was at the sink, furiously polishing a stainless steel surface that already glittered from the exertions of the cleaning lady the day before. The face she turned to Laura was puffy and blotched with patches of colour, like that of a small child that has been illicitly experimenting with its mother's make-up. Laura went to her and put her arms round her. They clung together speechlessly, and Laura felt her own eyes filling with tears.

'What happened?' she asked in the end. 'Whatever happened? I just can't believe it!'

'Nor can I.' Anna's smile wobbled, but she was making an effort. 'Thanks for coming. Daisy begged me not to tell anyone, but it's not the kind of secret you can keep, exactly, is it? Besides, she wouldn't have meant you. And I've got to have someone to tell it all to.' She sighed, and the long breath signalled to Laura that she was already coming to terms with what had happened. 'Good God, look at me, cleaning the sink in my silk dress. I'd better go and change. There's a bottle of wine in the fridge – open it, there's a love, while I go upstairs. I'll be down in a moment.'

Laura heard her slow footsteps on the stairs as she fetched the bottle and hunted out the corkscrew and two glasses. Like many large people, Anna was light and graceful on her feet, but today her tread was ponderous. Her misery weighed her down as the deposits of fat on her body had never done. The footsteps paused, and Laura knew that Anna was listening at Daisy's door, perhaps putting her head into the room. After a few moments they carried on, and Laura, who hadn't noticed she was holding her breath, started to breathe again.

When Anna came down she was wearing one of the loose cotton dresses she generally wore in summer, finding trousers uncomfortable and leggings unsuitable for her shape. She had also, Laura noted with relief, washed her face and brushed her hair, and had regained her usual composed manner. Laura handed her a glass of wine.

247

'Is Daisy all right?'

Anna nodded. 'Crying her eyes out on her bed. It's so easy for the young, isn't it? For girls, anyway. You have a good cry, and everyone's sorry for you, and then you feel better and life just carries on.'

'She knows I'm here?'

'Yes. She doesn't want you to know, but only because she doesn't want you to be shocked, or angry with her. I told her you'd understand. And I hope you do, because I certainly don't.' She took a gulp of wine. 'Thank God for alcohol, at least.'

So, it's not drink then, thought Laura. She picked up the bottle and her glass, and walked through to the conservatory. Less formal than the drawing room but more comfortable, for sitting, than the kitchen, it was full of light and colour from the rioting plants. The painted cane chairs creaked gently as they sat down, the bright flowered cushions soft and luxurious.

'The school rang me this morning,' said Anna abruptly, launching without preamble into her recital. 'The secretary, I suppose. Asked if I could come over to the school at once. Of course I was horrified, but she said Daisy wasn't ill or hurt, which was my first thought. She said it was a matter of discipline.'

She paused, and drank again, as if the wine had power to anaesthetise the memory. Discipline, thought Laura. A chilling word that had the power to strike terror into any parent's heart, particularly the parent of a child like Daisy, who was inclined to wilful disobedience over minor school rules. Refreshed, Anna continued, telling Laura how she had paused only to change into one of her better summer dresses (moral support), and had driven the thirty miles to the school. She had arrived with no very clear memory of the journey, and had been if anything more alarmed by Daisy's reception of her.

'Hello, Mum! What are you doing here?'

'I was summoned,' said Anna succinctly. 'By Mrs Woodman,' she added.

Daisy's brow furrowed. 'Why?'

'I rather assumed that you would be able to tell me about that,' Anna said grimly. She didn't know whether to be relieved or not. Daisy's conscience, quite obviously, was clear, so she had not committed any major crime – or at least, had not been caught out in one. At the same time, to be sent for like this indicated a serious matter, not just skipping breakfast, or a cigarette butt in the wastebin. Daisy, now, was beginning to look worried too.

'What are we supposed to do?' She looked helplessly round her study bedroom, as if seeking inspiration or enlightenment from the posters on the wall.

'Go and find Mrs Woodman, I suppose. I rather sneaked past her door when I came in. Thought I'd find you first, try to synchronise our stories, you know.' Anna fought to keep her tone light and encouraging, but Daisy looked if anything even more alarmed.

'What if I hadn't been here? I could have been at a class, or anything.'

'Well, you weren't, were you? Not that it's done us much good, if you're quite sure you don't know what it's about.'

'I don't. Truly, I don't. I've really been *good* recently.' Anna could have smiled at the astonishment in her voice, if she hadn't been so concerned.

'Perhaps that's it,' continued Daisy more cheerfully. 'I've been so good, they're worried about me. They probably think I'm ill.'

'They probably think it's too good to be true, and that you're covering up for something,' said Anna. She was careful not to make it sound like a question, but Daisy knew her too well.

'Honestly, Mum, what do I have to say to make you believe me?'

'I do believe you. It's just that you're not usually so well behaved, particularly at the end of the summer term and with the exams safely behind you.'

'No.' Daisy had to admit the truth of this. 'It's really since Jocasta was expelled. It gave us all rather a fright, actually. I mean, it's one thing when it's people in another year and another house, but when it's a friend, well . . .'

Jocasta had been expelled, three weeks earlier, for smoking pot. Anna knew she had not been a close friend of Daisy's, but they had been in the same year and house and were doing similar A-levels, so had inevitably seen quite a lot of one another. Anna, though naturally sympathetic with the girl and her family, had thought secretly that it would do Daisy no harm to see that, when it came to the rules, no one was immune. Jocasta herself had been very clever, one of the top scholars, although her wealthy father had declined the financial help involved, saying with truth but no grace that he was in no need of charity. It was no secret that he was a very rich man, since he invariably arrived at the school in a chauffeur-driven Rolls Royce with a metallic gold finish that was positively blinding on a sunny day. Jocasta herself had an allowance that would have kept an average family, if not in luxury, at least in some comfort, and it was generally felt to be greatly to her credit that she was as pleasant and relatively unspoiled as she was.

Anna looked at her watch. 'Well, I've been here for nearly a quarter of an hour. Mrs Woodman's probably been on the look-out for me, and she'll have seen my car by now. We'd better go down.'

Daisy twitched nervously at her uniform. 'I'm sorry you've had all this hassle, Mums,' she said. Anna gave her a quick, warm hug.

'Never mind. Now I'm here, let's go and get it over with.'

Down in the housemistress's study, Anna's misgivings returned in full force. While it could not be said that she and Mrs Woodman had ever achieved a friendship, Anna had thought that they were at least on reasonably good terms, and that there was an element of trust between them. Now, however, the housemistress seemed evasive, and even appeared reluctant to meet Anna's eyes, saying merely that the senior mistress needed to see Daisy, and that under the circumstances it had been thought better that her mother should be present.

'Under what circumstances?' asked Anna bluntly.

'I'm afraid I can't tell you.'

'Can't, or won't?' It was perhaps unfair to put this pressure on the woman, but Anna was fighting for her daughter.

'I think we'd better go straight away,' was the only reply. 'Miss Hill is expecting us.'

The senior mistress's position was a relatively new one, and had been created a few years earlier when it was decided to admit girls to the school. She was, in effect, the headmistress, and responsible for all matters of discipline relating to the girls in the school. Anna, walking beside Daisy and resisting a strong inclination to clutch her hand protectively, felt a heavy sensation of doom. Only something serious would justify a visit to the senior mistress.

In the event, it was very quick.

'It all happened so suddenly,' Anna said to Laura. 'Like a car accident – you know how afterwards you say it all happened so quickly . . . She just sat us down, and asked Daisy if she'd ever smoked cannabis. Why couldn't she say pot, like everyone else? And Daisy just looked at her and said yes, she had. And that was it. Out. Just like that. And I just sat there, stunned. I mean, I know Daisy smokes – I've smelt it on her clothes when she's been out with her friends, and even found the odd butt or empty cigarette packet. And I suppose I should have realised that she might have experimented with pot, though I'm absolutely certain she's never tried anything else. If she'd been caught, of course, that would have been it. We all know it means instant expulsion. But to make her condemn herself like that out of her own mouth . . .'

'Oh, Anna, I'm so sorry, it must have been awful for you both,' said Laura, herself near to tears at the sight of her friend's distress.

'And she had to pack up all her things there and then, and come home. We were both in floods of tears, she's left half her things behind, and the worst thing is that she didn't even get a chance to say goodbye to her friends. They were all in lunch when we left. I can't tell you how dreadful it was, driving out of the school with her and knowing that everyone else was carrying on with their normal school day, and that she wasn't part of it any more, and never would be again.'

'It's not fair,' raged Laura, knowing she sounded childish but too distressed to care. 'Catching her out like that.'

'It was a straight question, and she answered it,' said Anna with weary resignation.

'But why ask it in the first place? I mean, surely they weren't asking every boy and girl in the school, one after another? And if they'd never caught her or suspected her – or did they?'

'Apparently not.' Anna sighed. 'Mrs Woodman was almost as upset as I was. She said there were plenty of girls she would have suspected sooner than Daisy. And Daisy herself says she only tried it once or twice, and didn't much care for it.'

'So why ask her?'

'Mrs Woodman told me. The housemistress. Apparently the headmaster had had a letter, the day before, from the father of a girl who'd been expelled. Do you remember Jocasta?'

'Vaguely. The girl with pots of money.'

'That's the one. Now she was caught in the act, smoking pot. And when she was expelled her father made a tremendous fuss. Of course, it wasn't Mrs Woodman who told me this bit – Daisy told me about it at the time, you know how things get round in a place like that. First of all he said they should keep her because she was almost certain to get into Oxford or Cambridge – she was terribly clever, you know – and that the school needed her to keep up their image. Then, when that didn't work, he offered them money for the new theatre they're building. Quite a lot of money, I imagine, and it must have been tempting. I can't help admiring the headmaster for sticking to his guns and saying no, it would have been the end of all that fund-raising. Anyway, when they turned him down and insisted Jocasta had to leave, he turned nasty. Daisy said even Jocasta was frightened, and she's the apple of his eye. Threatened them with legal action, the lot. Of course, he hadn't a leg to stand on, and he must have realised that when he cooled down – or perhaps his solicitor pointed it out to him. But he was determined to make trouble, so he got a list of names out of Jocasta, of people she had smoked pot with.'

'And Jocasta gave them to him? I don't believe it.' Laura knew very well how strong was the unwritten rule against what *Neighbours* had taught her to call 'dobbing', but which in her and Anna's school days had been called sneaking.

'She did. After a while. And I have to say that in spite of everything I feel sorry for that poor child, because I hate to think of the kind of pressure he must have put on her.'

'He sounds a horrible man.'

'He is. Anyway, he got his beastly list, and sent it to the headmaster. With a letter, saying that if these kids weren't investigated also, and expelled, he would make sure it was all over the tabloids.'

'The devil! Why didn't they stand up to him? That's blackmail!'

'Of course it is. But you know how it is with these schools – they're terrified of publicity, and the papers are always delighted to get any bit of dirt about public schools. There was a boy a few years ago – a peer's son, I think – who was always in trouble, and every time it was reported in one of the papers. They found out afterwards he'd been selling the stories himself. Made thousands out of it, too. Anyway, that's neither here nor there. The point is that once the information had been given to the school, they were obliged to do something about it. I mean, they're always on about drugs, and how they do everything they can to keep them out of the school. So, there it was. As a matter of fact, one of the people on the list had already been expelled, and four of the others had taken their A-levels and were about to leave anyway, so it was only poor little Daisy left. The trouble was, you see, that the times she had tried it had actually been with Jocasta, wretched girl. Of course, her father was trying his best to put the blame on to somebody else.'

'It sounds to me as though it was Jocasta leading Daisy astray, rather than the other way round.'

'Yes, almost certainly, although of course Daisy would never say so. Oh, dear.' Anna sniffed, and wiped her eyes with a handkerchief that was already sodden. Laura tipped the last of the wine into their glasses.

'What a mess,' she said sadly. 'And what a waste. It seems a pity . . .' She paused, eyeing Anna dubiously.

'What does? In particular, that is,' added Anna bitterly.

'That she told the truth.' Laura said the words shamefacedly, but honestly. 'If only she'd just said, "No, I've never tried it" quite firmly, I should think everyone would have breathed deep sighs of relief, and that would have been that.'

'I know. I'm proud of her, really,' said Anna, shaking her head ruefully. 'Proud of her honesty, at any rate. But, I must admit, I thought the same myself. I mean, I know she's not perfect. I know she lies to me about this and that. All kids do. I did it myself, we both did. It's quite normal. As a matter of fact, I did ask her in the car. About the only thing I did say to her, actually. I was so upset, and so *angry* . . . And she said it was all so sudden, she was taken by surprise and couldn't think, and then she didn't like to lie in front of me . . .'

Her eyes flooded with tears again. 'Why didn't they warn her?' she railed. 'I know they had to check it out, but they know as well as I do that Daisy isn't into drugs the way some of them are. They didn't want to have to get rid of her. Why didn't that damned housemistress just say to her, "Think very carefully before you answer any questions." Something like that. Even criminals are warned when they're arrested that they don't have to say anything, but that whatever they do say may be taken down, and all that. Poor little Daisy never had a chance. What am I saying, poor little Daisy? I could kill the little wretch, really. How could she? How could she do this to me, to us, to herself? Where did I go wrong? Is it because of Michael? I keep thinking, if only he were here, everything would have been all right.' Anna put her face in her hands and sobbed.

'Oh, Anna.' Laura went to crouch at her feet, her hands on the shaking shoulders. It felt awkward, and she thought inconsequentially how bad the British were at this kind of thing. I don't know how to comfort her, and she doesn't really know how to receive comfort, she thought. If we were Spanish or Italian, would it be easier? She patted Anna helplessly.

'It's not your fault,' she said, trying to speak with authority. 'Daisy's seventeen now. Old enough to make choices. To take responsibility for her own actions. And it may not have felt like it at the time, but she made a choice today. She chose to tell the truth, to the school and to you. And what that tells me is that however many mistakes she may have made, or may make in the future, you've done a good job. You, and Michael too. He would have been proud of her.'

'*I'm* proud of her,' wept Anna in despair.

There was a small shuffling sound from the doorway. As they looked round the door opened, revealing a woebegone Daisy who seemed to have shrunk even smaller. She was still, poignantly, in school uniform – Daisy, who hated the sensible navy skirt, the white shirt and the school tie, and who would never allow herself to be seen in them if it were humanly possible.

'Please don't cry, Mums. Please don't.'

With an enormous effort, Anna stopped. She sat up straight, and scrubbed fiercely at her face before blowing her nose firmly.

Laura sat back on her heels.

'Shall I go?'

'No.' Anna's response was immediate and instinctive. Daisy shuffled her feet, unwilling to meet Laura's eyes.

Laura stood up. 'I think another glass of wine is called for,' she said tactfully. 'I'll go and fetch the other bottle from the fridge. And another glass.' As she passed Daisy she gave her a kiss and a quick hug. After a second's hesitation, Daisy rather convulsively returned the embrace. Laura took her time over opening the bottle and finding another glass. From the half-open door of the conservatory came a hesitant murmur of voices, Daisy's higher pitch mingling with Anna's lower tones. After that silent journey home, Laura judged, they had a fair bit to say to one another. The voices rose, Anna's in particular. Tactfully, Laura put the bottle back in the fridge and went out to the garden, where she walked aimlessly around. From the corner of her eye she could see the conservatory, Anna and Daisy standing confronting one another, and hear the muffled sound of Anna's anger. After a while the shouting died down, and a short glance showed her that mother and daughter were huddled together on the sofa, so closely entwined that Laura was reminded of monkeys at the zoo, and smiled.

When she went back, they both achieved rather tremulous smiles.

'That's better.' Laura put down the glass, poured wine for each of them. 'Here's to crime,' she said, lifting her own glass. Daisy gave a wild hoot of laughter, and put her hand to her mouth to stifle it.

'To crime,' repeated Anna, and drank.

By the time they had finished the second bottle, they had achieved the kind of desperate hilarity that comes in the aftermath of disasters.

'You should have seen The Green's face,' said Daisy with a giggle. 'She was so sure I was going to lie to her, she just didn't know what to say.'

'The Green?' asked Laura. Her head was buzzing. She never normally drank during the day, and because she had had very little lunch the wine was having more effect than usual.

'Yes. The senior mistress. You know – "There is a green hill far away" – I wish.'

'She was astonished,' agreed Anna. 'I'd like to think she was astonished that you'd done it at all, rather than by the fact you spoke the truth, but we'll never know. Actually,' she added, solemn as an owl, 'she was very nice. As far as you can be nice under those circumstances. At least, she did say I could choose to take you away from the school, rather than you being expelled.'

'Doesn't it come to much the same thing?' asked Laura innocently.

'Oh, no.' Daisy knew all about this. 'If you're expelled, it goes on your school record and follows you about wherever you go, and on to university too.'

'Maybe further,' put in Anna. 'Nobody has any secrets any more, do they? Everything's on a computer somewhere. Companies can check you out when you apply for a job. Or building societies, when you want a mortgage.' She shivered. 'I think we've been lucky.'

'Yes,' agreed Laura, with a shiver of her own. 'I hadn't thought about that. What about finding another school?'

She almost wished she hadn't asked when she saw the anxiety return to Anna's face. Her earlier blotchy pallor had gone, and now her face was flushed with wine and emotion.

'I could go to the comprehensive, with Candida,' said Daisy helpfully. 'You know it's a good school, and I'd like it, really. And I'd be at home,' she offered hopefully, as a bonus. Laura's eyes met Anna's in a moment of shared amusement. There were times during the holidays, Laura knew, when Anna felt she only coped with Daisy's moods by reminding herself that she would soon be back at school.

'That would be lovely, darling,' said Anna warmly, 'though I'm not sure you wouldn't find it a bit – limiting – being at home all the time, after the freedom of school.'

'Freedom! In that gulag?'

'In some ways, yes.' The freedom of being with her friends all the time, thought Anna sadly, was not something it would be wise to remind Daisy of at this moment. 'Anyway, the main problem isn't whether or not you live at home, it's the courses. I know Candy's doing different A-levels to you, but I rather think the state schools do different boards. And as there's no way you can change boards half-way through your syllabus, we've got to find you a school that does the same boards.'

'How do we find that out?' Daisy was looking worried again.

'The school will help,' said Anna, with more confidence than she felt. 'Abbotsford, I mean. Mrs Woodman told me to call her later, when I was free – meaning, I suppose, when I was able to talk to her without howling.

255

Don't worry, darling. We can sort something out. At least you got the timing right, for once. You're not missing anything but the last few days of this term, and we've got all the summer holidays to get everything organised.' Daisy nodded, but her head was drooping on her slender neck, and her eyes were on the floor. Anna looked at her watch. 'Why don't you go and see Candy?' she suggested gently. 'She'll be home by now.'

Daisy revived like a wilting plant. 'Oh, can I?' she asked childishly. 'I'd really like to. I mean, you've been great, you and Laura, but . . .'

'But you need to talk to Candy,' Anna finished for her. 'I know. Why d'you think I called Laura round the minute I set foot inside the door?'

'Will you be all right?' Daisy still hesitated.

'I'll be fine. Off you go, darling. Try not to worry about it too much. We'll get it sorted out, you'll see. This time next year we'll look back and wonder why we got in such a panic.'

Daisy gave her a quick hug and kiss, and whisked out of the room. Laura and Anna listened to the tattoo of her departing feet. Anna put up her hand, and rubbed her forehead with her fingers.

'Headache?' asked Laura sympathetically.

'Mm. And my face feels a bit numb. Too much wine, I expect. I'd better sober up a bit before I ring the housemistress.'

They sat in companionable silence for a while.

'You know,' said Laura eventually, 'awful though this is, I don't think it will do Daisy any harm. In fact, if anything I'd say it might do her a power of good.'

'I was just thinking,' agreed Anna, 'that we've talked more today, really talked, I mean, than we have for months. Years, even. I shouted at her, I'm afraid, I just couldn't help it. It's something I do try not to do, but . . . she seemed almost relieved when I did. As if she wanted me to be angry with her.'

'She knew you were angry. And that you had every right to be. Better out than in, as they say.'

'I got to know her today,' said Anna thoughtfully. 'Funny, that. You think you know your children. That little baby, you know the different cries, what they mean – I'm hungry, I'm bored, I hurt . . . and you feel you're the only one who can do it, the only one who *really* understands them . . . and then they grow up, and one day you look at them and they're strangers . . . and I thought, until today, we'd be strangers for ever . . . she was sorry for Jocasta. Still sorry for her, I mean, in spite of everything. That's . . . nice . . . isn't it?'

'Very nice. She's a dear girl. And if you've got to know her better

256

today, I think it works both ways. If she's still sorry for Jocasta, I know why. There are ways and ways of sticking up for your children. His way, and your way. I know which I'd rather have, and so does Daisy.'

'If you say so.'

'Yes, I do. There was never anything wrong with Daisy, fundamentally. She just needed something to make her think.'

'Everything happens for the best?' Anna's voice was wry, but she was smiling.

'That's it. Do you want me to break into song? "Always look on the bright si-ide of life, *fi foo, fi foo foo foo foo foo foo*",' Laura whistled breathily.

Anna laughed. 'Oh, that *song*!' she gasped. 'That *awful* song! Blast you, now I'll be singing it in my head for days!'

'Could be worse,' said Laura. 'Come on. "*When you're chewing on life's gristle, just give a little whistle . . .*"'

'Oh! Aah!' gasped Anna, doubled up with laughter. 'Don't!'

'Yes! Come on!' She pulled Anna to her feet. With their arms round each other's shoulders they hopped and danced round the room, Anna doing the words between gusts of laughter, and Laura the whistles. They were so absorbed that they didn't hear Tod's entrance, and the first thing they knew was that he was joining in, twirling his silver-headed walking stick to the peril of the plants, and booming out the song in his surprisingly deep baritone voice.

They carried on until they all ran out of breath, then Laura and Anna collapsed on to the two-seater sofa. Tod stood, wheezing but dapper, and looked down at them.

'Well, my dears, I'm glad to see you so jolly. Now, what's all this I hear about Daisy? Such a silly business, and so unnecessary. So, we'd better set to and find another school, hadn't we?'

He spoke as though they would be going to the supermarket to pick one off the shelves. Anna put her head back against the cushions and panted.

'Yes,' she said at last. 'Yes, we better had. Heavens, Tod, that was quick. You should have been a reporter, you'd have made a fortune. Goodness, I'm puffed. But I do feel better, though heaven knows what the senior mistress would have thought.'

'Senior mistress – huh,' said Tod, waving an elegant hand.

By the time Laura left them, they were deep in list-making. Anna kissed her goodbye.

'I don't know how to thank you for looking after me this afternoon,' she said. 'And you with enough problems of your own to worry about, too.'

'All part of the service,' said Laura airily. 'And you know perfectly well, there's nothing so therapeutic as someone else's problem. It's a wonderful distraction.'

'Yes, wonderful. Like breaking your ankle when you've got an abscess on your wisdom tooth.'

'That's right,' said Laura.

Chapter 22

Laura lay face down on her towel. The sun on her back was like a physical weight, as though she were being ironed by some hefty cosmic laundry-worker. Her skin prickled, and although she had only just put more high-factor sun cream all over it, it felt tight and scorched, as if the sea water had crusted her with salt crystals, each one concentrating the sun like a tiny magnifying glass.

Jane, next to her, was reading, but Laura felt too tired to read. Her eyes felt as gritty, as though half the sand from the beach was in them. She longed to sleep, but was too uncomfortable. As always, the reality of lying in the sun was less pleasant than the anticipation, the hired sun-loungers being formed of uncompromising wooden slats, the discomfort of which was only surpassed by the voids where they were missing. Laura decided that, however awkward it might be, she would bring one of the inflatable mattresses down tomorrow.

They had arrived in Turkey the previous week. The flight had been delayed by two hours, and the coach journey from airport to village had been long and hot, particularly since they had left home in pre-dawn chill and were accordingly overdressed. A spirit of determined holiday cheer had prevailed, more or less, among the adults, but the younger members of the group had found the early start difficult to bear, and were inclined to be morose.

The first sight of the villa, however, had cheered them all. For once, the idealised photographs in the brochure did not do justice to the reality. A long octagon in shape, the downstairs rooms opened directly on to an open cobbled courtyard with a marble fountain in the middle, while upstairs a windowed gallery round the same courtyard gave access to further bedrooms and a bathroom and, on the long side overlooking the garden, a large covered balcony. The whole building was constructed of golden wood in a garden lush with fig trees and pomegranates, oleander, bougainvillaea and pelargoniums. Even Toby, generally uninterested in architecture, was impressed, and Daisy's face had lost, for a few minutes,

259

its look of anxious withdrawal. Laura, who during the previous two weeks had wondered whether they should not just accept defeat and abandon the holiday, had been heartened.

Candida and Daisy were also sunbathing today, and had established themselves nearby, though with a subtle space round them that defined their separateness as clearly as if they had set up a moat and gun emplacements. Daisy clung to her friend, just now, as if she were her only support and protection. In the aftermath of leaving school, Anna and Daisy had spent hours talking, in between anxious telephone calls to schools. These had so far been fruitless, all the places approached by Anna, or by Abbotsford on her behalf, saying that they did different examining boards, or that they had no space.

'I suppose it's just a polite way of saying they don't want her,' Anna had said privately to Laura after the fifth such rejection.

'Oh no, surely not? I mean, why wouldn't they want her?'

'They don't really want the awkwardness of fitting someone in just for one year, who's already half-way through the courses, and has probably been taught different things in a different way,' worried Anna. 'Time's getting on, too. Most of the schools will be closed for the holidays soon.'

'Something will turn up,' was all that Laura could find to comfort her.

'And thank you, Mrs Micawber.'

Meanwhile, Anna and Daisy tried hard to put the problem out of their minds, but their inability to do so could be seen in both their faces.

Of all the group, perhaps only Toby and his friend Nick were enjoying their holiday. Ben, to Jane's dismay, seemed once again to have stopped eating. Try as she might, Jane could not persuade him to talk to her about it, or to admit that there was any problem. She had hoped that once they were away from home he would be able to put whatever was worrying him out of his head, but if anything he seemed quieter than ever, and the heat killed any appetite he might otherwise have had. As before, he made a show of being hungry and of enjoying his meals, but most of his portion ended up on Mark's plate, and he even said no to beer, saying he preferred water.

Still more worrying, from Jane's point of view, was his lack of energy. The small village offered no sophisticated water sports, but the previous year Ben had enjoyed snorkelling, hiring one of the small beach canoes and paddling up the river, or diving from the rocks at the side of the bay. This year he stayed in the sea for only a few minutes before coming back, shivering, to lie on his towel.

Jane shifted from her front to her side, and laid down her book.

'Hot,' she said unnecessarily. 'I'm having trouble concentrating on this book. It's so foreign, and I just can't concentrate in this heat. Who was it said that we're two cultures kept apart by a common language?'

'Oscar Wilde, I think. Why? Are they spreading jelly on to crackers?'

'Sort of. Well, no, not really. It's more my own ignorance, I suppose. I just don't know enough about American history. I know there are references I'm just not picking up, and words that are just words to me that have resonances I'm not aware of. I should have picked something lighter, a nice thriller, or a detective story.'

Laura sat up and reached for the cool bag that held a bottle of water. 'I know,' she agreed, pouring the water into two plastic beakers. 'It's very difficult to get holiday reading just right. You feel you ought to be using some of that lovely free time to improve your mind by reading something like *War and Peace* that you'd never get round to at home, but somehow it never seems to work out. Maybe if we were somewhere cooler – but then we'd probably feel obliged to take up sailing, or visit all the local stately homes or something.'

Jane took a drink of water. In spite of the cold-blocks in the bag it was already tepid.

'How do you pronounce "feisty"?' she asked idly. 'I've only ever seen it written down. Is it fay, or fie?'

'Fie, I think. Difficult, when you never hear anyone else say it. What about Auberon?' She spelled it out. 'Obe, or Orb?'

'Depends whether you're thinking of the king of the fairies, or someone with lovely red hair.'

'Neither. It's just another of those words. People get so upset if you don't pronounce their names correctly.'

'Well, it is irritating. It sort of makes you into someone else. But names are hell anyway, aren't they? I got into trouble with Candy, last year, because she'd just discovered her name was the Latin term for thrush. The medical variety, that is. I mean, I never gave it a thought when she was born! I'm not sure that I even knew that thrush was called anything but thrush, at that age.'

'Jane's all right. Nothing wrong with Jane.'

Jane wrinkled her nose. 'Plain Jane? That about sums it up. But I like yours. Petrarch, and the "Little House" books.'

'And so topical.'

'?'

'Laura Norder. The poor thing's always on the news, and no one ever has anything good to say about her.' Laura sat up. 'Where is everybody? I must have dozed for a while, after all. Anna was here last time I looked.'

'She went for a swim. I think she was going to swim round to the rocks, and see Toby and Nick diving in.' Jane shuddered. 'Rather her than me. It's bad enough watching them from the land. When you're in the sea it looks even more dangerous, the way they have to jump right out to miss the rocks underneath.'

'Edward's with them, though, isn't he?'

'Yes. He said he'd take some pictures of them in mid-air. I know they're all right, I just prefer not to watch them.'

Laura sympathised. Her own heart had missed several beats a few days earlier, watching Mark diving off the same place.

'What about Ben and Mark?'

Anna hesitated. 'Ben's over there,' she said at last. 'With Candy and Daisy.'

Laura looked round. The two girls lay head to head across the beach, and behind them Ben's skinny figure lurked like a reluctant soldier behind a barricade.

'Oh, yes,' she said. There was another pause.

'It's boring for Mark,' said Anna at last, her voice apologetic. 'Ben never wants to do anything.'

'They were supposed,' said Laura despondently, 'to be friends.'

'They don't really know one another very well. And you know what Ben can be like. It's a good thing Mark's met those other boys, so he's got someone to do things with. Although . . .' she hesitated again, glancing at Laura.

'I know. I don't like them much, either.'

'Poor things.' Anna was trying hard, but her tone was insincere.

'I suppose so. Yes.'

The two boys in question, twin brothers, were staying in the pretty little hotel that fronted the far end of the beach. Slightly older than Ben and Mark, they were in the nominal care of their mother, whose whole attention and time were taken up with a boyfriend who was almost young enough to be called a toy-boy. Blond and good looking, their appearance on the beach, which seldom happened before two in the afternoon, caused a frisson of interest among the sunbathing girls. Since the village had little by way of night-life, the girls were mostly rather young, and the two boys generally let their lofty gaze pass over them without interest. They had, in the beginning, showed signs of being prepared to speak to Daisy and Candida, but Daisy was too wrapped in her own misery to be interested. After one rebuff they had tossed their blond hair back from their eyes and lounged off to seek a more receptive audience.

They had met Ben and Mark on the second day of the holiday, at the diving place. Ben, after an hour in their company, privately wrote them off as bone-headed public-school yobs. Even if he had been well he would have had little time for them, and in his present state he found their arrogance distasteful. Although his feelings towards his father were bitter, he was far from sharing their creed that anyone over twenty-five was a waste of space, to be despised and ignored. To Mark, on the other hand, this view was only a short step beyond his already deeply ingrained belief that adults were a race apart. Bored by Ben's lethargy, excluded from Daisy's companionship because she wanted only Candida, he was drawn into the other boys' orbit.

Laura had taken a violent dislike to them. To Mark's ill-concealed annoyance she had insisted on meeting them.

'I don't see why. They're all right.'

'Of course they are, Mark. But if you're going to be wandering round the village half the night with them, I owe it to your mother at least to learn their names.'

'Dom and Cris. Dominic and Crispin,' he expanded, in a sarcastic upper-crust accent. 'All right?'

Laura looked at him. His arms were folded across his chest, his head was down and his shoulders up, his whole body-language eloquent of resentment. This was a Mark she had never seen before, though she supposed she had always known he existed. She sighed.

'Please don't be like that, Mark.'

'Like what?'

'Like . . . oh, damn it. Like I'm just an interfering old bag who's out to stop you enjoying yourself.'

He gave a shrug that was no more than a quick twitch of his shoulders. Laura bit her lip to hold back the angry words.

'All I want,' she said carefully, 'is to meet them. For a few minutes. If you like, they could join us for supper.'

'Could they?' For the first time he lifted his eyes to her face. 'All right. I'll ask them.'

Dom and Cris duly joined them that evening at the little restaurant near the beach that they had decided they liked the best. They were very polite to Laura and Edward, with 'Mr Melville' and 'Mrs Melville' scattered liberally over every remark. Their blue eyes, however, were cold, and had a disconcerting tendency to focus not on one's face but very slightly to one side of it. Laura found her hands straying to her ears, and her hair, checking that there was nothing strange about either. Their very politeness, after a while, seemed somehow insolent, a kind of thinly veiled contempt that was as unanswerable as it was unpleasant.

From that evening on, Mark spent more and more of his time with the twins. The result, from Laura's point of view, was an instant withdrawal, not so much physically as mentally, of Mark from all of them, and more particularly from herself. She told herself that she was being paranoid, that nothing had changed, but when Dom and Cris saw her and smiled politely, she read derision in their sidelong glances, and saw its reflection in Mark's eyes also.

The evening meals, the one time in the day when they were all together, became more and more uncomfortable as the group fragmented. Mark, though he had perforce to eat with them since Edward held all the money for meals in a wallet called The Housekeeping, sat silent and morose, grimly swallowing his food and leaving, without a word or a backward glance, as soon as he could. Sometimes, too, he would vanish in the lengthy pauses between courses, to slouch back after five or ten minutes smelling strongly of cigarettes. By the second to last evening, Laura felt she had had enough. Anna and Jane had long since given up finding excuses for Mark's behaviour, and Edward, to Laura's dismay, spoke of his son with dislike and contempt.

It was Sunday, and because the beaches were always crowded that day, they had arranged to go out on a boat. The previous weekend this had been a successful trip. The boat's owner, a tubby black, boasted a brilliant stripe of peroxided blond through the two-inch-high helmet of his hair, and his few words of English were more than supplemented by the broad friendliness of his smile. They had promptly christened him 'Captain Ahab', which soon became shortened to 'Captain', a soubriquet to which he cheerfully responded. During the week he had several times joined them on the beach, and Edward had once brought him back to the villa for lunch, during which conversation, supplemented by mime and drawings, flowed with uninhibited ease.

This Sunday, however, started badly and continued worse. The night before, Mark had as usual gone off with Dom and Cris, and Jane had privately begged Daisy and Candida to persuade Ben to go with them to a beach barbecue that someone was organising.

'Please, darlings, do try and get him to go with you. I'm so worried about him, he's nothing but skin and bone and he's got no energy at all.

He won't talk to me, but he just might to you if you can get a few beers down him.'

'I don't think Daddy would like to hear you say *that*,' said Candida primly, teasing. Bill had been shocked to hear from Toby that Ben had got drunk once or twice.

'Sod that,' said Jane robustly. 'Your father forgets he's not still thirteen. You know I don't like any of you to drink too much, but there are times when it helps. Ben's so *controlled*, he bottles everything up so.'

Ben was reluctant, but Jane stayed tactfully silent and indifferent while Daisy and Candida persuaded him, and he finally gave in. The adults went to bed, and at half past two Candida came knocking on Jane's door.

'Mummy? Mummy, wake up.'

'Urrh. Whatsmatter?' Jane mumbled.

'It's Ben. Nothing absolutely desperate, but I think you'd better come.'

Sleep vanished. Jane leaped from her bed. In the downstairs bathroom she found Ben not being sick, as she had imagined, but holding his hand under the cold tap. A litter of bloodstained paper towels on the floor was mute evidence of earlier attempts to halt the flow of blood that was turning the basin a nasty shade of pinky red. His face was pale and sweating.

'Sorry, Mum,' he mumbled. 'I think it's stopping now.'

'Let me see,' said Jane. She took his wrist and turned his hand from the water. A deep cut in the fleshy pad at the base of his thumb oozed sluggishly. 'It could probably do with a couple of stitches,' she said, worried, 'but at this time of night . . .'

'Oh, no!' Ben's eyes darkened with distress. 'It's all right, really it is. Look, it's hardly bleeding at all.'

Jane looked at him, thought of trying to find a taxi and a hospital, and quailed at the prospect almost as much as Ben.

'Tetanus . . .'

'I've had all my boosters. *Please*, Mum . . .'

'I suppose, if it's well disinfected and I bandage it together tightly – it's not as though it's a flap of flesh or anything – it should close up all right, and we'll be home in a couple of days if there's any trouble . . . Fetch me the first-aid bag, Candy. It's in the cupboard over there . . . How on earth did you do it?'

'Lost my temper.' Ben was typically laconic.

'You – you didn't get into a *fight*, did you?'

He drew in a shaky breath. 'No. Not exactly. I just got a bit upset, and . . . I'm sorry, Mum. I'm afraid I smashed a chair, and a table.'

Jane gaped at him. In her hand, the small bottle of antiseptic that Candida

265

had passed her slowly tilted between her nerveless fingers, and a thin stream of viscous yellow fluid poured over Ben's injured hand, still held in place by her grasp on his wrist. It trickled into the cut, turning fluorescent orange in the blood.

'Ow!' Ben's hand jerking from her grasp brought Jane back to life. 'That hurts! You're supposed to dilute it, Mum!'

Jane looked down. The water in the basin had turned cloudy, a milky pink. Like raki, she thought. All those aniseed drinks, going a nasty white when you add the water. She looked at Ben in suspicion.

'Have you been drinking? Is that why?'

'I had a few beers . . .' His eyes followed hers, looked at the basin. His quick mind made the connection. 'Oh, Mum, only two or three beers. Not raki. I don't even like the stuff. I'm not drunk.'

It was true that his eyes and voice were steady. Jane shook her head. 'Sorry, love. Well, it ought to be pretty thoroughly disinfected by now, anyway. We'll just rinse it off once more, and bandage it up, and hope for the best.'

Later, when she had seen him settled in his bed – Mark's, she noticed, was still empty – Jane went wearily back to her own room. Candy and Daisy were there, huddled together on her bed, and they had made her a cup of tea. Jane's eyes filled with tears.

'Oh, bless you, darlings. How very comforting!'

'Did he tell you what happened?'

Jane sipped her tea, realising that her mouth was dry. 'Not really. Only that he smashed some furniture. I thought that you would explain it all. Did he really do that? I can't believe it. I mean – Ben, of all people!'

'Well, it's not very strong furniture,' said Daisy soothingly. 'I know that doesn't make it any better, but it was so easy to do, you see. And he needed it. It was a – what was that thing? Like a cart-horse?'

Cart-horse? Jane thought wildly. Maybe we've all got sunstroke, and this is a hallucination. She took a large gulp of tea, in case it vanished or turned into something else.

'Catharsis, she means,' said sensible Candida. 'Daisy's right, though. And it was her that managed to get him talking.'

'Oh, Daisy, you miracle! What is it that's upsetting him so? You can tell me, can't you?'

'Yes, of course.' Daisy had no qualms. 'It's not a secret. It's just that someone told Ben that his father's girlfriend's pregnant.'

Candy shifted closer to her mother, offering wordless support. To Jane, however, the information was meaningless except in its effect on Ben.

'Oh, poor Ben! And he minded so much . . . yes, of course, he would. It's another rejection, isn't it? A new life, a new family . . . and nothing could ever be put back the way it was. Not that it could have been anyway, of course, but . . . poor old Ben.'

'The others were there,' said Candy. 'Dom and Cris and Mark. The beach party was stupid, really awful music, so we'd all left and gone to this bar. Daisy got Ben talking, and it all came flooding out. I thought he'd stop when they came to sit with us, but he didn't, and Dom and Cris started winding him up. I don't think they meant to,' she added fairly, 'in fact, I think they meant to help, but they hate their own father, and they despise their mother, and the things they said just made Ben more and more angry. Anyway, the boys managed to stop him before he smashed anything else, and they were really good with the bar owner, gave him some money and persuaded him we'd pay for the damage, and not to call the police.'

'Great,' said Jane hollowly. Daisy yawned suddenly, and at once the others did too. 'We must get to bed. We booked Captain's boat for ten tomorrow morning. Good-night, darlings. Thank you for looking after Ben.'

'You won't worry, will you?' Candy kissed her anxiously. 'He's all right, you know. In fact, I think he'll be better now.'

It seemed, the following morning, that Candida was right. Ben, though pale beneath his tan and with dark bruising shadows beneath his eyes, seemed calm and even cheerful. As the adults organised the picnic lunch, and all the paraphernalia deemed essential for a day out on a boat, he volunteered to go and apologise to the owner of the smashed furniture. Jane gave him some money.

'I'll pay it back,' he said earnestly. 'You can take it out of my allowance.'

'I'm afraid I'll have to,' said Jane. 'Are tables and chairs really so expensive round here? I think we're being taken for a ride.'

'I expect we are, a bit, but we're not really in a position to complain, are we?' Jane was so glad to hear him sounding relaxed about it that she refrained from asking Edward to go with Ben to sort things out. Better, she thought, to let him accept responsibility for his actions. Something, she thought, that his father had never learned to do.

'Give Mark another shake,' was all she said. 'Whatever time did he get in last night?'

Mark, when finally roused from his bed, showed all the signs of little sleep and much beer. Jane saw Laura eyeing him with anxious irritation as he trailed behind them down the hill to the pier where the boat was moored. When they reached it there was no sign of Captain Ahab, and when he did appear almost an hour later he, also, looked tired and hung-over. His apology, though profuse, was incomprehensible and seemed to involve something being wrong with his legs.

'Legless, I should think,' muttered Edward as they set off down the coast.

The day progressed with outward normality, though probably only Toby and Nick enjoyed it. Candida and Daisy sat up on the prow, sunbathing and talking to Ben, whose hand was clearly throbbing painfully, though he refused to admit it. Toby and Nick played a complicated game involving water pistols, a pair of dice and a system of scoring that nobody could understand, and Edward chatted laboriously to Captain, who was doing his best to make up for his late arrival. Jane, who was exhausted, talked quietly to Anna and Laura, whose eyes constantly strayed to Mark who, on reaching the boat, had lain down on the cushioned side bench and gone to sleep with his back to them.

'I did ask if he wanted to bring Dom and Cris,' said Laura, 'but he said it was too boring for them, and too early in the morning. I think he'd rather have stayed behind with them. I suppose I should have let him, but . . .'

'He's just tired,' said Jane encouragingly. 'He was very late last night. And I think he's better off away from those boys. What does Edward say?'

'The same as you, really.' Laura glanced at Edward, who was frowning as he listened intently to Captain Ahab's story. 'He doesn't like the twins, either. Well, nor do I. But he's rather cross with Mark.'

'I'm not surprised,' said Anna firmly. 'I think Mark's behaviour is disgraceful.' She saw the distress on her friend's face. 'I'm sorry, Laura,' she said more gently, 'but he is bloody rude. Especially to you, and that's what Edward minds about, I should think.'

'Oh dear, I know. And I don't like it either – in fact, I'm pretty fed up with Mark myself – but I think it's mostly those awful boys. They're a bad influence on him. He's not really like that.'

Anna looked as though she disagreed, and so did Jane, but neither of them could bring themselves to say so. Laura, however cross she might be with Mark at the moment, was still deeply fond of him and would resent any criticisms but her own.

They moored at a beach where the sand was so silvery white that the sea over it was a luminous turquoise so bright it almost hurt the eyes. They ate pizzas from the local bakery, only made on Sundays and still slightly warm from the wood-fired oven. Afterwards Edward and the boys played in the water, Edward as usual inventing the rules of a game that was a cross between rugby, water polo and volleyball. Ben forgot his sore hand, and even Mark, after watching dourly for ten minutes, allowed himself to be drawn into the game. Laura felt her spirits lift, but when they returned to the village at five o'clock Mark vanished almost as soon as they had left the boat. He went without a word or a backward look, and it was only by chance that Laura saw him, half-way down the beach, talking and laughing with Dom and Cris. Wearily, she hefted her beach bag and the picnic box, lighter than it had been but still awkward to carry, and set off up the hill.

That evening Mark again disappeared during the meal, only returning after the main course had been put on the table. As soon as this was eaten he was gone again, and this time he did not return. Back at the villa the adults as usual sat on the balcony. Toby and Nick were playing in the garden, and the two girls had taken Ben with them to a nearby bar for an ice cream.

'I hope they won't stay and drink,' said Jane.

'I don't think they will,' said Edward soothingly. 'They're tired, for one thing, and the girls will see that Ben comes to no harm. Not that he's likely to. I think he's got it out of his system, now, and he's sensible enough. Unlike some.'

'It was a fairly awful day, wasn't it? I'm sorry,' apologised Laura.

'Don't be silly.' Jane spoke robustly. 'It was a perfectly nice day, and if Mark didn't enjoy it he had nobody but himself to blame. Everyone else was perfectly all right. And don't look like that, Laura. I know you want to make excuses for him, but as far as I can see he's just a spoiled, selfish little rat, and you shouldn't allow him to spoil your holiday. Sorry, Edward.'

He shook his head and made a gesture of dismissal. 'It's all right. I agree with you. I've had just about enough of his moods and his rudeness. I think it's time we had a little talk with him, and with Dom and Cris too, if necessary.'

Afterwards, Laura wondered why she had agreed, why she had not stopped him. Was it because she was angry enough with Mark to want to punish him? Certainly if she had known the effect it would have, she would have done anything to prevent the confrontation. As it was, used to the arguments and discussions that were common in Jane's and Anna's households, she thought that it would be better to get the resentments out in the open, to clear the air. It was, she realised later, entirely the wrong course to take with Mark, who took the slightest hint of criticism as an attack and as a signal of dislike. Brought back from the bar by Edward, without Dom and Cris, who had excused themselves with exquisite and gleeful insolence, he sat silent and seething on the balcony, closing his ears to everything. Edward's reasoning, Anna's forthright criticisms, and Jane's appeal to his better nature, were treated alike with wordless scorn.

Throughout it all, Laura stood in the shadows with her back to the balcony rail. She felt cold, and found that her arms were crossed protectively across her body. She could think of nothing to say.

'There's no point in continuing this,' said Jane. 'It seems to me, Mark, that you have had nothing but kindness and love from Laura and Edward, and that they deserve to be treated better than this. I think you should think about that.'

Mark hunched his shoulders, refusing to speak.

'How on earth are we going to get through the rest of the holiday?' asked Laura desolately of all of them.

'Normally, I hope,' said Edward firmly. 'We've had our say, and Mark's had a chance to have one too, even if he doesn't want to. Let that be an end to it. No recriminations. Right?'

Silently, Mark stood up and left the balcony. They heard the bang of the front door as he went out. For the remaining two days of the holiday, he ignored them all. Although he could not avoid eating with them, he acknowledged their presence neither by look nor word. At Gatwick, where his mother was waiting for them, he said 'Goodbye' in their general direction, and was gone.

Chapter 23

Time, thought Laura. Time, the great healer. Come on, then, time. Do your stuff. Heal a bit.

The trouble with time was that it was so elastic, moving so slowly and yet hurrying so fast. She knew, of course, that in order to make it pass she must keep busy, and certainly there was plenty to be busy with. The house, for a start. She had hoped, secretly, that nobody would want to buy it, at least not for a long while. The newspapers were full of the recession, of the collapse of the housing market. Whether the bank manager would be satisfied with the fact that they were at least attempting to sell was something she had not cared to ask, not wanting to hear the likely answer that no, that would not be enough in itself.

But the recession, however much it might have damaged the building trade and those (like architects) associated with it, seemed to have passed over some sections of the population, like the angel of death over the children of Israel. What blood, Laura wondered, had they daubed on their lintels? What bitter herbs had they consumed with their unleavened bread? While she had been in Turkey the estate agent, as desperate as Edward to earn a commission, had been busy, and on their return laid not one but two good offers before them like a gun dog with a brace of pheasant hanging from its soft mouth.

One of the offers was from a young family with three children, the oldest five and the youngest only a few months old. The father was an accountant, already a partner in a good firm, secure and successful.

'Know what the kid said to me?' the estate agent asked Edward gloomily. 'He said "My Daddy's a very busy man. He says he's never had so much work to do." I said, that's nice, the way you do, and why was Daddy so specially busy now? And he said, "He does winding up for the receiver."' They shared a rueful smile. 'He didn't have a clue what it meant, of course. I think he thought it was winding things up with a key, like clockwork toys.'

'What universe have you been inhabiting?' asked Edward. 'They don't have clockwork toys any more. They have computers and electronic toys with micro-chips that do everything. Your average five-year-old is more sophisticated than we were at twelve.'

'I suppose so,' agreed the agent, whose grandchildren were still babies. 'What a ghastly prospect. Anyway, it's a good offer, slightly higher than the other, but they still have to sell their present house. It's the sort of thing that should go like a hot cake – medium-sized detached on a nice estate – but there are too many of them around. He could afford to drop his price, they've got a good lump sum put by to set against the greater value of your place, but he's reluctant to sell for too much less than he paid for it. I told him he'd do well to take what he can when he can, but of course I'm the Wicked Estate Agent, so he's not likely to take much notice. It's his wife who's really keen on moving, anyway. He's going to have to do a much longer journey to town every day from here, so while he wants to please her, he's not going to break his heart if they miss this one.'

'And the other offer?'

'Slightly lower, but a better bet. An older couple, retired early, selling their house to their son-in-law, ready to move as quickly as you like. No problems with money, they can afford to buy even without selling the other one. He was chairman of a company that went public two years ago, made him a nice little fortune.'

'You didn't like him?'

The agent grinned. 'Not much, since you ask. Jealousy, I expect. But he's arrogant as hell, and she's worse. They won't match the other offer – he knows he's in a strong bargaining position – but he'll stick to the one he's made. And quibble like mad over the fiddly bits, offer you four pounds instead of five for the greenhouse heater, that sort of thing.'

Edward sighed. 'I'd like to go for the others, and I know my wife would too. The village would like another young family; there are too many retired people here already. It's not really up to me, though. Can you let me have the details in writing? I'd better go and put it to the bank manager. In the end, the decision's his.'

As Edward had expected, the bank manager opted for present certainty rather than a possible future gain of a few thousand pounds. Laura, who by this time had met both families when they came for a second look round the house, was disappointed but resigned.

'I should have liked to have seen those children living here in this house,' she said. 'Those other people – what are they called? Snipe?' ('Snape,' put in Edward.) 'Snape, then, were so rude when they came round for a second look! Poking in all the cupboards, and making remarks about the furniture.'

'They're bound to want to see how big the cupboards are,' Edward pointed out mildly. 'Surely the Nicholsons did?'

'Yes, I know. But they said "Do you mind if I look in the cupboards?" That Snap woman' ("Snape," murmured Edward) 'just marched in and jerked all the doors open. I think she was hoping they would be untidy, and everything would tumble out. Then she looked all sniffy at the chest in the hall, and said she thought antiques were unhygienic. So I said in that case I'd better not offer them a cup of coffee, and they left.'

'Oh, Laura!' Edward could not help laughing. 'We need them, you know. If they pull out, the Nicholsons might not come up to scratch, and then . . .'

'I know. I'm sorry. Actually, I'm exaggerating a bit. Well, quite a lot, really. Not about the Snorts, they were awful. But I was perfectly polite to them. They were the ones who didn't want coffee. But I can't help thinking how much the village is going to hate them. I'm sure she's going to be just like Linda Snell in *The Archers*. Worse, probably. I feel so guilty about landing everyone with them.'

'They'll cope. Tod will sort them out.'

'I suppose so.' She saw his face, and came to lean against him. 'Sorry. I'm not being much help, am I? I know you hate this just as much as I do. I'm not really moaning.'

'You'd have every right to. I just feel so guilty.'

'Don't. It's not your fault. It's just . . . fate, I suppose. Bad luck. And we're better off than most. I don't really mind that much, anyway. Not about the house, or money. That's nothing, compared to . . . well, you know.'

'Mm.' He hugged her. The unspoken, unspeakable name hung in the air between them, a physical barrier. Mark.

For the first week after their return, Laura had been carried along like a surfer, on the crest of a wave of anger. Every time she thought of Mark, she made sure that what she visualised was the sulky face, the look of anger and resentment, the refusal even to return a greeting or pass anything at the table. The anger was hot and clean, it made things simple and easy to bear. The photographs came back from the processors. She chose several that showed him diving, or on the boat, or smiling beneath a waiter's Turkish fez, and one, taken on that last Sunday, where his shoulders were hunched and his face, half turned away in rejection, was sullen. She sent them to him, to remind him that the holiday had not all been bad, and put

273

the unpleasant one on the top, to punish him.

By the second week, that anger was dying down. It became an effort to produce it, to fan the sluggish embers into clear, bright flames. And beneath the heat was not so much pain as the knowledge that pain was to come. Laura dealt with it, as she had always done in the past when faced with unhappiness, by pushing it away from her. She could not prevent herself from thinking of Mark, but every time that she did she blanked him out, rejected the image of him with an effort and a finality that were almost physical. She worked furiously, clearing out cupboards, ruthlessly getting rid of anything that wasn't strictly necessary.

She managed to keep that phase going for three weeks, which made it a month since their return. During that time, particularly in the third and fourth weeks, she had expected to hear from Mark. Not during the first week – they were both still too angry then – but when, as she assumed, his first fury had cooled. Nor did she underestimate the strength of that fury, but she pinned her faith on Mark's innate honesty. Recalcitrant and stubborn he might be, but she knew he had a strongly developed sense of justice, and she firmly believed that he would be able to see that, if they had behaved wrongly, so had he.

That he was unused to self-criticism she knew, but he had occasionally in the past been brought to apologise when once he had been made to see and accept what he had done wrong. So sure was she that this would happen again that she even resolved not to be too quick to forgive him, believing that he would learn more that way than from forgiveness more lightly given. Having calmed down, she saw this episode as merely a phase of the relationship they were building, something unpleasant to experience but ultimately of benefit, just as Daisy's expulsion, though awful, had given her and Anna a new closeness and understanding.

It was not until the fourth week that it began to dawn on Laura that Mark might not get in touch. Until then, every time the telephone rang she jumped and felt a lurch of pleasure mixed with anxiety. By the end of that week, however, she had begun to realise that he might not be prepared to forgive them. On Friday afternoon, after several false starts when she dialled the number and then put the receiver down before it could ring, she swallowed her pride and rang him.

'Hello?' The sound of his voice, so familiar and dear, almost silenced her.

'Hello, Mark.' She drew a shaky breath. 'Mark, I think we should talk about what's happened. Mark, I'm sorry . . .' Before she had said even that much there was a click, and she was speaking into the echoing void.

At the sound of her voice he had hung up.

Once more, she was angry, but this time she knew that the anger would not help her. A temporary anaesthetic only, like taking a pain-killer for a decayed tooth. The rejection was so sudden and final, above all so unexpected. It had never occurred to her that he could put her and Edward out of his life so easily. The blame, she thought, must be hers. As an adult, and as a parent, she had failed Mark. If he could not forgive her, how could she forgive herself? Had there been time for him to hear her apologise? Would he, perhaps, relent?

Drearily, she tried to distract herself with the other things that should be so much more important. By then, the sale of the house was in the hands of the solicitors, and progressing rapidly. Laura and Edward had decided that, for the moment at least, they would not buy another house. Edward's office building, still unlet, had once had a small flat on the top floor. Deconverting it would be a simple matter, Edward would be able to do most of the work himself, and in that way they could pay off all the overdraft and the bank loans, wiping the slate clean.

'Oh, Laura,' said Anna sadly when she heard this. 'It sounds a very good idea. Very sensible.'

'Yes, isn't it?' said Laura, rather too brightly. 'And there are a lot of advantages. Edward won't have to spend time and money travelling in to work, and we'll be able to have lunch together. In fact, I may well take over some of the office work for him, as I'll be on the spot. Or perhaps see if I can't get some kind of job. I'll have to give up St Barbara's, I'm afraid, but it should be easier to find something in the town.'

'Your old dears will miss you.'

'Yes, and I shall miss them.' It was, of course, one of the least of the things that Laura was going to miss, but neither of them felt able to mention that. 'Now, what about Daisy? Is there any news?'

Anna's face brightened. 'Yes, that's what I came about. Danewood College say they'll have her.'

'Danewood? But wasn't that one of the first ones you tried? I thought they said no.'

'So they did, but it seems that one of their sixth-form girls has been pulled out at the last moment, without any warning. School fees crisis, I expect. Awful for them, of course, but wonderful for us, because the school's got an empty place they need to fill.'

'So it was true that they hadn't any room. There you are, you see, I told you they weren't just making excuses. Oh, Anna, I'm so pleased for you both. What a relief! And it's a good school, too.'

'Yes, it is, almost as good as Abbotsford, and the best thing about it from Daisy's point of view is that it's not too far from there, so she'll still be able to keep up with all her old friends. It's nearer here, too, so the travelling will be easier.'

'When does she start?'

'Next week. Monday.'

'Next Monday? But it's Thursday today! It certainly is the last moment, as you said. You must be frantic!'

'Just a bit. The worst thing is that the school shop won't be open until Saturday, so we can't do anything about her clothes. Still, it's only for one year and they have much more freedom in the sixth form, so she won't need too much in the way of uniform. I'm hoping to get most of it second-hand. There won't be much to do by way of name tapes – the worst things are socks and knickers and things, and of course they're all done already.'

'I could do some for you. I'd like to help.'

'Bless you, but I wouldn't dream of it. You've got more than enough to do here, and Daisy can perfectly well sew them all in herself. It certainly won't do her any harm.'

'She must be nervous.'

'She is, rather, but she's being very brave about it. I think she'll be all right. The headmistress is very nice, and so is her housemistress, and there are several girls she knew at Princess Mary's, too. She'll soon find her feet. And as she says, she'll have masses of street cred!'

'Yes.'

The telephone rang. They were in the garden. Anna had arrived to find Laura scrubbing the shelves in the understair cupboard, and had dragged her out into the sunshine. She had not noticed that Laura had brought the cordless phone with her, and when it rang under Laura's chair she jumped. Laura snatched it up, her face shuttered and intent.

'Hello? Hello?' There was a pause, then: 'That's all right. Goodbye.' Her eager tone was flattened, and she looked at the machine with dislike as she switched it off. 'Wrong number,' she explained, unnecessarily. Anna sighed. She knew Laura too well not to understand the tension she perceived in her friend, the air of desperation underlying the controlled exterior.

'You haven't heard from Mark at all?'

'No.'

'Rude little sod.'

Laura shook her head. With her face turned away, she said: 'Will you have the urns and those pots for your garden? I don't want to leave them for the Snakes, and I can't very well take them to the flat.'

'Of course I will. And when you get another house, you can have them back.' Anna studied her friend's face, seen in less than profile. In spite of the Turkish suntan, she looked pale and drawn, Anna thought.

'Don't be upset about Mark,' she said gently. 'He's not worth it, Laura. Not worth making yourself unhappy over.'

Laura turned back. Her eyes were stretched wide in an attempt to keep the glaze of tears from brimming over her lower lids. 'He is to me,' she said simply.

'Oh, Laura. Do you want to talk about it?'

'No. Yes. *I can't*!' Anna found herself clearing her throat in sympathy with the husky tightness in Laura's voice. Laura swallowed, her head dipping with the effort. 'It hurts,' she said, putting her hands to the vulnerable softness below her ribs. 'Physically hurts, I mean. As if I'd been stabbed, or kicked. Bruised, anyway. You know?'

'I know,' nodded Anna, remembering.

'It's so difficult to believe. I keep thinking about Turkey, and wondering how I could have let things go so wrong. I expected too much from him. Comfort, and support, and understanding. Adult things. And he's a child. Children are selfish.'

'He's fifteen. Old enough to be aware of other people's problems, and to make allowances. I get comfort and support from Daisy quite a lot of the time. Jane does from Candy and Ben. From Toby, even.'

'Yes, but they're your children. They've grown up with you, been through all the good and the bad things with you. Mark's not my child. I let myself think of him as if he was, but he isn't. I know that, with my mind, but . . . I feel bereaved. Unbalanced, as if I'd lost an arm, or a leg. If he'd died, like the baby, I could mourn him and get over it, but he's alive, and I can't bear the thought of him growing up and never seeing him again.'

'It's only been a few weeks. He'll get in touch.'

Laura shook her head. 'I don't think so. I do know him, you see. I know how he is. It's not so much that he won't forgive, as that he will simply put us out of his head. We just won't exist, in his world, any more. He never looks back, never considers the past. Just the present, and the immediate future.'

'Immature.' Anna tried to keep the criticism out of her voice, but Laura heard it.

'Yes. But that's how he *is*. It's not his fault. Not anyone's fault. I had thought, once, that it would be possible to teach him some self-awareness, to help him look inside his head and understand himself so that he could learn to understand other people and deal with them better. Now I'll never get the chance.'

Privately, Anna wondered if it would have been possible, but she had to admit that there had been a change for the better in Mark over the year they had known him.

'What does Edward say?'

'Nothing.' Laura sounded both despairing and resentful. 'He's so angry with him, he won't talk about him at all. I've begged him to get in touch, to try to put things right, but he won't. He never really loved Mark like I did. He felt guilty about it, I think, and of course that made it even harder to like him. Mark was never really more than a reminder of the things that had gone wrong in our life, and I'm afraid it began to seem to Edward as though, somehow, he was to blame for our problems. Sort of unlucky, you know? And yet he was stuck with the feeling of responsibility towards him. I suspect he's a bit relieved that Mark doesn't want to have anything more to do with us.'

Anna considered. 'Was he . . . do you think he might have been a bit jealous of Mark?' she asked hesitantly.

'Jealous? Of his own son?' Laura did not want to admit, even to herself, that she had once been aware of this possibility.

'It happens. Quite a lot, actually.'

'Yes, I suppose so. Perhaps he was. I know I used to make too much fuss of Mark. That was partly the trouble. I'd always put Mark first, whenever he was with us, always did everything I could think of to make him happy. I thought it was good for him. I still think so. But then, in Turkey, I was worried about the house, and about you and Daisy, and Edward of course, and I stopped doing that. I still wanted him to be happy, but I had other things on my mind. It was a kind of betrayal.'

Anna thought this was exaggerating the problem. 'You can't organise a holiday for ten people round the whims of one of them.'

'No, but I should have explained things to him. Talked to him. I never got the chance, though. He was always with those twins. They turned him against us, I'm sure they did.'

Anna, though sympathetic, was unsure what to say. She had known, of course, that Laura was very fond of Mark, but she had never realised how deep the feelings had gone. She was relieved when they heard a voice calling from the front garden, and recognised Cassandra coming down the side path pushing Eva in the opulent pram her parents had insisted on buying.

'You won't tell anyone, will you?' begged Laura in a low voice. 'I know I'm being – unbalanced.'

'Of course not. Hello, Cassie. How's that gorgeous girl, then?' She stood up, and bent to look in the pram. 'Fast asleep, the little cherub. I must get going – Laura will tell you my news. For goodness' sake get her to make you a cup of tea and keep her out in the garden for an hour, or she'll be back in there polishing the attics, or something daft.' She bent to kiss Laura. 'Ring me. Any time. I mean it.'

Laura nodded, knowing that she wouldn't. 'Thanks, Anna. And love to Daisy. I'll go and put the kettle on,' she added to Cassandra, pausing as she went by to bend over the pram for a moment. Gently she stroked the back of the downy head, entranced by its smooth roundness, breathing in the indefinable aroma of milk, talcum powder and clean washing that rose like incense from the sleeping baby. When she came back with the tea, Eva had woken up, and was sitting on a rug on the grass. She grinned up at Laura, displaying the small teeth that sat like little ornaments on the wide expanse of pink gums. She was teething again – her chin was glossily varnished with dribble – but as usual nothing marred the sunny placidity of her nature.

'She's still not crawling yet,' said Cassandra. 'I don't know whether to be sorry or relieved. After all, she's nearly nine months old now.'

'Be grateful,' recommended Laura. 'My mother always said this is the perfect age. You can sit them down and they stay where you put them, and they haven't learned to answer back. Make the most of it, it won't last.'

As they spoke, Eva reached for a daisy and overbalanced, toppling slowly sideways with an absurdly exaggerated expression of surprise, like a mime artist. Wasting no time in tears or regrets, she wriggled and rolled herself from her back to her rotund tummy where she paused for breath before getting her knees beneath her, her nappy-padded bottom lifting in a parody of abasement. Then, her chubby hands spread like starfish, she lifted up her front end until she was on hands and knees.

'What did I tell you?' said Laura, gasping with laughter that was still not far from tears. 'She's off!'

Breathing heavily with exertion and concentration, Eva moved.

'But she's going backwards!' said Cassandra.

It was true that the baby, her eyes still fixed on the daisy of her desire, was slowly inching away from her prey.

'An allegory of life,' murmured Laura, but her voice was drowned by Eva's wail of frustration as she collapsed flat on the rug. Laura scooped her up. 'Poor little Eva. Poor little love,' she murmured, nuzzling her neck until the screams of fury turned into chortles. 'There you are, then, you shall have it. Don't think it will always be like that. And don't eat it, for heaven's sake.' She inserted a questing finger into the dribbly mouth, and hooked out the daisy.

'They're not poisonous, are they?' Cassandra looked alarmed. 'She puts everything into her mouth.'

'No, I don't think so. Buttercups are, though. I remember being very sick, as a child, after eating a buttercup.'

'Goodness. I didn't know that.'

'Nor did I, for years afterwards. At the time nobody knew what was the matter with me. Then, long after I'd grown up, I read how poisonous they are, and I suddenly remembered that I'd eaten one, and a daisy, because I was bored of playing rounders. I always hated games at school.'

After Cassandra had left, Laura went back into the house. It was too late, now, to start any more cleaning or sorting. Edward would be home soon, and there was supper to make. Wearily she went upstairs to wash, and change out of the clothes that Eva had dribbled over. Her body still held on to the memory of Eva in her arms, the warmth, the solid weight of her, above all the confiding way she leaned into her embrace. She savoured the exquisite pain of it. No one, of course, would have been surprised that she should feel moments of anguish at the sight and feel of a baby who, they would assume, must remind her so poignantly of the child she had lost. The reminder was there, but the longing that was like a knife in her heart was not for that baby, who had never truly woken from the sleep of the womb, but for what she had never known, the infant that Mark had once been.

The night before she had dreamed so vividly that the dream had stayed with her all day, haunting her. She had met Georgia, who had told her she was moving a long way away, and that Mark was to be sent to the strictest school that could be found. Then she had had a letter from Mark, but somehow had been unable to read it, the only clear words being 'love, Mark' in his crabbed handwriting. Then, with one of those inconsequential changes that one accepts in dreams, she was in a school, and a small child had fallen from a staircase. The heavy thud of its head hitting a railing below still echoed in her ears. She had picked up the child, cradling it against her, feeling its limbs already cold but trying, desperately, to warm it back to life, and had woken in tears, unable to explain to Edward what was the matter.

Now, on the stairs, the dream came back to her and she closed her mind to it, distracting herself by looking about her. Already the house, though it would have looked much the same to anyone else, felt different. The knowledge that behind the closed doors lay empty cupboards, stripped and cleaned, created an echoing hollowness that produced, most of the time, a kind of ache in the middle of her forehead. Even the rooms, though still fully furnished, had the unreality of a stage set. Sometimes she found herself shutting doors carefully, to avoid the tell-tale wobble of painted canvas walls that would bring a ripple of laughter from an unseen audience.

Her own behaviour, too, had a similar theatrical quality. To the eyes of others (she hoped) she appeared to be behaving normally. She could chat to Cassandra, be pleased for Anna and Daisy; she could encourage Edward and try to keep him cheerful. She was, as always, the Laura who coped, who didn't let things get her down. But, for the first time in her life, it was an act.

My starring role, she thought. Playing the part of Laura Melville to the life, eat your heart out, Stanislavsky. There were no Oscars, however, for this performance. For how long, she wondered, would she be able to keep it up? Would the black slug of depression that coiled and stirred within her grow, one day, big enough to engulf the flimsy paper and paint of her constructed persona? She had hoped, at the beginning, that she could re-create herself, that by keeping the act going it would become reality. As days went by, however, she had less and less belief in that reality.

In the bathroom she stripped and showered. Wrapped in a towel, she brushed her hair and made up her face. She found herself looking at her reflection in the mirror with detached dislike. The Laura she saw still wore, in her own eyes, the smug, contented look of a person who believes she is in control of herself and of her life. But I'm not, thought Laura. The person I thought I was would never have inspired the degree of dislike, of hatred even, that I saw in Mark's face at the end of the holiday. It was the absolute finality of that rejection that had struck at the roots of her being, had shaken her trust in herself and in the world as being, fundamentally, beneficent.

And why should you be spared? she sneered at the face she saw. Why should you, over all the millions of people in the world, be granted immunity from the realities of life? It came to her that what she had taken, in herself, to be strength and courage, had been no more than a delusion born of ignorance. Sheltered by the fairy-tale towers of friendship and love, she had slumbered, like Sleeping Beauty in reverse, through the sunshine days of her innocence. Now, shocked from that sleep by what those around her regarded as a pinprick, she awoke to the knowledge of thorns and briars. They were so thick around her, so tangled and high, that the possibility of escape seemed unthinkable.

The stupid woman in the mirror was crying again. Laura saw without pity the red-rimmed, bloodshot eyes, the slack distorted mouth. Edward would be coming home soon, and he must not find her like this. Poor Edward, who would think she blamed him for the loss of their house when, in truth, the only thing she blamed him for was not trying to make peace with his son. Resolutely she breathed in, closing her eyes and gripping her lips together. Turning on the cold tap by long-accustomed feel, she cupped water in her hands and splashed it on her face.

The black slug stretched and stirred, then subsided. It might be the most real thing about her, she thought, but she would keep it hidden from everyone else for as long as possible. Out of shame, and pride, and a kind of perverse self-punishment that made her hug her pain to her like a baby, cherishing it, she would keep up her act while she could.

Chapter 24

With the passing of the months, it seemed to Laura that it was not her grief that was growing less, but that she herself was in some way ceasing to exist. She found herself glancing sideways to catch her reflection in shop windows or mirrors, not checking as she might once have done that her clothes and hair were tidy, but to see whether that reflection was still there. She was surprised, at times, that it was and that it appeared so solid when she felt herself to be faded and diminished. She took to reading the Deaths columns in newspapers, an activity she had hitherto regarded as morbid in someone of her age. When Anna was having coffee with her one day in March, she noticed Laura's eyes straying to the open pages she had abandoned on her arrival.

'Why on earth are you reading that?' Anna's voice was sharper than usual; she had noticed a change in Laura in the five months since she had left the village, and was concerned by it.

Laura raised unseeing eyes. 'Just checking,' she said vaguely.

'Checking for what?'

'To see whether I'm still alive.' Laura, only half aware of her, answered with disconcerting honesty.

'Laura!' Anna's anxious voice recalled Laura to reality.

'Oh, sorry, what a silly thing to say! I was miles away. It was just to see whether any of my old dears have died.'

It was the best she could do on the spur of the moment, though not very convincing because they both knew that if any of the residents of St Barbara's had died Laura would undoubtedly have heard about it straight away.

Anna frowned. 'Laura, are you all right?'

'Yes, yes, I'm fine. Really, fine. Well, a bit down, you know, but . . . fine.'

'Only, if you want to talk about anything . . .'

Laura looked at her rather desperately and shook her head. How could she say that yes, she longed to talk about it, but that it was impossible for her to find the words. They were all there in her head, but to bring them out and parade them in front of anyone else was more than she was capable of. Partly because she was afraid that they would think that she was unhinged, and be shocked or contemptuous, and partly because she felt that her misery was the only part of her that was still properly alive, and she clung to it as a lifeline against the nothingness that threatened her from within. Knowing that it was irrational, she still feared that if her friends, kindly and compassionately, should reason her out of her sadness, she would lose her last link with Mark and with the person she had once been.

She had always been told that the first year of bereavement was the worst, and bereaved was what she felt herself to be. It was certainly true that, although to outward appearance she had moved forward with the passage of time, in her mind she was constantly looking back. For her, the turn of the year was not January, but the end of July when they had returned from Turkey. Mark's visits had been so few, in the fifteen months that she had known him, that each one was distinct in her memory, each anniversary a moment of pain. Christmas, this year, had been strange and empty away from the village, but it had been New Year that had set her weeping. Now, in Lent, she was getting ready to face both Easter, when last year he had sat with them all and been happy, and the time when he had first arrived, literally, on her doorstep.

Laura had always felt that living in the past was permissible only in the very old, and despised people who looked back all the time. The tragedy of Orpheus roused no sympathy in her: she always thought how maddened Eurydice must have been by him, and how she must have wished that she, not he, had been the one leading the way. Eurydice would not have looked back in that idiotic way. She thought so even more, now, and despised herself even as she wondered whether Mark, too, ever looked back to the previous year with regret.

No, she could say none of this. Particularly not to Anna, who had been through a loss and a bereavement ten times worse than this, and survived it with courage and humour. Speaking of her feelings would not do any good. There had been a time, last summer, when Laura had hoped that Anna might intervene. When she had spoken to her in the garden of her old house that day, she had wondered afterwards whether Anna might say something to Edward, or even to Mark himself, to try to put things right. But Anna, no doubt rightly, had done nothing, and Laura had felt an unreasonable sense of betrayal. Now she shook her head again, pulling her face into a smile.

Anna sighed, and gave up. At once Laura found herself regretting, even resenting, her friend's acquiescence with her wishes. She knew that it was irrational, but feeling as she did that she was worthless and unlovable she badly wanted the reassurance of her friends' interest in her state of mind, even though she would have been unwilling to give them an answer.

'The flat looks nice.' Anna, feeling that they were not communicating but unable to find the right words, looked desperately around her for inspiration. 'You've done it beautifully.'

It was true that the flat had worked out unexpectedly well. Edward, needing to express and expiate his own feelings of guilt and failure, had used every atom of inspiration, skill and experience he had to transform the top floor of an uninspired thirties building into a new home. The rooms, fortunately, were already of a good size and pleasantly proportioned, with large windows which flooded them with light. The area had few tall buildings, and on the fourth floor they were high enough above everyone else to have no need of net curtains for privacy, to Laura's immense relief.

They had one large bedroom and one smaller one, a good-sized kitchen and bathroom, and a big living room stretching the width of the building, looking out on to an area of flat roof that he was hoping to enclose with a little conservatory. Meanwhile Laura kept it crammed with plants in pots and troughs which softened the view of the town below. Their furniture had fitted in surprisingly well – though much of it was being stored in Jane's attics and Anna's outbuildings – and the only thing Laura found significantly difficult was cooking. She kept forgetting that the oven had to be switched on.

'It does look good, doesn't it?' Laura pushed enthusiasm into her voice. It was like forcing a too-large pillow into a pillowcase that was just too small for it. 'One of Edward's triumphs. And it's very easy to run.' It was one of the things she found hardest to bear about the flat. At least, before, she had been able to use the anodyne of housework and gardening. Here there was little to do and it was getting more and more difficult to force herself out of bed in the mornings. She no longer went swimming, although the pool was a mere five minutes away. Cassandra, who would have nagged her into going, was herself tied with Eva. It was unpleasant feeling flabby and unfit, and some of her clothes were too tight to wear, but Laura found she did not care enough to do anything about it.

'Any luck with finding a job?' Anna laboured on.

'Not yet. I'm not qualified for much, and of course there's not much around.'

'It's a pity you gave up St Barbara's, in a way.'

'Yes. It seemed sensible at the time, though. A clean break, and all that. How's Mrs Snake getting on?'

'Don't ask!' Anna leaned forward in her chair, eager with appalled amusement. 'You wouldn't believe the trouble that woman's caused! I believe if people had known what they'd be like, they'd have taken up a collection to pay you not to sell the house! She seems to think she's the lady of the manor and Florence Nightingale rolled into one. How she ever persuaded them to let her take over your job I'll never know. Steam-rollered them, probably. Even Tod gives in to her from time to time. Not always, of course. He gives her a good run for her money, generally. The trouble is, he's so besotted with Eva that he doesn't have as much time for village activities as he used to have. Or, not as much interest in them, anyway. He's slowing up a bit, too, have you noticed? He doesn't say much, but I know his feet hurt, and he's having trouble with his knees – arthritis, I suppose.'

'He's happy, though. He loves being with Cassie and Eva, and he's good for them, too, don't you think? You don't mind?'

'Mind?' Anna looked surprised. 'Of course I don't mind. I'm delighted for them all. I just wish he'd stand up to that awful woman more, that's all.'

Mr and Mrs Snape, who had moved into Laura's old house the previous October, had fulfilled all the worst prophecies of the estate agent. While claiming to want a quick purchase and an early completion, they had obstructed its progress at every turn, and wasted days over decisions on whether they wanted to buy carpets, garden furniture or the freezer. They combined an obsessive attention to detail with an equally obsessive wish to save money on small things, though one of their first actions on taking possession of the house had been to replace all the period windows with modern sealed-unit ones in plastic-coated frames that Edward referred to as 'monstrosities' and which sat in the arched openings like baseball caps worn with a city suit.

Like Tod and James, they had at once thrown themselves into the social life of the village. Also like Tod and James, they had enthusiasm, time, and money, but somehow the effect was quite different. What, in Tod, was amusing exuberance, in the Snapes was interference and pushiness. It did not take them long to set the village seething with resentment at their high-handed ways, and if it was to their credit that they did not take offence at the snubs dealt them, it was generally felt that this was because, armoured in their self-esteem, they had failed to notice them.

Laura, with many good intentions about 'making a fresh start' had decided early on not to continue working at St Barbara's after moving to the flat. For one thing, now that they were living in town, they decided to get rid of Edward's estate car and keep only Laura's small car. Although there was a car park attached to the office building, Edward had let all the empty spaces in it. While he could not find tenants for the offices, there was always a need for parking, and though the income was not great it was better than nothing. Laura could use the car whenever she wanted, but she was reluctant to do so in case Edward needed to go anywhere. Also, and more importantly, she did not think she could bear to work in the village where she had been so happy, or to pass her old house twice a day getting to work.

Mrs Snape, wanting to make her mark, had found it difficult to push her way into a position of sufficient influence in the community. While she had no doubt that she would get herself on to all the major committees as soon as there were vacancies on them, this could not be done instantly. When she realised, however, that Laura's place at St Barbara's was empty, it seemed the most natural thing in the world for her to put herself forward for it, doing away with any hesitation on their part by offering to do the work for nothing. As an offer it was impossible to refuse, particularly as she obviously had the necessary organisational skills.

Laura tried hard not to feel pleased, but it was difficult not to experience some satisfaction when, virtually every time she visited the village, someone insisted on telling her how awful Mrs Snape was, and how much she, Laura, was missed. At St Barbara's one old lady had been almost spitting with fury as she told Laura how most of the original activities that had been set up had been changed or replaced.

'The local-history group is done for,' she mourned. 'Of course, it meant a great deal of work, finding books and getting copies of old records, but it was such an interest! That Woman said it was too much for us, all that mental effort, and that we could get all the intellectual stimulation we needed from the television. I ask you! She seems to think that just because we're old, and can't get about very well, we've lost the use of our brains! It's the same with the music. All we have now is sing-songs. She said the evenings of classical music were too depressing.'

'She means well . . .'

This feeble answer was treated with the contempt it deserved. 'Of course she doesn't. If she meant well by *us*, she'd make some effort to find out what we want. All she likes is the power. No wonder both her children live abroad.'

287

'Do they? I didn't know she had any.'

'Yes, two sons. One of them emigrated to New Zealand – and you can't get any further away than that, can you? – and the other one joined one of those communes and lives a sort of hippie existence in California. Poor kids. She must have been the worst kind of mother: never giving them a chance to be people in their own right, and loving them with that awful relentlessness, like a boa constrictor.'

As always, at the mention of such things, Laura's mind flew back to Mark. 'But surely children need love more than anything else?'

'Certainly they do. Like they need food, and drink, and shelter. But it must be the right kind of love. Just as it must be the right kind of food.'

Laura thought of the old lady's own three children, two of whom were happy and successful and visited her at least once every week. The third, the youngest, moved from job to job and from love affair to love affair, and visited her mother only when she wanted money.

'And what is a balanced diet, where love is concerned?'

The old woman gave a cackle of laughter. 'That's like asking how to be the perfect mother. No such thing. Love them enough to say no to them, I suppose. Love them enough to push them out of the nest, and enough to welcome them back to it when they need it. Love what they are, not what you would like them to be. How do I know? All I know is, I wish you would come back here again.'

'I know. I'm sorry. I miss all of you as well, but I don't see how I can, though.'

'I know that. Don't mind me, I'm just a cantankerous old woman, blowing off steam. Don't worry, Laura. It'll all come right in the end.'

'Do you think so?' Once, thought Laura, I would have agreed with her quite easily.

'Of course I do. And like you say, she's not all bad. For one thing, getting annoyed with Mrs S. gets us all going beautifully, takes years off us, sometimes, complaining about her. And we've all got a kind of wartime spirit, too – united against a common enemy, as you might say! Very stimulating!'

'Well, so long as it's not too stimulating. We don't want you all popping off with heart attacks.'

It was a relief to Laura when Edward's secretary decided to move to London and Laura took over her work. It was May, and she had been looking for seven months for a job without any success. There had been a few weeks here and there, filling in for holidays in local shops, but the work had been dull, and she was secretly glad that she was not committed to sitting at a till or behind a counter for any length of time.

'Are you sure I'll be any use?' she asked Edward anxiously. 'I can type, but that's about the limit of my competence.'

'You can spell, you can string words together into a coherent sentence, and you sound nice on the telephone. Those things alone put you in a different league from most school-leavers who apply for jobs like this,' he said wryly. 'I just hope you won't be too bored. There's not much going on, and I'm not sure it's very good for you to be stuck with me day and night, like this.'

'No, it *is* a difficult prospect,' she answered earnestly. 'I hardly know how I'll bear it. Tell you what, we'd better make a pact. No talking shop in the evenings.'

'You mean I can't come home and tell you about my day?' he asked in mock horror. 'I thought that was what wives were for?'

'Not this wife,' she answered firmly. 'And in return, I won't spend the evenings moaning about my awful boss. Deal?'

'Deal. Oh, Laura, I am sorry.'

She stifled a twinge of impatience. 'I don't mind. Honestly I don't. It doesn't matter to me.'

'But you're not happy.'

'No.' She had never been able to lie to him. 'Not very. But it's not because of that.'

He never asked her anything more, and she did not know whether it was because he knew the answer but felt unable to do anything about it, or because he preferred not to know. In any case, she would have been unable to tell him. At her insistence he had resumed his letters to Mark. He always showed them to her, and though they were friendly enough they were, she guessed, substantially the same as those he had written in the days when he had never set eyes on his son. Mark never answered the letters.

Living in the flat was, not unnaturally, more difficult in the summer than it had been in the winter, and Laura was selfishly relieved that the weather was poor, cool and cloudy days and evenings that made the loss of her garden easier to bear. Laura took up swimming again, encouraged by Edward who claimed he was getting a paunch, though Laura could see no sign of it. Together they walked through the quiet morning streets to the pool, which had undergone cosmetic surgery and was now known, rather grandly, as a leisure centre. Laura made a few friends nearby, and got to know the local shopkeepers. Like many urban areas, the little group of streets had a strong sense of community, and she soon found that in some respects it differed little from the village she had left. She took a pride in being able to amuse Edward with little snippets of local gossip, and even got him one or two small commissions from nearby shop-owners.

By the end of August, however, Laura felt exhausted. Not physically – as Edward had said there was no great pressure of work in his office, and she had more time on her hands than she knew what to do with. Mentally, however, she was drained with the effort of continuing to behave like the old Laura. When Tod was suddenly taken into hospital with prostate trouble, the relief of having someone to fuss over was tremendous. For although the operation itself had been both routine and successful, Tod had gone down with an infection afterwards and had been slow to get over it. Laura was shocked, when she first saw him, by the sight of his face that seemed suddenly drawn and yellowish. His tongue, however, was as sharp as ever.

'So tedious,' he said crossly when Laura visited him. 'I keep telling them I'm all right, but they won't let me go home. Can't they see that these *frightful* surroundings are positively *malignant* to me? Not to mention all these *tiresome* old men,' he added, glaring round the ward. 'The snoring, my dear! You simply wouldn't believe that their frail old bodies could produce such a volume of sound! And *worse*,' he added darkly. 'I wouldn't sully your ears, Laura, with descriptions, but the indignities to which one is subjected! Simply frightful!'

'Why didn't you go private?' asked Laura. A dreadful thought struck her. 'You're not broke too, are you, Tod?'

'Broke? My darling, I'm absolutely *rolling*,' he announced in sonorous tones. 'Stinking rich,' he elaborated cheerfully. 'But I don't really believe in all that private stuff. The National Health,' he said earnestly, 'was once the most glorious thing this poor old country ever created. And run down though it may be, I will stand by it to the end. Besides,' he added, 'I've been supporting it all these years with those *monstrous* taxes they keep laying on us. Might as well get my money's worth.'

'Oh Tod!' Laura laughed. 'You are ridiculous! But when are you allowed out? I can't believe they really want to keep you here, you must be driving them all to distraction.'

'Not at all. I am a *model* patient. The nurses are all *devoted* to me. They claim it's some kind of nonsense about my house not being suitable, no one to look after me, too many stairs, that kind of thing. They want me to go to some kind of nursing home. In fact, they suggested St Barbara's – can you imagine anything more humiliating? Being patronised by that frightful Snape person. I told them I wouldn't have it.'

'I should think not,' said Laura. 'Then won't you come to us? I'd love to look after you, and of course we're all on one floor.'

'Yes, but it's the fourth floor.'

'Of course it is, silly, but you know perfectly well there's a lift! Oh, do say yes. Please, Tod!'

'Well . . .' His reluctance, she saw, was pretend. 'If you insist. But only for a few days, mind. After that, I shall go home.'

In the end, he stayed for nearly two weeks. The short journey from the hospital tired him far more than he had anticipated, and, although he would not admit it, Laura could see that it had frightened him. Although he still spoke of going home in a day or two, it was easy to see that this was mere form. Laura was delighted to have someone to cherish, and Edward responded to her lift in spirits by a corresponding cheerfulness that reminded her how easily, before, he had been able to make her laugh. Worried that Tod would find the days too long and too empty, she issued invitations recklessly to their friends, and in keeping him amused found that she, also, was enjoying their company. It seemed a long time since she had taken pleasure in the kind of informal gatherings they had once taken for granted, and, although in the flat it was naturally different, she felt a renewed satisfaction in the preparation of large meals for all and sundry.

The young ones, too, seemed to have found an added dimension. Daisy, to everyone's pleasure, had managed good grades in her A-levels and had been given a place at Leeds for the following year. Since she was going to read modern languages she intended to spend some of her year out in France, Spain and Italy, but meanwhile she had found herself a job in a supermarket. Candida, whose exam results were less good, said placidly that she didn't really want to go to university, and that what she'd really like to do was to train as a nursery nurse. Meanwhile she was helping out at St Barbara's, where she was rapidly making herself indispensable. The two of them, with Ben who was eating well again (the rumour about his father's girlfriend proving to have been unfounded), had discovered the dubious joys of local night clubs, and regarded Laura's presence in the town with complacency.

'You don't mind us crashing out on your floor, do you, Laura?' Daisy regarded the answer as a foregone conclusion. 'I promise you we'll be as quiet as dear little mice; you won't hear a thing from us.'

'As long as you don't disturb Tod,' said Laura severely.

'No, no, of course we don't,' said Daisy earnestly, concealing the fact that Tod was frequently awake when they came in, and was not averse to

291

joining them in cups of coffee and late-night games of poker, a game which was their current fad and which they played viciously and for money.

'Should I be worrying about what time they get in?' Laura asked Tod.

'My *dear!* What good would it do? They're far too old for that!'

'Ben's only sixteen,' she pointed out.

There's nothing "only" about Ben's sixteen. Besides, if they thought you were keeping tabs on them they'd stop coming, and then where would we be?'

'True.'

'Anyway, it's good for you having them here. And me, come to that. Otherwise, of course, I wouldn't dream of imposing myself on you,' he finished with superb insouciance.

'Good for me?'

'Stops you moping. Don't think I haven't noticed.'

Laura looked down at the onions she was chopping. 'I thought I was hiding it rather well,' she said stiffly.

'So you have. But we've been worried about you, all the same.'

Laura's eyes flooded with tears. She sniffed. 'Damn these onions,' she said, clearing a husky throat.

'Onions, shmonions. You still miss that boy, don't you?'

Wordlessly Laura nodded.

'Would you have coped with it better if there hadn't been the other problems? Money, and having to sell the house?'

Laura's surprise at his question startled her out of her tearfulness. She put down the knife and thought about it.

'I don't know,' she said slowly, considering. 'But then, if there hadn't been the other problems, things wouldn't have gone wrong with Mark in the first place. It was because I was in a state about them that I handled him so badly.'

'Perhaps. So, we'll put it the other way round. If the other problems no longer existed, if you were to win a million pounds tomorrow, would that make you feel all right again?'

'I wish!' Laura laughed, then thought again. 'I suppose I might. I mean, if I had all that money I could buy back our house, and Edward would be all right, and everything would go back to being as it was . . . Only it wouldn't, would it? Money wouldn't bring Mark back. I just feel that if I could make things the same, I could somehow have another chance. Go back and put things right. Oh, Tod! I'd give anything to undo what happened! The house, the million pounds anything!'

'Only it can't be done. You can't go back.'

'No. I know. But I don't know how to go forward. I just seem to be sort of stuck.' Laura picked up the knife, and resumed her chopping with feverish energy.

He sighed. 'I can't tell you how to do it. We all have our own avenues of escape, our own ways of dealing with things that go wrong. You've done it before, picked yourself up and carried on. You can do it again.'

'I don't know that I can. I don't even know that I want to.'

'That's just self-indulgence. You don't mean it.'

'Yes, I do. I think I do. But I suppose I don't, do I? Or I wouldn't be here, now, chopping these onions. It just all seems rather pointless. And the onions are a mess, too. I've chopped them to a pulp.'

'They'll be all right. What you need, young woman, is someone else to look after.'

'I suppose so,' she admitted, 'but who? I did wonder about fostering, but . . . I don't think I could bear it. If I've learned anything about myself, it's that I'm not very good at letting go. I couldn't bear to look after them, knowing they'd end up being taken away from me.' She sniffed again, then tore off a piece of kitchen roll and blew her nose violently. 'Bother,' she said, as the onion juice on her hands got in her eyes.

Tod nodded. 'The most difficult thing In the world,' he agreed soberly. 'I thought I'd never forgive James for dying like that. But I've got over it, and now I've got Eva.'

Cassandra and Eva had been constant visitors, and Laura, who had never seen Tod with a small child before, had been amazed to see them together.

'You're lucky,' she said, not without envy. 'And so is Eva.'

'Perhaps.' He looked down at the cat on his knee. Laura had worried almost more about moving the cats to the flat than she had about her and Edward. Only the fact that they were relatively old had prevented her from leaving them in the village, and fortunately they seemed content enough. Tod stroked the cat, his hand moving slowly over the fur. 'I've left her my house,' he said, abruptly.

'Who, Eva? Oh, Tod, that's wonderful!'

'Do you think so?' He sounded rather shy. 'You don't think Cassandra will mind?'

'Mind? Why on earth should she? She'll be so grateful. Though of course it won't be for a long time yet,' she added bracingly.

'Mm. Well, nothing's certain. I went and made a new will before going into hospital. Just in case. I've no family left, only a few distant cousins

I never hear from, so I thought, why not? There's Anna and Daisy too, of course, only Anna's pretty wealthy already, and when her father dies she'll be very rich indeed. So I've just left them some keepsakes, things I know they like, and all the rest goes to Eva. Only I don't want them to know.' He glared at Laura.

'No, of course not, though I don't see why not.'

'I don't want *gratitude*,' he said fiercely. 'I don't want them to feel obliged . . . I want it to be a gift. This week's free offer.'

'Yes. Yes, I see.'

'Well, perhaps not *this* week's. I don't intend to shuffle off me mortals just yet. Though I have no intention,' he said firmly, 'of cluttering the place up. I'm not going to be one of those incontinent old wrecks. Nor am I going to put up with too much pain and discomfort. Is that clear?' He spoke as severely as if Laura were threatening to keep him alive at all costs.

'Quite clear, but I don't know what you expect me to do about it.'

'Just as long as you understand,' he said, more peacefully. 'It's all been great fun, but I don't want to outstay my welcome. Remember that, will you, Laura?'

'I'll remember,' she promised.

Letting go, she thought. Is that what it's all about? Can I do it? The most difficult thing in the world, Tod said. What was that thing I read? 'One of these days I'm going to get over this – why not start now?' That helped, before. The trouble is, I suppose, that I don't really want to get over it. So what do I do? How do I endure it? The trouble is, I don't believe that it is possible to get over Mark. But perhaps . . . perhaps I could believe that there might come a time when I might at least want to, and that would be a step forward.

She fried the onions, slushy and watery from being over-chopped so that they bubbled and spat. She felt surprisingly comforted, not least by the fact that Tod had seen and understood her unhappiness. What I need, she thought, is not an ending but a resolution. And to achieve that, I suppose, I must be resolute. For the first time, it seemed almost possible.

Chapter 25

It was Tod who first noticed the fire.

He had always suffered from insomnia, and since he had been in hospital he had found it increasingly hard to sleep for more than two or three hours at a stretch. His breathing, never very good, was worse since the anaesthetic, and he found lying down made him breathless. His joints were hurting, too, and in spite of the physiotherapist's efforts the enforced inactivity seemed to have silted them up with spiky grit, so that they crunched painfully with every movement. Keeping still seemed to make them worse, and since he seemed to spend so many of the night-time hours awake it appeared sensible to him to make use of them. He would wander round the house in his silk dressing-gown, toiling down the stairs to make cups of tea and back up again. He seldom bothered to turn on the lights because he didn't want anyone to know how badly he was sleeping. At first he had switched on the light in each room as he came to it, only to have Cassie on the telephone at three in the morning asking what was going on.

'Tod? Is everything all right? You haven't got burglars, have you?'

'Of course I haven't got burglars,' he snapped. 'And if I had, and they made me answer the phone, I'd have to say that anyway, wouldn't I?'

'Goodness, Tod! So have you or haven't you? Um, answer yes or no . . .'

'No! Why on earth should I have? Can't a man turn a light on in his own home without everyone thinking there's something wrong?' He was annoyed with himself for being irritable, but the sound of the telephone at that time of night had made him jump, and without thinking he had hurried from the landing, not to the bedside phone, but to the one in the hall. He had taken the stairs too fast, and his knees felt as though they were on fire. Cassandra, however, had no trouble holding her own.

'Ungrateful beast! Next time I'll let the burglars take all your treasures, then! Seriously, though, I was up with Eva, and I saw lights going on and off from one room to another, and it did look rather spooky.'

295

'I was just a bit restless. Sorry, Caz. It was lovely of you to ring, ducky. What's the matter with Eva?'

'Just a bit under the weather. She's still got that cold, and her nose gets so bunged up she can't breathe properly, and then she wakes up and wants company.'

'Poor little cherub. You'll have to rub her chest with Vick . . . I had a friend called Vic, many years ago, got very bored with jokes about chests . . .'

'Poor little nothing – unless, of course, you mean me. It's more a habit than anything else, and the ghastly thing is she thinks that three in the morning is the ideal time for a nice romp. She's full of beans, and I'm knackered.'

'You'll have to be *firm* with her, darling.'

'Not if you mean the kind of being firm with her that you practise – giving her everything she asks for, and not even scolding her when she breaks things.'

'Scold her!' His voice rose. 'How could I scold her?'

Cassandra laughed. 'You sound like Lady Bracknell – "*in a ha-a-a-ndbag*?"'

'*Dear* Lady Bracknell. Always such an *inspiration*. But enough of this idle chat. You must get back to amusing Eva, and I must get back to my burglars. Unless you want to come over and join us? We could have a party . . .'

'Burglars and babies? Tempting, but . . . no, I think I'll pass on that one. I don't want Eva picking up any more bad habits – she's already got a nice line in shop-lifting at the supermarket.'

'Splendid. I'll take her up to Bond Street next week, or Knightsbridge. We could have a crime spree.'

'Goodnight, Tod. Sleep tight. Mind the burglars . . .'

'. . . don't bite? I should be so lucky.' The sound of her laughing stayed with him as he replaced the receiver.

After that, Tod left the lights on all night in the hall, kitchen, stairs and landing, and for the rest only turned on his bedside light if he was wakeful. The other rooms he could navigate in the semi-darkness, and he soon learned to prefer it that way. The paintings and antiques that he and James had so carefully collected and so lovingly positioned took on a new and mysterious beauty in the dim light, and if he left the curtains open there was an additional glow from the night sky that was never, in this part of England, completely dark.

It was December, two days after Christmas. To Tod's enormous pleasure he had been invited to spend Christmas Day itself at Cassandra's house, where he had watched entranced as Eva, now two years old, had discovered the joys of tearing wrapping paper off parcels. On his best behaviour, he had refrained from teasing Cassandra's father, and had treated her mother with an old-fashioned courtesy that had her responding with coy delight, and meant that Cassandra had several times to retreat to another room before she asphyxiated with bottled-up laughter. Boxing Day had been spent at Anna's, along with Laura and Edward. On both days he had eaten and drunk unwisely, and by now he was paying for it with a digestion that felt as though he had swallowed a mixture of lead pellets and tin tacks, and joints that were swollen and aching. He had been thankful that he could spend the day quietly at home, and had passed much of it dozing by the fire, but as a result he was not sleepy, and at two in the morning he was still prowling restlessly round the house.

He had made a cup of tea and drunk it, sitting up in bed and listening to the World Service, as he so often did when wakeful. The programme, however, was one he had already heard on Radio 4, so he switched it off. The tea was having its inevitable effect, and cursing himself for drinking it, he struggled out of bed and along to the bathroom. Then, feeling no inclination to return to bed, he wandered into the back spare bedroom. It was seldom used, for there were two other larger and pleasanter spare rooms, and it had occurred to Tod that he might change some of the furniture around. There was a pretty Victorian chair in there which, if re-upholstered, would look really very nice in that empty corner of the best spare room. He bent over it, feeling it with his hands to estimate its width. Yes, it should fit very well. If only, he thought, he wasn't so very stiff, he might have carried it through there and then to try it out. He even put his hands on it as if to lift it, then thought better of it and straightened up.

As he did so, he caught sight of a glow of light through the window. Arrested, he paused half upright, then slowly straightened himself and went to look. Over the past months he had spent many minutes and hours looking out at the sleeping village and the night sky, and he knew at once that what he was seeing was something that should not be there. He put his face to the glass, and then opened the window to look out, cursing as he fumbled with the security lock.

Although he needed glasses, now, for reading, his long-range vision was as good as it had ever been. The window was at the side of the house, and in summer the trees in the garden next door screened the view from it, but now in the dead of winter the branches were bare of leaves, and through

297

them he could quite clearly see the bulk of St Barbara's, its turrets silhouetted against the dirty orange of the night sky so that it looked romantic but sinister, like something out of a cartoon fairy tale. And, to make the likeness complete, one of the windows was glowing a dull orange red. As he leaned out of the window the night air was cold and damp in his lungs and set him coughing, but even so he could catch the tang of smoke in it. Not wood smoke, either. Not the remains of someone's log fire or garden bonfire, but something altogether less pleasant. He slammed the window to and, aching joints forgotten, ran for the bedside telephone and dialled for the fire brigade.

The calm, almost bored voice at the other end, though it might have been intended to soothe, exacerbated his frantic anxiety. In his distress he was unable to remember the telephone number for the matron. From its position, the window had been an upstairs one. How had the fire managed to get so good a hold? The place was littered with smoke alarms – he had occasionally grumbled about their ugliness against the ornate plasterwork of the ceilings. With shaking hands he pulled on shoes and an overcoat and hurried downstairs. No time for phoning, now. It would take too many precious minutes to find his reading glasses, and decipher the number in his book, and in any case, if the alarms had failed, the telephone might not be working either. He snatched up his car keys and ran for the garage.

As he skidded to a crunching halt on the gravelled courtyard at the back of the building, he put his hand down on the hooter, holding it there for several seconds and thankful that James had fitted a loud, almost rudely aggressive horn instead of the politely apologetic toot-toot of earlier days. Then, without bothering to switch off lights or engine, he went for the back door that was near the matron's rooms, leaning on the bell and hammering with the other hand. He was too breathless to shout, and when the matron came to open the door he could only gasp out 'Fire!' in a strangled wheeze. She looked at him suspiciously. She was, he saw with a sinking heart, one of the relief staff, and he remembered that the usual matron, having spent Christmas itself on duty, had gone to stay with her family until after the New Year.

'Fire!' he said again, more firmly. 'The main building's on fire!'

'But . . . it can't be! The fire alarms . . .'

'I saw it,' he said succinctly. 'Forget the alarms, they must have a fault. For God's sake, woman, can't you smell it?'

'I've got a cold . . .' she wailed, but she leaned towards him and sniffed, clutching her quilted dressing-gown modestly round her. It might have been that she expected to smell drink on his breath, but one sniff of the night air was enough. 'Yes,' she said crisply, and he saw with relief that she was not the kind to panic. 'Have you rung for the fire brigade?'

'Yes, of course. We must get everyone out.'

He would have pushed past her and run into the building, but she grabbed at his sleeve.

'Wait . . . no use rushing around. The fire is in the main building?'

'Yes, somewhere upstairs – second floor.'

'Good. That part is empty. All the people who are fit enough to live in those rooms have gone to family or friends for Christmas. In fact, there's only the couple in the main suite on the first floor . . . I'll go and rouse them. Other than that it's the sick and the bedridden ones in the annexe, and I'd have thought the night staff would be . . . ah, there you are, Helen.' A nurse, indignant and flustered, came hurrying to the door.

'What on earth . . . ! That dreadful noise, half my old dears are awake and scared out of their wits . . . oh, it's you, Mr Tod. I might have known it.'

'The old house is on fire,' he said. 'Let me go and fetch the first-floor people. I know the way.'

Once again the matron grasped his sleeve. 'My responsibility,' she said firmly. 'If you want to help, help Helen. I don't want to move the patients out of the annexe unless we have to, but we must have them ready.' She issued swift instructions to the nurse, then ran towards the main house. In the distance, Tod heard the sound of engines. The fire brigade was arriving.

Everyone agreed, afterwards, that if there had to be a fire it could not have happened at a more fortunate time. At no other season of the year would there have been so few people in the house, and inevitably several of the inmates would have been at serious risk. It was true that, had the place been occupied, the fire might not have occurred at all or would certainly have been discovered sooner, but on the whole the occupants of the rooms and suites felt themselves to have had a narrow escape, and comforted themselves that, though they had lost treasured bits of furniture and other mementos, they were at least still alive. The occupants of the annexe, fortunately, did not have to be moved, and the only casualty of the evening (apart from the house), was Tod. The cold he caught that night turned to pneumonia, and he was dead within a week.

'I just can't believe it!' Cassandra sat in Laura's kitchen. Eva, oblivious, sat playing at their feet. Cassandra, like all of them, had visited Tod in hospital every day, and at her insistence they had called her when he became worse. She and Anna had sat all that day at his bedside as he slipped, by slow degrees, from coma to death, and Laura had looked after Eva. Anna, needing solitude, had preferred to go home, but, having come to collect Eva, Cassandra seemed to want to stay and talk. She looked pale; her eyes from which the make-up had long since been wiped away were puffy and red. She was composed, though, and Laura was glad to see that the extravagant paroxysm of grief that she would once have expected from Cassandra was being controlled. Motherhood, Laura thought, had brought an unexpected bonus of maturity and responsibility to her friend.

'He was so alive,' mourned Cassandra softly, her eyes on Eva as though she supplied some kind of reassurance. Certainly Eva, with her mother's dark curls and vivid colouring, looked like the embodiment of vitality in her red jumper and green dungarees. 'I just can't believe it.'

'I don't think any of us will be able to,' agreed Laura. 'Feisty, that was what Jane once called him.'

'Yes, he was!' Cassandra smiled. 'And maddening, sometimes! But so generous, and so kind-hearted.'

'Mm,' said Laura, remembering what he had told her about his will and wondering whether Cassandra knew about it.

'I shall miss him dreadfully,' continued Cassandra. 'He was such good company, so funny and light-hearted, and such a *support*, somehow. Does that sound ridiculous? I know I've got my parents, and that if I had any real problems I could go to them, but . . . Tod made me feel safe, in a different kind of way. Ever since he came to the hospital with me, when Eva was born. I always wanted Eva to think of him as a kind of grandparent – after all, she's short of two already. What I keep thinking is that now she won't ever know him. She won't remember him. It seems . . . such a waste.' Her lips trembled, and she firmed them together, pressing her eyelids closed. Eva, hearing her name, abandoned the toy animals she had been playing with and got up. With the rolling gait of one still wearing a nappy, she came to Cassandra and patted her with a chubby, starfish hand. Cassandra opened her eyes and smiled.

'Hello, darling! What a good girl, staying with Laura while I was busy. Have you had a lovely day? I hope you've behaved yourself.' In response to imperiously uplifted arms, she picked the little girl up.

'Where's Tod?' asked Eva. She sat straight-backed on her mother's knee, as upright as a Victorian woman in tightly laced stays. Her voice was clear, and having spent all her time with adults, her speech was well-developed and strangely mature for her age. 'I want to see Tod, too. Where's Tod?'

Cassandra looked helplessly at Laura.

'You can't go and see Tod just now,' said Laura firmly. 'Have you shown Mummy the Lego model we made?'

For a moment it looked as though this attempt at distraction might fail, but after a few seconds' frowning consideration Eva allowed her thoughts to be turned. She wriggled and slid from Cassandra's lap and trotted purposefully to the sitting room.

'She remembers him now,' said Laura softly. 'Perhaps, if you talk about him from time to time, something of what he meant in her life will remain with her.' Eva, after all, would have a great deal to remember him by, not least the financial security that the house and its contents would bring to her.

Cassandra duly admired the model, and seemed relieved when Laura asked her to stay to supper. Over the meal, with Eva asleep in a travel cot in the spare bedroom, their conversation returned inevitably to the fire.

'Have you seen the building?' Cassandra, after two glasses of wine, had more colour in her cheeks and was voluble with the relief of a crisis survived. 'It looks awful.'

'I haven't,' said Laura, spooning casserole on to their plates. 'Edward's been to have a look.'

'Professional curiosity,' admitted Edward. 'Frankly, if it hadn't been for Tod, I'd have said the whole affair has been a godsend. The house was an eyesore, to say the least.'

'It had character,' objected Laura. 'I was fond of it.'

'Only because you're sentimental about it,' said Edward, softening the criticism with a smile and a brief touch of his hand on her shoulder. 'And it wasn't really all that appropriate for the purpose. Whatever they put up – and I hope whoever gets the job of designing it doesn't put up another eyesore – will at least be purpose-built.'

'It's beyond saving, then?'

'Oh, yes. The roof fell in, and all those little turrets came crashing down . . . heavy little brutes, they were. It would cost more to reinstate it than to pull it down and start again. Quicker, too, probably. And of course it should all be covered by the insurance. Luckily they were pretty much over-insured, which is all to the good. As long as the insurance pays up, that is.'

'Why wouldn't they?' Cassandra, obviously, had not had to make an insurance claim recently. Edward smiled at her as if she had been Eva.

'If they can find any possible reason not to pay, they won't. In this case, the unknown quantity seems to have been the cause of the fire, and why the alarms failed to go off. If there were any question of negligence by the staff, it might invalidate the insurance. It's too soon to say, but the insurance investigators have been poking about in the ruins. If there's anything to find, they'll find it.'

There was a wistful look on his face. Laura knew that he hoped, even longed, to get this commission. Not merely because of the money involved – their overheads were now so much lower that things were far less desperate than they had been – but because it was the kind of work he was particularly interested in. The housing and care of the infirm and elderly was, as he had pointed out on several occasions, something of a growth industry.

'There are too many cowboys leaping on to this bandwagon,' he had said. 'For every good one, like St Barbara's, there are five dismal places where the poor old dears spend every day sitting in a line in front of a television. And part of the problem is the use of old houses which are inappropriate, but which can be bought up cheaply because no one else wants them. The relatives see a picture of the outside and are pleased, because it looks solid and attractive and reassuring, and they forget that those old places were designed to be run by an army of servants.'

'You're bound to have a good chance of getting this one,' Laura said now, encouragingly. 'Most of the committee know you, or at least know of you, and their suggestion will carry some weight with the charity. Have you got any ideas?'

'Lots,' he admitted. 'I've even sketched down a few preliminary drawings.'

'Well, I think you definitely should get it,' said Cassandra hotly. 'They'd be mad to choose anyone else! Tod would have been the first to say so!' Her eyes misted over. 'At least someone would benefit from all this horribleness.' A muffled wail reached them from the spare room. 'Blast it, that's Eva. I'm afraid she's getting more difficult to settle in that travel cot, it's not really big enough for her any more. I'll finish this and get her home, if you don't mind; it doesn't seem worth trying to get her back to sleep at this stage.'

Later, when they had cleared up the kitchen, Laura and Edward sat together in the sitting room. They sat close together on the sofa, the only light in the room coming from the remains of the Christmas candles that stood on tables and windowsills and which still had one evening of burning left in them, and from the little white lights on the Christmas tree.

'It's beginning to look a bit dusty and tired,' murmured Laura, knowing

302

that Edward was well enough in tune with her to know what she was talking about.

'Only three more days to Twelfth Night. Do you want to take it down sooner?'

'No,' said Laura, who loved Christmas decorations. 'The room always looks so dark and dismal when we do. And at least this kind doesn't drop. Remember the year when I tried spraying the tree with hairspray to keep the needles on?'

She felt the rumble of his laugh. 'As if I could ever forget! The smell! Tod kept calling the house "The Salon" for weeks afterwards. Dear Tod. We'll all miss him, won't we? Cassandra doesn't know, does she?'

'About his will?' Laura had no secrets from Edward. 'Absolutely not, I'd say. I've been thinking about that. What do you suppose she'll want to do with it? If she has any say, that is. I don't know how Tod set it up, but knowing him he wouldn't have tied it up too tightly. He'd want Cassandra to be able to benefit from it.'

'Do you suppose she'll want to live in it?' Edward asked.

'Haven't a clue. It's difficult to imagine her there, she's made that little cottage so much hers. I suppose she might want to, to give Eva more space. Why?'

'Well, she's got three choices: to live in it, to sell it, or to let it. If she sells it now, with prices so low, she might well regret it later. And I wondered . . .'

Laura pulled away from him so that she could turn and look up at his face. 'Not buy it? We couldn't afford it, could we?'

'Not at the moment, I'm afraid. But we might be able to rent it . . . part of the problem with letting a house is worrying about whether the tenants will take care of it. She'd know she wouldn't need to worry about that, with us. And we could easily let this flat, unfurnished, for quite a good rent. It's such a central position, and it does look nice, though I says it as shouldn't. What do you think? It's not quite the same as having our old house back, but we would be back in the village.'

Laura shut her eyes for a moment. 'I think it sounds almost too good to be true.'

'Perhaps I shouldn't have mentioned it. It's only an idea, love, it might not come off. We'd better not get too excited about it.'

'No, I know. I'm not. I mean, I'd love it, but I feel a bit . . . fatalistic about it, if you know what I mean. If it happens, then great, but if not . . . never mind. Kismet.'

'If you insist.' Deliberately mis-hearing, he kissed her.

'You know what they're saying in the village? About the fire, I mean?'

'No, what? Don't tell me – they're blaming it all on Mrs Snape?'

Laura pulled away from him again and turned to look at him suspiciously. 'You did know, then?'

He pulled her back against him. 'No, it was just an inspired guess. So how do they work that one out? Or is it just wishful thinking?'

'Well, from what Tod said before he was ill, the fire must have started in Mrs Anscombe's room. On the second floor, near the middle.'

'Yes.' Edward thought about it. 'Yes, that would be about right, I should think. And?'

'And Mrs Anscombe smoked.'

'Aha.'

'Aha indeed. She was practically the only person there who did – most of the others had given up, but she said there were so few things left that she really enjoyed, she didn't see why she should have to do without that as well. She didn't smoke downstairs, though, in the communal rooms – she knew the others would hate it – just in her bedroom.'

'Sounds fair enough. And they think she left a cigarette end smouldering in a bin, or something? I don't see why it should be Mrs Snape's fault.'

'Well, that's just it. Apparently Mrs Anscombe was always very careful – had large ashtrays everywhere and was meticulous about stubbing them out. She wasn't one of the forgetful ones, either, in fact she was very much on the ball and was one of the leading lights in the local-history group. She was really furious when that was abandoned, and had a big row with the Snake about it. Things were *said* – you know – and I rather gather she said something fairly outspoken about the Snakes' background which Mrs Snake took violent exception to. After that she took every opportunity to make a fuss about Mrs Anscombe's smoking. She actually got on to the charity, and the committee, to have smoking banned in the buildings altogether.'

'She'd never have done it. In the communal rooms, perhaps, but not in private bedrooms. It's not a prison they're running there, after all. That place is meant to be their home.'

'Precisely, and so they told her. So she was reduced to nagging and carping. So much so that Mrs Anscombe, apparently, took to hiding her cigarette if she heard her coming.'

'Oh lord.'

'Yes. Mrs Anscombe went to her niece for Christmas – her son lives in Brazil – and she says it was the Snake who came to tell her that her niece had arrived to collect her. Quite unnecessary, of course, as the niece was going up to fetch her case anyway, but like I said she always seemed to be looking for an opportunity to catch her smoking. Mrs Anscombe swears she remembers putting her cigarette out, but . . .'

'But her first instinct might have been to hide it, and then in the bustle of going she didn't remember it . . . It doesn't explain why the fire alarm didn't go off, but of course that's a separate issue.'

'Would it affect the insurance?' asked Laura anxiously. 'I mean, it would have been an accident. They wouldn't sue Mrs Anscombe or anything, would they?'

'Oh no, I'm sure they wouldn't. That sort of accident happens all the time. Of course, if they do ask her about it, it wouldn't do any harm to be a bit vague . . .'

'A bit gaga, you mean?'

'Well, yes. Just a bit. Not that I want to encourage anyone to defraud the insurance, but . . .'

'Quite. Anyway, I'm sure they've been collecting absolutely enormous premiums for years and years, so it won't hurt them to pay out. And then you can build them a lovely Old People's Xanadu.'

'A stately pleasure dome? Sounds like *Center Parcs*.'

'Well, stately anyway.'

'Don't cross your bridges . . .'

'. . . before they're hatched. I know. But I think it will happen. I know it will.'

Laura spoke with an optimism she had not felt for more than a year. Listening to her own words she recognised for the first time that, in spite of the fire and Tod's death, she had regained some of her faith in the possibility of some kind of benign future.

Chapter 26

'Guess what?'

Laura looked up from the dough she was kneading. Edward did not need her in the office, and she had taken the opportunity to make some bread, something she had recently gone back to. It was a beautiful day, clear and sunny and warm, with the special early summer warmth that April sometimes produces. Through the open door she could see the daffodils in the sitting room – country daffodils from Anna's garden that Daisy had brought her, sitting in an old jug of greenish glass that glowed in the sunlight like one of those pieces of glass on the beach that have been smoothed by sand and sea to velvet softness. Beyond them, on the little fourth-floor roof garden that Edward had never got round, as yet, to enclosing, were more bulbs in flower: dwarf daffodils and tulips, scillas, and grape hyacinths that flopped over, but which she grew for their scent.

They looked bright and fresh among the evergreens and climbing plants, but they were still to her eyes stiff and confined. Next spring, she thought, maybe this summer even, I'll have a garden again. Tod had never been interested in gardening – the house and its contents had taken up all his attention – and she rejoiced in the prospect of the work ahead. Just wait, she apostrophised the pot-grown bulbs mentally. Just wait, and as soon as I can I'll put you in some proper soil instead of that characterless compost. You'll have to put up with birds, and slugs, and all the hazards of nature, but you'll be free. And so will I.

Not that she had disliked the flat. On the contrary, it had supplied her with a kind of liberty all its own. It had been so undemanding, so characterless in its newness, and that had been restful. Nothing, here, carried her back to those 'before' days; even the furniture, though it was the same, took on a new and rather surprised appearance, looking light-hearted, as though it were on holiday. There had been an element of playing with a doll's house or a Wendy house that had given a patina of unreality to living there. Knowing that it was a temporary move, she had not really put down roots: she might have been living in a foreign country, enjoying the experience but never expecting any kind of permanence. Laura knew that once she moved out she would find it difficult to remember the eighteen months or so that she had lived here. Returning to the village, though not to her own house, the threads of her life would once again weave themselves into the familiar old patterns, their very familiarity enriched by the changes like the addition of strands of scarlet or gold, turning the sensible homespun, for a time, into taffeta or shot silk.

They were going back to Ashingly. Not yet, but soon, when the formalities had been dealt with. Back to Tod's little house that would be empty, then, of its clustering treasures. He would not have grudged her that emptiness: Tod, though he adored his paintings and antiques, had never expected them to stay together. He would have been thrilled by the prospect of them being auctioned in London, and Laura had a vision of his spirit hovering in gleeful excitement over the bidders, egging them on. She would buy, she hoped, one or two pieces in his memory, and put them back in their old places, but for the rest she would sweep through the house like a tornado with a paintbrush. Some of their own furniture would have to go, too – the rooms were much smaller – and it would be fun to hunt for replacements.

'Laura!'

She started, and withdrew her eyes from the daffodils through which, as through a curtain of yellow gauze, she had been seeing the home she would create.

'Sorry, darling. I was wool-gathering.'

'You don't say!' Daisy laughed at her. 'It was wonderful how your hands carried on turning and pushing the dough, as if they had a life of their own. I wish I could ask you to make some of it into pizza, and stay for lunch.'

'Do, if you can.'

'Just not possible, I'm afraid. I shouldn't really be here at all. I only meant to pop in for five minutes, but I can tell them I had an important meeting.'

'Who with?'

'The architect, of course! Well, the architect's p.a., anyway. And it's true! And I did pop my head in to say hi to Edward on my way up, so it's even truer!'

She sounded as triumphant over this small victory as if she had still been fourteen instead of nineteen. She perched on the stool just as she had always done, her legs twisted round it in the contortions she appeared to find comfortable, and her hand sneaked out to steal a pinch of dough. Her nails, however, were no longer painted black but were merely buffed to a soft shine, filed into neat short ovals that would not interfere with typing on a keyboard. Gone, at this moment, were the embroidered shirts and bead-encrusted waistcoats, though Laura was secretly relieved that these still appeared at evenings and weekends. Instead, Daisy, in a neat navy suit and a white silk blouse, radiated crisp efficiency from every pore.

She had spent three months the previous year working in a hotel in France, where they had raved over her English accent and her English-rose appearance. By the time she left in January, they had offered her a generous salary if she would stay on, but Daisy had never regarded it as more than a chance to improve her French before going up to Leeds in October. She intended to spend three or four months working in England, then go to Italy for the summer where she had booked herself on to an intensive Italian course as well as a course on Renaissance art.

Anna, she knew, would pay for the courses, but Daisy very much wanted to earn enough money at least for her fares and her living expenses. Coming home because she wanted to see Anna and her friends, she wondered if she was being stupid – she would be lucky to get work in a shop at home, and in France she could have been earning twice as much. Both fortune and the manager of the French hotel were on her side, however. The company that employed him specialised in refurbishing old country hotels, their emphasis being on keeping (or creating) the atmosphere of a high-quality, family-owned establishment, and combining it with sporting and fitness facilities. The opening of the Channel Tunnel had turned their attention to England, and they had recently bought a moderately successful hotel that had overreached itself by building a nine-hole golf course and then been struck by the recession.

Daisy, applying for a receptionist's job and armed with a glowing reference from the previous manager, was able to tip the scales in her favour because, as she was able truthfully to tell her interviewers, she had lived nearby all her life and, between her mother's friends and her own network of school friends, had a wide acquaintance among the kind of people who might well be interested in using the facilities of the about-to-be-created health suite, and the existing (but to be refurbished) tennis courts and golf course.

Using publicity ideas secretly culled from *The Archers*, she managed to organise several successful publicity events, and when she suggested that she knew an architect who would not only be able to extend the old house without destroying its atmosphere but would certainly be more reasonable than the London firm who had submitted preliminary ideas, she was listened to. Edward got the commission, partly on the strength of the drawings he had prepared for the new St Barbara's that was to arise, phoenix-like, from the ashes of the old.

'I think this just might be the turning of the tide,' he said to Laura, quietly exultant. 'This is the first hotel they've bought in England, but if it works out – and I think it will, they're fantastically successful in France – then they're planning to look for more. They've even asked me to keep my ear to the ground for suitable places . . .'

'Laura!' Daisy was looking affronted. 'You're *still* counting sheep!'

'Wool-gathering . . . sorry. I really am listening. It's just such a lovely day.'

'That's as may be,' said Daisy severely, 'but I haven't got very long, and I'm dying to tell you the news . . .'

'I'm all ears. I return,' said Laura in a fake French accent, 'to my muttons. *Oh speak, and make me listen, thou guardian of my soul.*'

'Goodness, you are in a silly mood, aren't you? Well, you'll be even more spring-fevered when I tell you that the Snapes are going to sell your house!'

'Their house,' corrected Laura automatically. 'Really? Are you sure? But why? They've only been there eighteen months. I thought they were planning to stay there until they had to move into St Barbara's, or were carried out in a box.'

'So they were, but they've changed their mind. Minds. Whatever. And of course, they can't possibly stay because it's all her fault that St Barbara's burnt down and poor darling Tod died. They might have been forgiven St Barbara's, since nobody's hurt and they're going to get Edward's lovely *lush* new building, but nobody will forgive her for Tod. And quite right too.' Daisy untwined her legs and straightened her spine, looking suddenly like Nemesis in modern dress, and spoke with capital letters. 'That Woman Is a Murderer.'

'Daisy! You shouldn't go round saying things like that! It's libel!'

'No it isn't.'

'But darling, it is! She could sue you, for calling her a murderer!'

'No, I mean it's slander, not libel. Libel's written. And of course I don't go round saying it to all and sundry, but if I can't trust my godmother not to tell on me, who can I trust?'

'But do people really think that? I know there was some idea about Mrs Anscombe's cigarette, but the insurance company were perfectly satisfied that everything was in order, and even that the fire alarm had somehow malfunctioned. Nobody said anything then . . . though of course they wouldn't, really. Not if it means Mrs Anscombe getting the blame, or the insurance not paying up.'

'Of course not, they all shut up like clams, but everyone knew. No one's said anything to her face, but there's an atmosphere, and everyone seems to be muttering . . . you know how it happens.'

'I know.' Laura did know: not for nothing had she lived in a village that was still, in spite of newcomers, a close-knit community. The days of rough-musicking, when country people banded together to sing rowdy songs beneath the windows of those who had transgressed, might have passed, but the people of Ashingly still knew how to make their feelings known.

'Nobody would have said anything until the insurance was settled, even if it did mean letting the Snarks off the hook. Mrs Anscombe was wonderful – all dithery and shaky, and stopping her sentences half-way through. In fact, they're thinking of setting up a drama club. When That Woman has gone.'

'And are they definitely going? Surely she could give up working at St Barbara's – and I must admit she's been a disaster there, and the sooner she stops the better – without selling the house?'

'I don't think she could.' Daisy, interested, unconsciously relaxed and twisted her legs again, one round the other with her toe hooked behind the cross-bar of the stool. 'I mean, just giving up the job is an admission, isn't it? If not of guilt, at least of knowing what everyone's saying about her. And she's one of those people who always have to be perfect. She couldn't exist in a place where she had to confront an image of herself as a woman who bullied an old lady.'

Laura looked at Daisy with dawning respect. This was not the child who had sat in her kitchen in Ashingly, even though her hand was once again sneaking towards the ball of dough. Laura scooped it back into its bowl, covered it, and set it aside in a patch of sunshine.

'That's very perceptive of you.'

Daisy grinned. 'You learn a lot about people, working in a hotel. But that's beside the point. Who cares why she goes, so long as she does? And then you can have your house back!'

'No.' Laura's response was immediate and instinctive.

'No?' Daisy looked disappointed, like a child that has had its proffered gift refused.

'No,' said Laura more gently. 'It's funny, it's not something I'd ever thought about at all. Well, I never thought they'd be selling it . . . but it would be, oh, I don't know, wrong, somehow.'

311

'But . . . it was your house! Your lovely house! Edward could have those repellent windows taken out, and you've got all the furniture here, and at home and in Jane's attics. You could put it all back, and it would all be just the same, just how it used to be.' Her voice was pleading. Laura went and put her arms round her, holding her hands at right angles to her wrists to keep them from marking the neat blue jacket of Daisy's suit.

'If I've learned anything, over the past year, it's that you can't go back,' she said, kissing the top of Daisy's head and laying her cheek against it.

'But you are going back! You're coming back to Ashingly!' Daisy's voice was muffled as she leaned her head into Laura's shoulder.

'Back to the village, yes. To rent Tod's house from Cassie, and maybe even buy it from her if we can. That's going back, but it's also moving on. I'm not going to try and recreate our old house in Tod's. I couldn't, any more than I could recreate it in this flat, though all the furniture is the same. The house is different, I'm different, Edward is different. It's another new beginning.'

'But the village is the same!'

'In a way. The buildings are the same, the church and the shop and the cottages round the green. Anna and Jane and Cassandra are there, but Tod is gone, and Eva has arrived; you and Candy are setting sail into the world, and though you'll come back to your home port between voyages you'll find new harbours, and that's as it should be.'

'I don't like changes.'

'That's what I used to think. But you can't stop them happening, they're how life progresses. Some of them are so painful you wonder how you'll ever survive them, but you do. You have to.'

'Like Daddy dying.'

'Exactly. And that experience is probably why you find the thought of things changing so upsetting.'

She felt Daisy's nod. 'Yes. I don't mind me changing – in fact, I couldn't wait to leave school, and now I can't wait to go on to university – but I don't like other people doing it.'

'I know.' Laura withdrew her arms, and went to wash her hands.

'Do you remember the heart-to-heart we had in your kitchen all those years ago? The day Edward came home and told you about Mark?'

Laura, who had been remembering it rather poignantly, nodded without speaking. 'That was April, too . . . doesn't it seem a long time ago?' Laura nodded again. 'For me, I feel as though everything began to be different when Daddy got ill, but for you it could have been that day, couldn't it? And for Candy, the day when Bill went off. Do you think you'll ever hear from him?'

'Bill?' asked Laura, deliberately obtuse.

'No, Mark. You don't mind so much now, do you? I know Mummy said you were very upset about it, but that was ages ago.'

'No, I don't mind so much,' said Laura steadily, cleaning round and round the sink for something to do. Liar! shrieked her mind. But how can I explain to Daisy that yes, I still mind just as much, but that I've got used to it?

Daisy, glancing at her watch, gave an anguished cry and leaped off the stool. 'I must fly, I'll be late. 'Bye, Laura! See you soon!'

She was gone. Laura glanced at her watch – ten o'clock. In half an hour she would make coffee, and take it down to the office. Having coffee and lunch together, even when she was not needed in the office, punctuated the day for them both. Meanwhile, she did something she seldom did during the day – went and sat on the sofa. I'll just enjoy the daffodils for a few minutes, she thought. For the last few days she had been feeling tired and slightly under the weather, though surprisingly this had not dimmed her optimism. It was, after all, so good to have something to be optimistic about.

Daisy's question had stirred up her mind. The difference was that, whereas a few months ago she would have had to find something to distract her, now she felt able to look within herself, to examine and dissect her feelings.

When she had said that she didn't mind so much about Mark, had it been the lie she had thought it? Perhaps not. There were still moments when it caught her unawares, when some trivial thing would send a flash of regret through her like an electric shock. At those times the pain was as great as it had ever been, but the difference was that she knew it would pass.

Would it have been better if he had never existed, or if she had never met him? The answer to that was still no. Although there might always be an aching, Mark-shaped void in her heart, the fact that he existed and lived in her world, breathed the same air, read (perhaps) Edward's letters, gave an added dimension to her own everyday existence. She thought, now, that there might never be a day when she did not think of him, and wonder how he was, but was content that it should be so. If good wishes and loving thoughts had any virtue in them – and she believed they did – then some intangible benefit might reach him, and did it really matter that

313

the Mark she sent them to was the boy of fourteen she had first met, and not the seventeen-year-old he must now be? As a young man she would have to let him go to live his own life: at fourteen, she could continue to cherish him in her mind as she cherished the memory of the baby.

Maybe, one day, he would need them again. That was the one thing that worried her, that he might be in trouble and not ask for help. Would he know that the door was always open for him? She could not deny herself that one small hope, that next week, next year, in ten years' time, the telephone would ring and it would be Mark.

The windows were open, and the air that came in through them was softly fragrant with the spring scent of the flowers outside, the heavy sweetness of the grape hyacinths contrasting with the clean light breath that came intermittently from Daisy's daffodils. Her eyelids were heavy – she had woken early with a feeling of unquiet inside her that had made her cast her mind back to supper the night before; had those mussels been all right? They had tasted fresh enough, but you never knew with shellfish. Perhaps she would just close her eyes for a moment. She kicked off her shoes and swung her feet up on the sofa, curling up on the cushions.

She did not think she had slept, but when she opened her eyes there was a smell of coffee in the air, and Edward was smiling down at her.

'Slacking, Mrs M?'

Laura blinked at him. 'I wasn't asleep,' she said with mock dignity. 'I just closed my eyes for a moment.'

He sat on the sofa next to her, and put out a hand to stroke her cheek.

'You're allowed, you know,' he said. 'I made the coffee. Do you want some, or is your tummy still dodgy?'

'My tummy's fine.' She put a hand on it. 'I was dreaming . . .'

She frowned, catching at the drifting wisps that remained in her mind, portions perhaps of her subconscious that had floated up as they often did in such brief, daytime sleeping. He actually saw the thought take shape in her mind, and afterwards it always seemed to him that that instant was the true moment of conception. Her eyes went blank and intent, and her fingers twitched as she used them to count. They looked at one another for a long moment, each seeing the incredulous hope in the other's eyes. There was no need for words. To say it aloud might be tempting fate. Their hands met and clasped, very gently, as though something infinitely precious was cradled between them.